Praise for Anna del Mar and *The Asset*

"The unexpected ———————————— ne enthralled until th ———————————— rful start to the series ———————————— ories continue to showc ———————————— n equally exciting ar ————————————
—N——————————— ————— and top pick

"I really REALLY loved *The Asset*, the first in the planned Wounded Warrior series. Ash was a freakin' fantastic hero, one that women can both swoon over and be in awe of. Lia was also incredible, such a survivor and a strong, independent woman despite the terribly shitty life hand she'd been dealt...The intrigue and danger elements of this book were extremely well written and played out. Additionally, the story was fast paced without being overdone. And when everything came to a head, I felt like I was balancing on a tight wire of tension, it was excellent!"
—*The Romance Reviews*

"*The Asset* by Anna del Mar will take our heroine on a dark, emotional rollercoaster in order to get her happily ever after...but she will get it! This is the debut novel for the Wounded Warrior series and I for one can't wait for the next book in the series. This author has captured my attention with her well-written words, strong characters, and vivid storyline."
—*Harlequin Junkie*

"Whether you are a character driven reader or a plot driven reader, *The Asset* will appeal to you. This is a kick butt book with a strong romance, strong characters and action galore."
—*Book Briefs*

**Also from Anna del Mar
and Carina Press**

The Wounded Warrior Novels

Romantic Suspense

The Asset
The Stranger

The At the Brink Novels

Erotic Romance

At the Brink
To the Edge

ANNA DEL MAR

THE ASSET

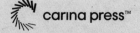
carina press™

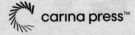 carina press™

Recycling programs
for this product may
not exist in your area.

ISBN-13: 978-0-373-00480-5

The Asset

Copyright © 2016 by Anna del Mar

www.CarinaPress.com

Printed in U.S.A.

Dear Reader,

A couple of years ago, I wasn't really thinking about writing romance novels. Sure, I'd had these stories in my mind for a long while, but the idea of putting them down intimidated the heck out of me. And then one day, while spending the holidays in Colorado, I gave myself permission to write. The floodgates opened.

Inspired by the Rocky Mountains and the heroes I met during my time as a navy wife, *The Asset* poured out of me. Thanks to the amazing folks at Carina Press, it became the first novel of my Wounded Warrior series, a collection of hot, smart, sexy romances about strong heroines fighting to find their place in the world and the kick-ass alphas who protect them with all they've got. After *The Asset* came *The Stranger*. Then more. It all goes to show what happens when you embrace your passions and write from the heart.

Thank you so much for choosing to read *The Asset*. My stories are always journeys and my readers are my favorite traveling companions. I'm thrilled to share this adventure with you.

AdM

To BTM, who made me do it.
To the wounded warriors who've sacrificed
so much to protect us. And to that special breed of
warrior, whose heroism often goes unrecognized.
They keep watch but are seldom seen.
For their service, I thank them.

THE
ASSET

ONE

MY FINGER TWITCHED on the trigger as I stared down the barrel of my shotgun. A stranger stood on my stoop. The mere sight of him shoved my heart into my throat and sent my brain into default. I widened my stance, tightened my grip on the gun and aimed at the stranger's chest. No way. He wasn't going to take me alive.

A sharp bark startled me. The largest, darkest, most handsome German shepherd I'd ever seen stood next to the stranger, head tilted, ears forward, nose quivering in the air. It uttered a quiet whimper and padded over to me without a trace of aggression, circling me once before it leaned against my legs.

I kept my shotgun leveled, but I spared another glance at the stunning dog. The plea in his eyes tempered the adrenaline jolting through my body, reined in my runaway heart and gave me pause to consider the stranger before me.

Framed by the Rocky Mountains and the lake, the man at the threshold blocked the morning's gray light and cast a huge shadow over my little porch. Raindrops tapped on his leather jacket, dripped from the rim of his cap and ran like tears down the sides of his face. Despite the exhaustion etched on his features, his glacial blue eyes narrowed on my gun.

"That's a pretty old Remington," he rumbled. "With the damn safety off, no less. Who the hell are you expecting, Jack the Ripper?"

"Stay back." I forced the words out. "I'll shoot if you come any closer."

"Damn it, girl," he said. "If you want us to leave, just say so."

The scowl on his face contributed to his dangerous appearance. So did the scruffy beard and the shaggy hair sticking out from under his baseball cap. If he hadn't come all the way out here to get to me—and that was still a big "if"—what on earth was he doing here?

I couldn't see any weapons on him. Was he a drifter? He didn't look dirty, but a metallic scent wafted from him, an odd, ripe trace I couldn't place.

He must have seen my nose wrinkle. His whole body stiffened. He drew taller than six feet by several inches, but it was the outrage I spotted in his eyes that reinforced my fears.

"Aren't you a spitfire?" He pulled out a rumpled piece of paper from his pocket, balled it and dropped it at my feet. "Secluded, cheap and quiet, that's what the ad said. But I don't think you want to rent out a room, at least not to me. Come on, Neil," he said to the dog. "Let's leave this little hellcat to count her bullets." He touched the rim of his baseball cap. "And a good day to you, ma'am."

He braced on a pair of sturdy crutches and hopped down from the stoop. *Crutches?* I should've noticed those before. The sable shepherd looked up at me, then nuzzled my hip and trotted off after his owner. The rubber bottoms of the man's crutches stabbed the ground as he shuffled to the black truck parked in my driveway, a supercharged Ram 3500 that matched its owner's brawn.

I exhaled the breath I'd been holding. Bad guys didn't knock at your door. They didn't back down, at-

tack while on crutches or hobble away after they came for you. They didn't call you ma'am, either. I picked up the crumpled paper and flattened it against the stair's wobbly baluster. It was indeed the one flyer I'd dared to post at Kailyn's convenience store, printed on pink paper, complete with the ten tear-off rectangles that listed my cell phone number.

The ad. My brain came on line. He was here about the ad?

Crap. Terror had a sure way of wiping reason from my mind. The ad talked about a stone cottage but didn't include the address. True, mine was the only stone cottage around. Still, my stomach churned.

I stared at the paper in my hands. He'd taken down the ad. Now I had exactly zero chance to rent out the room, which also meant that, since I'd have no money to make the rent, I was going to lose my little stone cottage. I was going to be homeless and I'd have to move on. Again.

But I liked it here. The place suited me well. People in this secluded valley were nice and I'd managed to build a semblance of a life hidden out here. And what about my little friends out back? Who'd take care of them if I wasn't around?

The pound, that's who.

I took a deep breath and looked down on my flannel pajama pants and my extra-large sweater. With my hair up in a messy tail, I was pretty sure I looked like a gun-toting, gray-eyed witch, brimming with hostility. I'd just scared away my first and only customer.

A top-notch German shepherd like that couldn't belong to a crook. It was obvious that the owner took excellent care of his dog. If that wasn't enough, the man got around on crutches. He couldn't hurt me and, if he

tried, I wouldn't need a shotgun to defend myself. I'd just have to trip him.

God, the things I thought about. Was I going to live in fear forever?

Yes, I would, but living in fear was better than not living at all.

Right?

I considered the paper in my hand. My rent was due next week.

"Wait!" I jammed my feet into my weathered rubber boots, gripped the gun in one hand and the umbrella in the other, and rushed out into the rain. I caught up with him as he slammed the door of his truck shut.

"Hey!" I waved the flyer in the air. "I didn't know that you came for this." I tapped on the window. "Could you please, like, talk to me…please?"

He rolled his eyes, but the window whirled down. "What now? You want to sue me for stinking up your stoop?"

"Oh, no." I blushed all the way down to my toes. "I just wanted to say—I'm sorry. I'm…um…skittish, you know? Living out here in the boonies all by myself…"

"I get it." The man's glare didn't waver. "Lots of folks don't like dogs. Or vets. Sorry I scared you."

"You didn't scare me," I lied. "I love dogs. I was just…being careful, that's all."

"Careful?" His mouth twisted into that terrible scowl. "Is that why you're still toting that thing around, cocked and loaded no less?"

My eyes shifted to the shotgun, still clutched in my hand, and then back to the stranger glaring at me. "Oh."

"That's what I thought." He turned the key on the ignition.

"Wait!"

On impulse, I stuck my hand through the window and placed it over his on the wheel. He flinched. I cringed. He was hot, and I mean scalding hot, to my touch. The look he fired in my direction burned just as bad.

"I... I..." I swallowed the lump in my throat. "I think you should come back inside."

"No way," he said. "I hate the wrong end of the barrel."

"It didn't register," I said. "I didn't realize that you were a vet."

He growled like a cranky bear. "I don't want your damn pity."

It was a good thing I recognized pride, fury and defiance when I saw it. Otherwise, I might have forgotten the whole thing and fled back to the cottage with my tail between my legs. Instead, I steeled my nerves and stuck out my chin.

"I'm not offering you any pity," I said. "But I do need to rent out a room. So let's start over. Okay? I'm Lia."

"Lia?" He lifted his cap and scratched his head. His eyebrows drew close together in a frown that deepened the two little vertical lines above his nose. "Have we met before?"

"Not in this lifetime."

He let out an exasperated sigh. "I don't think I'm the kind of tenant you were looking for."

"You might be right about that," I said. "You're grouchy and we didn't exactly get off to a good start. But right now, I'm offering you a cup of coffee. So follow me. If your references check, if you're not a serial killer or wanted by the FBI, then we'll talk."

The dog barked and, stepping over his owner, stuck his huge muzzle out the window and licked my face.

"Come on, boy." I opened the door. The German shepherd bounced out of the truck, running around me in an explosion of energy. I petted him as he loped beside me on the way to the cottage.

"Neil!" the man shouted. "You traitor. Come back right this minute!"

Neil sat on his hind legs halfway between the house and the truck and *woofed*.

"See?" I said. "Even your dog wants you to come in."

The man slapped the wheel and cursed some more. Oh, Lord. He was stubborn. All that anger stiffened my shoulders and churned up my belly. Did I really want a bundle of rage as a tenant?

But Neil wasn't moving either. This was a war of wills if I'd ever seen one. The umbrella sprang a leak so I got out of the rain, set it on the porch to dry and wiped my feet on the mat. I brought the shotgun into the kitchen and settled it on the counter for easy access. Better safe than sorry. I prayed that my instincts were right on this one.

The German shepherd trotted into the foyer, ears forward, mouth agape and long tongue lolling. He pawed at me, licked my hand and yapped in a way that sounded a lot like commiseration.

"That's a surly owner you've got there." I scratched him behind the ears. "He's lucky to have you, yes, he is. I would have shot him without batting an eyelash, but you? No way. You're too gorgeous."

I went into the kitchen, grabbed an old towel and laid it on the floor next to the stove. Neil shook his coat and settled on the towel. I set up the coffeepot as the man shuffled with his crutches into the foyer and hesitated at the threshold. I kept my face blank but my senses on alert.

"You look goddamn comfortable," he said to the dog, before his gaze zeroed in on me again. "He's never done this before. Go with a stranger? Never."

"Don't take it personally." I set out a pair of mugs. "Animals like me. I like them too. They're better than people any day."

"Amen to that," he muttered, his glare leaving no doubt that I belonged in his despicable human race category.

"Take a seat." I gestured toward the kitchen table and placed the clipboard at one end. "Fill that out. Coffee will be ready in a moment."

He set his jaw at a stubborn angle. Yikes. The guy was nothing if not ornery. Neil got up and pressed his body against his owner's legs. Bluster aside, the man couldn't resist the plea in the dog's eyes. He scratched Neil's head with unmistakable affection. I took that as a good sign, but even as I went about the kitchen, I kept my eye on the man and the shotgun within reach.

"You're a pain in the ass, Neil," the guy said as he took off his leather coat and hung it on the rack. "You're trained a lot better than that. We'll give this a try, but I'm telling you, this isn't going to end well. That gun-toting madwoman is not right in the head."

"I heard that." I poured some cream into a dish and stuck it in the microwave. "I'm not right in the head? What about you, Mr. Sourpuss who talks to dogs?"

"Neil isn't just any dog." He set the crutches against the wall and winced as he lowered himself into the chair. "He's got brains. He deserves to be talked to. As to the rest, I'm not the one going about in my pajamas aiming loaded shotguns at people."

"Sorry," I said, duly contrite. "I've only been up for

a bit. I'm a waitress, so I work late. But a girl's got to do what a girl's got to do—"

"Jesus Christ." He stared at the clipboard with open alarm. "How many applicants were you expecting? You do know that the nearest town is Copperhill, population two thousand? You've got like ten applications here and each one is five pages long."

"Maybe it was wishful thinking on my part, but I'm like the Boy Scouts, always prepared."

"I can see that." He glanced at the shotgun before returning his attention to the clipboard.

Hackles down, girl. I forced myself to breathe. He was only making a point. Still, the permanent knot of fear that churned at the center of my being tightened, an irrational impulse I couldn't always control. It may have won out, if the ancient microwave hadn't begun to clatter and rattle like my discombobulated, panic-prone brain.

"Come on." I pounded on the thing. "Please, don't break down now."

"Wow." The man shook his head. "You also talk to microwaves."

"If it makes any difference, I only beat naughty appliances that want to quit on me." I pounded some more until the microwave rattled back to life. "Yay." I kissed the old clunker.

He rolled his eyes, leaving no doubt that he considered me foolish, eccentric, or both. I watched him from the corner of my eye as I finished fixing the coffee. He pulled out his driver's license and began to write down his information with a shaky hand. After only a few pen strokes, he stopped midline and dug his fist into his thigh.

The lines on his face set with grim determination. He

grumbled something under his breath and jotted down a few more lines. I poured a cup of coffee and parked it in front of him. He squinted, clutching the pen with a white-knuckled grip.

"Are you okay?" I said.

"Fine," he muttered.

"Are you sure?" I said. "You don't look fine to me."

The pen snapped between his fingers.

"Christ." He stared at the pieces in his hand. "This was a stupid idea." He pushed away from the table. "I… I need to go."

He faltered as he tried to get up. I moved quickly. I tucked my shoulder beneath his arm to steady him, but he was heavy and I stumbled under his weight.

"Easy, now." I helped him to sit down again. *Ooof.* All that heat coming from his body. It enveloped me like a wave of steam. Neil whimpered. The man tried to stand up again, but he couldn't.

"Give me a sec." He slumped on the chair. "I'll go in a moment."

This man was sick and in a lot of pain, pain he concealed behind a mask of rage and gruff. He sat there, shivering like a penguin stranded on an iceberg, swaying dangerously in the chair. Who was he and why was he so ill?

I picked up the clipboard and read through the application. He'd only gotten far enough to fill out the top part, but the shaky script spelled a familiar name. I straightened. Holy cow. Could it be? I scanned the driver's license on the table for confirmation.

"Ash?" I studied the man sweating all over my kitchen table. "Are you really Ashton Hunter?"

I'd never met Ashton Hunter, but I'd heard an awful lot about the town's very own golden boy. I would have never recognized him from the pictures, but looking closely, seeing beyond the nearly healed scar that split his left eyebrow and all that facial hair...yes... I supposed it could be him. Wynona Hunter's grandson in the flesh, right there before me, sick as a dog and, judging by his terrible pallor, about to throw up.

I got the pail just in time.

He vomited—such a violent explosion. I almost threw up myself. I did okay with animals, but people? I wasn't so sure.

Man up, girl, this is Wynona Hunter's grandson getting sick in your kitchen.

Wynona was the reason I had the cottage in the first place, the one person who'd gone all out for me and possibly the only reason why I'd survived on the lam this long. She was also the closest thing to a grandma—or a friend—I'd ever had.

Losing her had torn me to pieces. Her death had deprived me the opportunity to return her incomparable kindnesses. Which was why now, holding on to her beloved Ash as he puked out his liver, the universe was giving me a second chance to pay her back for everything she'd done for me.

To think I'd confused Ashton Hunter for a drifter. Well, at least he was a local, which explained how he knew where to find my cottage. What was he doing here? Why was he looking to rent a room from a stranger so far away from town? And why was he sick?

"Christ," he mumbled. "This is embarrassing."

"Don't worry about it." I got a paper towel and wiped his mouth. "Are you really Wynona's grandson?"

"I am." He shuddered like a wet dog. "Ash."

"What's wrong with you?"

"I'm fine," he said before he heaved again.

"Hold on." I groped for my cell. "I'll call the ambulance. It'll take a little time to get out here, but they'll come."

"No ambulance." He snatched my hand and tightened his fingers around my wrist.

I jumped back, but I couldn't shake his hold. God, he was strong. Even as he shuddered with fever, no matter how hard I tried, I couldn't free my arm.

"Let go."

I choked on a wave of panic fueled by the perverse memories that ruled my subconscious. My heart rate sped into triple digits. My fight response kicked in and I threw my best punch. With the reflexes of a baseball player, he caught my fist in his other hand.

"Stop it," I said. "Let me go!"

His stare was cold, unfocused and remote, his face blank. He snarled some harsh words I couldn't understand. Nothing that I said registered in his expression, that is, until Neil barked, a set of sharp, loud yaps.

Neil's barks returned Ash to his senses. As if waking up from a dream, his eyes focused first on the dog, then on his hands, gripping my wrists, and finally on my face, surely frozen in a grimace of terror.

"Christ." He released his hold on me. "Did I hurt you? Jesus, I'm sorry."

I thrust myself away from him, against the wall. My knees shook like babies' rattles. My wrists throbbed with the memory of his grip. *Steady. Breathe. Cope.* I rubbed my wrists and stared at the man before me, trying to squelch the dread churning in my belly. He was really sick, I reminded myself. He couldn't harm me, not if he was truly Wynona's grandson, the boy she'd raised, the man she adored.

"I didn't mean to lose my cool." He braced his hands

on the table and tried to get up but his legs wouldn't hold him, so he sat down again. "I'm not like that, I swear. I just need my meds."

It took all I had to rally my wits and reclaim my courage—that, and the tremendous pain I spotted in Ash's eyes, plus the memory of Wynona Hunter opening her world to me.

"This medicine of yours," I said, cautiously. "Where is it? Is it in the truck?"

"Duffel bag," he muttered. "Front seat."

"Sit tight," I said. "I'll be right back."

"Don't call the ambulance. Don't call anybody. I'm not ready, not like this."

"Okay," I mumbled, but I wasn't sure.

Part of me understood what he meant. Wynona had told me that he was super smart, an extraordinary athlete and an officer in the United States Marine Corps. His family had been prominent in the area for several generations. I sensed he didn't want to be seen weakened and sick by the folks who'd watched him grow up. Still, the other part of me worried.

My best guess was that Ash had been wounded while serving in the military. It made sense. Other than a curt statement from his unit's commanding officer notifying us that he'd been "out of reach and on assignment" at the time of Wynona's death four months ago, no one had heard a word from him.

I'd resented him for missing the funeral. Ash had been Wynona's last living relative. She'd raised him. He'd been the center of her existence. He should have been there. Instead, he was here, now, four months late, in my house, sick and refusing to go to the hospital where he obviously belonged.

What would Wynona do if she was in my shoes?

I put on my coat, slipped on my boots and ran out to the truck. I grabbed the blue bag sporting the Marine Corps seal from the front seat. Neil waited by his owner when I came back, resting his chin on Ash's lap. Ash sat slumped over the table, forehead leaning on his crossed arms.

I plopped the bag down on the table and rushed to unzip it. My jaw dropped. A jumble of prescription medicines filled the duffel. There must have been twenty different bottles of pills, liquids and injectables in there, all labeled and marked with instructions.

I forced myself to get over the shock. "Which one do you need?"

He lifted his head painfully and groped through the bag, squinting at a bottle. "No, not this one. It liquefies my gut." He chucked it aside and picked up another bottle. "This one makes me drowsy. This one makes me stupid. This one, I think."

I twisted off the cap and handed him the two pills indicated on the label.

He washed down the pills with a gulp of coffee and then picked out a pack containing a loaded syringe. "I'm supposed to have this one too. At least that's what I think they said."

He fumbled with his belt. For a sick guy, he moved swiftly. Leaning to one side and then the other, he dropped his pants, ripped the syringe out of the sterile pack and without so much as a word, stabbed it into his thigh and pushed down on the plunger.

A hiss escaped between his clenched teeth. "Motherfucker burns."

I stared in horror as the veins in his neck bulged. My eyes shifted between the wicked syringe, dispensing its load of liquid fire, his muscular thighs, thick as tree trunks, and the bandage wrapped around his left calf. The ripe smell I'd detected earlier came from that bandage. Mother of God. I was no doctor, but Wynona's grandson was clearly sick with a full-fledged infection.

He dropped the empty syringe in the bag and pushed himself to his feet. "Let's go, Neil."

"You can't leave."

"Why not?" He wavered on his feet but managed to pull up his pants and buckle his belt.

"You can't drive like this."

"Sure I can," he said. "And I did."

He slung the bag over his shoulder, gripped his crutches and, with Neil at his heels, shuffled to the coat stand. How long had he been running around like this?

"But…" I didn't know what to say. "What about the room?"

He grabbed his jacket and sneered. "You don't want to rent me a room any more than you want me to puke all over your damn kitchen again."

"Well…" I gulped. "I'd prefer it if you kept your breakfast to yourself, but…um…you did say you were looking for peace and quiet. So if you want the room, you can have it."

His blue eyes lasered through my brain, his gaze dulled with pain but alert all the same. This guy wouldn't accept help from me, from anybody. He would get in that truck, pass out from the fever and kill himself—and his dog—in the process.

He more or less growled. "Why the hell would you want to rent me a room when that upturned nose of yours finds my stink so offensive?"

I fingered my nose, a little self-conscious. "I knew your grandmother. Wynona."

"You knew her?" He frowned, a familiar gesture now. "How?"

"She—um—she helped me when I first arrived in Copperhill." I measured my words carefully. "She took me under her wing, found me this place to live and helped me get a job. She was the kindest, most loving person I've ever met."

He closed his eyes and leaned his head against the wall. "That she was."

I had a moment of hope that he would reason with me, but then the grim expression reclaimed his face and he clutched the crutches with new resolve.

"Nona is dead." His eyes darkened to indigo. "I don't need help from you or from anyone else. Neil and I, we can take care of ourselves. So get the hell out of my way."

I had to make a conscious effort to overcome my fears and differentiate violence from desperation, pain from danger. Helping Ash was a bad idea, but could I really let him leave in this condition, knowing that he had no place to go to and no family to take care of him?

"Your grandma and I were good friends," I said, against my best judgment. "She told me lots of stories about you. And she gave me this."

I pulled out the chain buried beneath my sweater and showed him the pendant I wore around my neck. I flinched when he reached out, but I got hold of my fear before he noticed. His square-tipped fingers closed over the pendant, a highly polished obsidian crystal mounted on a silver frame. His eyes narrowed on the stylized frog skeleton carved in the center of the stone. It had the look of an ancient fossil, but it was actually one of Wynona's edgiest designs.

"Damn." His broken eyebrow rose in surprise. "She gave this to you?"

I nodded, all too aware of his proximity as he leaned in closer to examine the pendant. A wave of intense, metallic-scented heat radiated from him. His pain-sharpened breaths came out in blustery bursts.

"Courage," I mumbled.

"What?" he said.

"Wynona told me that obsidian was the stone of courage." I rallied. "She told me it would balance and restore, calm and soothe."

"Lia." His eyes narrowed. "Now I remember. Nona emailed me. About you. You took care of her when she broke her hip last year."

"It was the least I could do."

He took off his cap and raked his hair with his fingers. "Damn meds. They muddle my brain. But I know who you are now."

"Will you stay?"

His brows clashed over his nose. "I don't need you to feel sorry for me."

"I don't, but I think your grandmother would have liked it if you stayed, and I need to pay my rent."

"Ah."

That last bit was the type of rationale I could sell to the proud and the stubborn.

The meds were kicking in. Ash's eyelids drooped and his legs wobbled. His gaunt complexion matched his nickname. He looked like one of those giant lodgepole pines infected with beetles, colorless and brittle, swaying in the wind and about to topple over.

His words came out slow and slurred. "The house burned down."

I swallowed hard. "I remember."

"She was in there."

I shivered inside.

"I was in goddamn Afghanistan."

I reached out and squeezed his shoulder. "There was nothing you could've done."

He tensed beneath my touch like a feral cat, but he didn't pull back. He stared at my hand with an odd expression on his face, as if he expected me to recoil in horror, as if he hadn't been touched with kindness in a long time.

"I think Wynona would've really liked it if you stayed with me," I said. "Let's do this, for her, at least while you get your act together?"

He fingered the pendant once again. "I don't know."

"You must have had a really good reason to come back, even if you don't feel so good."

"The property," he mumbled, thumbing the stone. "I have to deal with that. This place is close. It's nice here. Not so many people around. Besides..." His stare drifted out the window. "I grew up on that lake. I like looking at it."

"I do too," I said. "It's peaceful and beautiful. Wynona told me that the two of you loved to hike around it."

"She did?"

I nodded and held my breath. Maybe he would go along with my suggestion. Or maybe I was out of my freaking mind. His presence spelled only trouble for me. My life didn't have room for complications or mistakes. If he stayed, I'd have to worry about his safety on top of mine.

If all of that wasn't enough, he came across as proud, stubborn and bitter. He scared me, especially when he got angry. It would be so much easier if he just moved along. If I was smart, I'd let him leave in his fancy truck and be done with it. But how could I let Wynona's grandson walk out when he needed help?

It was a bad idea. It was a dangerous idea, and reckless. I opened my mouth to send him on his way, but what came out of my lips had nothing to do with my impeccable logic.

"What's it going to be?"

Ash hesitated for moment, then he squinted down at me. "You still want me to fill out that application?"

"That won't be necessary."

"What the hell," he said. "I do need a place to crash. No one wants dogs. Or screwed-up vets."

Way to go. I'd just persuaded Ashton Hunter to barge into my carefully conceived, little farce of a life. To my astonishment, he pulled out his wallet from his pocket, and, after counting out a few crisp, hundred-dollar bills, pressed them into my hand.

"First, last and deposit," he said.

It was already spent, but it was more money than I'd seen all month.

Was I doing the right thing? I hoped so. Damage aside, I was basically a decent human being. But kindness was at the heart of catastrophe and evil thrived on good intentions. The danger in my life was very real. If I was going to come through unscathed, I needed to heal him quickly and then send him on his way. But first I had to think of a way of getting him up the stairs.

"Would you like to check out the room?" I said.

"Damn it." He looked at the steps. "It's up that way, isn't it?"

"Yeah," I said. "I don't know if you can make it."

Even in his drug-induced stupor, he wasn't one to pass up a challenge. He tucked the crutches under one arm and, gripping the balustrade, tackled the staircase.

Neil whimpered.

"I know," I mumbled. "This isn't going to be easy."

Ash nearly fainted on the landing, then regained his senses long enough to get his arm over my shoulder and make it to the bathroom at the top of the stairs, where he did faint. I managed to get him gently to the floor. He came to as I filled up the bathtub.

"What the hell?"

"Two choices." I knelt on the tiles next to him. "Either I take you to the hospital or we get your fever down the old-fashion way."

He lifted his head from the floor and contemplated the old claw-foot bathtub with trepidation. "No hospital."

"Okay, then."

He groaned when I took off his boots. I bit down on my lips and suppressed the grimace that tried to overtake my face. *Ouch*. His left foot was riddled with scars and swollen like a rotten gourd. He unbuckled his belt and, between the two of us, we managed to lower his pants. The swelling in his foot connected with his lower leg, which was also flushed and inflamed. I helped him to take off his shirt. I tried to keep my eyes averted from the other scars on his body, but they were many and most of them were still raw and red. My God. He'd been seriously injured.

He hunched over his arms, hugging himself, shaking uncontrollably, glowering at me through lidded eyes. He snapped when I tried to loosen the bandage around his calf.

"Forget this."

He heaved himself from the floor to the toilet and from the toilet to the tub and, perching his calf on the ledge, slid into the bath, groaning as he immersed the bulk of his body in the tub, shivering nonstop. A tide of displaced water swelled and spilled over the edges, splashing on the floor and drenching my feet. Within moments, his teeth began to chatter.

"Are you sure you don't want me to call the ambulance?"

"Sure as shit."

"I could drive you to the hospital or call the sheriff for help."

He snarled. "No."

A tiger trapped in my bathtub might have been a safer bet. A swipe of his paw could take my head off.

Perhaps this was about more than embarrassment. "Ash," I said. "Why don't you want me to take you to the hospital or call the sheriff? Are you in trouble?"

"Yeah," he mumbled. "I'm in trouble all right."

"With the law?" I said, fearing his enemies as much as mine.

"No, not with the law," he muttered before he closed his eyes. "With someone a lot more dangerous than the law."

TWO

ASH'S LISTLESS BODY dwarfed the bed's iron frame. He was a big man and even though it was a double bed, he seemed to take up all of the space in it. I pressed my hand against his forehead and exhaled in relief. The fever had finally broken.

I crossed the room and added a log to the hearth. The flames crackled, filling the bedroom with a sound that reminded me of quiet laughter. Maybe it was God—if he really existed—laughing at the irony of me trying to protect a stranger when everyone I'd ever cared for was dead.

The past three days had been intense. The fever had refused to cave. Now, after days fighting the stubborn infection, I reeled with exhaustion, but Ash was getting better. Maybe I wasn't so bad at the business of caring. Perhaps I could help people after all, instead of getting them killed.

I cracked open the front window, just an inch or so to let in some of the crisp morning air. The scent of pine, rich loam and dew-moistened forest freshened my lungs—autumn's fragrant perfume, the smell of freedom to me. I'd arrived at Copperhill and met Wynona Hunter in the fall, exactly two years ago. Back then, I couldn't have imagined I'd be alive today, thriving in such a stunning place among such kind people. I celebrated my unlikely anniversary by watching the sun's birth behind the mountains to ignite a brand-new day over the cobalt lake. I let out a sigh. To think that I was still free.

I'd brought my shotgun upstairs to clean it—okay, fine, maybe I felt a little safer having it nearby—but Neil had other plans. The big German shepherd padded over to the basket where I'd stowed his belongings and, carrying the brush between his teeth, dropped it on my lap.

"Oh, I see what this bright boy wants."

The dog replied with a series of modulated vocalizations, expressive whimpers that made him sound strikingly humanlike.

I laughed. "You're a big talker, aren't you?"

He *woofed*. I set aside the gun, plopped down on the floor and ran the brush over the dog's obsidian coat. Neil just lay there, luxuriating under my care with a puppy's joy. His paws seemed too large for his body, so I assumed he was still a juvenile.

I recalled what I knew about the breed. German shepherds were hardworking, intelligent and loyal, traits that made them ideal working partners for humans. Many of them were highly vocal, like Neil. Judging by his behavior and the service vest I'd found among the dog's carefully packed belongings, Neil had been trained to assist his owner, although in what capacity, I wasn't sure.

The cell I'd found in Ash's pocket rattled on the night table again. It had been going off a lot lately, but I didn't see any use in answering it at the moment. I mean, what was I supposed to do, take a message?

The dog lifted his head, rose and padded over to the bed. Trusting Neil's instincts, I followed. As if on cue, Ash opened his eyes and scanned the room with systematic efficiency. His vivid blue eyes settled on me.

He tried several times before he found his voice. "What the hell happened?"

"Relax," I said, pouring a cup of broth from the thermos I'd kept warm next to the fire. "I've got it all under control. Neil has been really worried about you."

The dog nuzzled Ash's hand.

"Hey." Ash petted Neil, but his eyes remained on me. "How long was I out?"

"Oh, not too long," I said. "A couple of days, that's all."

"Two days?" He seemed horrified.

"More like three," I said. "What? You missed a hot date?"

"Very funny." He examined the dog. "You look good, boy. Did you…did you take care of Neil while I was out?"

"Ask him yourself. He's a pleasure to work with, unlike some other mammals in the room." I helped Ash to sit up against the pillow and then pressed the cup against his lips. "Drink up. The doctor said you'd need lots of liquids."

"A doctor came?" He choked on the broth and broke out into a coughing fit. "Here?"

"Why, sure." I set the cup aside and pounded gently on his back. "Who the heck do you think did that?"

His eyes fell on the IV hanging from the bed frame and followed the line all the way down to his arm. He coughed some more before he got the fit under control.

"That little plastic tube and the antibiotics running through it did the heavy lifting," I said, fluffing his pillows. "Now your job is simple, drink and rest." I offered him the cup. "Can you hold on to that?"

He wrapped his big, calloused fingers around the

cup and frowned. "I can't remember anything that happened after the bathtub."

"Consider that a blessing." I arranged his covers. "The doctor had to drain the wound in your calf. You put up a racket, but that's all done now."

He peeked under the covers and sniffed. "Smells better."

"Much better," I agreed, remembering the awful sight. It had been such a shock to me. Ugh. So much pus. "How long had you been fighting that infection?"

"A week maybe."

"You needed to be in the hospital," I said, gathering his first dose of pills.

"I was in the goddamn hospital." A fearsome scowl etched his face. "Where the hell do you think my wounds got infected in the first place? Those morons fix one thing and break another."

"Jordan said you should take these." I handed the pills to Ash.

He cupped the meds in his palm. "Who's Jordan?"

"Jordan is the doctor."

"Why the hell would he agree to come out here to see me?"

"Oh, believe me, he wasn't exactly happy about that." The understatement of the day. "But he loved your grandmother. Had it not been for her, he would have been working at some low quality, run-of-the mill clinic in the Midwest. Instead, thanks to Wynona, he got to live his lifelong dream of practicing in the Rockies." I eyed the pills in his hands. "How about getting those out of the way?"

He stared at the tablets in his hand and wrinkled his nose. "They make me drowsy. Or sick to my stomach.

That stuff fucks with my brain. I've got no intention of ending up addicted to all that junk."

"Brilliant idea." The mere prospect of having to deal with a junkie rattled my courage. "Jordan thinks that you were taking too much of the heavy psych stuff anyway. Were you giving them hell at the hospital?"

One of his shoulders rose in a noncommittal half shrug.

"I knew it." I smirked. "I bet you were a royal pain in the ass."

He flashed me an affronted look. "Hey!"

"Just saying." I cocked my head. "Do you get them very often?"

"Get what?" he said.

"The nightmares. They seemed pretty bad."

He shrugged again.

"Or perhaps you were hallucinating?"

He glared. "I don't hallucinate."

"Then maybe you were having flashbacks," I said. "I wonder, what's the difference?"

"Nightmares are bad dreams," he explained, clearly annoyed by my ignorance. "Hallucinations are perceptions that aren't real. Flashbacks are vivid memories that feel like they're happening in real time."

"So you don't hallucinate," I said, "but you do have nightmares and flashbacks."

"I didn't say that."

"No need to get cranky."

"Damn it." He cursed under his breath. "Why do I feel like you arm-wrestled me with your pinkie?"

"Relax." I sat at the edge of his bed and, making a huge effort to overcome my fears, squeezed his arm. "I'm not the enemy. You're doing great, so much better than when you first got here. Jordan thinks you should

keep taking these pills and maybe something to sleep—
but only at night. It was the infection, combined with
the excess medication that had you feeling all wrong.
He thinks the leg needs some additional medical attention. Rest, food and fresh air will help too. Now, will
you please take the pills?"

"He actually sounds like a doctor I might like instead of those quacks who just want to pump me full
of drugs." He gulped down the pills and washed them
down with a swig of broth. "Sorry if I got out of control."

"It was only an old vase," I said. "And the doctor's
nose. No worries."

He gawked. "I broke the doctor's nose?"

"It wasn't intentional."

"Jesus Christ," he grumbled. "I told you not to call
anybody."

"You told me not to call the ambulance or the sheriff, and I didn't. You also told me not to take you to the
hospital, which narrowed my options considerably, especially when you started to get worse."

His eyebrows rose. "I got worse?"

"South of worse."

"Christ, I usually stay north of worse, at least most
of the time."

This time, when he met my eyes, he smirked, a lopsided smile that brightened the room and gave me a
glimpse of the man hidden beneath the grouch. Maybe
there was a little bit more than pain, anger and violence
in Ash Hunter.

"How long have you been back?" I asked.

"Over three months," he said, gulping down the rest
of the broth.

"Did you get hurt in Afghanistan?"

"Where else?"

"What happened?"

He snarled. "I was walking in the park and tripped. What the hell do you think happened?"

His anger hit me like a wallop to the face. My instinct was to run. I lurched inside, but I managed to keep my cool outside. *Steady. Breathe. Cope.* He didn't want to talk about what happened to him. I could relate to that. I didn't like to talk about my past either. But still, all that anger got my bile churning. Back straight as a steel rod, I got up and refilled his cup.

He must have noticed my distress.

"Sorry," he mumbled. "I didn't mean to snap at you."

"It's okay," I said, even though I wasn't.

"I still don't understand how you got this doctor to come all the way out here. Nona's gone and he doesn't owe me anything."

"But he owes me big." I blew on the broth to cool it off. "I've done Jordan lots of favors before."

"Favors?" His jaw tightened. "What kind of favors?"

"I subbed at his office when his assistant went out on maternity leave last summer." I handed him the refilled cup. "And I always volunteer for the free events and the health fairs. Not to mention that I'm his last-ditch contingency plan. If everything else fails, he knows I'll take in his patients."

"So it's like a professional relationship?"

"Exactly."

"Still, I don't know too many doctors who do house calls these days."

"Jordan does for some of his patients." He had to, since some of them were hard to transport. "I'll admit that he was a little reluctant to treat you at first. But I told him that we'd pay his full fee. I also assured him that you wouldn't hold any grudges, or sue him, or tell anybody about this."

"Sue him?" He frowned. "No, of course, not. Why would I sue him?"

"Oh, I don't know." I chewed on my pinkie nail.

"I'm curious," he said. "How did you meet this doctor?"

"He treated Ozzie, Izzy, Ivy and Ike, and he did a great job at it."

He scratched his beard. "You seem kind of young to have four kids."

"Kids?" I tittered nervously. "No, not kids. Ozzie and Izzy are goats, rescued goats, to be precise."

"Goats?" His eyes rounded into moons. "What about Ivy and Ike? Are they kids? Please tell me that they're people."

"Sorry." I shrugged. "Ivy is a donkey and Ike—he's a miniature Shetland pony. Which reminds me…" I checked the time. "Oh, yes, we'll be hearing from Ozzie in three, two, one…"

Ozzie bleated with all the might of his powerful little lungs.

"And here's Izzy," I blabbered on, just as she joined Ozzie, followed by a donkey's loud braying. "That would be Ike. You're listening to the breakfast symphony. Ozzie and Izzy were abandoned by their owners when they got hoof disease. Ivy was rescued from a farm, severely abused and emaciated. Ike used to work at a circus but his owner ditched him at the national park in lieu of financing his retirement. I've got to go feed them right away, otherwise the racket becomes unbearable—"

"Lia?" Ash said. "If these friends of yours are rescued animals, are you saying—I mean, am I right thinking that maybe your friend the doctor isn't really a doctor?"

"For real?" I perched my hands on my hips. "You wouldn't let me call the ambulance or drive you to the hospital. You would've been really pissed off if I called the sheriff. What was I supposed to do?"

"Oh, shit." Ash shook his head and dipped his face in his hands. "The doctor is a veterinarian, isn't he?"

"It was the best I could do on short notice."

The bed started to shake, creaking beneath his weight as if complaining. Outside, Ozzie bleated his heart out and Izzy and Ivy escalated the racket. I had to strain to hear over the ruckus, but the sound spilling from Ash took me by surprise. Soft and musical, deeply masculine, but also contagious. He was laughing, hard.

"Those sons of bitches were talking about taking my leg." He wiped tears of hilarity from his eyes. "And you got a vet to treat the infection. A vet? He probably used meds for horses instead of people."

"Well…" I might as well tell him the whole truth. "He didn't want to treat you at first, but I begged him. His brother is a famous wound care specialist in Boulder. They tackled the infection together."

"Wow." Ash's blue eyes beamed with a mixture of incredulity and glee. "You're unbelievable, you know that? It couldn't have been easy. Convincing a vet to treat a vet and then persuading some famous doctor from Boulder to help the vet to treat the vet. A vet for the vet!" He laughed some more.

"Whew." I let out the breath I'd been holding. "I'm so glad you're not mad at me. I knew for sure you'd be in good hands."

"You've got guts, girl." His eyes fell on the pendant

hanging from my neck. "You're something different all right."

My hand wrapped around the little obsidian stone. It felt oddly warm to my fingers, kind of like his eyes. I don't know why, but I flushed under his stare.

"Thanks for watching my six," he said. "We Hunters honor our friends. I've got your back, Lia."

Those eyes. My brain slowed down to a crawl. Strange. I fumbled for words, *umming* and *ahhing* like a fool.

"I'll go feed those troublemakers." I forced my brain to catch up. "While I'm gone, you're going to stay in bed and finish your broth. Is that clear?"

"Clear as mud, ma'am." He gave me a smart salute.

I turned on my heels and fled the room as if it was on fire. I ran down the stairs and into the backyard. When Ash smiled, he didn't seem half as daunting as before. And his laughter… I smiled. Contagious.

The goats, the donkey, the pony and an assorted variety of homeless or maimed chickens waited for me by the kitchen door.

"I know I'm late, guys, but I'm here."

I went into the old shed and mixed some pellets and oats. I set the buckets on the far side of the fenced field and filled the chicken feed dishes. While the animals ate, I put the hose to the trough and filled it with fresh water.

My ears registered the danger first. The absence of sound struck me as absurd, especially given the commotion just moments before. I looked up to see the animals huddled together by the barn. Ike's nostrils flared as he sniffed the air and hoofed the ground. My body tingled. The hair on the back of my neck stood on end.

I glanced up at the hills and the forest around the cottage. Nothing. I turned around, knowing in my heart that I'd been discovered. My shotgun. Where was it? Oh, crap. I couldn't believe it. I'd been so confounded by my reaction to Ash when I fled the room that I'd forgotten it upstairs.

Fatal mistake.

From afar, I spotted Neil, paws perched on the second-story windowsill. Ash stood next to him, holding my shotgun. He pumped the gun and pointed it in my direction.

I was going to die. I had no doubt about it. Wynona had told me that he was an excellent hunter and an extraordinary shooter. I could've run, that's true, but I wouldn't have made it to the kitchen or the barn before he shot me three times. Besides, my feet seemed to have grown roots. Time stopped. A thousand thoughts zipped through my overloaded brain. Had he been hired to get to me after all? Had I allowed my killer into my home?

Kindness killed. I'd always known that. I would die for the same mistake that had killed my father.

My pulse went into arrest. The emotions shredded me from the inside out. Confusion. Ash's eyes didn't seem like they belonged on a killer's face. Terror. I faced some deadly foes. Relief. No more running. No more hiding. No more fear. It was done. I'd gained a few years in the bargain, but the outcome hadn't changed from the start.

Ash frowned, squinted through one eye and, abruptly shifting his aim, pulled the trigger. The shots blasted one after the other, echoing in the forest, but the shot that would end me didn't come. Instead, the bullets struck on a spot higher to my left on the hill. A ferocious growl echoed from the rock ledge and a sudden burst of movement shook the underbrush.

For a moment, I couldn't move. Then the goats started to bleat again. Ivy brayed, the chickens clucked and all of the animals gathered around me. Ike pushed his head against me. I held on to the pony's speckled mane because my knees had turned to lard.

Neil burst through the kitchen door and darted toward the woods, barking. Ash followed, barefoot, wearing only a pair of Levi's with the zipper undone. He clutched the shotgun and the crutches at the same time, moving more swiftly than any other man in his condition could've done. He halted, put his fingers to his mouth and whistled.

"Back here, boy," he shouted. "Now."

The dog returned right away, although he kept bouncing about the yard and barking, a deep, resonant bass.

Ash made his way toward me, tore through the goats, pushed aside the pony and, bracing on his crutches, grabbed me by the shoulder. "Are you hurt?" he said. "Are you all right?"

I opened my mouth only to close it again. I had no spit to make words, no air to breathe. My legs gave way.

"You're okay." He dropped his hand to my waist and helped me lean against the trough. "You're going to be okay."

"What was it?" I managed to mutter.

"A mountain lion," he said. "Biggest fucker I've ever seen around here. It was getting ready to pounce."

"A mountain lion?" I shuddered. "Stalking my animals?"

"Stalking you too," he said. "It wasn't scared of you."

I pressed my hand against my chest and tried to slow down my pulse. "Did you hit it?"

"I didn't shoot to hit it," he said. "It was out of the twelve gauge's range. If there's anything worse than a mountain lion stalking your backyard, it's a wounded, pissed-off mountain lion hanging around. I shot to scare the hell out of it. I figured the sound and some flying shards would do the trick."

"I have to call Fish and Wildlife." My voice sounded like an automated teller. "I'll have to lock the animals in the barn when I go out. And I'll have to keep watch or something." I couldn't allow anything to happen to my crew.

"Neil will let us know if the mountain lion comes back," Ash said. "That's how I knew. He started to growl. He pulled on my covers until I got up and followed him to the window. I saw the fucker low to the ground, sneaking in through the woods."

"Thank you, Neil." I hugged the big black dog to my chest. "If it wasn't for the two of you, we could've been mauled or worse."

Ash's eyes scoured the woods. It was as if he existed at three levels, intense, super intense and hyper intense. I took in the full sight of him, his brown hair stirring in the wind; his feet, large and bare against the mottled grass; his waist, tapering into his jeans; his broad chest, still heaving from the strain of the dash down the stairs; those scars...

He was the same person who'd been so ill only hours ago. He had to be hurting, and yet by the looks of him, no one would ever know. He wasn't really dressed for the morning chill and he certainly shouldn't be out of bed straining his leg. The IV's needle was still taped to his forearm.

I realized three things about Ash Hunter at that moment: he was stronger than most, he was trained to withstand pain and injury beyond the norm, and he was capable of functioning at the highest level in the harshest circumstances.

My brain jump-started.

"We need to get you back to bed."

"I'm fine," he said. "But there's one thing bothering the hell out of me."

"What?"

His stare fixed on my face. "You thought I was going to kill you. I saw it in your eyes. You think I'm a cold-blooded murderer."

For an instant, I didn't know what to do. The alarms ringing in my head announced all kinds of dangers. No, I hadn't mistaken him for a cold-blooded killer. I'd mistaken him for a *hired* cold-blooded killer. But how could I explain the difference to him?

I had a strange impulse to tell him everything, how I'd gotten here and why I lived the way I did. Then reason kicked in.

The only thing standing between me and disaster was silence. It was the only reason I was still alive. I didn't want to endanger his life too.

"Well?" he said.

"Of course I thought nothing of the sort." My voice always sounded shrill when I lied. I rose on my toes and settled my hand on his forehead. "Is the fever back?"

"The fever's gone." His eyes burned through me. "And you're a sorry-ass liar. Why the hell would you think that I—or any other dipshit for that matter— would want to kill you?"

"This discussion is silly." I tried to modulate my high pitch with no success. "It's back to bed for you, mister."

I made a controlled dash for the kitchen, but even with the crutches, he beat me to the door and blocked my path.

"I don't like it when people confuse me with murderers."

"I didn't say—"

"But you thought it," he said. "And after you decided I was going to kill you, you made another bad decision."

I shook my head, afraid to hear him say it.

"You were ready to die."

He was way too perceptive for his own good, too smart to live with the likes of me. How could he know all of that about me when he didn't know me at all?

The sound of tires crunching on the gravel announced a visitor. For a woman who avoided both strangers and visitors, today was turning out to be a bit much. My already elevated panic rating went up a notch.

His head tilted in the direction of the driveway. "Are you expecting someone?"

"No," I said. "You?"

He shook his head.

With a deep breath, I steeled my nerves and took the shotgun from him. "I'll go see."

His hand landed on my arm, a contact that flustered every cell in my body. That stare. Lord. For all I knew he could be drilling directly into my brain to get the truth out of my head. Given enough time, he might succeed.

The pounding on the door startled me, stern, urgent and loud. I almost dropped the shotgun.

"You're afraid," he said, and it wasn't a question. "You live in terror. You think someone's out to harm you. Why?"

"Please," I said. "You're off the mark."

"I'm right on target," he said. "Don't lie to me. I don't know what your story is, but that thing you did, that was really fucked up."

"What are you talking about?"

"Giving up," he said. "You don't do that. You're still alive. You're still in the fight."

Was he right? I wasn't so sure. The only reason I'd survived so far was because I'd fled the fight and found a place to hide.

The door rattled with a new set of blows, harder and louder. Bad guys usually didn't knock, but the insistent pounding shoved me to the edge of my anxieties. Or was it the know-it-all expression on Ash's face that frightened me out of my wits?

"I better get the door," I said, "before it falls off the hinges."

"Go ahead, then, keep your secrets," he said. "But don't make the mistake of underestimating me. I might be down at the moment, but I'm not dumb. Don't ever underestimate yourself, either."

"I didn't—"

"You did and I want to know why."

His glare twisted my guts. "I… I don't have to answer your questions."

"Do you always welcome your guests with a shotgun?"

"Enough with this interrogation." I found my backbone. "It's none of your business."

His eyes darkened. "So you don't like questions?"

I stuck out my chin. "No."

"Questions are part of my nature."

"Then you'll have to change your nature." I snapped. "Or leave."

"Fine." He let go of my arm. "If that's what you want, I'll go."

Part of me regretted my words instantly. His fever was down, but he was still sick. He was Wynona's grandson and he had just saved me from the mountain lion. Besides, I really liked his dog.

But pushing him away was also the right thing to do. For myself. For his safety. I could take care of my animals. I'd done it this long and I didn't need him—well, with the mountain lion around, maybe Neil could be helpful. But I didn't like the way Ash had crash-landed into my life, upsetting my balance, upsetting me.

"I won't stay where I'm not wanted." He opened the kitchen door. "But know this: no matter what happened to you, you don't give up. You never quit. You fight and you go out fighting. You got that?"

He shuffled away, pounding the floor with his crutches. Waves of regret washed over me. I could only imagine Wynona's disappointment. I'd driven her grandson away while he still needed me.

But maybe I hadn't lost it at all. Maybe I'd just regained my wits and made the right decision for both of us. Maybe he needed to go, because without knowing anything, he knew everything, and that was way more risk than I could handle.

THREE

THE WOMAN CLOBBERING my door was as wide as she was tall, built like a tank, dressed in woodland combat fatigues and carrying a briefcase almost as big as a suitcase. Her sparkling brown eyes and flawless complexion matched a set of lips that would have made Angelina Jolie jealous. But the bulldog expression etched on her face frightened me, and so did the perfect teeth she gnashed at me, a grimace that had all the hallmarks of an officially fake smile.

She stared at the shotgun in my hand and raised an eyebrow. "Is that a loaded firearm?"

"Oh, there was a mountain lion—never mind." I pointed the shotgun toward the floor. "What can I do for you?"

"Are you Lia Stuart?"

My heart plummeted to my feet. "Who's asking?"

"Soraya Watkins." She offered a hand and checked me out from head to toe. "Gunnery Sergeant, United States Marine Corps, District Injury Support Coordinator. You may call me Gunny Watkins."

The long title meant nothing to me, but my hand nearly cracked like a nut in her grip. I glanced at the uniformed pair standing behind her, noting the weapons in their holsters.

"These fellows are military police," the gunny said. "Do you know why we're here?

Ash? "No clue."

"We're here to speak to Major Ashton Hunter."

"Who?"

"Ah, ah, ah." She waggled a stern finger in the air. "No lying and no pretending either. We know he's here. We've verified the plates, make and model of his truck out there. We haven't driven halfway across the state to go back empty-handed. Am I making myself clear?"

"Very."

"May we come in?" she said.

"Do I have a choice?"

Her smile widened unpleasantly. "No."

"In that case…" I stepped aside and gestured for her to come in.

She signaled for the MPs to stand by before she rolled into the cottage. Her head swiveled like a rotating turret. She considered the kitchen to the left then turned right, marched into my sitting room and took command of the space.

I hung the shotgun on the coat stand. "Coffee?"

The gunny's stare fell on me like a pair of hammers. "Just get Major Hunter down here stat."

"Um, okay." I hesitated. "He's not in trouble, is he?"

"That depends on your definition of trouble." She plopped down her case on the coffee table and, with a double click, flipped it open. "In the Corps, a UA marine is considered in very bad trouble."

"UA?"

"Unauthorized absence."

"He's sick, you know," I said. "He should be excused from work."

"Major Hunter is assigned to Wounded Warrior Battalion East," she said in a clipped tone. "As such, his current duty station should be in the neighborhood of

Bethesda. To be more precise, in the very hospital from which he walked away without a medical release."

"Oh." That explained a lot of things. "I'm sure he didn't mean to break the rules."

"Spare me your civilian platitudes," Gunny Watkins said. "The Marine Corps has policies and procedures that apply equally to all marines, including Major Hunter. Just get the major, will you?"

"Perhaps you should have called instead of coming all the way out here."

"Oh, I've been calling, and texting, and emailing," she said. "Believe you me, I had high hopes that the major would turn himself in and spare me the mountains of paperwork I'm now required to complete. But no such luck. Not only has he lingered, but he has chosen to ignore my contacts and reject my advice."

She pulled out a tablet from her case and plunked it down on my rickety coffee table.

"Major Hunter has the interest of the Marine Corps and the Navy at the highest levels," she said. "His reckless cross-country drive has created quite a stir. I might be new at my job, but I will *not* fail."

Yikes. Gunny Watkins was something else. I suddenly understood why Ash had said that he was in trouble with someone much more dangerous than the law. She was like G.I. Joe on steroids.

Gunny crossed her arms and stared at me "Three choices: I go up there, the boys drag him down here, or you go get him. What will it be?"

"I'll be right back."

I retreated upstairs, totally intimidated. The door stood ajar, but I knocked before I stepped into Ash's room. Neil whimpered when he saw me. Ash didn't spare me a look, focusing instead on his efforts to prop up the old window. He was dressed, wearing combat boots and a black T-shirt in addition to his blue jeans. His bags were packed, everything except his medications.

I rested my hand on the pile of medicines. "Leaving without these?"

He secured a rope to his duffel. "I don't need all that shit."

"Maybe you don't need all of it, but you certainly need some of it," I said. "And where on earth did you get that rope from?"

"I had it with my gear." He glared. "What's it to you anyway?"

I sighed. "Stalin is downstairs waiting for you."

He lowered the duffel on the rope out the window. "We'll be gone before she knows."

"We?" I said. "You don't intend to hurl poor Neil out the window, do you?"

"Neil's a pro and a trouper." He deposited the bag on the ground below, pulled on the quick release hitch and retrieved the rope. "I'll get us down."

As if on cue, Neil lay down on the floor and whimpered.

"Oh, come on," Ash said to Neil. "Don't be a wimp."

"Poor thing." I crouched next to the dog and petted him. "He's terrified. You can't do this to him. Besides, that lady has backup, two MPs watching the doors and the truck."

"Motherfuckers." He tripped on his bad foot and winced. "I can take them."

"Ash, please, you're in no condition to fight anyone, let alone a couple of armed MPs. Heck, Gunny Watkins might be short and wide, but I bet you she's got a mean hook. Besides, you can't climb down."

"Of course I can," he said, knotting the rope into a harness.

"Well, maybe you could, but you shouldn't," I said. "You'll hurt your leg. You're not out of the woods yet. What are you going to do if the infection returns?"

"I can figure it out."

"Don't do this," I said. "Please?"

He flashed me an ornery glance. "You said you wanted me out of your house."

"Not like this."

"I'm *not* going back to the hospital," he said. "I'm not."

Neil uttered a pitiful groan.

"Ash, be reasonable." I stood up from the floor. "You're going to break your neck."

"I don't get you," he said. "One minute you're throwing me out, the next minute you're trying to talk me out of leaving."

I didn't get me either, but I supposed schizophrenic behavior happened when one's survival instinct clashed with one's human decency.

"Please, Ash, go downstairs," I said. "Surely you can reason with that lady."

"Reason with Gunny Watkins?" He scoffed. "Impossible. She's the most obstinate, stubborn, pig-headed jarhead I've ever met."

"I beg to disagree," a voice announced at the door.

Ash and I turned in unison. Gunny Watkins stood at the threshold. Neither he nor I had heard her come up the stairs. She held her tablet in one hand and Ash's bag in the other, the same duffel he'd lowered out the window only a few minutes before. She marched into the bedroom and dropped the duffel at Ash's feet.

"*You're* the most obstinate, stubborn, pig-headed jarhead I've ever met," she said. "And you're not going anywhere, sir."

Ash glanced at the window. There was a good chance he could make it and, by God, he longed to try. Neil circled around him, pressing his body to his legs. Taking my cues from the dog, I inched closer to Ash, wound my arm through his elbow and squeezed his arm.

"Easy now," I muttered. "Don't do anything rash."

He gave me the strangest look.

"Gunny," I said, "Major Hunter doesn't want to go back to the hospital."

"Then perhaps he'll agree to go to the nursing home."

"No fucking way," Ash said.

"Sir, are you set on giving me hell?" The gunny plopped her hefty frame in the chair. "Please, sir, sit down."

My knees bent automatically and my bum hit the mattress, but Ash didn't budge. He stood his ground and locked stares with Gunny Watson.

"Sir, with all due respect, what part of sit your ass down don't you understand?"

I tugged on Ash's arm. "Please?"

He let out a sigh and, wincing, lowered himself next to me. His fingers clamped around the edge of the mattress. Neil settled his paw on Ash's lap. I worried.

Sure, Ash had extraordinary stamina, but he'd gotten out of bed prematurely, he hadn't eaten anything substantial in days and he wasn't getting his antibiotics at the moment. Plus, he probably hurt a lot, not to mention that he was under a lot of stress.

"Excuse me?" I lifted a finger in the air and pointed to the desk. "May I?"

"Proceed," the gunny said.

I got up, retrieved the next dose of pills, poured a

glass of water and handed it to Ash. For the first time, he didn't argue with me. He downed the pills and the water in a gulp. I unknotted the plastic hose on the IV stand and connected it to the needle in his arm as Jordan had taught me.

"If it'll get you off my back," Ash said, "I'll resign my commission." The way he just sat there with his shoulders bunched up reminded me of a cornered animal waiting for a chance to strike.

"You can resign your commission all you want, sir," the gunny said, "but I don't see the Marine Corps accepting your resignation just yet. You're a highly trained asset, a big-ticket investment. Besides, paperwork takes time. Even if someone were to approve your request—which I doubt it—it would take months before it took effect, sir."

Ash's knuckles whitened around the mattress. "You enjoy this exercise in petty power, don't you?"

"Is that how you see it, sir?" Gunny Watkins scoffed. "I thought I was doing my job."

"To keep me trapped in that hospital?"

"My mission is to ensure that you heal, sir, and that hospital, along with the doctors and nurses in it, provide the best possible setting for you to do that."

"They wanted to chop off my leg."

"Amputation was only one of a number of options," the gunny said. "You need to go back so they can decide what the best course of treatment is for you."

"I'm *not* going back."

"Sir, I've got orders and so do you," the gunny said. "You will follow those orders or I'll take you into custody for insubordination. You're a war hero, sir. The Purple Heart, the Navy Cross, so many awards, so many commendations. Your superiors are recommending you for the Medal of Honor. Did you know that?"

Ash grumbled. "I don't want any more medals."

"With all due respect, sir, the Marine Corps doesn't take orders from you."

"Medals should be given to those who really deserve it," Ash said. "And that's not me, since I'm alive and my friends are dead."

Survivor's guilt. I carried it deep inside. So many people had died instead of me. I stared at Ash. I understood how he felt. How had he earned all those medals? What did Gunny Watkins mean when she said he was a war hero and a high investment asset?

Whatever it was, I could almost hear Wynona's voice in the back of my head, urging me to help her grandson.

"Um, Gunny?" I said. "Surely you wouldn't throw a wounded war hero in the brig?"

"We'd prefer that the major come with us voluntarily," the gunny admitted. "But if I have to take him into custody for his own safety, I'll do it."

Ash rumbled. "That's a load of crap and you know it."

"Would you prefer to be declared unfit for service, sir?"

"You wouldn't dare."

"Oh, yes, I would, if it's in your best interest. Respectfully, sir, your state of mind is questionable at best."

"Bullshit."

"In addition, if you refuse to cooperate, I'll have to remove the dog from your custody."

Ash's hands curled into fists. "You will *not* take my dog."

"Sir, the dog was given to you by the Wounded Warrior Animal Companion Program. The policies of that program state that you must be capable of caring for him—"

"I take excellent care of my dog."

"How can you take care of your dog if you can barely manage to take care of yourself?" the gunny said. "One call to the program director and he's gone."

"You just want to fuck with my head."

Ash was too proud and upset to help himself, and Gunny Watkins would've been better suited to lead a charge or a firing squad than to reason with someone as stubborn as Ash. But maybe if I put my wits to it, I could somehow maneuver the woman into a compromise.

"Let's be logical about this," I said. "You don't want to take this man's service dog any more than you want to throw him in the brig. There's got to be an alternative to returning Major Hunter to the hospital. Surely a marine should be allowed to convalesce closer to home?"

"Ah, now, an intelligent question." The gunny let out a blustery breath. "That's true for a marine who has been medically released from the hospital—not the case for Major Hunter."

The gunny perched a pair of reading glasses on her nose and, punching the screen with a stout finger, brought up a file and scrolled down the document.

"Let's see," she said. "The major's leg and foot require additional medical treatment. According to the records, they've suffered several staph infections. The ruptured eardrum was healing, but needed to be evaluated for recurrent infections and hearing loss. Same with the collapsed lung. There's also the issue of Major Hunter's kidney function, which requires regular follow-up to ensure that the remaining kidney stabilizes."

I looked to Ash. "You're missing a kidney?"

"You only need one," he said defensively.

"The major's TBI also requires long-term monitoring and regular evaluations."

"TBI?" I asked.

"Traumatic brain injury," the gunny said.

I opened my mouth and closed it. "You suffered a traumatic brain injury?"

"My head got banged up in the explosion," Ash said. "That's all."

"Explosion?"

"Major Hunter was in a coma for three weeks."

Holy Mother. That's why he hadn't come back to Copperhill for the funeral, because he'd been in a coma on the day we buried Wynona.

"I'm not nuts, if that's what you're getting at." Ash turned to me. "I swear I'm not fucking nuts."

"I know that," I said. "You're just naturally profane, stubborn and irritating."

"Sounds about right," Gunny Watkins said. "I didn't say that you were nuts, sir, but you've got unresolved medical issues. You refused to talk to the therapist and you haven't undergone your premedical release evaluation. As far as the doctors are concerned, you're not safe to be on your own recognizance."

"What now?" Ash shook his head. "Do you think I'm going to turn into a mass murderer?"

"No, sir, I do not," she said in her exacting tone. "But you haven't followed the standard protocols and you refuse to follow orders. You may have tricked the hospital staff into letting you go, but you're not officially discharged. You're not even supposed to be driving. Even if you were able to straighten the hospital situation, according to regulations, you'd need a caregiver. We can't have you running around without supervision, sir."

"That's a really long way of saying that I'm fucked."

"Not necessarily," I said. "What's the Corps's definition of a caregiver?"

"A caregiver is a person who provides direct care, protection and supervision for a marine who's injured or ill," the gunny explained. "Given Major Hunter's conditions and stage of treatment—not to mention his recent history of insubordination and noncompliance—he requires a full-time caregiver."

Ash swore under his breath. "That's the biggest load of shit I've ever heard."

"What about a home health care agency?" I asked.

"He needs ongoing observation," the gunny said.

"So what you're saying is not that I need a caregiver," Ash said, "but rather a caretaker, someone to watch over me, as if I were a useless, decrepit, dilapidated old building, a nonoperating military installation waiting to be decommissioned and demolished."

"That's not what I said, sir."

"That's exactly what you implied."

"Caregiver, caretaker, call it what you will."

"I don't need a fucking caretaker!"

These two were about to come to blows.

"Gunny," I said. "Couldn't you designate a caregiver for Major Hunter and let him be?"

"Therein lies the problem," the gunny said. "In his case, there are no family members to provide ongoing care, so the Corps must assume responsibility."

Life was throwing some hard pitches at me and I couldn't dodge them all. My thoughts wavered from one extreme to the other. A few days ago I'd taken in Ash Hunter. Thirty minutes ago I'd asked him to leave my house for some very valid reasons. What the heck was I thinking now?

As if sensing my unease, Neil padded over to me and settled his head on my lap. I petted him between the ears. Part of me understood exactly how Ash felt—trapped, isolated and without recourse—confused, desperate and afraid. He was as alone in the world as I was. He'd come here to heal but couldn't, because his home had burned down and his grandmother was dead. The other part of me wanted to throttle my empathic version.

I fingered the obsidian pendant hanging around my neck. If the dead could speak from their graves, Wynona Hunter would be shouting my ear off just about now. I'd already set aside my safety to help out her grandson once. But this…this could be even more dangerous.

"I'm Major Hunter's landlord," I said tentatively. "Couldn't I care for him?"

Ash stared at me. "Why the hell would you do that?"

Gunny Watkins adjusted her glasses and tapped on her tablet. "I'm afraid that under the current rules, landlords don't qualify as viable caregivers."

Ash shook his head. "So it's back to I'm fucked all over again."

"Watch your temper, will you?" I said. "So, Gunny, the caregiver has to be a family member?"

"Exactly."

"I see." *Don't ask. It won't work. Bad idea.*

"Is a girlfriend considered a family member?"

Both Ash and Gunny Watkins stared at me as if I'd lost my mind, which I probably had. Ash started to say something.

"Hush." I looked to Gunny. "Well?"

"I believe so." She scrolled down her screen. "Yes, here it is. Girlfriends can become official caregivers."

"Well, then, that settles it," I said. "I'm Ash's girl-friend and I'm willing to be his caretaker—I mean, caregiver."

The silence in the room was deafening. Ash stared at me as if frogs and snakes had just leaped out of my mouth. Gunny Watkins eyed me as if she'd never seen me until this second. The internal throttling had already started. Such a freaking fool.

The gunny shook her head. "I don't know about this…"

"Yeah, me neither," Ash muttered.

"Wait." The gunny consulted her file. "Didn't I read something about a girlfriend in the record? Yes, here it is. There was a girlfriend. She declined our approach."

From the corner of my eye, I saw Ash flinch. He'd had a girlfriend, but she'd wanted nothing to do with him after he got wounded. That had to hurt.

"Um…well… I'm not that girlfriend," I said. "I came after."

Ash rumbled. "Lia…"

"Hard to believe that you two are in any kind of re-lationship." Gunny's shrewd little eyes shifted between Ash and me. "You don't seem to like each other much."

"We quarrel sometimes." I groped for Ash's hand. "But every couple does. Isn't that true, honey?"

"Honey?" Ash's hand went rigid in my hold. For a moment I feared the idiot would ruin my good work. He stared at me long and hard, bewildered blue eyes dark like the roiling sea. He was about to say something, when the gunny's cell rang.

She looked at the number on the screen and got up. "Excuse me. I've got brass on the line. I'll be right back." She put her cell to her ear and stepped out of the room.

"What the hell do you think you're doing?" Ash demanded as soon as the gunny was out of earshot.

"I'm trying to keep your ass out of that hospital you hate so much."

"No way," he said. "I don't need your help."

"You might be wrong about that."

"If it wasn't for you, I would've gotten away."

"Excuse me for sparing your neck, not to mention your leg and Neil," I whispered testily. "I'm sorry if you find the idea of me being your girlfriend insulting."

"Insulting?" he said. "More like infuriating."

"Well," I said, "I couldn't think of anything else and I didn't hear a single, helpful, original thought coming from you."

He let out an exasperated breath.

"It's your choice," I said, "If the idea rankles you so much, you can go back the hospital."

"No."

"Then what's your problem?"

He hesitated. "I don't want a pity girlfriend."

"A what?"

"A pity girlfriend, you know, the girl that hangs out with the crippled grunt 'cause she feels sorry for him."

I raised my hands to the sky and dropped them to my lap in frustration. "I can't be your pity girlfriend," I said. "It's impossible."

He frowned. "Why not?"

"Because a, I'm not your real girlfriend and b, I don't pity you."

"Then why the hell are you trying to help me?"

"I told you, because your grandmother was very kind to me."

"If that's true, why did you throw me out?"

I groaned. "Because of this!"

"What?"

"This," I said. "You ask too many questions."

"Lady, I can't keep up," he said. "This conversation is giving me whiplash."

"Hush." I gestured toward the landing, where the gunny spoke on the phone. "Do you want to make this even harder than it is?"

"Look, Lia." He lowered his voice. "I don't want your charity. I'm not that kind of a guy."

"Fine," I said. "Here's the deal. I'm willing to rent you a room and I'll sign on to be your caretaker—sorry, caregiver—until you're able to be on your own. But I've got a couple of conditions and you've got to swear you'll abide by them."

He rolled his eyes. "Here we go again."

"First, if we pull this off, you'll go see the doctors and you'll work hard to get better. This is a temporary arrangement, a limited-time engagement. Understand? The objective is for you to get well as fast as possible so that you can be on your own."

"And out of your hair, I get that," he said. "Here's the trouble with all of this: I don't believe in one-way tickets. What's in it for you?"

"I get my rent, which I need in order to make ends meet. I also get the benefit of having you and Neil around to protect my rescued animals when I'm at work."

He looked mildly encouraged. "You want me to shoot that mountain lion?"

"No, I don't want you to shoot anything or anyone," I said pointedly. "I just need you to protect my animals and keep the danger away, at least until Fish and Wildlife show up."

"I could do that," he said tentatively.

"I also need you to control your temper," I said. "You're moody and you've got a short fuse. You snap faster than a rubber band. I don't like it. It frightens me."

"Do you think I enjoy being angry?"

"It's hard to be around you when you want to snarl and roar all the time."

"Hell." He slumped. "Is it that bad?"

I shrugged. I'd gotten through to him, but I'd also hurt his feelings.

"I could try, I guess." He massaged his thigh. "I never did have a lot of patience, and these days I'm down to zero. What's your other condition?"

"No more questions about me. Past, present or future."

"Why not?"

"Because you're driving me crazy."

He smirked, a shrewd half smile. "Do you want to know what I think?"

"Not really."

"You're an illegal alien. You're terrified you're going to get deported."

I flashed him my nastiest look.

"I swear, I won't tell anyone."

"I'm *not* an illegal alien," I said. "I was born in the USA and I'm going to die here if I can manage it."

"Really?"

"Really."

He frowned. "So if you're not an illegal alien, what's your problem?"

"You're my problem."

"Me?"

"If this is going to work out, you've got to promise me—no more questions. Period." I went mum as the gunny returned to the bedroom.

"That was your CO on the line," she said. "He was pleased to learn that I found you. He suggested we could wipe the slate clean *if* you agree to fix your mess."

"See?" I smiled at Ash. "All is not lost."

"So," the gunny said. "Where were we? Ah, yes, you star-crossed lovers were trying to convince me that the two of you were a pair."

"Well, did we?" I asked.

"Oh, come on." The gunny looked mighty skeptical. "You're gutsy, but you're a lousy liar. How long have you two been dating?"

"Not long," I said. "It just happened, very fast."

"Is that true, sir?"

"It was instant, really," Ash muttered.

"Gunny," I said, "this is probably the only conflict-free accommodation for all involved."

The woman's jaw set like a brick. "Are you threatening me?"

"Me? Gosh, no, no way, never." I smiled sweetly. "I have nothing but the utmost respect for the very difficult job you do. But imagine what people would say around here if they heard that a wounded war hero had been sent back to the hospital or thrown in the brig because he wanted to heal at home."

"What do we have here?" The gunny sneered. "A tiger in disguise?"

"Wow." Ash glanced at me with genuine admiration. "She's good."

"Much better than you, sir." The gunny contemplated her options for a moment. "The role of caregiver is demanding. Frankly, Ms. Stuart, I don't know if you've got the mettle for it."

If there was one thing that riled me at this point in

my life, it was someone thinking that I was powerless, inept or incompetent.

"The major arrived here in a sorry state and look at him now," I said. "The infection is a lot better. I'd say I've done the job."

"Is that so, sir?"

"Yes, ma'am." He actually smirked. "She's got a gift for rehabbing animals."

It was my turn to roll my eyes.

"All wounded marines are heroes in my book," the gunny said, "but not all of them are agreeable. Major Hunter here might be less agreeable than most."

"No kidding," I said.

The gunny's stare narrowed on me. "Are you doing this to get the stipend?"

"What stipend?"

"There's a stipend," she said, "for civilians who care for service personnel."

"No," I said automatically. "I don't want any stipend."

"By the looks of this place, you could use a few extra bucks." The gunny pulled up a document on her screen and handed me the tablet, along with a stylus. "It's not much, but it's something."

"No, thanks." I refused the tablet. "That won't be necessary."

Ash started. "You might as well take the money."

"I don't want it," I said firmly. "It's fine as it is."

"If you don't want me to put in a subsidy request, that's fine," the gunny said. "But you still have to fill out the forms in order to register as an official caregiver."

My name on a government document. Great. I needed that like I needed a bullet to the brain. But it was too late to backtrack now. I filled out the forms and penned my signature.

"You'll also need to complete the online caregiver education program by the end of the month," she said. "It's optional for most people, but in this case, I need some serious CYA."

"CYA?"

"Cover your ass," Ash said. "Standard protocol for bureaucratic shit shifters."

"Hilarious." The gunny didn't smile. "Major Hunter, sir, consider yourself a very lucky marine. If I were in your boots, I'd suck up to Ms. Stuart here. If she's willing to vouch for you, then the least you can do is follow her instructions. You could also try to clean up, shave, get a haircut and stop howling at the moon. And if I catch a whiff of insubordination, negligence, or if you miss any of your appointments, it's back to the hospital. Do you understand, sir?"

Ash glared. I elbowed him and he muttered an insincere, "Yes, ma'am."

The gunny closed her documents and powered down her tablet. The realization of what I'd just done smacked me like a slap to the face.

"Um, Gunny?" I said. "Before you go, one last question?"

"Yes?"

I dodged Ash's stare. "How long do you think that the major will need an 'official' caretaker—I mean caregiver?"

"Until he's better, of course. Until he gets his medical release."

"And...well...who determines when that is?"

The gunny removed her glasses and looked me in the eye. "In this case, I do."

Shucks.

Ash's face turned to granite. "I don't know about this."

"Too late." The gunny tucked her tablet under her arm and stood up. "Ms. Stuart, good luck to you."

The expression on the woman's face transformed. Gone was the bulldog frown, in was the Cheshire cat smile. I hadn't bullied Gunny Watkins into doing what I wanted. Quite the contrary, she was the tiger in disguise. She'd maneuvered both Ash and I into doing something that neither one of us would've agreed to do under any other circumstance. And now I was stuck with Ash and he was stuck with me.

FOUR

IT WAS VERY cold in my room when I woke up. The tiny fireplace in the bedroom had long since been walled off and the cottage's ancient furnace worked only sporadically. I had to remember to do something about that, although what, I wasn't sure. The furnace was too old to be repaired and Silas Ford didn't have a dime to his name to fix up the cottage. And to think it was only the beginning of September.

I was almost afraid to get out from under the covers. Exhausted from working at the bar until late last night, the notion of staying in bed a little longer tempted me; but my animals would start the breakfast ruckus anytime and I had a lot to do, including following up on Gunny Watkins's list.

With a groan, I dragged my butt out of bed, slipped into a pair of yoga pants and piled an extra layer on top of my tank top before I shuffled to the bathroom. God, I looked worn-out. Dark smudges underscored my eyes. Not that it helped much, but I washed my face, brushed my teeth and combed my shoulder-length bob into a semblance of order. My artificially blackened hair struck a harsh contrast against my skin, making me look sickly, gothic or both. My pale roots were showing.

I went to stoke the fire in Ash's room, but when I tiptoed to the door, I found it ajar. I peeked in. A robust fire already burned in the hearth. Ash looked very different from the drifter who'd showed up at my door. Not only had his health and pallor improved, but he'd shaved, transforming his features from shabby chic to contemporary elegant. He had a wide face, a straight nose and a nicely defined mouth. His grandmother had always said he was a handsome kid. She hadn't been boasting.

Metallica blared from his earphones. Wearing only a pair of sweats, he did sit-ups on the braided carpet, crisp, fast, picture-perfect sit-ups that might have split me in half or killed me on the spot. His wide shoulders and his abs revealed little need for such rigorous exercise, even though he didn't look like a bodybuilder or a punk on steroids. His body came across as balanced, flexible and resilient, despite the scars and even after several months in the hospital.

Dear God. Men like him shouldn't be allowed to go shirtless. Or maybe they should be required to go shirtless all the time?

"Good morning," he said, startling me.

"Oh, hi," I said, blushing like a tween.

Standing there, enduring Ash's scrutiny as he continued to exercise, my skin flushed, my pulse raced and my belly fluttered. And I don't mean fluttered as if I had a couple of butterflies in there—no—nothing like that, nothing soft, benign or pure. I mean *fluttered*, as if a rabble of migratory butterflies numbering in the millions had overtaken my body with lust all the way to the cellular level.

What the heck was wrong with me?

I disguised my reaction by petting Neil, who greeted me with a doggy smile and a wagging tail. I avoided Ash's stare, afraid of partial brain failure. My eyes wandered the room as I tried to focus my attention on anything that wasn't a physical part of Ashton Hunter, like the IV bag. He'd rigged it on the bedpost so that he could exercise with the needle in his arm.

"Do you think that's such a hot idea?" I said.

"What?" he said, without missing a beat.

"Exercising so hard when you're still hooked up to an IV?"

"I can't stand the bed anymore," he said. "I've got to move."

"You're supposed to be resting."

"Only a few more to go."

I tore my eyes away from the human sit-up machine and took in the room. He'd settled in for sure, organizing his belongings with military precision. His backpack and gear hung from the pegs on the wall. A pull-up bar was wedged on the door above my head. A formidable-looking rifle hung on an improvised rack by the window.

I approached the window cautiously. "What's this?"

"That's my personal MK11 Sniper rifle," he said, coming to a stop and resting his elbows on his knees. "I had it locked in the truck. Don't worry, I didn't steal it from the navy or anything like that. I own it, permit and all."

"Do you think the Taliban will attack today?"

"Not the Taliban."

Did he know? Had he figured out my secrets? For a second, I was sure he had. My stomach plummeted to my feet. My blood turned into iced water. Then he smirked.

"Rent and protection," he said.

"Excuse me?"

"Rent and protection." He pulled himself up from the floor and hopped gracefully on his uninjured foot.

"That's why I'm here. Right? That's the deal you put on the table."

"Protection?"

"Protection. Mountain lion, remember?" He lifted his arms over his head and stretched like a lion himself.

"Oh, yeah, sure, I remember." Why couldn't I think straight? "Okay, protect away. I'm off to feed the crew."

"Wait." He grabbed the IV, hopped to the window and hung the bag on the curtain rod. He picked up the rifle and, putting his eye to the scope, swept it in a slow arc as he scanned the hills and the woods. "Let me do some recon. Give me a sec."

"Fine," I said, "but if you spot the mountain lion and it's like, really far away, chasing butterflies or doing something harmless, don't shoot. If it's not endangering my animals, I don't want you to kill it. Promise? It deserves to live too."

"Yes, ma'am," he said. "Rules of engagement: I shoot only if it threatens you or your animals. Otherwise, the son of a bitch can live forever."

"Good."

Eye on the scope, he swept the grounds again while I stood over him, keenly aware of his proximity. I breathed in his scent, heated iron, boiling water and something darker and slightly spicy that enticed my senses and discombobulated my body.

This had to stop. Now.

"I sure hope that mountain lion stays out of your way," I said.

"Sometimes you've got to make shitty choices."

I had a feeling we weren't talking about mountain lions anymore. "Must be really hard to make choices like that for a living."

"It comes down to some simple facts, really." The

lines between his eyes deepened as his eyes narrowed when he slowed down to scour a distant thicket of trees. "It's whether you want to make your own decisions or play someone else's game; whether they're gonna kill your guys or you're gonna to kill the ones who want to kill your guys. The rest is just bullshit."

I seized the chance to snoop. "So you were a sniper with the Marines?"

"Sometimes," he said cryptically.

"Did you ever regret one of your kills?"

"That's a hard-ass question."

"Sorry," I said. "I didn't mean to intrude."

He glanced at me then put his eye back to the scope. "Are you sure about that?"

The flush on my face confirmed my guilt. "I better go."

"Stand by," he said, scanning the far hills. "For someone who doesn't like to answer questions, you've got a wicked double standard."

"Forget I asked."

"I could, but I think I won't."

"Excuse me?"

"There was this one time," he said, one eye shut, the other squinting against the scope. "It was a while back. We were doing over watches for the Marines. This woman steps out of a mosque tugging this kid by the hand. The kid is crying. I can see them clearly through my scope. My marines are coming around the corner and the woman sets an intercept course. My spotter is like, 'She's got a kid,' but I track her with the scope, and the kid is still crying, and my guys are about to meet her in ninety seconds…"

I couldn't even imagine the pressure of a situation like that. "And?"

"She pulls out an AK-47 from under her burka. I get a glimpse of the bulk beneath her robes and some wires. It's not an easy shot or a done deal at over two thousand yards. It's got to be final, you see, or else she'll have time to pull the wire. My marines, they're less than ten yards around the corner."

I nibbled on my pinkie nail. "What did you do?"

"So I light her up and take her down. My spotter is like 'What did you do?' He never saw the AK-47 or the bulk under the burka, and he's losing it. He thinks I just killed a woman for no reason at all. That's the moment when I regret pulling the trigger. Did I really see what I saw? Did I kill an innocent woman?"

Holy Mother.

"Lia?" Ash stared at my hand. "You're going to draw blood if you keep biting your nail."

I pulled my finger from my mouth and clasped my hands together. "What happened?"

"Through the scope, I see the marine's advance element checking out the kill," he said. "Sure enough, she's wired with enough explosives to take out the entire unit. The news comes over the radio. The kid's not even hers. She stole him from another woman and she was going to use him as a shield and blow him up too."

"God."

"That's what I said too—well—I added a few choice words. My spotter, he went home stateside after that."

"And you?"

"I didn't like killing that woman and yet I can't say I regret it. She killed herself with her actions. It was either her or my guys. But I made my decision and I get to live with it."

He looked up from his scope. "Are you horrified?"

"No."

"No?" The split eyebrow came up. "Lots of people would find tons of material for moral and ethical commentary in that story."

"Not me," I said. "I wish life was different, but beyond opinions, perspectives and politics, there are some evil people in this world."

"Some would call you judgmental and self-righteous," he pointed out.

"Sure," I said. "That's because they haven't suffered at the hands of evil, or because they don't know anyone who has, or because they don't understand that evil can look cool, nice and even trendy sometimes."

He flashed me a curious glance. "But you do."

"I do what?"

"You understand evil quite well," he said. "Why is that?"

The memories slammed me all at once. The darkness lunged at me like a hungry beast. I battled it back, rejecting the gloom and suppressing my emotions behind the wall I'd built in my mind. *Steady. Breathe. Cope.* I was getting better at this. My stomach roiled, but I managed to keep it together.

"Are you okay?" Ash eyed me with concern. "You're looking a little shaky on your feet."

"Me?" I let out a manufactured titter. "Nah. I'm good. What were we talking about?"

He frowned. "Evil and why you understand it so well?"

Crap.

I cleared my throat. "I guess I'm just a realist. At the end of the day, your guys went home to their parents, wives and kids. That's what matters to me."

His eyes lingered on my face for a few seconds too long. "Clear."

"What?" I said.

"You can go now," he said. "To feed your animals."

"Oh, yes." I charged for the door, but his voice stopped me at the threshold.

"You never walk to the door," he mumbled, looking through his scope. "You run for it."

"Pardon me?"

"Never mind." He glanced at Neil, snapped his fingers and motioned for the German shepherd to follow me. "Go with her."

"Come on, lover." I patted my thigh.

The dog trotted over to me, but hesitated at the door and grumbled a drawn-out *woof.*

"Neil doesn't like to leave you behind," I said. "Is he trained to stick by you?"

Ash sighed and, turning from the scope, fixed his gaze on me. "And you say *I* ask too many questions."

"If you don't want to talk about it, you don't have to."

"I don't like certain places and situations with lots of people these days," he said, straightening on his feet. "That's why I came out here. I'm not crazy or psychotic or anything like that."

Post-traumatic stress disorder. "I know."

"He helps with that stuff."

"You didn't have to tell me."

"But I did tell you about Neil, just as I told you about that woman in Iraq, and for a very specific reason." He set his rifle aside and leaned against the windowsill. "I don't want you to fear me. I don't want you to feel unsafe in your own house, and I mean more unsafe than you already feel."

I shifted from one foot to the other. I wrung my hands until they hurt. How could I reply to a statement like that without breaking into a billion little pieces?

His words did reassure me, but I couldn't acknowledge his kindness or deviate from my path. Silence was the safer course of action, even if it disappointed the expectations I spotted in his eyes.

"Neil and I will bring you breakfast after we feed the guys," I finally said.

He gave me a curt nod. "I'll be watching."

He was indeed watching when I went out to the backyard. Maybe I was a fool, but as I crossed the pasture and let the animals out of the barn, the world around me seemed like a safer place.

I fed and watered the animals. I cleaned the stalls, laid out some fresh straw and groomed both the pony and the donkey. I added some nectar to the busy hummingbird feeders throughout the backyard. Neil had a blast terrorizing the chickens.

By the time I made it back to the kitchen, Ash hopped about on his crutches downstairs. Thankfully, he wore a T-shirt, which meant I could think with a degree of clarity. He'd fitted the IV to his camelback and strapped it to his back so he could move about hands free.

The good news? He welcomed me with a steaming mug of freshly brewed coffee. The bad news? He rummaged through my pantry like a marine with a mission.

"What the hell do you eat for breakfast around here?" He inspected my cupboard, holding the sparse offerings he found at arm's length as if they were nuclear waste. "Are you a junk food addict?"

"I've got some cereal somewhere in there." I grabbed a couple of boxes and shook the empty one. "Well, maybe not Lucky Charms, but you can have some Cocoa Puffs if you'd like."

"Have you heard of proteins, fresh fruits and vegetables?" he said "They're food groups, the kind that provide some nutritional value to your body?"

"Ha," I said. "Are you also a comedian?"

"You can't live on junk like this," he said. "No wonder you look like a little breeze could topple you over."

"I don't need much," I said. "Besides, that stuff is cheap and it tastes good. Who doesn't like Lucky Charms?"

"You've got the palate of a three year old." He looked in the old Frigidaire. "There isn't enough food here to sustain a grown-up, let alone two of us. And how about some fresh milk to go with the kiddie cereal that no mom in her right mind would allow her child to eat?"

"Sorry, but your first, last and deposit are already spent," I said. "I had to catch up with the rent and stock up on feed for the animals." No sense telling him about my escape fund. "Milk is next week when I get paid."

"Looks like I'll need to do a food intervention before that," he said. "Maybe you can pick up some things at the convenience store when you go into town?"

"I guess I could do that."

"Also, I scheduled the cable guy to come out this afternoon. Please don't shoot him when he knocks on the door."

"Have you mistaken me for a Rockefeller?" I smashed the empty cereal box in the trash can and grabbed my cup of coffee. "I can't afford cable out here. It's crazy expensive."

"It'll be under my name and on my dime," he said. "I can't be a proper hermit without internet and you've got to complete your online caregiver class."

"But—"

Out in the yard, Neil barked. My heart broke out into

a wild gallop. I leaped to the window, splashing coffee all over, straining to see who was coming up the hill.

"At ease." Ash grabbed a rag and wiped the floor with mind-boggling efficiency. "It's just one car and he's not sneaking around."

"Is that what your Spidey senses are telling you?"

"Neil wouldn't allow anyone to sneak up on us," he said. "He knows I don't like surprises."

I didn't like surprises either. They made me sick to my stomach. I suppressed the urge to lunge for the shotgun, but only because Ash's studious gaze stuck with me as I pressed my nose to the window.

Sixty seconds later, a car came up the hill. I breathed a sigh of relief when I spotted Jordan Meddler in his convertible. He got out of the car and came to door, trailed by Neil, who wagged his tail and sported his best doggy smile. Those two were meant to be lifelong friends.

Tall, lean and lanky, Jordan ran marathons in his time off, which also accounted for the tan that darkened his otherwise fair complexion and the blond streaking his short hair. I met him at the door. The smile froze on his lips when he caught sight of Ash in the kitchen.

"Jordan, this is Ash," I said. "Ash, this is Jordan, the doctor I told you about."

"Hey," Ash said. "Sorry about your nose."

Jordan fingered the bony bridge of his nose self-consciously. It was made even more prominent by the Band-Aid he wore over it and the bruises underscoring his hazel eyes. "What's he doing out of bed?"

"Oh, he's got his own crazy ideas about convalescing," I said. "Guess what? They don't include a bed."

"Mr. Hunter—"

"Call me Ash." He shuffled on the crutches to the

coat stand and groped through his coat's pockets. "Everybody else does."

"Ash," Jordan said, setting his vet bag on the table. "You really shouldn't try to undo Lia's efforts. She worked hard to make you better."

"You're right about that one." Ash fished out a couple of protein bars from his coat and, after opening one, tossed it in my direction. "Try this for nutrition, Lia. Doc?"

Jordan shook his head. "I already had breakfast."

"Are you perchance a Lucky Charms kind of guy?" Ash asked.

Jordan grimaced. "I'd rather eat dirt."

"Great news." Ash winked at me. "You'll live a lot longer than Lia."

The wink shot through my body like a steel ball in a pinball machine. It raced, spun and bounced up and down my spine, lighting up my body's gates all the way down to my toes. Alarms rang in my head. Jackpot.

Oh, no, not this type of a reaction again. I made a conscious effort to ignore my wild emotions. I bit into the protein bar and made a face. "Speaking of dirt…"

Ash laughed. "I said nutrition, not flavor." He tore open the wrapper with his teeth and spat out the foil. "Lia tells me that you and your brother got me out of trouble, Doc. So I thank you. I'll have to think of a way to pay you back in addition to taking care of the bill."

"That was a nasty little infection you had going there." Jordan's gaze fell on me. "I wouldn't have touched it if it hadn't been for Lia. She can be very persuasive."

"Oh, yeah." Ash chomped down on his protein bar. "No arguments there. One look at those stunning gray eyes and you just want to do whatever the hell she says."

Stunning? My eyes? Had I heard right? I had to force my heart to beat in sync again. Surely, I'd heard wrong. Yes, that had to be it.

Jordan cleared his throat. "I'm glad you're feeling better, Mr. Hunter—Ash. Perhaps now you can be persuaded to seek proper treatment elsewhere?"

"Lia's got it covered," Ash said. "She's trying to get through to the VA to arrange for regular doctor's appointments. If anybody can do it, it's her. She's got grit."

"Is that so?" Jordan said stiffly. "Well, until then, I'd keep the antibiotics going." He put a hand on my back and motioned toward the kitchen door. "Lia, may I speak to you privately?"

"Sure." I started for the door. "If it's about Izzy's hoof, I think it's getting better—"

"It's not about Izzy's hoof," Ash said. "I guarantee it."

"No?" I halted in my tracks, confused.

"No," Ash said.

Jordan's eyebrows drew together. "Is there something bothering you?"

"Not yet." Ash eyed the other man with a glimmer in his eye. "But soon."

Jordan's hand wilted off my back. "I don't follow."

"Nothing's bothering me yet, but something will bother me in a moment," Ash explained, leaning casually against the counter.

"You mean because I asked to speak with Lia privately?" Jordan said.

"That too."

I stared from one man to the other. "What's going on?"

"I'm thankful that the doc here helped me out, I really am." Ash downed the last of the protein bar and licked his fingers. "Far be it for me to act like an ungrateful son of a bitch. But I don't like this next part where he pulls you aside and tells you that now that I'm better you should ask me to leave."

"Leave?" I said.

"Yes, ma'am." He sipped on his coffee. "This is the part where he says he's not sure about me. I could be off. I could be dangerous too."

Jordan opened his mouth and closed it.

"Admit it, Doc." Ash flashed his wicked smirk. "Isn't that what you were about to say?"

"Someone has to look after Lia's interests," Jordan said. "She's a woman living alone, away from town. She's kind and caring and it would be a real shame if someone tried to take advantage of her."

"Jordan?" I said. "Ash is not trying to take advantage of me. I asked him to stay. He's actually helping me out by paying rent. He's Wynona's grandkid, for God's sake."

"When you care for dangerous species," Jordan said, "you're bound to get hurt."

"What on earth are you talking about?"

"Reptiles," Ash said. "More specifically, venomous ones like cobras and rattlers, the sort of vicious, unpredictable snakes that will bite the hand that feeds them. Ain't that right, Doc?"

"It was just a figure of speech," Jordan said.

"See, Lia, the doc wants to warn you," Ash said. "Guys like me, coming back from Iraq and Afghanistan, we're iffy. If there's a shooting somewhere, everybody thinks it's one of us. The studies aren't conclusive yet, but we could be off. Doc wants you to know that."

"Jordan knows better than to make huge generalizations like that," I said. "Don't you, Jordan?"

"I'm not saying that Ash is a bad person or anything like that, but…"

"But what?" I said.

"You told me you wanted a woman tenant, remember?" Jordan said. "You were wary and rightly so. You never expected a guy like him to show up at your door. Think about what people in town will say when they find out."

I stared at Jordan for a full thirty seconds, until the full implication of his insinuation hit me. "I don't care what people say." My cheeks burned. "If people want to jump to the wrong conclusion, that's their problem."

"I don't want you to get hurt."

"Jordan, stop," I said. "Ash has been through a difficult time. He's come home and he deserves a fair welcome."

"Actually," Ash said, "the more the doc talks, the more I like him."

It was my turn to stare at Ash. "You do?"

"I wasn't trying to get you to like me," Jordan muttered.

"I know." Ash crumpled up the foil wrap and, with a flick of his wrist, tossed it into the trash can. "But, still, I appreciate a guy who watches over his friends, especially if that friend is Lia."

"I worry about her." Jordan's tone sounded less like concern and more like a warning.

"That makes two of us," Ash said, matching Jordan's tone.

"I'm standing right here," I said, not a little irritated. "I don't need anybody to worry about me." Especially when I did enough of that for the three of us.

"Well, see, I'm not really convinced that Lia's well-being is foremost in your mind." Jordan flashed a joy-less smile.

Ash's smirk was equally mirthless. "I'm not out to convince you, Doc, but since I'm around, you don't have to worry so much."

What the heck? I looked from one man to the other. It was like watching a Ping-Pong match. The mood in my kitchen had taken a turn for the worse and I couldn't figure out why.

"Come on, Lia." Jordan appropriated my elbow. "Let's go check on Izzy."

"Um, okay."

"Yes, by all means, kids, go check on Izzy." Ash twirled his fingers goodbye. "I'll make some fresh coffee and I'll be waiting, right here, when you two come back."

JORDAN LEFT IN a rush after examining Izzy's hoof, avoiding the cottage altogether, declining the cup of coffee that Ash offered. I lingered in the barn, determined to fit a workout into my busy day. I'd missed my exercise while taking care of Ash, a routine that helped me to keep fit and control my anxieties. I stripped down to my tank top. With the mountain lion around and Fish and Wildlife not answering my calls, I forwent trail running for the moment.

Instead, I mounted the rusted treadmill I'd picked up at Goodwill, and, cranking the speed setting, went at it with all I had. Every time fatigue threatened to slow me down, I reminded myself that, as per my own experiences, cardiovascular endurance was vital to any successful escape. *Run, Lia, run.* That's what I'd done for a while. That's what I was destined to do for as long as I lived.

Forty minutes later, I stepped down, sweaty and breathless. My muscles twitched from the strain. Holding my side, I studied the diagrams I'd pinned on the back wall, before I began to practice my strikes on the straw-filled sack I'd recently strung on the beam.

The tricky heel kick I'd been trying to perfect sent the bag swinging wide. It bounced against the wall and came back at me with a vengeance. It struck me square on the chest and shoved me butt-first into the ground. I hit the dirt with a grunt. The air swooshed out of my lungs. I sprawled on the floor for a full sixty seconds, struggling for breath, staring at the rippling ceiling beams.

"Score one for the bag."

I craned my neck and made upside down eye contact with Ash. He grinned then shuffled forward on the crutches. Neil trotted over, sniffed me and promptly began to lap at my neck and shoulder. I caught his face in my hands to prevent him from licking me to death. I flushed. Maybe I could be the cover girl for *The Idiot's Self-Defense Guide*.

"How long have you two been watching?"

"Long enough." Ash stood over me, offered a hand and pulled me up.

I groaned like an old lady and bent over my knees, trying to catch my breath.

"Don't just lay there like a stationary target," Ash said. "You've got to counterattack right away. You've got to keep moving, even if you can't breathe."

"It's hard to think without oxygen flowing to your brain."

"If you don't think, you die." He examined the diagrams on the wall. "Krav Maga?"

I nodded, still sucking for breath.

"Interesting," he said. "I don't know too many civilians who practice it."

"It's all the rage in urban gyms."

"Shows what I know after years of consecutive deployments," he said. "How long have you been training?"

"Apparently, not long enough." I straightened and slapped the dirt off my butt. "What's the point if even the punching bag can beat me?"

"It's all about muscle memory." He inspected my improvised punching bag. "You start with the simple movements and repeat them until you have them down pat. Then you build on that. But first, your bag is too light. You've got to find a proper opponent."

His eyes scanned the barn. He grabbed a three-legged stool and, after plunking it behind the punching bag, bent his knee and balanced his injured leg on it. He braced the bag between his arms. "Let's see you throw a cross-body punch."

"Oh, no," I said. "I don't want to hurt you."

"You won't hurt me," he said. "Come on, little girl, give it a try."

Little girl?

I hurled my fist at the bag. Ash moved it slightly to one side. My knuckles skimmed the burlap and burned with the brief contact.

"Your opponent won't be standing still waiting for a hit," he said. "Be aware. Plant your feet first, claim your real estate. Krav Maga is about speed, maximum effectiveness and preemptive attack."

"You know Krav Maga?"

"Expert level," he said. "Don't react, attack with the end in mind and anticipate your opponent's range of responses. Try it. Feet apart, feel the earth beneath your feet."

I landed a solid punch on the bag, which didn't move this time around. A jolt shot up my arm. "Ow." I grimaced and shook off the pain.

"Contact means pain," Ash said. "It's a lesson you have to embrace. Your opponent is constructed of bones and muscles. He'll be bigger than you, and stronger too, which is why you have to be faster and smarter if you're going to win the fight."

He went through the basic combinations, teaching me how to turn my elbows, knees and heels into weapons and where a hit could make the biggest difference.

"Go for the body's vulnerable spots," he said. "Eyes, throat, face, groin, feet, toes. Show me a hair grab escape." He watched me critically. "Not bad, but you need to build speed, range of movement and endurance."

"I just need to be able to defend myself."

"The most effective defense is an intelligent attack," he said, "and the most effective attack is the one that disables your opponent fast and for good. Why are you so keen to learn to fight anyway?"

"No questions," I said. "Remember?"

"You're a gutsy gal with lots of brainpower." He challenged me with a smirk. "Why are you afraid?"

"Is that how you want it?" I front-kicked the punching bag. "What were you doing in Afghanistan when you got wounded?"

He absorbed the energy of the hit without so much as a grunt. "That's classified information," he said. "Why is it that you don't like questions at all?"

"For your own good, that's classified too."

"Come on, Lia." His eyes darkened. "Tell me the truth."

"The truth?" I stepped away from the bag and wiped the sweat off my brow. "Okay, I'll give you the truth. The truth kills, Ash, it kills with astonishing regularity. So be happy that you don't know anything about it, and heal fast. The sooner you get away from me, the safer you'll be."

FIVE

I PACED THE end of the old dock with my cell glued to my ear, grateful that I had reception. Otherwise, I might have had to spend the entire glorious day indoors trying to get my job done. On the lakeshore, I spotted Neil trotting toward me with a giant stick held fast between his jaws. Ash followed, maneuvering his crutches onto the dock's creaking boards, face set into straight lines. I hated it when he was in pain. I waved at him, greeted the sweet German shepherd with a side hug and returned my attention to the phone call in progress.

"What do you mean *four* months?" I said.

"Major Hunter is not registered as critical," the bureaucrat on the other side of the line said. "It's the best we can do."

"Major Hunter may not be classified as critical, but he's in pain," I said. "He needs to be seen right away."

"Hey." Ash set his crutches aside, lowered himself to sit on the dock and swung his legs over the edge. "What's up?"

"VA," I mouthed.

He waved his hand dismissively and, after prying the stick from Neil's jaws, flung it far on the beach. Neil took off like a rocket after the stick.

"A four-month wait is not reasonable," I told the woman on the phone. "These are our country's heroes, surely there's something you can do."

"Maybe I can fit him into one of the waiting lists," the woman said.

"I don't want him on a waiting list," I said. "I want him on an appointment list."

"No need to get prissy."

"I'm not prissy," I said. "What do I have to do to get my boyfriend out of pain?"

"I'm afraid I'm going to hang up now."

"Don't you dare…"

"Goodbye," the woman said. "And thank you for calling Veterans Affairs."

The line went dead. I groaned in frustration. Neil, who'd just returned from fetching his stick, dropped it on Ash's lap and yapped.

"You tell 'em boy." I plopped down next to Ash.

"Man," Ash said. "You're fierce on the phone, maybe even a little scary."

"But it didn't get me anywhere." I huffed in frustration.

"I can make my own appointments." Ash hurled the stick for Neil again. "You work hard enough as it is and I can afford to see a private doctor if I need to. Besides, there are other guys out there that need those appointments more than I do."

"Maybe," I said, "but nobody should have to put up with this crap. Wait a minute." I had an idea. I sifted through my notes, found the number I needed and, after dialing, waited as the line rang.

"How about a picnic?" Ash unzipped his backpack, pulled out a Tupperware container and, popping off the top, offered me a perfectly layered, crust-free, peanut butter and jelly sandwich.

"Oh." I was a little tempted. "I don't want to eat you out of your food."

"Two slices of bread, how's that going to make a dent?" He pressed the sandwich into my hand. "Besides, you went and got the bread and the peanut butter from the convenience store." He picked another sandwich and bit into it. "Call it a service fee."

The cell clicked and a voice came on the line. "Watkins."

"Lia Stuart here," I said. "I need a favor."

"Is Major Hunter misbehaving?"

"Only occasionally." I smirked at him.

Ash grinned, then his tongue slid over his lips, licking the excess peanut butter from the corners of his mouth. He might as well have licked my brain clean of thoughts. And the heat between my legs…for all I knew, his tongue had visited there, as well. Why was he looking at me like that? Dear God. When had I turned into a wanton freak of nature?

"Ms. Stuart?" The gunny cleared her throat. "And the reason for your call is?"

"Oh, yes, of course." I pushed the shameless thoughts out of my malfunctioning brain. "I've been trying to get those appointments on your list for days now. I'm getting nowhere."

She grumbled under her breath with familiar frustration. "I'll call you right back." She hung up.

"Ha!" I smiled. "Now they're going to get an earful."

"Yes, ma'am," Ash said. "I have a feeling you're about to terrorize those bureaucrats."

"Do you know what they're going to get?" I clawed my fingers, gnashed my teeth and lowered my voice into a spectral bass. "The wrath of Gunny Watkins."

Ash burst into his contagious laughter. "You don't give up easily, do you?"

I growled. "I'm as dangerous as Godzilla."

"You are pretty formidable," he said, laughing some more. "I like that about you. You're funny too. Neil and I, we're not into people these days, but we like hanging out with you."

My skin flushed under his scrutiny. He liked being with me. If he only knew how much I enjoyed coming home every night to lit windows and waking up to the sounds of his jarring workout playlist. I enjoyed having someone to talk to, even if I did most of the talking and he did most of the listening.

During the past two weeks, we'd fallen into an easy routine: breakfast together, chores, long morning walks to enhance Ash's recovery and Krav Maga training for me. It wasn't all nice all the time. Sometimes he struggled with his temper. Other times, he could be moody or infuriatingly stubborn. Once he made up his mind, there was no reasoning with him. Moving Mount Everest would've been easier than changing his mind any day. But Mount Everest aside, he was honest, straightforward and intelligent.

The smarter part of me knew that this was a temporary situation. I needed to heal him and move him out of my life as soon as possible. The balance of my emotions, those inexplicable pangs of madness that hit me unexpectedly—like at this very moment, when he licked the jelly off his fingertips—those were forced aside and ignored, although they tended to ambush me in my dreams.

Neil returned with his stick and plopped down next to Ash, fur wet, chest heaving, tongue hanging. Ash praised the dog and scratched his belly, smiling with the kind of affection that would reassure any and all of God's creatures on earth.

"Neil was worried that you didn't think he carried his weight around here," Ash said.

"Oh, please." I reached over and scratched Neil's soft under chin. "Neil is an awesome guard dog."

Ash wasn't bad to have around either. He kept busy with projects around the cottage—fixing the fences, tweaking the plumbing, repairing the barn, rewiring the microwave, shuffling on his crutches around the lake with Neil at his heels. On patrol, as he liked to say.

"There, buddy," Ash said to the dog. "Does that make you feel any better?"

Neil barked, a light, happy *woof*.

"Without a doubt," I said. "You're the most handsome dog I've ever met."

"Did you hear that, boy?" Ash said. "She likes you." He took out two milk boxes from his backpack, fitted the straws into them and offered one to me. "Why don't you have a dog?"

"Oh, well, I… I had one. Once. A little dog. His name was Pepe. It was a long time ago. He died."

"Sorry." Ash drew on his milk quietly.

I nibbled on my sandwich and sipped on my milk box, fighting off the memories. The sound of yelping filled my head, my little Pepe dying a gruesome death because I made a mistake. *Steady. Cope. Breathe.* I had to force the awful sounds out of my head.

"You okay?" Ash said. "You got real quiet there all of the sudden."

"I'm fine." No flashbacks allowed.

I concentrated on the present. I made myself take a bite of the sandwich and then another. Focus on the positive. That's how I made it from one day to the next. The food settled well in my stomach and reminded me that eating regular meals was a healthy habit I'd forsaken too many times in my life. This moment was nice, sitting on the dock under the sun with Ash and Neil, taking in the osprey's acrobatic flights over the lake.

Neil barked when one of the birds grabbed a fish nearby.

"Go on, boy," Ash said. "You've worked hard today. You can take your break now. Twenty minutes of just being a dog and then you're back. But remember, no porcupines."

Neil barked again and trotted off as if he'd understood every single word that Ash had said. I was pretty sure that there were no porcupines in his near future.

"He's also got to be the smartest dog I've ever met," I said.

"Kind of like his owner?" Ash flashed me a goofy smile.

"A bit more modest."

Ash laughed, but the smile wilted quickly on his face. His eyes darkened and he winced as he dug his fist in his thigh.

"Hurting?" I said.

"Not much."

In Ash-speak, that meant he was hurting like hell.

"Do you want me to run to the cottage and get you some meds?"

"You know how I feel about all that junk."

God, he was stubborn. His appointment could still be weeks away. "Maybe I can help."

"How?"

"Maybe I could try to stretch the leg muscles."

"Have you done it before?"

"Well, I rehabbed a lame mule last year. Does that count?"

"A mule?" He laughed his quiet cackles. "Very

appropriate. Why not?" He scooted backward and stretched on his back. "Experiment away."

"But don't blame me if you end up worse off."

"You're hereby released of all liability."

That smile. It liquefied me on contact. *Stop it.* I couldn't afford to feel like this. Not only was the attraction dangerous and inconvenient, it was also inappropriate. He was my charge and I was his caregiver. I was supposed to heal him, not ogle over him like a hormonal adolescent.

Worse, what if I was malfunctioning? What if my past was influencing my behavior?

I was no ignorant chick. I'd done research and read a lot about my situation. I strove to make myself into an educated survivor. Lots of people developed hypersexual behaviors after experiencing what I had, but my reaction had been the complete opposite. I hadn't been attracted to anyone, hadn't connected with anyone physically or emotionally in years, and I avoided intimacy at all cost.

Why was this happening to me now?

I pushed the troubling thoughts out of my head. After all, there was no real danger. I was barren inside and not much to look at on the outside. No one in their right mind would be attracted to someone as damaged and scarred as me, especially not Ash, who'd have the pick of the litter. Surely his finely honed brain steered him clear of broken people like me.

I worked my fingers carefully through Ash's sweats, feeling along his thigh. His quads contracted in a massive spasm. His hamstring was stiff as a blade. With care, I bent his knee, perched his injured foot over my back and tucked my shoulder beneath the back of his knee. Then I pressed forward, slowly stretching the quads.

"How does that feel?" I asked.

"Hurts good." He winced. "Keep going."

"Let's do it in small increments." I eased the pressure before I slowly increased it again. "We don't want to kill you."

His face came closer when I pressed forward. I caught a whiff of his scent: boiling water, fresh clay and cold granite imbued with a hint of cedar from the shampoo he kept in the shower. Shards of dark blue and obsidian black flecked his blue irises, which focused on my face with laser-beam intensity.

"I know you don't like questions," he said, "but could you just answer one?"

I leaned away from him. "And if I say no, will you stop asking?"

"But you didn't say no." He grinned. "Do you perchance have a history of paranoia?"

"What?" I stared at him. "No!"

"It'd be okay if you did," he said. "You don't mind hanging out with me, and I'm a firm believer in the law of reciprocity—"

"I'm not paranoid."

"Yeah," he said. "I didn't think so either. Most of the time, you're a pretty rational lady. You've got a big brain and you use it frequently. Besides, there are no psychotropic meds anywhere in the house."

I straightened on my knees. "You looked?"

He offered a sheepish smile. "Sorry?"

"You're *not* sorry."

"I am, I swear," he said in a strangled voice. "You don't have to press the stretch so hard."

"Oh, sorry." I released the pressure and tried to cope with the idea that he'd looked through my cupboards.

"Don't get mad at me," he said. "You have to admit that scouting was the smart thing to do."

"Really?" I scoffed. "You wouldn't think so if I'd been the one looking through all your stuff."

"Just because you haven't admitted to it, doesn't mean you haven't done it."

The heat that blushed my face served as a signed and sealed confession.

"See?"

"Turn around," I said, trying to disguise my embarrassment.

"I don't blame you," he said, shifting to his belly. "Being thorough is always wise. The way I see it, I've done us a favor. I've eliminated madness from the equation. Which leaves two outstanding possibilities: either you're running from the law or…"

"Or what?"

"Or you're running away from a specific someone."

Two out of two. My heart skipped a whole lot of beats. My lungs failed to process the air. I was running away from a very specific, dangerous, savage someone—someone who wouldn't hesitate to kill me and anyone associated with me on sight. Despite the brisk day, a cold sweat broke out on my forehead. The less Ash knew, the better. It was imperative for his safety.

I forced myself to breathe and focused on the moment. My fingers dug into the hip insertion as I pressed down in search of a release. The feel of his muscular glutes warmed my belly. His mind might be too sharp for my liking, but it was true: he had a very nice ass.

"On your side, mister."

He shifted toward me at the same time that I leaned

into him and ended up accidentally brushing his lips against my chin. His breath rushed against my neck. Judging by the shiver that shook me, the guy's lungs were fashioned from pure ice. My nipples poked through my shirt like a pair of frozen spikes.

He stared at me as only Ash could. "Are you trying to distract me?"

"Impossible," I said. "Your mind is a one-way track."

"It's a great strategy," he said, "that is, if you meant to distract me."

Had he just made a pass at me? No way. Maybe? I suppressed the subversive part of me that wanted to believe he'd made a pass at me. I was not that delusional.

He sighed as if in resignation. "Back to my theories, then. My grandmother was a law-abiding citizen. She would have never aided a criminal. On the other hand, she was known for taking on impossible odds. She would have gone out of her way to help someone trying to escape from an abusive relationship, for example."

Not a word made it through my tightly pressed lips. I didn't want to lie to him, but I couldn't tell him the truth either. Fortunately, my phone rang.

I released his leg and scrambled on all fours for the cell. "Yes?"

"You're going to get a call from a supervisor in ten minutes," Gunny Watkins said. "Make the most out of it."

"A million thanks," I said before she hung up.

Ash sat up. "Sounds like somebody somewhere is getting his ass kicked."

"How does your leg feel?"

"A lot better, actually."

"Good."

I rubbed his thigh, just to take off the sting of the

stretches, but it didn't quite work the way I expected. In the neighborhood of my hand, the bulk between his legs rose to notable proportions. The worst part? I was curious. I really wanted to know how he would feel to my touch.

He caught me looking. My face burned. I prayed for someone to please pluck me out of the moment and spare me from those eyes full of questions.

He cleared his throat. "Lia?"

I stuck out my finger. "Not a word from you."

"But—"

"Nope," I said, collecting my cell and my pad. "Don't want to hear it."

"There's no need to get upset."

"I'm not upset," I said as I got to my feet.

"Talk to me," he said, reaching for his crutches, struggling to get up. "It's what adults do."

Steady. Breathe. Cope. Or run. Run like hell.

"Wait," Ash called after me. "Lia, damn it. Stop!"

Talk about a pair of obedient feet. They halted at the sound of his voice. I turned around slowly.

Ash stared at me with unbearable intensity. "Where the hell are you going?"

"I've got an important phone call from the VA coming in," I said in my best business tone. "I'm going to take it at the house. After that, I'm going to work." And after that, I might have to find my way to the moon in order to avoid the glare he leveled on me.

"Lia…" I couldn't read the emotion in his eyes. Skepticism? Frustration? Anger? "You can't run away all the time."

I stuck out my chin. "Who says I'm running away?"

"You're bailing."

"No, Ash, I'm busy."

"What about our previous conversation?"

"What conversation?"

"The one we were having when the gunny called."

"Oh, that one." I turned on my heels and marched down the dock. "Consider it finished."

LIKE MOST FRIDAY NIGHTS, Mario's bustled with a rowdy crowd, faithful locals who drank by the gallon during the weekend, plus the gas company's field crews, a handful of permanent employees from the nearby ski resort and a few truckers detoured from the highway.

I wove between the crowded tables and the bar, heaving full trays of oversize mugs brimming with tap beer. It wasn't my dream job, but it paid cash and it took care of the bills. It allowed me to feed my rescued animals and have a place of my own, both great sources of joy to me. Besides, I really liked Mario and the majority of the townies who frequented the bar.

At the mike, Jimmy Martin—looking like a young Bob Marley—rasped on his guitar like a cat scratching a pole, hurling his folksy interpretation of "Story of My Life" above the noise, fitting in my name every few lines. It didn't rhyme, but what the heck.

"Marry me, lovely Lia," he added at the end of the song, á la Elvis Presley.

I lifted my hand in the air, encouraging a group response.

"Not tonight," the crowd intoned in unison, mimicking my usual reply. "But maybe tomorrow."

The place dissolved into laughter. I smiled. The regulars got such a kick out of my little trials and tribulations.

I plunked down the mugs on the VIP table. "Here you go."

Sheriff Wilkins tipped his hat. "Thanks, Lia."

"Yeah, thanks," Jordan said. "Put it on my tab, will you?"

"This round is on me." The diminutive Reverend Martin took out his wallet.

"Be quiet, all of you." Gary Woods, the owner of the local gas company, slipped a twenty into my apron's pocket. "It's my turn."

Ouch. The pinch of a bruising set of fingers stung on my butt. I whirled around to confront Charlie Nowak, Wood's foreman in Copperhill. He sat behind me on his usual stool, belly spilling over his belt, staring at the ceiling.

God, he made me so mad! I sizzled inside. He was well into his cups, but it was beyond me how he managed to pinch me with such stealth in front of everybody. I took my vengeance and poured half his beer on his lap.

"Oops," I said and I wasn't sorry. "I'll get you some napkins."

"Never mind that." Gary's wife, Barb, a busty blonde with a preference for big hair and neon-red lipstick, threw a whole stack of napkins on Charlie's lap, then turned to me. "Is it true that Ash Hunter is back in town? Rumor is he's staying at your place."

"Is that so?" Charlie shifted his bulk on the stool, suddenly interested in the conversation.

Crap. The last thing I wanted to do was draw attention to myself by becoming the target of Barb Wood's enterprising rumor mill. Never one to miss a chance to make a point, Jordan waggled his fair eyebrows. Amusement twinkled in his eyes.

"It's no rumor," I said. "He's renting out a room at my place while he tackles his grandmother's affairs."

"How long will he be staying with you?" Barbara said.

"Not long," I said. "A few weeks maybe?"

"Is it true he's wounded?" she said. "Somebody said he's lame, scarred and deformed. He might be a little off too."

This time, when Jordan's stare met mine, he leaned back on his chair and flashed me a smug smile that blared *I told you so*.

"Jesus, Barb," Gary said. "There you go again, wagging your tongue."

"Gossip is a delicious sin," the reverend put in.

"I talked to Ash the other day on the phone," the sheriff said. "He sounded perfectly rational, like his old self."

"He called me too," the reverend said. "He's a kind soul. He takes after his grandmother."

Ash had talked to the sheriff? And to the reverend as well? What about?

None of my freaking business. I should be glad he had reached out. Ash was getting better every day, but so far, he showed little interest in venturing beyond the cottage, accepting my company but otherwise keeping to himself. His medical appointments were finally coming up. He'd have to leave the cottage for sure then.

"Wynona did a great job with the boy," the sheriff said. "He was always a bright one, a real winner. Unlike you, Nowak."

Charlie let out a laugh. "I bet I can hunt elk just as good as that SOB."

"In your dreams," the sheriff said.

"Well?" Barb demanded. "Is he lame, scarred or deformed?"

"Of course not," I said a bit too sharply. "He's recovering from his wounds—that's true—but he's fine. He's doing really well."

"When do we get to see him?" Gary said. "I'd like to talk to him, if I could."

"Maybe we ought to drive to your place," Barb suggested. "A visit may cheer him up."

I imagined Ash's displeasure at finding Barb on our stoop.

"Oh, no, really," I said. "That won't be necessary."

"Give the boy some time," the sheriff said. "He'll be out and about when he's ready."

"Hot tamale," Barb said, squinting toward the door. "Who's that? I don't think I've seen that hunk around here before."

I turned around. A stranger scanned the room at the door as if looking for someone. His temples were streaked with white but he was lean and fit, and he wore a designer sports jacket that said both *urban* and *moneyed*. My mind's alarms screeched a lot louder than Jimmy Martin's chords. My belly sank to my feet. I ducked behind my tray and scrambled away, tracking the stranger all the way until I made it to the back room. Tucked behind the wall, I studied the man unseen. The fear. God, it tore into my guts like a rusted blade.

The man whose name I'd tried to erase from my mind had the means to hire people that looked just like this stranger—wealthy, competent, alert.

The newcomer settled on a stool, ordered a beer and struck up conversation with Mario. I couldn't hear what he said over the loud music, but it was obvious he asked a lot questions. Not a good sign. I hesitated in the shadows. I couldn't hide all night, but I didn't want to show my face either. I was trying to decide what to do next when Mario came around the corner and startled me.

"You okay, hon?" he said. "You're jumpier than a mountain goat tonight."

"You took me by surprise, that's all." I wrung my hands together. "Who's he?"

"You mean the looker in the mucho-money jacket?" Mario's dimples deepened with his smile. "Is that why you don't pay attention to our guys? You like them rich urban types instead?"

"Oh, no, it's not that. I mean—"

"Don't get so flustered." Mario chuckled on his way to the cellar. "I was joking. You've got the right to like whoever you like, and I do hope you like someone nice, someone who deserves you, Lia. But this one's asking about Ash and nobody's telling him anything."

Ash? I was relieved but also instantly curious. Was he with the Marines? No, Gunny Watkins had already straightened all of that out. I breathed a little easier. At least he wasn't after me.

I lingered in the back room until the guy got a call on his cell, finished his beer and left without further trouble. By then, my customers had grown really thirsty. I jumped back into the fray even though my nerves felt like jagged shards of glass. Terror spin. That's what strangers did to me. My life pitched up and down like a wild roller coaster ride. These days, I lived on hope, luck and faith. I needed an awful lot of all three to remain free and alive.

SIX

I SAT IN the waiting room at the VA hospital with Neil at my feet, sipping on my fifth cup of coffee, bundled up in my coat despite the fact that the room was quite warm. Occasionally, a drop of sweat trickled down my back. I wore my hat and my big sunglasses and kept my back to the security cameras the entire time. I didn't think anyone would recognize me here, but I didn't take any chances.

It had been a long morning. After innumerable phone calls, a week's wait and an hour-and-a-half drive, Ash faced a grueling schedule that included multiple appointments with several specialists. I'd nearly told Ash about his visitor at Mario's a dozen times. But every time I opened my mouth, I thought about how anxious he was about going to the hospital. I couldn't get the words out.

I'd accompanied him to most of his appointments, including the one with the orthopedic surgeon, where I'd seen the X-ray of Ash's leg for the first time. The femur had fractured in half, snapped in two as if it was but a toothpick. The tibia and the fibula showed two breaks, healed, thank God. The foot was the worst. It had been shattered in the explosion and rebuilt with plates, pins, mesh and wires. It was a miracle that the doctors had been able to reconstruct it in the first place.

"The marvels of modern medicine," the doctor had

said as he turned from the screen to examine Ash's leg. "From one to ten, what's your pain level?"

"Two," Ash said.

"Eleven," I put in. "If he were human, he'd tell you. He doesn't take the pain meds, so he hurts a lot. And by the way, the leg cramps all the time."

"There's the honest answer," the doctor said.

"Tattletale," Ash mouthed.

"Damn IEDs have done their share of damage," the doctor said. "It's like stepping on barbed wire every time you put your foot down."

Ash snapped. "How the hell would you know?"

I squeezed his hand and chastened him with my best "watch your temper" look.

The doctor sighed and, pushing off from his stool, lifted up the cuff of his pant to display a futuristic prosthesis springing from his shoe.

"Sorry," Ash muttered. "I'm such an asshole. Where?"

"Fallujah," the doctor said. "Are we good now?"

"We're good," Ash said.

"I gave up the limb to live pain free," the doctor said. "You may not be ready yet, but remember, you have options. There are no guarantees that your leg—especially your foot—will hold up for long-term daily use. I don't know that it can stand the additional wear and tear that a full return to the service would entail."

The doctor went on to rattle off a long list of possible complications that could require surgical interventions and amputation, including stress breaks, faulty calcifications and more infections. The spiel was enough to make me frantic with worry. I started to bite my pinkie nail, but Ash shook his head and I dropped my hand, at least for the moment.

After that, Ash went to do his mental health evaluation. He was now attending the last appointment of the morning with the orthopedist while I got copies of his medical reports. Sitting in the waiting room, I ruffled through the thick folder and took a deep breath. I'd be happy when we got out of the city and returned to the relative safety of my little valley.

A very pregnant woman plopped down next to me. "Husband? Brother? Sister?" she asked.

"Excuse me?"

"Are you here waiting for your husband?" She pulled out a set of needles and some yellow yarn from her quilted bag.

"Oh, no," I said. "He's not my—well—I guess he's my boyfriend."

"Aw, how sweet." The woman knitted as she spoke. "I'm waiting for my husband. Afghanistan. Where did your guy get wounded?"

"Afghanistan too, I think."

"Helmand, Kandahar or Kunar province?"

I had no clue.

"Don't take it personally," the woman said. "It's hard for them to talk about these things."

Any additional attempts that I'd made to talk to Ash about his time abroad had been met by silence and gruff. I didn't push him. His silence seemed fair, since I didn't want to talk about my past either. Besides, we were getting along. Some days, he didn't even ask too many questions.

"Is this your first time at the VA?" the woman said.

"Yep." I folded and refolded Ash's leather jacket on my lap.

"It's going to be okay." She eyed my jittery foot. "Try to relax."

I tried to repress the impulse. "I'm super caffein-ated."

"If it gets you through the day, caffeine is better than drugs and alcohol." She knitted furiously. "Our guys, they survived. We're the lucky ones. The rest is just gravy. Think about all of those who didn't make it back home."

My own problems had insulated me from the pain and hardship of families like hers. A war fought so far away seemed like a movie on TV. It was easy to forget the sacrifices of these men and women when one didn't have to worry about improvised explosive devices in the streets or terrorists in one's backyard.

"There he is!" The woman put away her knitting needles and, flashing a dazzling smile, got up to meet her husband. He balanced on prosthetic legs, wore dark sunglasses and carried a white cane, but his face lit up when he wrapped his arm around the woman's waist. She gave me a little wave. I waved back. My gaze lingered on them as, together, they made their way out of the clinic.

"Hey."

Ash stood before me, wearing blue jeans and a plaid snap front shirt, looking incredibly tall, strong and whole by comparison.

I jumped to my feet and hugged him.

He looked startled, but he hugged me back. "What was that for?"

"For surviving." I wiped a tear from my eye. "I don't think I've ever thanked you for your service."

His eyebrows drew close together. "Are you okay?"

"Yeah." I stepped back, a little embarrassed. I was probably PMSing. "Where are your crutches?" I asked, belatedly noting their absence.

"Gone." He showed me a cane. "I graduated to this plus a brace instead. I'm cleared to drive and I'm cleared for a round of rehab too."

"Awesome news." I high-fived him. "I feel like we just won the lottery."

The smile on his face could have illuminated the whole of the Front Range. There I went again. Rules, I had rules. No ogling or gawking allowed. No dreaming or fantasizing either, and no cheesy metaphors, period.

That was how smart, competent, independent women dealt with inconvenient—not to mention dangerous—attractions. Sure, Ash was cute and he had a strange, powerful effect on me, but he wasn't part of the plan. Step one, heal him. Step two, send him on his merry way.

I set a course toward the parking lot. "Time to go home."

"How about pizza?" he said, taking his coat and Neil's leash from me and leaning on his new cane. "I'm starving."

"Sorry," I said. "I don't have spare change to buy bread, let alone for eating out."

"It'll be my treat," he said. "We got up at the crack of dawn. We've been here all morning and you must be hungry too."

I hesitated, torn between hunger and caution. "I don't want you to waste your money on me."

"After everything you've done for me, the least I can do is buy you lunch."

He waited patiently for me to make up my mind. Being out and about wasn't easy for him. He'd adapted nicely to the cottage, but the city and the clinic put him on edge. His eyes scanned the spaces around him constantly, as if tracking some invisible enemy.

"Are you sure you want to go a restaurant?" I asked.

"The shrink says I need to be out." He sighed. "She says I need to make an honest effort. So I'll be damned if I don't try."

His determination to get better impressed me. Besides, he deserved the little splurge.

THE RESTAURANT WAS cozy, but the red silk rose adorning the table had to go. I banished it to another table when Ash went to the bathroom. I hated roses. Roses reminded me of the monster I wanted to forget. I had the sense he was always watching me, reading my mind, monitoring my heart. Sometimes I imagined that if I let my guard down, he would see through my eyes, target the people I liked and strike yet another devastating blow to my life.

Steady. I took a deep breath. *Cope.*

With the rose gone, I sat down on my chair and struggled to regain my balance. It became easier when Ash came back to the table and filled my senses with his presence. He anchored me to the here and now. Plus, he was nice to look at.

Maybe it was because I hadn't eaten out in a long time, but the pizza was out of this world. Ash downed several slices at an impressive pace. I nibbled my way through half my slice and kept at it. Wearing his service vest, Neil lay quietly under the white-and-red checkered tablecloth as Ash and I enjoyed our lunch.

"So what's with the costume?" he said, adding a fresh slice to my plate.

"Costume?" I set aside the slice. My appetite vanished, knowing what was coming.

"The Cold War theme—coat, hat, dark glasses indoors, that sort of thing. You don't wear those in town."

"Oh." I fished the mushroom pieces from the slice. "I'm just cold."

"Right," he said. "Are you going to eat those?"

"Mushrooms, ugh." I crossed my eyes and stuck out my tongue.

"What a face." He laughed. "May I?"

"Sure."

He reached over and stabbed the mushrooms with his fork. "I bet the movie-star look explains your aversion to security cameras too."

Not again. "Ash, I—"

"I remember: no questions." He wolfed down the mushrooms. "I'm not brain-dead. But you do have to admit that nobody in their right mind would go through all of the trouble you've gone through unless they were really afraid. You may not always be forthcoming about the truth, but you don't lie either. In the last few weeks, I've learned quite a few things about you."

I didn't want to go down this path, but curiosity got the best of me. "Like what?"

"Well, let's see." He wiped his mouth with the napkin and set it aside. "You love those animals of yours more than you love yourself. You don't mind that they're sick, lame or old. No one wants them, but you do. You're hardworking, diligent, punctual and organized. You can't cook. In fact, you're a pyromaniac's dream date, but you're honest to a fault and you're fair. Do I have it right?"

"I can too cook." I faked about half of my outrage. "Okay, only in the microwave, but that's something."

"You had no cable or internet service until I arrived," he said. "You don't appear on any of the social media sites. You carry the oldest prepaid cell in the history of civilization. You don't use credit cards, or banks, only cash. Your carbon footprint is almost nonexistent."

He'd been paying attention. A fringe of unease prickled my sensitive hackles. I wrung the napkin in my hand. "I'm frugal," I said. "So what?"

"You're educated," he said. "I can tell by the way you speak, the paperbacks on your shelves and the way you look at the world. If you had free access to the job market, you'd be running something for sure."

"Something like what?"

"A company, a program, a classroom, a country," he said. "The bar is work, but it isn't your calling."

Now my hackles were definitely up and sharp as quills.

"My job at the bar pays the bills," I said. "How about we talk about you instead of me?"

"Sure." He flashed me the lopsided smirk that said he was on to me. "When we're finished talking about you. The thing is, I don't think you like working at Mario's."

"I like Mario's," I said. "Your grandma got me that job."

"I bet he pays you under the table."

I glared.

"I know, none of my business." He eyed the slice on my plate. "Are you going to eat that?"

I pushed the plate over to him.

"Being at the bar drains you." He sprinkled a mind-boggling amount of parmesan cheese on the slice. "I can see it when you come home."

"I get tired, that's all."

"I think there's more to it than that." He tore into the pizza.

My stomach squeezed. "What on earth are you talking about?"

He wolfed down a mouthful before he spoke. "You don't like men."

Now my stomach hurt. "I like men fine."

"Jordan said you wanted to rent out the room to a female and you don't have a boyfriend."

"So what?"

"A girl like you, working at a bar, would probably attract lots of men."

"Maybe I have a boyfriend and you just don't know about it."

"Well?" He set down the crust on his plate and wiped his mouth. "Do you?"

Not in this lifetime. "Can you stop asking all these questions?"

He smirked again. "See what I mean?"

"I told you I like men fine, maybe not all of them, maybe not all the time, but—"

"That's it." His eyes lit up. "There's an asshole giving you trouble at work."

Was he a mind reader? A drop of sweat ran down my back. I stretched my turtleneck to allow some circulation in there. I had to stop this conversation. It had already gone too far out-of-bounds.

"Those bruises," he said. "The ones I spotted on your ass the other day when you were wearing those khaki shorts and bent over to clean the fireplace? Are they the work of the creep at the bar?"

I opened my mouth and closed it. "Ashton Hunter, have you been staring at my butt?"

"It's nice to look at," he said, "when it's not covered in bruises."

I reached across the table and smacked him on the arm. "You pervert."

"No, ma'am, I'm just a guy grateful to have two

working eyes. If you bend over and show me your assets, you can't expect me to look away."

My mind spun, engaged in a dangerous game of Russian roulette. I didn't know if the bullet that would destroy me was the one marked "secretly delighted," or the one marked "don't even think about it."

"We're done talking about me," I said. "Turnabout is fair play. What should we address first? Your absent girlfriend?"

"Ouch," he said. "You're going for blood today. Not everybody is cut out to hang out at a hospital or to look after sick people, you know."

"So you're not mad at her?"

"She knew what she wanted and it wasn't me. Besides, it wasn't going to last anyway. We were for fun, not for life."

"You knew that?" I drew on my soda. "You understood the difference?"

He nodded. "The mission was the most important thing in my life. In between missions, it was just R & R."

"Wow," I said. "That shrink you saw today is a magician."

He grinned. "Maybe you ought to talk to her."

"She'd have to be a miracle worker to set me straight," I said, "and even then, I'd still be weird and eccentric."

"Weird and eccentric is cool," Ash said. "I could dig weird and eccentric."

The butterflies in my stomach were off like racing greyhounds and I had little hope to cram them back into the starting gate. And then I remembered a dead man hanging from a gate, a puddle of blood growing at his feet. Just because he'd talked to me.

"What's the matter?" Ash said. "Did I say something wrong? You've got the *look*."

"What look?"

"The one that says you're about to bolt."

"No, no." I pushed the horrible image out of my mind. "I'm fine, fine and amazed at your grand understanding of all things deep."

"If you really have to know," he said. "I'd rather forget my ex."

I waved my hand in the air. "Erased, moving on."

He laughed and I smiled like a fool.

"My turn again," I said. "Inasmuch as I have a lot of respect for the Marines, I'm pretty sure you're more than your average major."

"Is that so?"

"You're not just a foulmouthed, empty-headed hunk either."

His split eyebrow rose. "You think I'm a hunk?"

"You strive to hide it behind that cranky charade, but I'm not fooled. You're also well educated. Your grandmother told me you went to grad school and you've been sending me to buy *The Wall Street Journal* for you every day."

"So?" he said. "A guy can't be interested in the economy?"

"Gunny Watkins said that you were a highly trained asset and a big-ticket investment." I plucked the straw out of my drink and, splashing soda all over the table, pointed it in his direction. "You're a Krav Maga expert. Your powers of observation are impressive. I think you're some sort of special operations kind of guy. Am I right?"

"How about we make a deal?" He stared at me for

a little too long. "I tell you a bit about myself and you tell me about your troubles."

I twisted on the straw until it broke. "I just…can't."

A whimper echoed from under the table. Neil's face popped up by my side. Ash's eyes shifted from the dog to the crumpled straw in my hands to my face.

"Something—or someone," he said in an exacting tone, "has frightened the hell out of you. There's the shotgun and the fact that you jump ten feet high every time someone comes to the door. You dress like that when you go out of town and you train like a soldier. You're not on the wanted or missing lists—"

I gasped. "You looked?"

"If you haven't noticed," he said, "I'm a thorough kind of a guy."

"More like scary."

"The fact that you're not on the lists tells me that whoever you fear doesn't want anyone else to know they're looking for you."

Out. I needed out. I looked over my shoulder and fought an urge to run for the door. Neil laid his paw on my lap and licked my hand.

"You've got no knickknacks." He kept going like a bulldozer without brakes. "You've got no references to your past anywhere in the cottage, no pictures, no mementos, nothing. You never talk about the past. You own very little, your work clothes and the bare essentials. A quick look at your keychain redefines the meaning of self-defense. And then, of course, there's the go bag. Very thorough. Well conceived."

My lungs deflated like punctured balloons. "Go bag?"

"It couldn't be anything other than an escape bag," Ash said. "A backup prepaid cell, a hundred bucks, two wigs, a few sets of high-quality fake IDs. Those are impressive, by the way. Want to tell me where and how you got them?"

God almighty.

Neil thrust his big head between my hands and tried to lick my face.

"Stop it, boy, she should be able to handle truth every once in a while." Ash pulled on the leash before aiming his stare back on me. "I must congratulate you on the disguise concept. It'd be hard for anyone to think of you as a boy, never mind a hipster type. It could work."

My fingers clawed under the table. My nails sank into my thighs. I knew he'd gone through the kitchen cabinets. I suspected he'd looked elsewhere, as well. But my go bag? My jaw ached from clenching it. Who the hell did he think he was?

"You have no idea what you're meddling in."

"My point exactly," he said. "Care to enlighten me?"

I wanted to scream at him. I wanted to accuse him of interfering with my plans and endangering my life and—oh, by the way—his, since he was living with me. Mine wasn't a great life, it might even be a poor excuse for a life, but it was the best life I'd known, and it was *my* life, something I'd never take for granted.

"See?" He shook his head. "You leave me to figure out things all on my own. How else will I be able to minimize risk factors and establish factual operational parameters?"

"Listen to yourself." I squeezed my temples and kept my voice down. "Are you even speaking English? What are you talking about?"

"I can't ask questions and you won't tell me who you fear or why," he fired back. "What other option did you leave me?"

"You want options?" I said. "How about leaving my stuff alone and minding your own business?"

"I tried." He had the gall to look chastened. "Would you believe me if I said I tried?"

"No." I pushed my chair back and, bracing my hands and leaning forward, faced Ash across the table. "I've tried to warn you. But you're choosing not to listen. Let me be clear. People die when they associate with me, people suffer. You got that?"

I pushed away from the table and, sidestepping Neil, stormed out of the restaurant. The German shepherd barked and tried to follow me.

"I know, boy." Ash's voice trailed after me. "She's upset."

I shoved the door out of my way and made it onto the sidewalk. *Steady. Breathe. Cope.* My stomach ached, my teeth hurt from grinding and fury colored the world with a red haze. But my bluster was for naught. Ash had the keys to the truck and I didn't have any other way home. Even though he eventually followed me, I had to wait for him to pay the bill.

I paced around the truck in the parking lot. My life must seem absurd to him. Had the situation been reversed, I would have been curious too. But the monster that stalked me had an IQ in the genius range, the looks, charm and sensibilities of a global tycoon, and the soul of a cold-blooded killer. The combination made him lethal to me, dangerous to his enemies and immune to justice, especially considering his multibillion-dollar cash flow. Nobody, not even his fiercest and most able opponents, had ever managed to best him, which is why my only alternative was to run like hell whenever I sensed he was getting near. He'd killed men for just looking at me. I might be furious with Ash at the moment, but I didn't want anything bad to happen to him.

When he finally came out of the restaurant with Neil on the leash, he opened the door of the truck for me, before limping around and taking his place in the driver's seat. I flashed him a glare before I buckled my seat belt, crossed my arms and fixed my gaze out the window. Neil jumped in the backseat and settled, caramel eyes shifting between us.

"I'm sorry," Ash said, driving out of the parking lot. "I didn't mean to make you mad."

"Just let it be."

"How about we establish some new communication parameters?"

I frowned. "Do you always speak like that or is it just me?"

"We can agree that certain parts of our lives are classified," he explained, braking at a red light. "You set your terms. I set mine. But beyond that, we can talk about the rest."

"Why would we do that?"

"Because we're two human beings living together?" he said. "Because we're friends? Because we're both trying to get better?"

"I'm not sick," I said. "There's nothing wrong with me."

He flashed me a glance. "Are you sure about that?"

I met his eyes. "What are you saying?"

"That anybody who lives through a traumatic experience can suffer from PTSD."

The anxiety. The fear. The nightmares. The fact that my world wobbled on the hinge of my nerves like a fragile crystal globe liable to shatter at any time. Was he right?

"You know, Lia," he offered as the light turned green and he pressed his foot to the accelerator. "We can't operate out of fear. We must operate out of our strengths. We all have to make an effort to get better."

Easier said than done. "You think?"

"Hell, that's what the shrink told me today, which reminds me, do you mind if I stop by the grocery store?"

"You want to go to the grocery store?" I eyed him in disbelief. "The big giant one, here in town?"

"I don't want to go," he said. "But I need to do it. Besides, I live with a woman who feeds exclusively on air and sugary cereals. Remember?"

Once again, I didn't want to sabotage his efforts to get better, or mine, maybe, if I accepted everything he said. I took a deep breath. "Okay."

He pulled into the parking lot, parked the truck and turned off the ignition, but he didn't get out. He stared at the store, at the neon sign flashing above the door and at all those people, streaming in and out. Neil rested his chin on Ash's shoulder. My stomach tightened into a knot. In my own way, I knew how Ash felt.

"Sorry if I pressed you too hard." Ash's fingers wrapped around the wheel. "Sometimes, when I'm fixed on something, I can be such a jerk. Now I feel like I owe you some answers."

"You don't owe me anything."

"You were right," he said. "In addition to being a marine, I am—was—" His Adam's apple bounced on his throat. "Hell, I don't know what I am anymore—I guess I'm in limbo. But before I got wounded, I was a navy SEAL."

The words came out of his mouth softly, reverently. I got a glimpse of his anguish. It erased any traces of residual anger in me and reset me into my caregiver role. He didn't know if he could be the person he was before again. He didn't know if he could exist as someone else either. If anyone in the universe understood his predicament, it was me.

"Did your grandmother know?" I asked.

"Yes, but we decided it would be better if we didn't tell anyone else."

"Do you think you'll go back?"

He shook his head. "I don't know if they'll want me now, lame and all…"

I hesitated. "You don't have to stand the pain, you know."

"I do if I want the foot and I need the foot if I'm going back." He gave me a half shrug.

"I saw several guys at the hospital wearing prosthetic limbs," I said. "They seem to be getting along fine. You saw the doctor. And I met this woman today. Her husband lost both legs and his sight. Despite all of that, they're getting ready to have a baby."

"She must be someone really special," Ash said.

"Maybe he's the one who's really special."

He gave me a probing stare.

"Look, I'm no expert at this, but you have options," I said. "You don't have to hurt."

"Lia, don't." He grappled for words. "You've been living with me lately. Can you imagine me in a wheelchair for weeks—months—at a time? Can you see me crippled for good, an invalid, depending on strangers for everything? I'd be a total jackass, unbearable, much worse than I've been lately, a wretched, miserable ass."

"You can be a little testy at times, but you're not so bad."

He shook his head. "I don't think I could stand it."

"It'd be a temporary situation."

"Who the hell knows for sure?"

Pain gleamed in his stare. His brow wrinkled and the lines of his mouth tightened, making him look older, grimmer. All that sadness clobbered me. How could I, of all people, console the inconsolable?

Well, at least I had to try.

I wet my parched lips. "You're one of the strongest, most determined people I know."

"Then you've been hanging around with losers all your life."

He was probably right on that one, but I stood my ground. "You're smart, skilled and disciplined. You're the original overachiever. Whatever goal you set your mind to, you will reach it."

He scoffed. "Don't be so sure of that."

"What if the best is yet to come?"

"Jesus, Lia, that's a huge cliché and you know it."

"Well?" I said. "What if it's true? What if the life you haven't lived yet holds as much adventure, challenge and satisfaction as your old life did? What if the future holds the same, or even more, promise than your past? Wouldn't you want to see the changes through if it gave you the chance to discover your alternative future?"

He rolled his eyes. "What if all of this talking is psychobabble or wishful thinking?"

"What if it isn't?" I countered. "People get hurt all the time and they still have happy and productive lives, like that guy whose wife is having a baby."

"He'll never serve again," Ash said somberly. "They won't want him."

"I suppose you're right," I said. "But maybe he'll be happy doing something else."

He shrugged. "What if he doesn't want to do anything other than what he did before?"

Ah, now we were getting at the crux of Ash's worries. "Life is all about change. We all suffer. We all fail. We pick up the pieces and try again. We have to forget about the past and reinvent ourselves."

He fixed his eyes on me. "Is that what you did?"

I shrugged. "Sometimes, that's all there's to do."

"Well, at least you're not denying your fucked-up truth, whatever that is." He exhaled a long breath. "Do you want to come into the store or would you rather wait in the truck? You don't have to come in if you don't want to. It's up to you."

I considered the supermarket before me. I hadn't been to one in ages. It was tempting, but there were a lot of people in there, not to mention a lot of cameras.

Was I being paranoid? Surely, after all this time, I could venture out for a few minutes. What were the chances that a random one-time stop at a supermarket could hurt?

I put my hat and sunglasses back on. "Okay."

We walked through the automated doors together. For a moment, we both stood there like petrified trees, blinded by the fluorescent lights. Neil stood between us, looking from Ash to me. I don't know who was more nervous, Ash or me, but Ash's eyes worked the place as if the grocery carts were piled with IEDs and the Taliban waited in ambush somewhere behind aisle three.

The muscles between my shoulders knotted into tight wads, but I offered my hand. Or did I need his hand to tap into his courage?

He seized my hand and clung to it with a grip that surprised me. "Let's roll."

It took a few minutes, but as we wandered down the aisles, Ash began to relax. Eventually, after we got a cart, so did I. The store was huge and full of interesting things. Hat low on my brow, sunglasses on, I enjoyed browsing, pushing the cart as Ash filled it with all sorts of stuff.

"Do you like oranges?" he said, grabbing a two-pound sack.

"I love oranges," I said, "but I'm on ramen until I get paid next week."

"Not while I'm around." He dropped the sack in the cart.

I stared up and down the long cereal aisle. "They don't have this many brands of cereal at Kailyn's convenience store."

"They don't have these many choices in Afghanistan either." He examined the boxes. "What do you think, Almond Clusters or Honey Bunches?"

I shrugged. "No clue."

"Fuck it." He dropped both boxes in the cart. "Let's go see how many types of milk they can squeeze out of the same cow."

It was a measure of our respective situations that two really screwed-up people could find such fun at the grocery store. On the leash, Neil trotted alongside, wagging his tail and sporting his red vest and his dog-at-work happy smile. We were at the register, checking out, when the display next to the magazine racks caught my attention.

Small red packets sat by the register in tidy rows. Botanical Incense, big bold letters announced at the front of the display. Catch the Rush. There was something familiar about the little red packets, but I couldn't quite figure out what it was.

I pulled one out of the rack. On the back, a yellow happy face with crossed-out eyes hovered above a line that said *not for human consumption*. I turned the packet around. The product was called Red Rush. The stylized *R*s in the name were reversed.

My fingertips burned as if singed. The packet fell out of my hand. A shot of adrenaline quickened my pulse. I couldn't breathe. My knees rattled, my throat went dry, my stomach pitched and roiled. It was as if a black hole had opened beneath my feet. My hand went to the back of my neck, where the same inverted *R* had once been inked into my flesh. A patch of thickened skin was the only remnant of a time I wanted to forget. I'd hoped never to see that brand ever again.

"Lia?" Ash said. "Why are you upset?"

I squeaked. "Me?"

Ash gestured with his chin to the German shepherd, pressing his body against my legs. "If Neil thinks you're upset then let me tell you, you're upset." He reached out and took my hands. "You're shaking."

"I…" A bomb had gone off in my mind. My capacity to think had been shattered. I gagged on the bile that surged up my throat. I wrenched my hands from Ash, squeezed between him and the register, and ran.

"Lia!"

I stumbled out of the store and made a straight line for the trash can in the parking lot. I barely made it. I retched like a drunk after a binge.

What should I do? What could I do? The fact that Red Rush was being sold as incense in a national supermarket chain meant that Red was in expansion mode once again. *Red.* How I hated to even think of his name. It felt like a knife stabbing at my brain.

I'd been forced to take Red Rush once, when it was but one of many of Red's "prototypes." He'd tied me down and strapped a mask over my nose and mouth. It'd been the last time he tried one of his prototypes on me. My heart raced in my chest as if it was about to explode. My blood pressure shot up and my head felt as if it was about to blow. My pupils had dilated until I could barely see. I'd suffered tremors, hallucinations and violent seizures that landed me in the hospital. Afterward, I'd been sick with nausea, vomiting and an excruciating migraine that wouldn't let up for days.

Red Rush was most definitively not a harmless pack of botanical incense as marketed. It wasn't a simple variation of marijuana either, but something much worse: a dangerous, powerful, addictive synthetic drug that enslaved its users, ruined lives and was responsible for accidental overdoses, many of which had resulted in deaths. The addictive nature of Red Rush guaranteed Red's market share. I thought of the kids and families that could be destroyed. My stomach churned all over again.

I couldn't stop it. Could I? I'd tried before and lost everything in the attempt.

Walk away. Don't think about it. There was nothing I could do about it. Worry about surviving. Surely someone else could deal with this. If they figured it out before it was too late. If they could. I retched some more.

I spotted Ash and Neil making their way toward me. I wiped my mouth and tried to suppress my emotions. I'd already paid the price. It wasn't my fight anymore.

Neil shoved his head into my hands. Petting the dog calmed my nerves. Ash parked the shopping cart next to the truck and met me by the trash cans.

He queried me with a grim stare. "What the hell happened back there?"

"My stomach," I said. "I think I ate too much."

"You didn't eat that much," he said. "Can you walk?"

"I'm fine," I said.

"And I'm Peter Pan, high on Tinker Bell's dust." He offered his arm. "Are you sure you're all right?"

"Yes." But I took his arm.

"You're such an awful liar."

Ash unlocked the truck's door and lifted me up to the seat. He grabbed a Gatorade from the grocery bags, opened it and handed it to me. I sipped on the Gatorade, nursing my queasy stomach while he loaded the groceries. My nerves were shot.

"Lia," he said once we were back on the road. "What happened back there?"

"Nothing," I said.

I curled up on the seat and closed my eyes, if only to escape his probing gaze. I leaned my head against the window and pretended to sleep. It wasn't easy. For the entire hour-and-a-half drive, I kept seeing Red's brand as if it had been seared inside my eyelids.

SEVEN

WHEN WE RETURNED to the cottage, I stuffed the milk
in the fridge, the vegetables in the pantry and the fresh
fruit in a basket. I was about done when I spotted something at the bottom of one of the empty bags. With two
squeamish fingers, I lifted up the little packet marked
with the inverted *R* and set it down on the counter. How
on earth had my nightmare followed me home?

"You dropped it on the conveyor belt," Ash said,
stacking a set of steaks in the freezer. "I thought you
wanted it."

"Oh, no—well—I guess…"

If nothing else, the glaring red packet on my kitchen
counter was a sign. The entire ride home, I'd tried to
convince myself that Red Rush wasn't my problem anymore. But I failed, probably because I'd been brought
up right and taught to care about other human beings. I
couldn't justify other people's suffering with my puny
excuse for a life.

I waited until Ash went upstairs. Reluctantly, I found
an envelope and addressed it to the one person I knew
who could raise the alarm. *This is it*, I wrote on the
red packet. *I warned you this would happen. Do something about it.*

I dropped the packet in the envelope and sealed it. I
added a postage stamp, but left the return address blank.
I might be reckless, but I wasn't stupid. I'd have to drive
across state lines before I could mail the warning and,

even then, I'd have to take precautions to ensure that the envelope couldn't be traced back to me. The whole thing was a huge, dangerous gamble that increased the odds against me. But how could I just stand by in silence when so many innocent people—kids especially—stood to lose from Red's machinations?

"What are you doing?"

I jumped three feet in the air.

Ash leaned against the threshold, watching me.

I dropped the envelope in my purse and picked up my keys. "Going to work."

"I thought you didn't start until later today."

"Mario needs me early."

"Is that so?" Ash cocked his eyebrows and crossed his arms. "Maybe you ought to skip work tonight. You've had a long day and you were sick earlier."

"I'm fine," I said, avoiding his gaze.

My cheeks were on fire as I mumbled a rushed farewell and bolted to my car. I drove as fast and far as my clunker could go. Two hours and seventeen minutes later, somewhere around the neighborhood of Cheyenne, Wyoming, I pulled into a rural subdivision, found an isolated postal pavilion and dropped the envelope in the mailbox. At least I could breathe a little easier now. With my mission accomplished, I rushed back to Copperhill.

By the time I got to Mario's, it was already past seven and the bar was in full swing. Gas crews from three states had gathered at Copperhill for the night and Charlie Nowak showed up to add to my bruise collection. It was my turn to close, so I was relieved when it was time to lock up around 2:00 a.m.

When I turned the ignition, the car wouldn't start. To be fair, it was a 1980 Chevy Citation, way past its

expiration point and I'd added too many new miles to
an odometer that didn't even turn anymore. I'd bought
the car at an auction for two hundred and eight dollars cash. If it had been headed for the scrap pile back
then, it was beyond scrap now, more like total crap. It
had never run well, but lately, it really wanted to go to
car heaven.

I slapped the wheel and groaned. "Oh, come on."

I popped open the hood and got out. I took off my
shoe, banged it against the carburetor and slipped it back
on. As if my troubles weren't enough, Charlie Nowak's
truck pulled into the parking lot. Two of his drunken
buddies slumped in the vehicle as Charlie climbed out
and stumbled crookedly across the asphalt.

I slammed the hood down and dove for the door, but
Charlie beat me there.

"Does our little Lia need help?" he slurred, pulling
up his pants. "I can help, yes I can."

"It's late, Charlie." I edged around him. "Go home."

"If you come home with me," he said, "I can help
you out really well."

"Charlie," I said, "You're a nasty drunk. I don't want
to hurt you, but if you try anything, I might have to."

Charlie's cackles echoed in the night. "You? Hurt
me? That's hilarious. Let's be friends, Lia. Let's be real
close friends. I can take you home and show you my
baseball cap collection. I think you'd like my basement."

The fine hairs on the back of my neck stood on end.
The word *basement* threatened to push me over some
proverbial cliff. I clutched my keychain and clenched
my fist. I'd decided long ago that I would never be a
victim again.

"Be decent, Charlie," I said. "Step out of my way."

"Sure." He opened the driver's side door and, giving

his friends in the truck the thumbs-up, stepped away. "Whatever you say."

As I went to get in the car, he lunged. He grabbed my wrists with one hand and pinned me against the side of the car with his body.

"You're so fucking hot." He planted a slobbering kiss in the vicinity of my mouth, reeking of stale beer and cigarettes. "Girls like you play hard to get, but you're no frigid bitch. I told my friends. There's a real woman under that hide and I'm gonna skin her out tonight."

"Get off me." I struggled against his bulk. "Let me go, right now!"

"This ass, these boobs." His free hand rubbed all over me, pulling and squeezing. "Come on, honey. I'm gonna give you what you need."

I glanced at the truck, hoping his friends would come to my aid or at least try to talk some sense into Charlie. No such luck. They were as drunk as him, if not worse, hollering obscenities out the window.

Charlie doubled me in size and weight, but he was drunk and panic lent me the strength to claim my real estate. Drawing on Ash's training, I planted one foot forward and smashed my knee against Charlie's groin.

He bent over and hollered. In that instant, I turned my wrists and snatched them out of his hand. I found the small tube hanging from my key chain, flipped the safety switch and squeezed.

The pepper spray hit him fully on the face. He stumbled, enraged, and groped for me blindly. I dove into my car, shut and locked the door, and turned the ignition.

"Please, God. Please."

The clunker rattled to life and I stepped on the accelerator. The wheels spun on the blacktop, then gained traction. The sounds of my frantic breath filled my ears as the staggering drunk grew small in my rearview mirror. A new bruise formed on my wrists, where Charlie had clutched too hard.

I forced myself to breathe and pay attention to the road. I didn't want to end up in a ditch tonight. Why did stuff like this happen to me? Did I have a target painted on my forehead? Had I been born just to be someone's victim?

Breathe and cope. I couldn't afford to think like this. It was the emotional response that could sink me for good. I pushed back on the black hole that threatened to swallow me. No panic, no hysterics. I tried to still my shaking hands. It had been a long day and I was exhausted, but I was alive and basically unhurt. My safety measures had worked, Ash's training paid off and the pepper spray had done its job.

The car conked out for good at the bottom of the cottage's driveway. No amount of pleading and banging could revive it. I trekked uphill under the freezing rain for half a mile. By the time I got to the cottage I was exhausted, sore and drenched.

I went around to the barn and checked on the animals. They were settled for the night. Neil met me at the door with a happy *woof*, but not even the handsome dog could cheer me up.

It was frigid downstairs.

"What now?" I muttered to myself.

"Is that you, Lia?" Ash called out from his room at the top of the stairs.

"The one and only," I said. "I'll be up in a moment."

I took off my muddy shoes and stomped down the cellar's rickety steps. The ancient furnace had given up just in time to welcome the first epic freeze of the season.

I groaned. "Give me a break."

I filled up a basket with firewood from the back porch, climbed the stairs and peeked into Ash's room. He lay on his bed, propped up on the pillows, working on his laptop.

"What the hell happened to you?" He motioned me in and set his computer aside. "You look like you've been to hell and back. And you're really late. I was worried."

"Car broke down." I set a log in the hearth and stoked the fire.

"Christ," he said. "Does that happen often?"

"Too often if you ask me."

"Why didn't you call me?"

I stared at him for a moment then told him the truth. "It didn't occur to me."

The hurt in his eyes reactivated the churn in my stomach.

"You know I'm cleared to drive," he said. "Hell, for all you know, I could've been in the neighborhood."

"I'm fine. I didn't need any help." I wiped my hand on my pants and made my way to the door. I hesitated. Anxiety squeezed my chest, but he needed to know. "The other day, a guy showed up at Mario's. He was looking for you."

"I know," he said.

I gawked. "You do?"

He nodded.

"What did he want?" I asked, curious.

"If you have to know, he's an old skipper of mine. We have a business together and he wants me to become active in it."

"How do you feel about that?" I said, leaning against the threshold.

"It'd be an interesting job—you know—if I couldn't do what I did before."

"That's great, Ash. You're keeping your options open."

"He wanted to meet me again tonight. I drove all the way over to Mario's, but then…" He paused and fisted his hands. "Why the hell would anybody want me to work with them if I can't even muster the balls to walk into a fucking bar?"

He was really upset with himself. For a moment, I forgot about my lousy night. I went over to the bed, sat down next to him and uncurled his fist.

"He wants you because you're excellent at what you do." I squeezed his hand. "You're getting better every day. You just have to be patient with yourself."

"You're right." He intertwined his big fingers between my smaller ones. "I'll get better. I have to. Thanks, Lia."

"For what?" I said.

"For teaching me patience."

He brought my hand to his mouth and brushed his lips against my knuckles. The contact was slight, sweet and brief and yet my brain went into default. Total meltdown. My body, on the other hand came online with a burst of electricity. A switch flipped inside me. I was utterly and completely tuned in to him.

His eyebrows dipped when he noticed the bruises on my wrists. "What happened?"

"I'm just clumsy." I reclaimed my hand and, face burning, made for the door. No question about it, I was in a bolting mood again. "The fire should last you through the night. It's a cold one out there."

"Lia?" He hesitated. "Do you want to talk?"

"About what?"

"About what happened tonight," he said. "About those bruises on your wrists. About anything, everything or just some things."

I stood at the threshold for a moment, keenly aware of him. What would it be like to put my day into words and free the emotions trapped so deep inside me?

Disaster.

If I opened my heart, Red would know. He would find us. Ash would die.

"No, thanks."

I went to my room and closed the door, suppressing the tsunami of tears that wanted to burst out of the bottom of my being. There was no point in talking about anything. I'd been on my own for so long that I didn't count on anyone else. Couldn't. Trust had been wrung out of my DNA. I didn't want to depend on anyone and that included Ash, who'd move on from my life as soon as Gunny Watkins decided he was fit to be on his own.

IN THE NIGHTMARE, I lay naked on the cold cement floor of Charlie Nowak's basement, staked to the ground and unable to move while Charlie—wearing only a baseball cap from his collection—squashed me beneath his heft.

"This ass, these boobs." He groped me with harsh hands. "He's caught your scent, bitch, and he's coming for you."

I tried not to feel, not to care—the only way I knew to survive—but I was freezing and couldn't stop shivering. My soul ached and my bones crumpled beneath the man's crushing weight. There weren't enough steel plates, pins and wires to repair the damage. Broken as I was, no miracle of science could keep me together. And yet I held on, because someone, somewhere, was calling my name.

"You won't get away this time around," Charlie said. "He's coming, right now, and he's gonna teach you a new level of pain."

The basement around me transformed into a meticulously landscaped garden crisscrossed by a river. The sound of artificial cascades muted the sobs escaping my throat. I lay facedown on the terrace's warm limestone floors. A vindictive presence weighted me down, a savage whose malevolence dwarfed Charlie's drunken stunts. Even without seeing him, I knew who he was.

I wrenched my neck and spotted the face that terrorized my life, the harmonious features that masked the workings of a putrid mind. He sat on my back and, forcing my forehead against the floor, stabbed the nape of my neck with the sharpened bone needles he preferred.

He chiseled at my spine, tapping directly into my nerves. He laughed every time I flinched in pain. From the corner of my eye, I could see him dip the needles into a rich pool of red pigment sloshing at the bottom of a wooden saucer. Red. It wasn't only his name. It was his favorite color too. The pigment was mixed with fresh blood. My blood.

"Did you think you could escape me?" His caw-like laughter was the sound of my life gone wrong. "You're such a fool. This time around, I'm gonna mark you mine for good."

It didn't matter that I'd gone to great lengths to remove his brand from my body. The needles savaged my skin. Blood dripped down my back and pooled over the limestone. I cried and begged and yet he wouldn't stop. The inverted *R* replicated over my body like a gruesome virus.

"It's a nightmare," a calm voice said. "You can stop it, Lia. You just have to wake up."

The voice fueled my inner strength. In the nightmare, I broke the ropes around my wrists, bucked from under my captor and ran, following the sound of my name. I darted out of the garden, through Charlie's stark basement and up the stairs, barreling through an open door I hadn't seen before.

I woke up crying and gasping. I saw the German shepherd first, head tilted, brow wrinkled, caramel eyes gleaming with concern. Then Ash's face overtook the space before my eyes.

"Lia?" he said, caressing my hair. "Are you awake, sweetness?"

I lay on my side with my nails digging into my palms and my body curled around my knees, shivering for real. I must have kicked off the blankets. I didn't think I could move even if I tried.

"It's really cold in here," Ash said. "It's too cold for you to get warm. I'm going to take you to my room. Okay?"

I nodded and tried to get up, but my body refused to uncoil and the shivers made me an uncoordinated mess. Ash picked me up and carried me as if I were made of air and light. He limped out of my room, across the hallway and into his room, and deposited me gently in his bed.

The mattress was still warm from his body. The covers he tucked around me helped. Neil lay on top of my legs, lending me his doggy heat. Ash stoked the fire and then got under the covers, slipped his bare shoulder beneath my head and gathered me against him.

The heat of his body permeated through me, unknotting my muscles and defrosting the frozen fear.

I don't know how long I lay there, listless and thawing, enjoying the soft strokes of his fingers running through my hair. He didn't ask any questions and I was grateful for his silence. The nightmare haunted me and, when I closed my eyes, little red packets of incense streamed in my mind like an electronic news ticker.

"Try to relax," Ash murmured in my ear. "No need to be upset. Go to sleep, Lia. You're going to be all right."

Eventually, my exhaustion prevailed. I succumbed to the calming rhythm of Ash's heart. I had no fears, nightmares or dreams. For once, I simply slept.

I WOKE UP to the smell of coffee and something else, something delicious that my stomach recognized with a loud growl. I stretched beneath the blankets. The fire roared in the little hearth. I was surprised to find myself in Ash's bed, but then memories from last night flooded in.

Inasmuch as I avoided sharing beds with anyone, how on earth had I managed to sleep with him all night?

A glance at the alarm clock on the night table showed that it was almost eleven. What about my animals? I must have slept so soundly I didn't hear the breakfast racket. I threw the covers aside and rushed down the stairs, stopping only to don my galoshes before careening into the kitchen.

"Hey, wait, whoa." Ash caught me by the waist. "Where do you think you're going without a coat? It's freezing out there."

"I forgot to feed the animals." I tried to disentangle from his arms. "They must be starving—"

"Calm down, Lia," he said. "They're not starving. I fed them."

I froze. "You fed them?"

"It's not so hard to do." He let go of me, turning his

attention to the pan on the stove. "Camels, now those are a pain in the ass. They're the nastiest sons of bitches."

"You fed all of them?" I said.

"I did." He turned the eggs with the spatula. "Nobody out there is complaining."

"I'll go check."

"*After* you have your breakfast." He plated the eggs.

"But—"

"Sit." He pointed at the table. "Food first, animals later."

With my brain still in a fog, I plopped down on the chair. He parked a full plate in front of me before he took his place beside me. I didn't know how hungry I was until the eggs eased down my throat and warmed my empty stomach. My mouth exploded with the taste of bacon.

"This is amazing," I mumbled with a mouthful of breakfast goodness.

Ash added a buttered biscuit to my plate. "Try this."

"Hmm." I swallowed. "It tastes just like your grandma's."

"She taught me all I know about cooking."

I washed it down with a gulp of coffee and a sip of freshly squeezed orange juice.

"Better?" He dug into his breakfast.

"Much."

"And the nightmare last night?"

"Gone."

"You get those often?"

"Sometimes." I glanced at Ash tentatively.

He sighed. "Nightmares suck."

I caught a rare glimpse of his intimate pain. My heart sank a little. Nightmares were the mind's ultimate hauntings, perverse, recurring and relentless. That's why he slept so little. Heck, that's why I slept so badly too. I wished I could do away with all of his nightmares.

"I hope I wasn't too loud," I said. "Did I wake you?"

"You weren't loud enough," he said, "until the end."

"But…how did you know?"

"Neil is trained to recognize nightmares." He bit into his biscuit, chewed and swallowed. "He alerted me that something was wrong. I knocked on your door, but you didn't answer. When I opened the door, he went straight to you. That's when I knew."

"Thanks, Neil." I sneaked a strip of bacon to the dog under the table.

"What happened to the furnace?" Ash said.

"It stopped working last night."

He put another biscuit on my plate. "And you didn't think to say anything?"

"The problem doesn't affect your room," I said. "The fireplace kept it toasty all through last winter. That's why I rented out that room and not the other. To be honest, I didn't realize how cold it would get in there."

The little lines between his eyebrows deepened. "So my room used to be your room?"

"Yeah," I said. "Who'd pay to stay in the other one?"

"You would," he said crossly. "You paid a high price last night."

"I have another blanket I can add to the pile."

"You can't possibly be thinking about sleeping in that freezer all winter."

"I can try weatherizing the windows," I said. "Or I can sleep downstairs on the couch."

Ash made a face. "That old thing will likely wreck your spine for good."

"Silas Ford doesn't have the money to replace the

furnace, but I'll stop in when I go into town today and ask him again."

"Why are you going into town?" he said. "I thought it was your day off."

"I volunteer for Reverend Martin when I can. I deliver hot meals to some of the church members." I checked the clock. "I'll need to get going soon."

"Mind if I go with you?" he asked.

I was surprised. "Do you really want to go into town?"

"No, but I've got some errands to run and I might as well get them out of the way."

"All right," I said. "I'll do the dishes, get dressed and then see if I can get my car started."

"Your car's no longer at the bottom of the hill," he said. "I jump-started it this morning and drove it up."

"You did?" I gave Ash a hug that got shortened on the spot when it had a big impact on my body. "Um…" I reeled from the contact, but rallied. "That's great, thank you."

"And by the way," he said. "There's no way in hell you or I are ever getting into that death trap again. I survived the jungles of South America, Iraq and Afghanistan. I'm not riding in that rusted piece of shit and neither are you."

"Hush, don't let the car hear you talking like that." I lowered my voice. "She's easy to offend and highly temperamental. She might just quit altogether. What would I do without her?"

He rolled his eyes. "You should make her into scrap metal, that's what you should do."

"But—"

"It's final," he said. "I'm driving and we're taking

my truck. From now on, the truck is the designated primary transportation asset in and out of here."

Right. I gave him a mock salute. Like he was going to take me everywhere I needed to go.

We drove to town in Ash's immaculate truck, a smooth ride on winding backcountry roads. The sun ignited the aspens, which lit the hills with flaring reds and luminescent yellows. I lowered my window, enjoying the crisp mountain air and the stunning views with Queen's "Princes of the Universe" blasting in all of its orchestral glory.

Ash looked relaxed at the wheel, reveling in the simple joy of driving, maneuvering the curves with obvious ease. Sticking out from beneath his knit cap, the ends of his hair fluttered in the breeze. He grinned whenever I smiled in his direction. The universe was playing with me again. Why did he have to be so darn good-looking?

Neil stuck his nose out the window and wagged his tail. His fur, tongue and lips flapped in the wind. I leaned back on the heated leather seat and shared in the moment's perfection. I even dared to imagine that this could have been my life in some other dimension. I couldn't remember a more beautiful day.

Our arrival to town put an end to the ride, but I stored the moment in my mind, eager to add to my limited collection of precious memories.

"Thanks," I said. "That was awesome."

He gave me the oddest look. "I don't know many people who'd think of a drive as if it were a gift."

"Well, I do."

"We'll do it again," he said. "And wait until I take you to Heaven."

"Heaven?"

"You'll see."

The mood in the cab changed when Ash parked the truck on Main Street. I opened the door and got out, but Ash lingered in his seat, toying with the leash while Neil hovered by his shoulder. No force in the world would get him to admit that he was having flashbacks, but he eyed the storefronts and the folks strolling by as if an attack was imminent.

I came around to the driver's side door and leaned into the window. "You don't have to get down if you don't want to."

He reached out and gently trailed my chin with his knuckles, a faint, brief caress. Was I imagining this? No. The buzzing in my spine proved that he'd disturbed my body's molecular hive. The eyes that centered on my lips turned into pure cobalt. My knees buckled. I clung to the door. The lush look of his mouth pulled on my body like a magnet.

"Ah, Lia." He took a deep breath. "What would I do without you? But I need to do this. I made an appointment."

I forced my eyes away from his mouth. "Where are we going?"

"We?" His gaze met mine.

"I have some time yet before the meals are ready," I said. "And if it helps…"

He put the leash on Neil, opened the door and limped out of the truck and onto the sidewalk, leaning on his cane as we made our way down the street.

It was unavoidable that people in Copperhill would notice Ash. Despite his limp, he made for a striking figure. Mrs. White, who ran the Laundromat, was the first one to come out on the street to say hello. He greeted her kindly. Mr. Stewart, the pharmacist, joined us at the curb. Ahead of us, the librarian pulled out her cell phone and called someone, before she too joined the group gathering around us.

I could tell the crowd tested Ash, but only because I'd learned to decipher his body's language. Neil also offered me clues. The German shepherd circled Ash, trying to interpose himself between his owner and the others without much success. In a place where rumors flew as easily as text messages, more people kept coming out of the woodwork.

"Good to see you." The owner of the hardware store shook Ash's hand.

"Welcome back." The stylists from the hair salon smiled in unison.

Reverend Martin pounded on Ash's back. "It's great to have you in town." He beamed at Ash then turned to me. "Hi, Lia. The meals are almost ready. See you at the church in an hour or so?"

"I'll be there," I said.

I caught a glimpse of Charlie Nowak coming out of the coffee shop with Sheriff Wilkins. Charlie shot me a menacing look, something between "if you tell anybody" and "when I get my hands on you..." The blood drained from my face. He didn't look much worse from our confrontation, but fear tightened the permanent knot clenching the pit of my stomach.

Ash leaned over and, excusing himself from the conversation, tugged at my sleeve. "You okay?"

"Sure." I exhaled a sigh of relief as Charlie got into his truck.

Ash scanned the street before turning to greet Sheriff Wilkins. The tires of Charlie's truck screeched when he swerved to avoid Barb Woods, who ran recklessly across the street to get a closer look at Ash. As she ap-

proached, I wished I had a sword and shield to repel
her morbid curiosity.

"Why, Ash." She hugged him way too tightly. "You
look whole—I mean great—just that tiny itsy-bitsy scar
on your face." She traced the scar that split Ash's eyebrow with her long witch's nails. "Oh, don't worry. I'm
sure the scar will go away. In time, you'll be your handsome, heartbreaker self all over again. Tell me." She
inched closer to Ash. "How many of those hajjis did
you kill? Dozens? Hundreds?"

A muscle flinched on Ash's face. Did Barb ever think
before she spoke? She must have noticed my scathing
glare, because she tried to dig herself out of the hole.

"I think the scar gives you character and the cane
makes you look elegant." She pinched an invisible speck
of lint from Ash's jacket. "Does the leg hurt? Does it
hang limply, you know, like when you have a stroke?"

"Barb!" I had a mental image of me clawing out
her eyes.

Ash tugged on my elbow. "It's okay, Lia. Barb is
just curious, that's all. I can feel my leg fine, Barb. As
for the cane and the scar, they weren't my first choice,
but I manage quite well and I don't mind being ugly
for a change."

The half smirk, half grin he beamed on us could've
melted glaciers. The small crowd chuckled, Barb included. Boy, he handled the situation with charm and
poise. His temper was firmly under control. At that
moment, if Ash had asked, every single person in the
crowd would have followed him to Afghanistan's highest passes. Me included.

"If you'll excuse us," Ash said, shaking hands and
kissing cheeks. "We need to go."

As soon as we turned the corner, I hugged him. "Well-done, Major Hunter."

"Don't patronize me, not right now." He took off his beanie and wiped the sweat off his brow.

"I'm not patronizing you in the least," I said. "I'm proud of you. You handled that like a pro, an officer and a gentleman. I might have punched that broad in the nose, but you scored a perfect ten on that one."

He laughed.

"What's so funny?" I said. "You said I needed practice *and* a new punching bag."

"You're funny." He kissed the top of my head. "You're just good to have around."

My pulse quickened, a light, happy drumming, kind of like an Irish jig. I'd never had anyone say that to me. And then the little dance in my heart came to a screeching halt. Reality check. It had never been good for anybody on this earth to have me around and, delusions aside, my harsh reality was never going to change.

EIGHT

Ash turned into a building and halted by the door. "Why so sad all of the sudden?"

"Sad? Me? Nah." Who the heck was he? My very own mood monitor?

He sighed and opened the door for me. "Lying is just not you, Lia."

But what choice did I have?

We entered an office. Ash introduced himself to the receptionist, who guided us to an expansive suite furnished with imitation leather couches. A slight gentleman wearing a twill jacket with leather elbow patches sat in an enormous executive chair that dwarfed him by comparison. He was an Isaac Newton look-alike, sporting an exuberant salt-and-pepper mane and a dark mustache that curved down his chin.

"My boy!" He leaped out of his chair and pumped Ash's hand. "It's so good to see you. I've been leaving messages and sending emails, trying to contact you every which way. I was so glad to hear you'd made an appointment." He slapped Ash on the back. "And look at you. Your father would've been so proud."

Ash granted him one of his warm smiles and turned to me. "Lia, this is Jack Latoya. Jack, have you met Lia Stuart?"

"Ah, Lia, yes, of course." Jack shook my hand. "We've met before. Lia was a great friend to your grandmother. She helped Wynona when she broke her hip last year."

"It was nothing, really," I mumbled embarrassedly.

"Lia here is being too modest," Jack said to Ash. "Wynona told everyone who'd listen that she couldn't have gotten along without Lia's help. And so that you know, Lia aided me with the arrangements when Wynona passed. She was very helpful."

"Is that so?" Ash's gaze caressed my face.

It was as if the lush lashes that fringed his eyes tickled my soul. God almighty. When he looked at me like that the rest of the world faded from my sight. I had to make a conscious effort to focus on the attorney.

Jack eyed Neil with a hint of fear. "That's a big-ass wolf."

"Don't worry," Ash said. "He doesn't bite."

Neil tilted his head and, ears forward, wagged his tail.

"Thank goodness for small favors," Jack said. "Now, please, sit down."

Ash lowered himself into the club chair across the desk with a measure of care. Jack tried to help, but Ash waved him away. For a moment, Jack just stood there, shifting on his feet, looking uncomfortable, like people often do when they first meet someone sick or disabled.

I eyed Ash with growing concern. He was hurting again. The cane slipped from his hold and clattered on the floor, but Jack retrieved it and tucked it into an umbrella stand by the door. Ash tapped the chair next to him, so I sat down, despite feeling completely out of place.

"I'm glad you're back." Jack went over to the wall cabinet. "I worried about you. You just, *pfft*, fell off the continent."

"I'm here now," Ash said. "I'm fine."

"Of course you are." Jack opened a cabinet door that concealed a mirrored bar. "You always were tough as nails. Do you remember that time when you, your father and I were riding out at the ranch and that surly mustang of yours threw you into the barbed wire fence?"

"I remember quite well." Ash chuckled. "I have the scars to prove it."

"It took your father and me a whole twenty minutes to cut you out of that mess. Lia, you should've seen it. He looked like a goddamn porcupine. He was no taller than my waist, but do you think the little son of a bitch cried? Nary a tear, I tell you."

I had no trouble believing that.

"How about a drink?" Jack picked out a crystal tumbler from the shelves.

I shook my head.

"Pass," Ash said. "I keep the tank on clean and sober these days."

Jack poured for himself then raised the tumbler in the air. "To your health." He took a sip and looked at Ash with kind eyes. "Son, it gives my old heart joy to see you again. But why didn't you call to tell me that you were in the hospital? Why didn't you come stay with me instead of renting a room so far away from town?"

"I didn't want to bother anyone," Ash said. "I really like it out by the lake."

"You were always an independent young buck." Jack balanced his drink in one hand as he sat down. "'You can't put a yoke on a wild steed,' Wynona used to say. How I miss the old gal."

Tears swelled in the man's eyes. Tears stung my eyes too, but I held them back in deference to Ash, who acknowledged Jack's grief with a blank-faced nod.

"I'm sorry." The attorney cleared his throat. "I'm a doddering old fool. I suppose there's no way around this. After all, Wynona trusted me with her legal affairs. We have much to discuss, private family business. I'm sure you understand, dear?"

"Sure, yes." I stood up. "How about I wait outside?"

"Splendid," Jack said.

"No need," Ash said. "Lia, please, stay."

I looked from one man to the other. Jack's expression left no doubt that he wanted me gone, but if Ash wanted me to stay, then I'd stay. After all, I was his caretaker. I sat down again, in spite of Jack's poorly disguised frown.

Jack opened a folder and consulted his notes. "The will is the first order of business. Your grandmother left all her cash assets and worldly possessions to you and appointed you as the executor of the trust. Do you know what you want to do with the ranch?"

"Not yet," Ash said.

"The county is cracking down on vacant and abandoned properties. You'll need to clean up and secure it by the end of the month. They're willing to waive the fines, since you're a wounded veteran currently listed as disabled."

Ash stiffened in his chair. I winced. Jack had managed to prickle Ash's pride three ways and he didn't even notice.

"I don't expect any kind of exceptions," Ash said. "The ranch will be in compliance by the end of the month. I've already set the wheels into motion."

"Good," Jack said. "Next on the agenda, the contract with Gas General expires at the end of the year. You need to decide whether you'll be renewing it. Gary

Woods has called many times to discuss the matter. He's looking to talk to you directly."

"What's your take on this?" Ash said.

"You hold the cards." The attorney took a sip of his drink and leaned back in his chair. "Prices have sky-rocketed and your yields have multiplied. You're in a position to negotiate a killer deal, that is, if you want to stick with Gas General and good old Woods."

"I need to think about it," Ash said.

Jack pushed a sheaf of papers across his desk and parked them before Ash. "There's also this."

"What is it?"

"The reason why I've been calling you day and night." Jack grinned excitedly.

"A proposal that can take care of all your headaches."

Ash leafed through the document. "What kind of a proposal?"

"A good one," Jack said. "From Aenergies Global."

"*The* Aenergies Global?"

"*The* largest provider of gas-based energy services in the world." Jack's blue eyes sparkled. "They want to buy your lands, the existing gas fields and the property in its entirety, without any contingencies or conditions. In cash."

Ash scanned the first page and whistled. "That's a hell of a lot of money."

"More zeroes than the average American can count."

"But the property has been in my family all the way back to the settlement."

"This is a once-in-a-lifetime opportunity."

"My grandmother wouldn't have liked the idea."

"Wynona was a woman of her world," Jack said. "Yours is a different world. How much time have you spent here since you went away for college?"

"Not a lot," Ash conceded.

"With that kind of money, you could live in luxury and travel at leisure. You could fund some other start-ups or you could capitalize on some of the other businesses and investments you've got going. You, your children and your grandchildren could live like kings. Hell, you could buy half of Colorado if you really wanted to stick around here with us losers."

Wow. I was astonished. Wynona was rich? And Ash stood to become even richer with this Aenergies deal?

I'd known the Hunters were a prominent local family, but I hadn't realized the extent of their wealth until that very moment. Wynona had lived in the old ranch house, a fine, comfortable home, but not huge or luxurious. She lived simply, selling her custom-made jewelry to a few shops and over the internet. Her biggest expense was her charity work.

From what I'd seen so far, Ash didn't lack for anything, but didn't live extravagantly either. He'd chosen to live in the cottage not because it was cheap, but because it was out-of-the-way, on the lake and peaceful. I had assumed he lived on his military benefits, so it was a shock to learn that the Hunter family trust was so significant and that beyond his military career, Ash was also an accomplished businessman. It explained all the time he spent on his cell and working on his computer. Every time I blinked, I discovered a brand-new facet of the man.

On the other hand, I couldn't help wonder what Wynona would have said about the Aenergies proposal. She loved Ash but she also loved the land.

"I don't know." Ash scanned the document. "This goes against my grain."

"Grain can be shaped, stained and polished," Jack

said. "And you could join the ranks of the world's mega rich. This is a limited-time proposal, son. Let me explain."

Jack rattled out the terms, but Ash wasn't paying attention. Maybe the pain was getting to him. Maybe his emotions had finally gotten the best of him, or perhaps he was having flashbacks. Neil's ears were swiveling every which way. He stared at his owner with what looked to me like canine concern, grumbling occasionally. Jack was too involved in his explanations to notice, but I could tell that Ash was perturbed.

"I need to go." Ash tucked the contract under his arm, braced his hands on the desk and got up. "I'll call you."

He looked around for his cane, but he couldn't reach it all the way in the corner. For a moment he just stood there, balancing on his good foot, looking pained and trapped. Instinct and habit kicked in. I sprang to my feet, grabbed the cane from the stand and gave it to him. He leaned on the cane and, with Neil at his heels, headed for the door at top limping velocity.

"Where are you going?" Jack said. "What do you want me to tell these people?"

"I'll let you know," Ash said, before fleeing the room. "Later, Jack."

Jack stared at the door, then at me, shaking his head. "The boy's changed." He tsked. "Traumatic brain injury. It can affect even the brightest minds."

The heat that ignited my face represented only a fraction of my outrage. Couldn't Jack recognize the huge effort Ash had to make just to be here?

No, he couldn't. Like most people, Jack didn't have a clue. I had to suppress my temper before I was able to address Jack with a measure of civility.

"Ash is fine," I said as evenly as I could manage. "He's the most rational person I know and he's perfectly capable of making his own decisions."

"I sure hope so." He handed me a small key from the file. "Wynona left this for him. She said he'd know what it was for. Will you give it to him?"

"Sure."

I said my farewells and left the office. It wasn't Ash's traumatic brain injury acting up. It was his PTSD. It pained me to admit it, but he faced a steep learning curve, because according to everything I'd read and studied in the past few weeks, before he could conquer his PTSD, he had to learn to live with it.

I knew what it was like to live with memories that tore you up every day. I knew what it felt like to live with the enemy inside, always watching, always waiting to pounce when you least expected. It was like being hooked on Red Rush, like having poison in your system all the time, blood gushing through your veins at blinding speed, brain high on adrenaline, heart pounding in your ears. It was a different kind of slavery than I had suffered, but it was slavery all the same.

I HALF EXPECTED to find Ash slumped over the wheel or locked in the truck. I didn't. A note stuck beneath the windshield wipers announced that he would meet me at this spot in a couple of hours. He left the truck's keys under the driver's side mat so I could run my errands. Since I was running late, I headed over to the church, picked up the meals and drove on to distribute them to the regulars on my list.

Mrs. Pearson welcomed me joyfully, as always. I sat with her while she ate, noting that she had a good appetite today. Her canaries trilled happily, but I took

a moment to clean the cage before I left. At the trailer
park, my landlord, Silas Ford, was next on the list. He
put down his chow in five minutes, confirming between gulps that no, he didn't have any money to put
into the cottage's broken furnace. Mr. Poden refused to
open the door as usual, but accepted the meal through
the window. When I popped open the cans of cat food
I'd picked up at the convenience store, his eleven cats
showed up for dinner.

As soon as I finished, I drove back into town. Ash
waited for me on a bench around the corner, with Neil
sitting next to him on the leash. I noticed a top-of-the
line RV parked nearby and three men standing with Ash
as I pulled up. The guys reminded me of Ash when he
first came to my door. Each was fit in their own way,
and maybe even good-looking, but there was something
haunted about their eyes, about the way they stared at
me, at the world, as they shook hands with Ash.

One of the guys looked like a kid with thick glasses,
despite a scruffy goatee. The tallest one hugged his
arms close to his body and wore his long curly hair tied
in a bushy ponytail. The guy with the high and tight sat
in a high-tech wheelchair.

"Hey," Ash said, climbing into the cab.

"Hey to you too." I slid over as Neil jumped in the
back and Ash took my place at the wheel. "Who are
those fellows?"

"Some old friends I hadn't seen in a while." Ash
buckled in, waved and drove off.

I checked out the men in the rearview mirror.
"Friends from the Navy?"

"Aye-aye, Herr Kommandant."

I laughed. "You can't blame me for being curious."

"Of course, not, Miss Holmes."

"You haven't been seeing too many people lately."

"These guys are different," he said. "They're my friends."

I liked the idea of Ash having friends around. Good friends could only be helpful to Ash's recovery. They'd also be helpful if I had to leave in a hurry. My heart sank at the thought.

"We ought to have them over for dinner," I said.

"Awesome idea." He flashed his best smile. "We could grill steaks."

"What are they doing in this neck of the woods?"

"I heard through the grapevine that they were looking for work."

"All vets?"

He nodded. "They're going to set up camp at the ranch and help me clear the charred ruins so that we won't fit the county's categories for abandoned or unsafe anymore."

"Great, that makes sense, although…"

"What?"

"Nothing."

He glanced at me. "You—preacher of 'People get hurt all the time and they still have happy and productive lives'—you're now wondering how a guy stuck in a wheelchair can be of help. Admit it. You have your hang-ups too."

"Perhaps I am wondering a little."

"Manny Rivera is the most brilliant technical mind you'll ever meet," Ash said. "Christ knows, the old tractor at the ranch needs all the help it can get. He can fix, rig and operate any piece of equipment, high-tech or not. Like that wheelchair of his. He drives it like an ATV. And that customized RV he uses to travel around the country? It's a goddamn work of art."

"Impressive," I said. "Where's his family?"

"His wife divorced him," Ash said. "She said she wanted children."

"Oh." How was that for a rotten deal? "What about the tall one with the ponytail? What's his story?"

"Wang Ho was possibly the best marksman of our generation until he lost his right arm in an ambush in Afghanistan."

"What a terrible loss."

"More like a national tragedy."

"And the one that looks like he's fourteen years old?"

"Will 'Kid' Jackson may look deceivingly young, but in his time, he could hack his way into the Ayatollah's hearing aid if need be. He still can hack with the best of them, but a TBI left him with a disability that makes him virtually unemployable."

"How so?"

"Will suffers from a very specific form of brain damage that affects only the verbal section of the brain. It's similar to Tourette's syndrome. Sometimes, when he's excited or stressed, he blurts out stuff."

"What do you mean 'stuff?'"

"Rude comments, inappropriate behaviors, songs. But other than that, his IQ still rules the MENSA charts."

"That's a lot of brainpower between the four of you."

"I think maybe we could find a way to clear a bunch of debris, don't you?"

"Absolutely," I said. "I didn't mean to put down your friends."

"We all do it." He let out a long breath. "Besides, you don't have to tiptoe around me. I can manage my moods."

"Too much for one day?"

"Maybe," he admitted reluctantly.

"It's good to know one's limits," I said. "What else did you do today?"

"I visited with a couple of locals, set up my rehab schedule, went to the bank." He took off his knit cap. "Oh, and I went to the barber shop."

"Wow." I reached over and ran my fingers through his freshly cut hair. "Looks great."

Touching him released the swarm in my tummy. What was it about the way he looked at me that made me feel warm and fuzzy inside?

Warm and fuzzy? I hadn't been warm and fuzzy since I was fourteen and had developed a serious crush on the boys of *NSYNC. I wanted to slap myself.

Ash's eyes darkened. "I also went to the cemetery."

"Oh." My throat tightened. "Are you…all right?"

"I'll live." His eyes were fixed on the road. "She's where she would have wanted to be, between Gramps and Dad. The groundskeeper said you insisted that's where she had to be buried. Thanks, Lia."

"You're welcome."

"I'm curious," he said. "Did Nona ever mention anything to you about selling the ranch?"

"No, we never talked about stuff like that."

"What did you two talk about?"

"Well, let's see, she loved to talk shop about her jewelry designs. The news, she had tons of commentary on world affairs. Her charity work. It was very important to her. But by far her favorite subject was you. She loved to tell me stories about you and how wonderful, smart and handsome you were."

"Really?" He flashed his lopsided grin. "And was she right about any of those things?"

I laughed. "What are you, on a fishing expedition?"

"I'm clearly using the wrong lure on this trout." He grinned, then sobered up. "A lot of people in town would lose their jobs if I sold to Aenergies. Call me a fool, but that bothers me."

"I don't think you're a fool."

"I don't like it," he said, all of the sudden.

"You don't like what?"

"The way people look at you when they think there's something wrong with you. Like Jack. He doesn't think I'm the same guy as before."

"And that bothers you?"

"I feel like I have to prove myself all the time."

"Don't fall into the temptation then," I said. "You don't need to prove anything to anybody. Speaking of Jack." I pulled out the key from my purse. "He asked me to give you this. He told me that Wynona said you'd know what it was for."

"Hmm." He fingered the key in his hand. "Mind if we take a detour?"

I didn't like detours. They messed with my head. They messed with my resolutions, my plans and my heart too. But Ash accelerated around a curve and veered right instead of left at the junction.

Within a few minutes, we turned into a private road that opened up to a striking valley surrounded by derelict pastures. Beyond the pastures, forests of aspen, spruce and lodgepole pines spread over hills that grew into ragged mountains. As we went around the bend and sighted the river, the charred remains of the Hunter house came into view. Autumn's splendid colors couldn't soften the terrible sight.

I waited by the truck, granting Ash his space while he surveyed the outbuildings. Neil stuck to him as if his fur was made out of Velcro. Together, they approached the ruins. My heart fisted in my chest.

The fire had consumed most of the home, leaving only a crumbling section of the chimney and a pile of rubble strewn over the foundation. Gas leak, the fire chief had said. Wynona had probably passed out well before the place burned down.

When it first happened, I'd wondered if it was my fault. She was my friend, and, God knew, bad things happened to my friends. I made all kinds of inquiries, but Jack had hired a high-profile investigative team that confirmed the chief's conclusion and the sheriff agreed with their findings. He'd assured me it had been an accident. I'd been heartbroken. I could only begin to imagine how Ash felt.

Ash circled the house and got lost behind the pile. I heard the hollow sound of metal hitting metal and a crash. Worried, I followed his tracks and found the cellar's trapdoor thrown open and Neil fidgeting at the top of a set of questionable stairs, ears swiveling in all directions.

"Ash?" I peered into the dark. "Are you down there?"

No answer.

"Come back," I said. "I don't think that's such a hot idea."

Something rustled in the darkness. I heard tugging, dragging and then another crash. A cloud of dirt and ashes blew out of the trapdoors.

Neil whined.

"Don't worry," I muttered to the dog. "You wait here. I'll go find him."

I worked my way down the rickety stairs, avoiding the carbonized wood piles and stepping around the collapsed sections. I groped for the little flashlight I kept on my keychain, only to remember it had no batteries.

Darn it.

I floundered about, tripping on stuff, clambering over a collapsed ceiling beam. A sound caught my attention. A light bounced off a wall around the corner. Groping like a blind woman, I went toward the light.

Ash crouched next to the safe lying on the floor. The little key Jack had given me protruded from the lock. He was reading a piece of paper. Two or three high-powered hunting rifles and three handguns were neatly stacked in there, along with some ammunition. Wearing a blank expression on his face, Ash folded the paper, tucked it in his pocket and looked up.

"You shouldn't have come down here," he said. "It's not safe."

"Yep," I said. "You shouldn't be here either."

"The safe is fireproof," he said as a way of explanation. "Catch."

His flashlight landed between my hands. I held it up, illuminating the scene. He grabbed one of the guns and, pointing it safely away, checked it to ensure it wasn't loaded. He tested each weapon methodically, before tucking them into a case that had also been stowed in the safe. When he was done, he slung the case over his shoulder and stood up with the help of his cane. Lugging the heavy load, he came to stand beside me.

"What was in the safe?" I said. "I mean, in addition to the weapons?"

"Old pictures," he said. "Some small things Nona wanted to preserve for me. And this."

He pulled the paper out of his pocket and showed me what was written on it. *Remember to trust your instincts.*

"She used to tell me to trust my instincts all the time."

"She was right," I said. "You've got a good brain."

"I'm glad you think that's the case." He refolded Wynona's note and tucked it in his pocket. "Because you don't trust your instincts at all, or anyone else's for that matter, which leaves the guesswork up to me." He fixed his eyes on my face. "Lia," he said. "I need to know. For sure."

"Know what?"

His eyes gleamed under the flashlight's beam. The scent of him rose above the smell of ashes and soot. His face gave nothing away, but his intensity ratcheted up. I was suddenly very aware of him, of how close he was, of how much closer he got to me when he leaned over, until the glow became a tiny circle reflecting the minute creases on his leather jacket.

His mouth found my lips without trouble. His lips brushed against mine with exquisite gentleness and yet the contact struck me like a jolt. The glimmer reflected in his eyes became my only point of reference. Then I closed my eyes and needed no light, because even with my eyes closed, he lit up my world.

It shouldn't be, couldn't be. The flashlight fell out of my hands. It clanged on the ground, but I didn't care. He deepened his kiss, savoring my mouth, lending me a taste of his body by way of his tongue and challenging my resolutions. He never touched me. He did nothing to prevent me from bolting and yet I couldn't move. My feet melted into the ground. I had a vision of my body combusting from the heat flaring in me, bursting into ashes, joining with the soot clinging to the walls.

I don't know how long he kissed me. Seconds? Minutes? Hours? But I knew the exact moment when the kiss ended. My body went dark. Total outage. All the light in the world died when his lips broke contact with mine.

He left me gasping for breath. The sound of our ragged breaths echoed in the cellar.

"Jesus," he rasped.

"Ash, I can't—"

"Lia?" He kissed me again, another delicious, brain-melting event. "I know what you mean to say, about the danger and all of that? But it is what it is."

He bent down, picked up the flashlight from the floor and, after turning it back on, pointed the light in the direction of the stairs. "There's nothing I can do about this. I won't apologize and neither will you. Go on. Before I kiss you again."

I didn't stop running until I was back in the truck, whole, hale and safe—well, maybe not exactly safe, not considering my circumstances, and especially not safe from my newest worst enemy: myself.

NINE

ASH DIDN'T SAY a word. He stowed his load in the back of the truck and we drove off as if we'd never detoured to the ranch. There seemed to be an awful lot on his mind. He kneaded his leg as he drove, while Neil grumbled and paced from one window to the other on the backseat, ears shifting like a pair of radar dishes scanning for signals.

I looked out the window, running my fingertips over my lips. My lips hurt, not from the force of his kisses—no way, he'd been way too gentle—but rather from his mouth's absence. He'd kissed me. And he'd liked it. So had I. Oh, Lord.

Ash's cell rang. "Hunter," he answered and then an official "Yes, ma'am."

"Who is it?" I mouthed.

"Gunny Watkins," he mouthed back.

"Be nice," I reminded him.

It was a one-way conversation, with the gunny doing most of the talking. I couldn't hear what she was saying, but Ash's contributions were limited to the occasional "yes, ma'am," a single "thank you, ma'am," and a final "I'll tell her ma'am."

"What did she say?" I asked when he hung up.

"She was checking on us." Ash kept his eyes on the road. "She said she'd reviewed my chart and was pleased with my progress."

I gave him a fist bump. "We've appeased Godzilla."

He smiled. "She sent her regards."

"We should feel mighty accomplished."

"*You* should feel accomplished," Ash said. "The gunny isn't easy to impress. She reminded me of what a phenomenal asset you are. Now if I could only get you to believe it."

Me? An asset? No way. He was the asset in my life. He guarded my house, protected my animals, eased my hardships and enriched my life with company and friendship. Whereas I was a huge, walking, talking liability, even if he refused to accept me as such.

When Ash and Neil went out for their evening walk, I slipped on a T-shirt and my old pajama pants and arranged my pillow and blanket on the couch. I was in the process of starting a fire in the living room's hearth when they came back. Neil made a straight line for me, splayed on the ground and, pawing the air, flashed his belly.

Ash's stare shifted from the couch to me. He sighed, stepped to the couch and, after bundling my pillow and blankets, threw them over his shoulder and started up the stairs.

"Hello?" I followed him. "That's my pillow."

"You're *not* sleeping downstairs."

"Who gave you the power to decide where I sleep?"

"Reason and common sense." He plodded to his room and, without hesitation, added my blankets to his bed and propped my pillow next to his.

"Ashton Hunter," I said. "You're definitively crossing a line here."

He flashed me a stoic look. "Then can we please cross it quickly?"

I opened my mouth and closed it. What on earth was one supposed to say to that? As if I wasn't standing right there, he pulled his sweater and T-shirt over his head, unbuckled his belt, dropped his jeans on the floor and grappled with his foot brace. Wearing only his boxer briefs, he got in bed and patted the mattress next to him.

"No way." My defective sense for self-preservation finally made an appearance. That kiss today? It was the kind of catastrophic mistake I couldn't afford. "I don't want to sleep with you."

"Lia, sweetness—"

"Don't you dare 'Lia, sweetness' me."

"I've waited for days at a time in a cradle to take a single shot."

"What's that supposed to mean?"

"I have the patience to stalk my target and the perseverance to stick with it for however long is necessary to accomplish the mission."

I wheeled on my heels. "I don't care if you have my pillow. I'm sleeping on the couch."

"Go ahead," he said. "I'll come down and carry you back up if I have to. I'll do it later when you're asleep, whether my foot hurts or not."

It was a cheap shot. I glared at him. I wasn't going to be swayed by theatrics. The problem was that, coming from him, it wasn't theatrics. His foot did hurt. His entire leg hurt.

I gritted my teeth and stomped to the door.

"Have it your way," he said. "By the end of the night, we're both going to be sick and tired of that damn staircase and you'll be sleeping right here, in this room, in this bed."

Everest had spoken.

"Let's be reasonable," I said. "I don't think this is wise."

"Lia…" He groaned. "I'm not good at bullshit. I'm not going to explain what you already know."

"And what is it that I'm supposed to know?"

"Everything."

"That would make me the smartest woman on the planet."

"Really?" He rolled his eyes. "Okay, I'll just say it, then. *I* want *you* to sleep in *my* bed."

My heart did that Irish jig thing again, but my mind crushed it like a giant mallet. "No."

"Why not?" he said. "We did it last night and you didn't complain."

"Last night was an exception."

"Or a first time."

Every cell in my body twinkled like the brightest stars, but the realist in me wasn't fooled by things like joy and anticipation. "Let's just leave it like it is."

"Let's not," he said. "Come to bed. Think of it as therapy."

"Therapy?"

"Yes, Lia, therapy." He huffed, not a little exasperated. "I don't know what happened before I met you, but I know trauma when I see it, and you're really screwed up. The only way to get over your fears is to confront them. You fear getting in bed with me? Then you need to do exactly that."

Holy Mother.

"Choose," he said. "You can sleep here with me or sleep here without me."

I didn't know what to do.

"Come on, Neil." Ash got up from the bed and grabbed his pillow and his cane. "We'll go sleep in the freezer next door."

That room got too cold. He wouldn't get a wink of

rest. He'd have nightmares for sure. He could get sick just from sleeping in there…

"Wait."

Both Ash and Neil froze in place.

"If I get in bed with you," I said, "there will be none of that kissing stuff and no hanky-panky."

He straightened and crossed his arms. "You don't like kissing?"

"I like kissing fine."

"Then you have some specific grievances about the way I kissed you today?"

"No, I mean, that's not the point."

"Yeah," he said. "What *is* the point of this discussion?"

"We have an arrangement," I said. "I'm your caretaker—I mean, caregiver—and you'll be moving on as soon as Gunny Watkins gives you your medical release."

He sighed, dropped the pillow on the bed and plopped down on the mattress. "What am I going to do with you? Please, come to bed. I promise: no kissing and no hanky-panky, unless you decide that's exactly what you want, in which case, I'll be happy to oblige."

"I'm serious," I said. "You and I—we can't get involved."

"Newsflash," he said. "We're already involved."

"What?"

"You were there," he said. "This afternoon. When I kissed you? You know."

The shiver that fringed my spine teased every part of me. It tickled my belly, curled my toes and tightened my nipples. They poked through my T-shirt as if I'd been hit with a burst of arctic air. Ash noticed, no doubt about it. His stare only aggravated my condition. I blushed to the roots of my hair.

"And modest to boot." Ash lifted the bedcovers. "Come on."

The fear, it was like Red Rush, barreling through my veins. It raked my guts and wiped out my brain. But this was Ash. I'd cared for Ash. I trusted him. And he was not going to go to sleep in this bed unless I did too.

I hesitated. I drew in a great gulp of courage then marched across the room, got in the bed and slid between the sheets.

"That a girl." He tucked the covers around me, slid his shoulder beneath my head and scooped me close to him. "That wasn't so hard."

"Good night," I said in a tone that forbade talk or touch.

"Good night." He chuckled quietly.

I WOKE UP later that night, snug in Ash's bed, firmly ensconced in his arms. Basking in his body's heat, I was beyond warm. I was really hot. I shed one of the blankets and tucked the remaining sheet beneath my armpits. That's when I noticed the blue eyes beaming at me and something else, something much more alarming.

I launched out of the bed like a gold-medal sprinter, but I got snared in Ash's hold before I managed to hit the floor. I ended up clinging to my pillow with my backside pressed to him, no less exposed to his offending parts.

"Sorry about that." He held me tightly and gently at the same time. "But I swear, you're safe. Please, don't go. You've got to know that I'd never hurt you."

My heart pumped at a mad rate. My lungs refused to draw in the air. I had to try to set aside the fear. From his doggy bed, Neil raised his head briefly then lowered it back onto his paws. He would have alerted if I was in danger. Right? He would have alerted me, even if the danger came from Ash.

"Give me a moment," Ash said. "Let me see what the hell I can do about this. I'm thinking triangles and squares, cold showers and icy lakes. In the meanwhile, try to relax. You don't have a thing to fear from me. Okay?"

"Okay," I squeaked, scooting away on the mattress, putting some space between his body and mine, breathing, always breathing. "Do you—um—do you have to do that?"

"Christ, Lia, the things you ask." He scooped me right back against his chest. "It's a biological response, a natural reflex. It's not so easy to suppress when you're lying next to someone you want."

If I had been woolly before, now I was wide-awake. He wanted me? Beyond a kiss, *he* wanted *me*?

"I'm not a beast," he said. "Wanting is one thing. Taking is quite the other. I don't have to act on my impulses. I promise."

At a rational level, I understood what he meant, but a jolt of stomach-turning fear reminded me that other people out there had no such restraint.

"To be honest, it's not such bad news," he said. "At least not for me."

"What do you mean?"

"It's sort of a relief."

I shifted in his arms and craned my neck to lay eyes on his face. "Relief?"

"Lying in that hospital bed, one had to wonder if all the plumbing is going to work right. Lots of guys do."

Had I become the most selfish, self-centered witch

in the universe? I hadn't thought about him after the explosion, coming out of months of painful treatment in the hospital, about his injuries and how they would have impacted his body's natural functions, his state of mind and his confidence. I forced aside my fears to pay attention to his. I remembered that day at the dock. His plumbing seemed to be working just fine and his reaction had echoed in my body in a way that warmed me all over again now.

"Well," I mumbled. "Now you know that you can load the old cannon."

He laughed so hard that the whole bed shook. "True," he said, "at least when you're around. It's not what you want to hear, I know, but it's the God's honest truth."

A new front opened up in the battle raging inside me. I gnawed on my lips until they hurt. On one side, reason argued on behalf of common sense and survival. On the other side, my heart longed to break free and my body craved what my heart wanted.

I turned ever so slightly in his arms. The pretext of helping him to heal lent me the strength I needed. But it was just a pretext. As I reached out under the covers, I wanted to touch him. I wanted to touch him intimately. I wanted to touch him…there.

My fingers slid over the fabric of his boxers, outlining the bulk of his erection. Something stirred deep inside me, something primal and powerful capable of giving my fear a run for its money. He was already hard, but when my hand brushed against it, his cock tightened.

"Lia?" His body went as rigid as his erection. "What the hell are you doing?"

"Um…" I gulped dryly. "Helping out?"

He rumbled quietly. "Is that so?"

"Uh-huh."

"In that case… Take your hand off me."

"But—"

"That's not how it works." He grabbed my hand and placed it over the covers. "And I won't have it like that."

"I… I just wanted to help."

"Don't."

He might as well have punched me in the gut. He didn't really want me to touch him after all. My blush was so hot that my face was probably glowing in the dark.

"Sorry," I mumbled. "I just thought that you—that maybe you wanted me to…"

He scoffed, "The understatement of the century."

I frowned in the darkness.

"Look at me." He turned me around in his arms and tilted up my chin until I was doing exactly that. "That's better. Don't be afraid and don't be mad at me either. Get this through your thick skull: I don't want your pity and I sure as hell don't want you to make out with me out of a twisted sense of obligation."

"I don't understand," I said. "What do you want then?"

"I want *you* to want *me*."

"Oh."

"Anything less is a bust." He planted a quick kiss on my lips. "Now go to sleep. Don't be afraid. I don't know what kind of life you lived before this one, but I'm not going to force, coax or seduce you. On the other hand, I do plan to be around when you're ready for me."

TEN

MARIO'S BUSTLED FRIDAY EVENING, buzzing like a frantic hive, jammed with people from wall to wall, loud with conversation and laughter. Jimmy Martin kept the dance floor crowded, belting out his folksy version of "Some Nights." An accident had closed the interstate, kept the gas crews in town and brought in the employees seeking to escape the resort's expensive bubble.

I was busy. The night promised aching feet but good tips. The money would be good. Maybe I could help pay for the cottage's internet after all. My heart tripped when Charlie Nowak showed up with some of his friends. He'd been staying away lately. I took their order and served them a few pitchers of beer without suffering for it. Maybe he'd gotten the message and learned a good lesson.

As always, I kept my eyes on the door and my senses on alert. Jordan came in, a little later than usual. He smiled at me as he walked toward the bar. I poured for him and plunked down the mug in front of him.

"Thanks." He took a sip of his beer. "Listen, I just wanted to tell you—he's not so bad."

"Who?" I said.

"Ash," Jordan said. "I might have been a little tough on him. The guy's got his shortcomings, but he's not an ungrateful fool. And since I've gotten to know him, I like him."

"You've gotten to know him?" Really? "When?"

"He stopped by my office a few weeks ago to pay his bill," Jordan said. "I'd never had a human for a patient before. I charged him as if he was his dog. He got a kick out of that. We've had a few beers since. I've gone out to the ranch a couple of times to help with the cleanup. He's a good one, Lia."

A few beers? Ash and Jordan had struck a friendship without my knowledge. Why did the association feel subversive? And why on earth was Jordan telling me that Ash was 'a good one?'

Jordan's jaw tightened. "You could've given me a chance."

"Huh?" I was really having trouble following.

"You could've at least considered me," Jordan said. "You know, pre-Ash?"

"Pre-Ash?"

Jordan just stared at me.

"Oh, no." My stomach squeezed with fear. I would've never considered endangering Jordan like that, just as I couldn't endanger Ash now. "I couldn't… I can't…" Panic. I swallowed around the lump in my throat. I had to dispel the dangerous notion on the spot. "You think that Ash and I…?" My snort sounded as fake as it was. "No way. You've gotten the wrong impression."

Jordan's mouth twisted into a smirk. "Ash said that's exactly what you would say. He said you'd deny everything. You really are a lot like his great-grandfather's mare."

"Excuse me?"

"It's a good story." Jordan's smirk shifted into a genuine smile. "Hasn't he told it to you?"

"Nope."

"One day, Ash's great-grandfather found this wild mare grazing in his pastures," Jordan said. "She was a beauty, but she wouldn't let him come close, biting and kicking whenever he tried to approach her, except when he brought her apples."

"Apples?"

"She liked apples," Jordan said. "So for three years, Ash's great-grandfather brought the skittish mare apples every afternoon, until one day, after all that time, the mare followed him to the stables and took up residence."

A skittish mare? I gritted my teeth. The gall of that man.

"Hey, Jordan," the sheriff called from his perch at the VIP table. "Come settle a bet. What's the difference between an ass and a mule?"

"I'm coming." Jordan chugged down his beer then smirked at me. "All this time, I thought you just weren't interested in me. Now I know better. You're oblivious, not to mention skittish as hell. But I suppose that's Ash's problem now. Got to go." Jordan offered his hand. "Are we cool?"

We shook. "We're cool."

Jordan went to set aright the nuances of the equine world. My mind was going in circles and my belly churned. How was I going to keep Ash safe when he went around telling people we were together?

I couldn't think of a thing, probably because I'd grown so comfortable with Ash's presence in my life. Sure, he drove out to the ranch every day, where he and the guys worked to clear the fire's debris, but he always returned to take a late lunch with me by the lake before he went to rehab. My car was off-limits, so he insisted on driving me to work and picking me up every night. Dinner was a late-night meal—Ash's best efforts to meld my limited palate with his lofty nutritional expectations.

It was the best life I'd ever lived and it seemed to work well for Ash, who was getting better by leaps and bounds. My only regret was that it had to end and soon. The problem wasn't Ash, who kept his word at every turn. The problem was me.

I woke up at night in his arms, yearning for more of him, longing for his affection and haunted by desires I hadn't known I had until I landed in his bed. I craved his mouth like an addict, but as promised, he behaved like a gentleman, especially in bed, where every night, I wished he made an exception. His body called to mine. Or was it my body screaming for his?

A poke from Mario startled me.

"You look like you're about to combust with worry," he said. "Need a break?"

"Do I ever." I made for the back door, fanning my face.

As soon as I stepped out, I breathed in great quantities of crisp air, but even the brisk Colorado breeze failed to cool down my anxiety. I paced back and forth in the alley, feeling restless, nervous and irritable, not unlike…a skittish mare.

Shoot.

A screech interrupted my thoughts. I recognized the sound immediately. Animal screams. They came from the huge Dumpster parked under a flickering security light at the far end of the building. I looked up and down the blind alley. Nobody was about.

I dragged a crate over to the industrial-size garbage bin and climbed on it. The metal lid weighed a ton, but I managed to lift one of the halves. No critters shot out, so I peered inside. The light was tenuous at best, but what I saw broke my heart: a raccoon entangled in a mess of ropes struggling in the corner. One of the ropes was coiled tightly around its neck.

"You're in a heap of trouble."

I had no idea how the raccoon had gotten there, but it was obvious that the small bandit, probably a juvenile, was in distress. If he managed to survive the night, the garbage truck's compactor would surely kill him in the morning.

"All right, buddy." I straddled one leg over the edge of the Dumpster and then the other. "I'm coming." Hanging over the edge, I couldn't reach the bottom. I let go, dropped down and landed on my feet. God almighty, this was a big-ass Dumpster. It didn't smell great either. Thank heavens that the weather was cool. The stench would have been unbearable in the summer. I stepped over only a few scattered trash bags and made my way to the corner. The frightened animal growled at me.

"I know," I said. "You're really scared. I'm going to try to help you, but can you please try not to bite me?"

I crouched out of striking distance. I pulled on the ropes, but the noose actually tightened around the raccoon's neck. Perhaps if I pulled from the other side…

"Who do we have here?" A voice from above startled me.

I looked up. Charlie Nowak smirked down on me from his perch on the crate.

"Why, if it isn't Lia," he said. "What a surprise. It never occurred to me that you'd go out of your way to rescue a pest. No sir, never crossed my mind."

My stare shifted between Charlie and the raccoon. The animal hadn't gotten into the garbage bin all by itself. It had been trapped and transported here for one purpose only: revenge.

I rose to my feet slowly, keeping my eyes on the man looming above me.

"Charlie," I said. "I don't want any more trouble with you."

"Then you shouldn't have kneed me in the balls," he said. "You should have skipped the pepper spray and accepted my invitation."

"You were drunk. Go back to the bar and forget about it."

"No fucking way," he said. "You're gonna pay your dues. My friends saw what happened. Beat by a fucking woman…"

Oh, my God. He was serious.

He pulled down on the lid. With a running start, I leaped, trying to keep it from closing, but my effort was for naught. It crashed down with a ground-rattling *boom*. Darkness and terror slammed on me at the same time. Confinement was one of my worst fears. The memories. All those hours spent trapped and alone came back to haunt me. My pulse broke out into a gallop. Don't panic. Keep it together, even if my legs were reduced to rattling sticks.

I forced my voice out of my throat. "This is not funny, Charlie. Let me out."

"No problem." Charlie's voice came muffled but clear. "I'll come back in a few hours."

A few hours? My heart about gave out. I tried jumping to push out the lid, but it didn't work. The sound of a chain rattling over metal chilled my blood.

"Hear that?" A rattle of keys came from the outside. "These keys are going in my pocket."

The jackass had come prepared. I wanted to kick myself. Charlie had chosen his bait well, a defenseless animal calling for help, the one lure I couldn't ignore.

"You need to let me out before I start screaming." I tried to sound reasonable. "If you let me go now, I won't press charges against you."

"Scream all you want," Charlie said. "I told Mario you went home for the night. Nobody is looking for you."

The bad news kept coming. Charlie was determined to get his revenge. The darkness compressed all around me. The raccoon whinnied.

"Try not to be afraid," I murmured.

Memories of Red's dark cellar began to trickle out, rivulets seeping through the cracks of the dam I'd built in my mind. Oh, Lord. I strained to contain the horrors and yet the memories dribbled out in fickle spurts—bloodied fingers, scraping against thick concrete walls, wails resonating in the darkness, and screams too, my past's terrifying echoes.

"Hola, querida," Red's voice whispered in my ear. *"My naughty girl is back where she belongs."*

"Go away," I said aloud. "You're not here."

"But I'm here, always here, always with you," the silky voice said. *"You can pretend all you want, but you belong to me."*

No. He wasn't here. I wasn't his. I broke out into a cold sweat. Once the flashbacks started, they were hard to stop. I needed to get out of the Dumpster and fast. *Steady. Breathe. Cope.* I tried not to think about Red or his cellar.

"Charlie," I called out. "What do you want from me?"

"Payback's a bitch," Charlie said.

"Fine," I said. "You got me. You're the man, Charlie. Now, please." My voice cracked. "Let me out of here. Please?"

"I like to hear you beg," Charlie said. "You wanna get out?"

"Yes."

"Then say the magic words."

"Please?"

"Not that," he said. "Beg me to fuck you, Lia. Tell me you want my cock in your cunt."

What a sick bastard. "That's a lie and you know it."

"It's what you have to say if you want out." Charlie snickered. "I'll make you a deal. You take off your clothes and get down on your knees, naked as God put you on this earth. Then you call out to me, nice and sweet, and beg me to fuck you."

A bastard like him would want to have the show on record. He'd film the whole thing on his cell so he could show it to his friends. He might even put it on the internet.

"Come on," Charlie said. "You do that and I'll let your ass out."

He was enjoying this. The lust in his voice scared me as much as the darkness and the confinement. But I knew better. No deals with bullies and drunks. I piled a few bags of trash in the corner and tried climbing on top of them. The lid didn't budge. The bags broke beneath my feet and trash spilled everywhere.

"Showtime," Charlie taunted me. "Tell me you want me to ride you on all fours, like those animals you like so much."

Helpless and trapped all over again. The walls closed in. The darkness and the smell conspired to make me sick. For a moment, I didn't know where I was, stuck in the Dumpster behind Mario's or entombed in Red's cellar for days at a time.

Don't freak out. Breathe and cope. I was about to lose it.

I kicked the walls and banged my fists against the metal wall until my knuckles hurt. "Let. Me. Out!"

"Querida, it's for your own good." Red's rumbling bass echoed in my head. *"Obedience is a hard lesson to learn. When I come back, you can beg me to forgive you."*

Pepe's yelps filled the darkness, the sound of unspeakable violence. Red's fingers slid over my face, smearing something hot and wet on my cheeks.

"You know what that is?" Red asked. *"It's Pepe's blood, Lia. Poor puppy. You killed him with your carelessness. You should've never tried to run. Now poor Pepe's gone and I have to punish you for your behavior."*

I couldn't breathe anymore. Cope, just try to cope. A sob escaped my lips. My knees failed. I dropped to the floor, folded my legs against my chest and leaned my forehead on my knees. The raccoon's shrieks chiseled at my brain. I pressed my hands over my ears and dug my nails into my scalp. Pain. I needed the pain to stay sane. It was the only way to remind myself that I wasn't dead, buried and forgotten. It was my way of surviving the torture all over again.

Charlie pounded on the wall. "Are you naked yet?"

A blow. A grunt. A crash and a quake. Something big, something like a body, bounced off the Dumpster.

"You should have never run from me." Red spoke in my head. *"Now you're going to pay."*

A violent boom announced another crash. More grunting and lots of clanging and banging. Dread. A muffled voice called my name.

I made myself small in the corner and kept quiet.

Maybe if I didn't move he wouldn't find me. Maybe if I didn't make a peep he'd go away.

The jingle of keys. A rattle of chains. The groan of the lid opening. A sliver of light penetrated the darkness. The shadow of a figure's outline rose against the night sky.

Oh, please, not him, not Red.

"Lia?" a familiar voice called out gently. "Are you okay?"

But Red had a caring voice too, a soft, sinuous, melodic voice he used when it suited him, one that had tricked me sometimes, especially at the beginning.

"Come on," he said. "I'll help you out."

He was lying. Again. Pleasantries were Red's preamble. They came right before the horror. He was up to no good whenever he was nice to me. Poor Pepe. He'd been just a puppy. All those deaths. Red said they were my fault. I dug my nails deeper into my scalp.

"What's wrong? Are you hurt? Lia?"

Smooth, his voice was so smooth. I resisted the urge to do as he said. He'd kill at will, regardless of what I did. He'd kill me too and, some days, I wished he'd do so, sooner rather than later. I rocked back and forth on my heels, shivering. If only I were invisible.

"Jesus, Lia, hang on."

The metal floor rattled with a thud. Steps. Silence. Someone crouched next to me. I braced for the blow. Instead, a gentle hand landed on my shoulder. I shrank into the corner.

"Lia, baby, don't be afraid." The smooth voice again. "It's me. Ash. Can you hear me?"

Lia. Red never called me that. He didn't know. He never knew. Red's touch hurt. This touch didn't hurt. Fear made it very hard to think straight.

Ash knew my real name. I hadn't told him anything, but he'd known everything about me from the very beginning. I opened my eyes.

"I need you to let go, baby." He pried my nails away from my head one finger at a time. "Can you feel it? You're hurting yourself."

Oh, yeah, I could feel where my nails had sunk into my scalp and drawn blood. I wanted to explain how pain was necessary to sanity, but I was shivering too hard. I had no voice left in me, no strength to spare beyond breathing.

"Those damn flashbacks, they seem so real, don't they?" Ash kissed my hands and tucked them into my lap. "You're in shock, but it's fine, we can deal with shock." He examined my scalp, blotting the scrapes with his fingers. "If you have to hurt yourself, the scalp is a good spot. Nobody can see the tiny cuts, but you can feel them so good."

Did he really understand?

"When we got hit, pain was the only way I knew I was alive." He wiped off a bit of blood dribbling down my forehead. "I looked around and saw the wounded and the dying, the mess of blood, gore and body parts. The pain told me I was dying, but it also told me that I was alive."

He knew. He knew!

"You're alive, Lia," he said. "You're still in the fight. You're going to be fine. But we do need to get you out of here. Can you help me, please?"

Help him? Yes. That's what I was supposed to do. Help Ash. My brain responded to that and so did my body. I reached out with a trembling hand and touched his face, tracing the grim lines bracketing his mouth and the worry lines etched between his eyes.

"Is it really you?" I said. "Are you sure?"

"It's me." He held out his cane. "Remember this?"

Ash carried a cane. But Red was tricky. Red was cunning and sly.

"The man who hurt you," Ash said. "Did he speak to you like I do?"

I shuddered. "Sometimes he pretended to be nice."

"But did he like talking to you? Did he like listening to your voice like I do? Did he tell you the truth, like I always do?"

"No truth," I mumbled. "Never the truth."

"Did he cuddle you in bed every night?" Ash put his arms around my shoulder and, rubbing the cold out of my arms, drew me against him. "Did he watch you dream while you slept? Did he love holding you like I do?"

My eyes queried his. "You love holding me?"

"I do," he said.

I looked down on my knees. "You like holding me even though you know I'm dirty?"

"You might be a little smelly at the moment." He lifted up my chin, made eye contact and smiled. "Nothing a shower can't fix."

"Not dirty outside," I mumbled. "Dirty inside."

He frowned. "Inside?"

"Like dirty laundry, you know, used and stained."

"Oh." His Adam's apple bounced up and down his throat.

I looked away. Why had I brought this up, here and now? It was something I'd never said before, something I hadn't acknowledged until this very moment, not even to myself.

"Lia, baby, look at me." He thumbed the line of my jaw and waited until I met his stare. "Whatever happened to you, you're none of those things. You'll never be that to me."

"But you know, right?"

"I got blown to pieces by an IED that killed some of the best men I knew." He wiped the tears from my cheeks. "You got messed up by a son of a bitch who fucked up your life. No lies. No pretenses."

I leaned my head against his shoulder and breathed in his scent, which was hard, because the stink of the Dumpster had poisoned my sense of smell. Still, I recognized water, earth and cedar; consolation, shelter and courage.

"Just in case you still have doubts…" He lowered his head and kissed me, a soft brush of lips that confirmed his identity for good. My body ratified his DNA as the only person on this earth who could make me feel like life was worth the pain even as we sat at the bottom of a giant garbage bin in a poorly lit back alley.

"It *is* you," I whispered.

"Now you know." He braced his hands under my elbows. "Can you get up?"

I got to my feet. My knees were iffy. I clung to him until I found my balance. Everything looked hazy, undefined and out of focus. I shuffled toward the light as if I was ancient.

Ash clasped his hands and offered a stirrup to my foot. "Ready?"

My brain sputtered an afterthought. I remembered something important. I turned around in circles until I spotted the little raccoon. By now, the creature panted with exhaustion. Its little pink tongue stuck out of its mouth. Its eyes flickered with desperation.

"I don't know if that's a good idea," Ash cautioned.

"Raccoons carry lots of diseases and this one could maul you."

"He's tired." I approached the creature tentatively. "I doubt he has much fight left in him."

"Let me do it," Ash said.

"I can do it."

He glanced at my shaky hands. "Are you sure?"

"I *need* to do it."

"Okay." He handed me his utility knife. "But you can't go at it all alone." He took off his jacket and circled the growling raccoon. "You've got to learn to rely on your friends. You've got to learn to trust your team."

In one swift movement, he flung his jacket over the raccoon, dove to the ground and held it down. "Now," he said. "Be careful."

"Easy." I knelt next to the raccoon. "Let's get out of here."

My fingers quaked like aspen leaves, but the ropes were frayed and easy to cut through. My knuckles brushed against the raccoon's coat. It was so soft and it reminded me of poor Pepe. Damn the tears streaming down my face. The old wounds gaped and oozed, but I forced myself to breathe and cut the last rope.

"Ready?" Ash said.

I stepped away. "Go home, buddy."

Ash went from knees to feet in a flash. The raccoon leaped and, hackles raised, lunged toward me. Ash intercepted it with his cane, which ended up getting the brunt of the critter's frustrations, before it bounced off the walls and darted out of the Dumpster.

"You're welcome," I called after him.

"That was close." Ash cocked his eyebrows. "Better?"

"Much." My knees locked and my mind flowed with a measure of clarity.

"Up," he said and this time I accepted the boost and vaulted over the side.

Behind me, Ash wrapped his fingers over the edge of the metal wall and pulled himself up and out like the athlete he was. He landed on his good foot without a sound.

The cool air freshened my lungs and cleared my mind. The night was quiet. I gawked. Charlie Nowak was fastened to the lamppost by the chain coiled around his neck. His jacket was ripped in several places. Bruises darkened his face and blood oozed from his violently crooked nose. He wasn't breathing too comfortably either.

"Once a bully, always a bully," Ash said. "If I remember right, you were also the class clown."

"Please," Charlie rasped. "I can't breathe!"

"A pile of shit like you is a waste of good air." Ash undid the chains from the lamppost. "If you ever bother Lia again, I'll kill you. Do you understand?"

"Y-yes."

It wasn't a threat or a boast. It was a promise. There was no violence to Ash's voice, no showing off, bluster or excess testosterone. He meant exactly what he said.

"Walk." He led Charlie by the chain. "Climb up the crates."

"But why?" Charlie struggled to scramble up the crates with his hands fastened behind his back.

"Genius." Ash boosted Charlie up. "You're about to get a dose of your own medicine."

"Ash?"

"Stay out of this, Lia."

"But—"

"No buts," Ash said.

"It was a joke," Charlie said. "I never meant to hurt her."

"But you did," Ash said. "You frightened her, and for that, you'll pay."

Ash grabbed his cane by the ends and, wedging it beneath Charlie, pushed him up as if he was a barbell. Charlie teetered on his belly at the edge of the Dumpster, babbling senseless pleas. With a final thrust Ash pushed him in. Charlie made a monumental racket when he landed. Ash closed the lid and jammed it shut.

"That's done." He wiped the dirt off his hands.

"Remind me never to piss you off." I wavered. "We can't leave him there all night."

"After what he did to you, I could."

The fury I spotted in his eyes frightened me. It brought memories of Red's simmering violence, always boiling beneath his skin. I stumbled away from Ash. Were all men vicious at heart?

Ash pulled me into his embrace. "Don't run away from me." He kissed the top of my head. "I said I *could* leave him there to be shredded by the garbage truck. But I won't."

I let out a long breath and held on to him with all I had. I didn't realize how stiff and cold I was until I made contact with his body.

"Repeat after me." He placed his jacket over my shoulders. "I will not get into a smelly Dumpster all by myself. I'll count on other people to help to solve my problems."

It was a credo that went against everything I believed.

"Others can help," Ash said. "You don't have to go at it alone."

But I did have to go at it alone, if I wanted my friends—and Ash—to survive.

I gulped down the fear and forced my thoughts to flow. "How did you end up showing up when you did?"

"I had some informal meetings with a couple of people tonight, including the sheriff."

"You went in the bar?"

"I did," he said.

"Wow," I said. "I bet that took some serious effort on your part."

"The one time I manage to go in there and sit for a while, and you're nowhere to be found."

"Why do I have a feeling that you being around wasn't a coincidence?"

Ash ignored the question and whistled instead. Neil sprang from the darkness, trailing his service leash.

"Where was he?" I said.

"I wanted him to hang back, so I left him in the truck." Ash picked up the leash and patted Neil behind the ears. "You did good, boy. It's something we've been working on. I didn't want him in a fight."

I squeezed his hand. "I didn't want you in a fight either."

"Most fights are better fought sooner, rather than later."

"But how did you know about Charlie?"

"It wasn't so hard to figure out," Ash said. "I put my ear to the wind. The day after you came home with those bruises on your wrists, his guys were calling him 'Blue Balls.'"

"You did more than put your ear to the wind," I realized. "You decided he would try again. That's why you insisted on driving me to and from work. Have you been waiting all these nights for him to make his move?"

"I told you I'd watch your back and I meant it."

"But Ash—"

"If all the intelligence suggests that an attack is coming, then it's coming," he said. "I'd rather fight on my own terms and turf, than when it suits the other guy best."

"You can't do this."

"What?"

"Fight my battles, come to my defense."

He rolled his eyes. "So now you've graduated from being my caretaker to acting as my personal shrink, and you're drawing all kinds of conclusions, including the one that infers that I'm somehow craving fights."

"If it fits…"

"Then you don't know squat about me," he said. "You're also blind as a bat."

"You have to stop coming to my aid," I said. "It's dangerous. I don't want your apples."

"Apples?"

"Great-grandfather's skittish mare?"

"Ah, that old story." He had the grace to look chastened. "I thought Jordan would get it."

"He got it all right," I said. "But you don't. I want you to stop trying to help me. It'll kill you."

"And that matters to you? Whether I live or die?"

"Of course," I said. "A lot."

"Lia Stuart." He smiled. "That's the sweetest thing you've ever said to me."

He kissed me again, a hard kiss that had glorious music playing in my ears. I swear. I couldn't reason when he kissed me. I couldn't even stand on my own two feet without swaying like a drunk.

He wrenched his lips from mine. "Christ, kissing you is like an ambush to my body."

"Lobotomy," I muttered, almost incoherent with want. "Electroshock."

He smiled. "We'd better stop. I can't be held responsible for my actions otherwise. Come along."

"Where are we going?"

He squeezed my hand. "Try to roll with the punches. Okay?"

ELEVEN

ASH, NEIL AND I walked out of alleyway and around to the parking lot where the truck was parked. The sheriff, Mario and Barb and Gary Woods were having a smoke outside the bar. I tried to shake off Ash's hold but he clung to my hand as we approached the little group.

"Phew." Barb waved her hand in front of her nose. "What's that smell? Something's stinking up this joint tonight."

Ash ignored Barb's remarks and walked right up to the sheriff. "You might want to have a look at the Dumpster behind the building," he said. "I took care of some trash that might be of interest to you."

"Dang it, boy." The sheriff dropped his cigarette on the ground and squashed it with his boot. "You didn't do anything silly, did you, son?"

"Only what had to be done to protect my girl."

His girl?

The eyes of everyone in the group turned to me. Barb gawked. I'd tried to prevent this very thing from happening, but Ash had disregarded all my warnings. How was I supposed to keep him safe when he did stuff like this?

"Gary," Ash said, "I've known you for a long time. You're a decent man. I haven't decided yet what to do about the lease, but I can't do business with you if your foreman's out of control."

"Excuse me?" Gary said.

"You heard me. Charlie Nowak has been harassing Lia. Today, he tried to trap her in the Dumpster. I judge a man by the quality of his friends, and Charlie is rotten piece of shit." Ash turned to Mario. "I'm going to take Lia home now."

"By all means," Mario said. "You okay, hon?"

I nodded, because I couldn't speak. The night had rattled me in all kinds of violent ways, but my brain was stuck on two words. *His girl.* I'd never been anybody's girlfriend. People had died just for being my friends.

We drove out of town with our windows cracked open to dispel the smell clinging to us. Neil found the stink fascinating. From his perch on the backseat, he kept trying to bury his nose in my hair.

The darkness hurled a dusting of fine snow at us. The truck's headlights illuminated thin flakes swirling in the wind like silver. Ash concentrated on the driving. My heart and my brain waged a fierce battle. It hurt like hell, but the brain won at the expense of the heart.

"We need to clarify some things," I said.

He glanced at me. "I was afraid of that."

"Tonight you called me your girl in front of all those people."

"Yes."

"It was a dangerous thing to do," I said. "And it's not true."

His knuckles whitened about the wheel. "Here we go again."

"I mean it," I said. "I appreciate your help. I don't know what would have happened if you hadn't showed up. But you don't have to tell everyone and their mothers that I'm your girlfriend in order to protect me. Now we have to do something drastic to dispel that very dangerous myth."

"Lia," he said in that stubborn tone of his. "You *are* my girlfriend."

"I'm not."

"But you are," he insisted. "You told Gunny Watkins. It was your idea in the first place."

"I'm your caretaker. Remember? I'm not your real girlfriend. I'm your pretend girlfriend."

"Maybe at the beginning," he said. "But you don't like pretending and neither do I. I might be a tad literal sometimes, but here's how it goes. I promised you I've got your back and I do. You said you were my girlfriend and, as it turned out, you are."

"Ash, please," I said. "You can't even flirt with the notion. I can't love anybody."

"I know." Resignation tainted his voice. "Because people suffer when they love you, people die. I admit it, it's pretty damn grim."

"Don't you dare make light of the danger."

"I'm not minimizing the danger. I believe you. But right this minute, you've got another problem."

"What is it?"

His eyes burrowed into my head. "You like me."

"I don't."

"I don't mean to be cocky, but you have feelings for me. You take care of me, but you also care for me."

"How would you know that?"

"I've got ears to hear and eyes to see," he said. "I'm not a total fool. The things you do for me? You care for me. I think you may even love me. I'm not letting go of that. For the life of me, I can't figure out how I got so lucky, but hell, I can't complain."

I willed my mouth to close. "It's not true. It's not possible. It's not safe."

"Sorry," he said. "You. Love. Me."

"Don't say it, Ash, please. He'll come. You'll die."

"Who, Lia? Tell me: who will come?"

The memory hit me, Red's chilling grin as he squeezed the trigger and killed a stranger right before my eyes. *"Did you see the way the motherfucker looked at you?"* Red had asked me as the man bled out in the alleyway. *"No respect."*

"Ash, you have to leave now." I panicked. "Or maybe I'll leave. Yes, that may be the safest course of action. He'll never have any reason to come here if I take off."

He stared at me as if I'd grown horns. "I'm talking about love here and you're talking about bolting?"

"Stop it, Ash."

"Then help me out, please. I'm dating a girl who keeps her go bag packed."

"You're not dating me and I'm not your girlfriend," I snapped. "Don't you understand?"

He shrugged. "You love me and there's nothing you can say or do that'll change that. So I think we should just accept that and move on."

I threw my hands up in the air. I'd squared off with Mount Everest and it wasn't about to move. "You're crazy, you know that? You drive the right kind of truck, because your skull is thick as a ram's. You're reckless."

"And you look pretty when you're mad, even if at this moment you're also very stinky."

He turned the truck onto a snow-dusted gravel road. I realized I hadn't been paying attention to our route or to the fact that the snow had ceased falling and the night had cleared.

"Where are we?" I said. "Where are we going?"

"You'll see." He parked before a rusted gate topped by a sign that said Trespassers Will Be Shot.

"What are you doing?" I said when he opened the door. "I don't want to be shot."

He hopped down from the truck, limped over to the gate and, after fiddling with the lock, opened it and motioned for me to drive the truck through.

"What now?" I said to Neil as I slid over to the driver's seat. "Your owner is the most maddening human on the planet."

Neil grumbled in what I interpreted as complete agreement.

Ash closed the gate behind us and climbed on the seat next to me. I drove the truck for a while, edging potholes as big as moon craters and mounting rock beds that tested the Ram's clearing. We passed an abandoned rock quarry and the remains of an old mine.

"What's all this?" I said. "The road to the end of the world?"

"Almost there," he said.

At last, the headlights illuminated the end of the abysmal road, where an old cabin stood like a relic of a time gone by. The rocky slopes of a spectacular mountain rose behind the cabin, framed by the brilliance of a million stars.

"Wow." I turned off the ignition and took in the extraordinary sight. "What's this place?"

"Welcome to Heaven." Ash too stared at the sky. "This was our family's original homestead. We've been using it as a hunting cabin for generations."

"Is this part of your lands?"

"The best part, if you ask me," he said. "Come on."

We stopped by the rustic cabin but only briefly. It was one room, with an old heating stove and a pair of bunk beds at one end. I was surprised because even though it was obviously very old, it was clean and provisioned. The cabin had no electricity or running water, which probably explained why Ash had chosen not to live there when he returned to Copperhill. He lit a miner's lamp and, after grabbing a bag from an old cabinet, motioned for me to follow him.

The night was clear but cold. The stars lit our path, along with the lamp. Neil led the way down a deer track that ran along a tumbling creek. The song of water on stone enlivened the narrowing canyon and appeased my frazzled nerves. The track dead-ended at the base of the mountain. Neil, Ash and the light disappeared into what looked like a crack in the mountain.

I peered into the fissure suspiciously. A cave? Not another dark, confined place. I couldn't handle any more of that tonight.

Ash reappeared briefly, holding up the lamp and grinning like a toddler with a secret. "Come on."

"But—"

"I promise, you're going to like it," he said, before disappearing again.

I stepped into the crack with trepidation. My steps crunched on a bed of gravel and sand. I took a deep breath and scurried across a short, natural tunnel to emerge at the other side, where I came to a dead stop and gawked.

I stood in a hanging valley perched between high peaks that rose dark and silent all around me. The valley opened up to what would have been an expansive view of the range during the day. In the darkness, it looked like a roiling sea, frozen beneath the stars. A tumbling creek crossed the vale and dropped over the edge. Neil stood like Simba on top of a boulder at the crook of the valley, framed by a cloud of steam.

I edged my way around the boulders and entered

yet another world, where three hot springs bubbled and
steamed to the side of the creek where they formed
deep pools. The air filled my lungs with the bland scent
of rock and minerals. The miner's lamp burned at the
edge of the middle pool, casting a magical glow on the
frothy water.

Ash stood waist deep in the center of the spring.
Steam wafted from his upper body. He looked like
some divine creature fashioned from granite, a spawn
of rock and water, nature's exquisite work of art. The
scars made elegant patterns on his body, like mineral
veins on marble. The pool hissed and gurgled around
him, warbling the same jubilant notes that played in
my heart. Water dripped from his head and torso, wor-
shipped his body and celebrated his existence, claiming him as surely as I longed to claim him. The current
foamed and fizzled against his skin, an intimate caress
that had me dripping too.

"That pool over there is too hot," he said. "That one
over there is not hot enough for a night like this one.
But this one, this one's perfect."

It was perfect, but only because he was in it.

"What are you waiting for?" Ash said. "Come in."

Two sets of old arguments seesawed in my mind.
Not in the plan. Very tempting. Not smart. But I stank.
It was a great reason to justify my impulse. I'd have to
take off my clothes. The mere thought had my stomach
churning and my face burning.

"I won't look." Ash turned his back to me. "I promise."

The disconnect between my brain and body widened. The sight of his broad shoulders and back didn't
help. Then my brain kicked in. *Don't do it. Bad idea.
Run, run now.* I turned around to go back to the cabin,

but instead, I found myself shedding my clothes with astonishing swiftness. In my head, a fresh new voice cheered me on, urging me to seize the moment, to live beyond survival, to live for the sake of living.

The spring welcomed my body with a delicious embrace. I immersed myself in the hot pool until the water closed above my head. I held my breath and stayed underwater for as long as I could. The tiny scrapes I'd inflicted on my scalp stung at first. Then the sting went away, replaced by an increasing sense of full-body healing. My muscles relaxed. The knot in my stomach loosened up. The cold fused into my bones melted along with the fear. I looked up. Beyond the layers of flowing water, the galaxy smiled down on me.

When I finally came up for breath, the air that poured in cleared my lungs and refreshed my senses. The stink of the Dumpster was gone for good. Where I stood, the water covered me comfortably all the way to my armpits. Across the spring, Ash sat on a rocky ledge, staring at me with a look that curled my toes.

"Nice?" he said.

"More like magical."

His smile rivaled the sky. "Want to come over?"

"I... I don't know." I gulped loudly. "Yes and no?"

"Okay," he said. "I get that."

It was only a flicker in his stare, but I was like a satellite tuned exclusively to his channel. Despite his best efforts to conceal it, a look of resignation dulled his eyes. So many questions. Should I? Could I? I was tired of fighting myself, eroded from resisting my impulses. I knew what he wanted—no—what he needed. I needed it too. Could I do it for him? Could I do it for myself?

I traced the spring's swirling whirlpools with my hands. "I'm really scared."

"Because you think someone will try to hurt me if he thinks we're together?"

"Yes."

"I've been to war," he said. "I've volunteered to go on missions with piss-poor odds for success. This is my life too. Don't I get to pick the risks I take? Don't I get a choice?"

"You've been away for a long time," I said. "You were hurt. You were in the hospital for a while. Have you considered that maybe this isn't a choice on your part?"

"Ah." His lips pressed into a tight, white line. "Let me get this straight: my personal shrink thinks I'm drawn to her out of necessity or reaction rather than choice."

"Admit it," I said. "Given our situation, it could be."

"Christ, Lia." He shook his head. "You're so smart and yet you can be so clueless. It's like you're tone-deaf or something. You never know how people really feel about you."

"What are you talking about?"

"Jordan," he said. "The guys at the bar. Me. We're all into you, and you don't even notice."

"That's not true." Why would anyone in their right mind want me? "But here's something that's true: you're healing quickly. Anytime now, Gunny Watkins will grant you a full medical release. You'll be able to meet new people, go places—"

"And where would you have me go?"

"Wherever you like," I said. "You'll be healthy and free."

"What about you?"

"I can never be free."

"Hear me out," he said. "And try not to be mad at me."

"Mad at you?"

"Gunny Watkins gave me the medical release when she called that day in the truck a while back."

My mouth fell open. "What?"

"She said the doctors were very pleased with my progress. The evaluations all agreed that I'd met the major milestones, physically and psychologically. She said I should be able to manage my own recovery."

I'd been out of a job for a while and didn't even know it. He'd gotten his coveted medical release. Days ago. The sand shifted beneath my feet. I wasn't sure where I stood.

"Why didn't you tell me?"

He shrugged. "Why do you think?"

"I don't know." I reeled. "You never wanted a caretaker—I mean, caregiver. You should've been delirious with joy on hearing the news."

"You're right. I never wanted a caretaker, that is, until I met you." The look in his eyes softened. "I didn't tell you about it because I didn't want you to bolt the moment you learned I'd been released from your care."

I tried to wrap my mind around that. "I… I don't understand."

"You're going to make me talk about it, aren't you?" He took a deep breath. "Okay, I guess I'll have to make the effort. I'm not good at saying stuff people want to hear. I'm no good at talking, period. I do, Lia. That's who I am. Can you understand that?"

Perhaps I could.

"All my adult life, it was all about being a SEAL," he said. "I lived for the mission. I gave each mission my all. Nothing else mattered. Then we got ambushed and blown apart, and all hell broke loose and we fought like devils to get out alive, but not all of us did—"

His voice fractured. The pain in his eyes was more than I could bear.

"What I'm trying to say is that life becomes very clear when you're dying," he said. "The golden hour is a century of pain and wisdom. You don't regret what you did. You regret what you didn't get to do. Four months is a lifetime in a hospital bed. Plenty of time to think. When the pain allows it, you spend a lot of time figuring out what you're going to do differently if you survive. You think about who you'd want to spend your time with if you could, about what matters."

He paused, wet his lips and continued. "I swore to myself that given the chance, I'd live differently the next time around. It was hard to come home, but I did. It was the first step. And there you were, at the lake, in the cottage, at the one place I could bear to be, my only possible destination, where only *I* could find *you*."

I swallowed the lump in my throat. "Maybe I was just in the right time at the right place?"

"Oh, yeah," he said. "You were there, waiting for me, as if God Himself had executed a precision drop and delivered me an exclusive lifeline." His gaze slid down my neck. "And just in case I missed the point—'cause He knows, and everyone else in my life knows, that I'm as dense as they come—you were wearing *my* stone."

"Your stone?" My hand followed his eyes to the little pendant I wore around my neck, the one Wynona had made for me. My fingers closed around the carved obsidian.

"I found that stone when I was a child," Ash said. "It was shortly after my parents died. Nona and I were walking around the lake and I thought it was precious. Nona laughed and convinced me that it was rare but only because it was special to me. I didn't know she'd kept it all this time until I saw it embedded in your pendant. She made sure with the design that even if I was out of my mind and mad with pain, I'd notice it."

"How?"

"Do you know what they used to call SEALs when the program was first established?"

I shook my head.

"Frogmen," he said. "Some still call us that. The skulled frog is a respected symbol for SEALs. That's why Nona carved her stylized version of it on that stone."

"Are you saying that Wynona chose me for you?"

"Chose you?" He laughed. "No, she'd never admit to that. She raised a rebel. I've always made my own choices and they were very different from hers. But I think she saw something in you. She even left me that note in the safe, reminding me to trust my judgment. She wanted me to notice that you were special. And I did."

That Irish jig? It blared in my head to the tune of a full orchestra. And my heart? It joined in the ruckus, swelled to impossible proportions, full with the emotions rocking my world. I sent my gratitude to the stars, where I was sure Wynona's soul looked down on us tonight. I sent a good scolding her way too. She'd been party to this mess.

"Lia, I know what I want," Ash said. "The question is whether you want the same thing."

"Ash…" I faltered. "You may need a new mission, but I'm not it."

"You're absolutely right." His eyes fastened on me. "I'm crazy about you, but you can't be my new mission. That would be screwed up. Our new mission—should you choose to accept it—would be *us*."

My heart exploded in my chest. My inner self danced wildly beneath the stars' fireworks. Not even in my most elaborate dreams could I have imagined I'd love a man, a marine, a SEAL. And that he'd love me.

"I... I don't think you understand." I gnawed on my lips. "If something bad happened to you, I wouldn't forgive myself. I wouldn't want to go on. I don't think I could."

"Lia." He started toward me then reversed the impulse and held back. "Give me the choice. In time, we'll deal with the rest. You've got to trust that I know what I'm doing. I want the choice. Please."

The look on his face scattered the last of my defenses. My resolve dissolved into the hot springs. It was as if the minerals in the water were corroding the shell I'd painstakingly built around myself. But there was something else, something I didn't know if he could understand.

"I don't know if I can..." God, I didn't even know how to say it. "I don't know if I can—you know—stand it."

"It?"

It took him a moment to realize what I meant. Who could blame him? It was beyond me why anybody in their right mind would want to grapple with a screwed-up mess like me. Sex terrified me. Memories of pain and humiliation shaped my only knowledge of it. But since I'd met Ash, sex had also begun to intrigue me and, even now, as I looked into Ash's eyes, something shifted in me.

I'd tried. I'd read everything I could get my hands on. I'd researched the matter at length. I'd even talked to a counselor at the shelter for a few sessions. She'd taught me the *steady, breathe, cope* technique that allowed me to get by most of the time.

The trauma had been difficult to overcome, but I'd been determined to free myself from Red's hold at every level. I'd worked hard to transform myself from victim to survivor. I'd tackled each step on my way toward recovery, but this moment was the summit of all of those steps and I didn't know if I could stand the final test. Was I ready?

"There's something else…" The words refused to come out of my parched throat. I tried to explain several times, then lowered my eyes and slumped in defeat.

"What is it?" Ash asked softly. "Whatever it is, you can tell me."

"That's the problem," I mumbled. "I… I can't."

Ash's stare caressed my face and perused my soul, deconstructing me as he tried to make sense of me, my reluctance, my fears. I groaned inside, wallowing in a surge of desperation. He needed to know, but I couldn't explain, not now. If I did, I could fall apart for good.

"Perhaps we can table this one for later," he suggested.

I shook my head. "You need to know…before…before you make your decision."

"My decision has already been made," he said with mind-boggling certainty.

"You could change your mind." I gulped dryly. "*This* could change your mind."

Mount Everest rumbled. "I doubt it."

"I understand if it does." I took a step back and then another, until I crouched in the shallow end of the pool, with my knees bent beneath me and my heart pumping hard in my throat. "But you deserve better. You should have a choice too."

I turned around and straightened my knees. I rose from the pool until the water lapped at my hips. The night's cold fingers tickled my skin despite the waves of steam wafting from me. Water trickled down my body like tears. I wrapped my arms around myself and shivered, baring my back for him.

I knew what he saw, grooves, notches and nicks from the belt and buckle that had permanently scarred my back, the little round blotches from the burns that puckered between my ribs and the countless other scars that littered my skin. He saw my shame too, a life of pain, and all the things I couldn't talk about.

After a little while, I dared a glance over my shoulder. Ash wasn't shying from the sight. On the contrary, mouth straight and brow furrowed, he stared at me, taking a hard look indeed, absorbing the dreadful story written on my body.

"Lia?" The restraint in his voice was a mix of compassion, outrage and kindness. "Turn around. Look at me."

I submerged myself in the pool and concealed the scars beneath the water, banishing them to the realm of anonymity, where they belonged. I took a deep breath and turned to face Ash. The warmth beaming from his eyes soothed my stiff shoulders as surely as the steaming current.

"I've seen what you wanted me to see," he said. "I won't lie. It makes me mad as hell to know that you had to live through that. But those scars on your back? They don't change the way I feel about you. They do, however, help me to understand the depth of your fears."

I didn't repulse him. The sight of me didn't dissuade him. He didn't judge me, didn't think less of me, didn't reject me outright. I let out the long breath I'd been holding.

"You're so brave," Ash said from his side of the pool. "I love that about you. But you don't have to be brave all the time. Not when I'm around. We can wait."

The only man I'd ever been with would have never said anything remotely like that to me. Red didn't believe in delays, consideration or patience. His methods of operation relied on brute force, torture and blackmail, on coaxing and tricking people into doing what he wanted. He enjoyed the suffering that came with it, the pain of others, especially mine.

The contrast between one man and the other was almost too much to bear.

But the fear. God, I quaked inside and out. Could I really wipe the memories clean from my mind's hard drive? Could I overcome the terror trained into my body? Could I conquer the fear, dread and anxiety that permanently knotted my soul?

Steady. Ash was there, just on the other side of the pool. *Breathe.* I dug my toes in the sandy bottom and pushed my body through the spring. *Cope.* I took a second step, and then another. The intensity in his eyes sustained me through the crossing. I focused on those eyes and kept going, until I stood before him, with only a few inches of churning water between our bodies. He didn't move. He didn't even blink. He was as still as he could be, as if he feared that if he moved, I might scatter and fly away like a frightened little sparrow.

In truth, part of me wanted to bolt. Fleeing was something I was used to doing. Staying, now that was hard. But there was another new part of me that refused to run, emboldened by desire and driven by need. And that part of me? It was determined to stay for the night.

I took a deep breath, reached out and caressed his face. He closed his eyes. I trailed the dark stubble growing along the line of his jaw and traced his lips' defined lines. He kissed my fingertips. I leaned closer and breathed in the air he exhaled, before I pressed my lips to his.

I kissed him. *I* kissed *him*. And I kept kissing him, allowing my lips to explore his mouth, persuading him with my kisses that I wanted this for him, but also for myself.

He groaned against my mouth. "Jesus, Lia."

I was familiar with his body. How could I not be, after tending to his wounds and helping him heal? I'd slept with him for many nights. I was used to his shape, slumbering next to me in the darkness, to his scent, mixing with mine on the bed's sheets, to the steady cadence of his respiration, as familiar to me as my favorite song.

But this was different. My hands explored him in a new way, openly and directly. I enjoyed the width of his shoulders beneath my palms, the span of his chest rising and falling under my hand and the raised outline of his nipples tripping against my fingers. I gave myself permission to follow his body's tapering lines, trailing the water dripping down his chest. I inched closer. His arms opened like a gate.

I stepped into those arms of my own volition. I trembled when our skins met. For a moment I just stood there as if perched at the edge of a great abyss. Then his arms closed around me and he drew me against his body, where I discovered firm ground and safe anchorage. It was as if my flesh was made of malleable putty. My body molded to his. My breasts snuggled against his chest, my belly nuzzled against his stomach and my thighs brushed against his thighs.

"You can't expect me to keep my word if you do that," he murmured.

I looked into his eyes. "I want to please you. I need to please you."

"Sweet Jesus." His eyes sparked with blue fire. "Are you sure?"

I kissed him.

"Lia…"

The way he said my name was a poem. How could a sound hold so much power, passion and warmth?

"Don't be scared." He caressed my hair away from my face and brought me even closer, until his erection pressed hot and hard against my groin. "It's just me, wanting you."

He wanted me. Me. And I wanted him too. I could do this. I would do this. I set the fear aside. There was no need to be scared. This was Ash, the man I'd pledged to heal. This was his way of needing me and my way of healing him—and myself. I softened against his hardness, as drenched inside as I was outside.

His lips seized my mouth and stole all of my breath. His body burned, and my body—it flared with the contact. I swear the spring got hotter from the furnace burning in my lower belly.

The feel of his hands traveling down my back made me dizzy. His fingers flowed over my spine, accepting the ugly scars, soothing the old shame. His hands were hot and strong as they cupped the halves of my ass and rubbed his cock against me. My body's jolts of pleasure reflected in his eyes.

He gathered me in his arms and cradled me on his lap, caressing my body with his gaze. The contrast between the hot water and the cold air tightened my nipples. My impulse was to cover my breasts.

"Don't." He lowered his head and kissed my hands. His perusal was as gentle as his touch and without judgment. "You're so beautiful." He kissed one of my breasts. "You're like a gift from heaven."

I let out a nervous giggle. "Given that we're in Heaven, that might be a bit over the top."

"Over the top?" He smiled. "No, Lia. You just can't see yourself right now. Beautiful doesn't begin to describe you. Beautiful doesn't do you justice tonight."

If the world had ended at that moment, my life would've been perfect. If lightning would've struck me down, I would have died a happy woman. God knew, I was already humming with need, buzzing with the thrill of being in his arms, still a little afraid but fully engaged. It was his smile that fueled the fire melting my heart like a marshmallow on a stick.

Ash's hand claimed one of my breasts. His touch was a promise of joy. He lowered his mouth and secured my nipple between his tongue and his palate. He suckled on it, first gently, then with more suction. Both of my nipples bloomed like spring buds. My body replied with bursts of pleasure to every tug. It was as if he'd found the secret dial to my need.

His hand slid between my legs. His fingers glided over my sex, soft but earnest. I startled, but he held me in place. "Just learning the lay of land," he murmured between kisses.

"But—"

"Hush, baby, let me do my recon. You're going to feel really good."

I could sense his need, not just his physical need, which was strong and tugged on my desire like a powerful magnet, but also his need to be trusted. So I let him touch me.

"There it is." He appropriated my clit between two fingers and rubbed around it, before stroking it ever so lightly while he kissed me. "Doesn't that feel good?"

Good? More like superb, fantastic and phenomenal all at the same time. I didn't know that my body could feel that much pleasure. Moreover, I didn't know he could crank up my need with nothing but his touch.

His strokes were gentle. His finger meandered. "No, don't close your legs. If you don't like it, just tell me."

It was only a knuckle at best, but his touch sent me to the very edge of an orgasm.

"Christ, you're so warm and slick." A shiver rattled his body. "Do you want to show me how you like it? Do you want to show me where you like it best?"

I pressed my face against his neck. "I think you're doing just fine. Can I… I mean, may I touch you?"

He smiled, took my hand and guided it beneath the water. He hissed quietly when my hand slid over him. He was hard and yet straightened and thickened even more between my fingers. I swear, every part of me sizzled with the contact. The effect I had on him built my confidence. I ran my hand up and down his cock, enjoying the feel of him, growing his bulk as surely as I was growing my own excitement.

He kissed me some more and murmured. "I won't last too long if you do that."

"Then don't."

His gaze was glued to my face. "You sure?"

"I'm sure." And for once, I was completely and utterly convinced.

Still caressing his cock, I braced my knees on the ledge at either side of his lap. He brought me closer and, spreading his hands over my ass, took command of my hips. I lay my forehead on his shoulder as he nestled his swollen tip against my sex.

"We'll take it real slow." He kissed me. "Say the word, and we'll stop."

My body tensed. A moment of sudden panic had me clenching all my muscles. But any fears I harbored scattered as he lowered me onto his cock and entered me. I was stunned. There was no violence to our coming together, no pain. Instead, safe in the fold of his embrace, I expanded and deepened for him, moistening his way with the sort of private oil I didn't know my body was capable of making. Outside, the spring water bubbled hot, harsh and playful. Inside, my body's primal spring flowed thick, lush and rich with liquid pleasure.

It was the most amazing sensation I'd ever experienced and it left both of us breathless.

His eyes met mine. "Okay?" he said gruffly.

"Okay," I rasped, enthralled.

"Just a little more…"

Oh, my God. Having him in me was incredible. We fit nicely, like two pieces of a multidimensional puzzle designed to join together. I felt whole, grounded, centered. He felt solid in me, firmly entrenched, fundamental.

"Jesus, Lia." The stars sparkled in his eyes. "You feel so good. You're so wet and tight. Do you want to move for me?" His hands nudged my hips. "I'd really like it if you moved for me. I need you to move for me."

I rolled my hips and smiled when I spotted the thrill on his face. I rocked on his lap and he grew inside me. I was the earth to his root and he was the root to my tree. He groaned and I moaned, and together we climbed up desire's steep ladder, three rungs up, one down, trying to prolong the pleasure that raked us, trying to push each other to feel beyond reason, until we were both at the very edge of someplace I'd never been to before. I clung to him as if he was the only rail between me and the abyss.

His face was control's strained mask. "I want you to come for me."

"I want you to come with me," I managed to say as he thrust in me.

"After you—"

"Together." I whimpered, nearly out of my mind. "I want you to come *in* me."

"Oh hell, there's nothing I want to do more than that," he muttered hoarsely. "Are you sure?"

He was asking a long, complex, relevant set of questions, but for once I knew what I wanted and I couldn't stop to explain.

"Please?"

The way he bore down on my body had me gasping for breath. There was no holding back now, no illusion of control, no sane way to prevent the blast that launched us into the space we could only share with each other.

I clung to Ash through the journey. I broke through my mind's boundaries, shattered my old limits and freed myself from my body's sorrows. My sex grasped, clenched, gripped, experiencing glory, convulsing with bliss. I vaulted from one orgasm to the next, convinced I'd reached my highest peak, only to launch higher, even if I wasn't sure I could survive the thrill.

And then Ash closed his eyes and shuddered. A quiet groan rattled his breath and escaped between his lips. He came deep inside me, his essence dissolving into my being, his goodness erasing the past, his seed extinguishing my body's dread, washing away terror with joy and anguish with elation. I came again, for him, for me, for the pure joy of it.

When it was done, I relished every ounce of pleasure he enjoyed, every shudder, groan and caress, every drop he contributed to my being. I couldn't fathom how I'd survived the pleasure, because every part of me had been touched, kissed and moved, and I wasn't the same.

He helped me out of the pool, or perhaps I should say we helped each other, because his legs seemed as unsteady as mine even though his hold on me was stronger than ever. I liked the way I smelled—fiery, like molded metal newly steamed from the forge; metallic, like the hot spring itself; strong, like Ash. I liked the way I felt too, clean, inside and out.

Ash enveloped me in a towel he pulled out of the bag and, hugging me to his chest, kissed me. "Jesus, Lia. That was…"

"Good?" I hoped it had been as powerful for him as it had been for me.

"No, not good," he said. "Incredible, out of this world, extraordinary."

"Extraordinary is good." I stood on the tip of my toes and kissed him. "Thank you."

"For what?" he said, gathering me in his arms.

"For teaching me joy," I said. "And for bringing me to Heaven."

WE WENT BACK to the cabin and made love several times after that, if only for the pleasure of discovering pleasure itself. Perhaps we were making up for the nights we'd wasted, for they'd been a waste, I was convinced of it now. We slept on and off, distracted from our dreams by the novelty of being together. I'd been loveless and

scared of sex most of my life, but now, in between bouts
of pleasure, I learned that love and sex entailed different emotions, but when they happened at the same time,
as they did when Ash and I were together, they were an
extraordinary force.

Somewhere in the early morning hours, when I lay
on my side with Ash curled about me on the bottom
bunk, I opened my eyes and heard him sigh.

"Such a deep sigh," I murmured in the darkness.

"If you only knew."

"What?"

He shrugged behind me.

"No, I mean it, I want to know."

"It's sort of silly."

I kissed his callused fingertips. "Tell me."

"Okay, but don't laugh."

"No laughs guaranteed."

His arms tightened around me. "I dreamed of this."

"You dreamed of you and me crammed into a narrow bed in the middle of nowhere?"

He chuckled. "More or less."

"When?"

"In the jungles of South America, in Iraq and then
in Afghanistan. At night, when I lay in my bunk waiting for a mission, or in the field, when we took turns
napping. And later in the hospital, when I didn't think
there'd be a day without pain and sorrow in my future."

I'd felt the same way so many times in my life, and
yet here I was, with him, my body delirious with pleasure, my heart brimming with joy.

"You mean to tell me that you fierce warriors of the
world don't spend every free second fantasizing about
having wild sex with a triple D centerfold?"

"No, ma'am." He kissed my ear. "I dreamed of this,

exactly this, lying with someone soft and beautiful, craving her body and her craving me. I dreamed of you, even though I didn't know your name back then."

I blinked away the tears. My gut tightened. The fear came back, fear that this exquisite moment was just a passing fad; that Ash wouldn't be in my bed tomorrow; that he'd die; that I'd die.

"Ash—" My throat tightened.

"Stop it, Lia, that part where you tell me off wasn't in my dream, so don't say anything. Can't a guy get to live his dream every once in a while?"

A dream. I was a dream to him. "Whatever you want, you can have it."

"Don't make me idle promises," he cautioned. "I'm addicted to you. If you were one of those prescription pills? I'd be completely hooked on your body and I'd have to have you all the time. Think about it. Despite the excess, I wouldn't mind more of you right this minute."

"What excess?" I said.

He tilted my face and found my mouth. His hands came around to stoke need that didn't need encouragement. He glided into me and pleasure deleted everything but him from my brain.

Hours later, my mind registered the distant sound of a rattling cell, but I was too far into my dreams to care. When I next opened my eyes, Ash's kisses tickled my face and the tricolor horizon on the window announced the sun's glorious rebirth.

"Come on, sleepyhead." Ash propped me up and slid my arms into an enormous flannel shirt. "Got to go."

"Go where?" I knuckled my eyes, half-asleep.

"To the cottage." He put on my shoes, picked me up and, still bundled in the sheets, carried me out into the morning chill and perched me on the truck's front seat.

I could sense the change in him as he clicked on my seat belt. He'd gone from sweet lover to all business and I was too woolly to figure out why.

"Your owner is in a hurry today," I mumbled to Neil, when the dog climbed on the seat behind me. Neil wagged his tail and licked my ear while I smoothed out my tangled hair and tried to make sense of our rush.

Ash got in the cab, drew a handgun from the glove compartment and tucked it in the back of his pants. I frowned. What on earth was going on? I started to ask, but he flew out of Heaven, driving the jarring road as if it was a six-lane highway. The truck rattled like a can full of dominoes and all I could do was hang on for dear life.

His phone rang as we shot out of the gate and turned onto the much smoother country road. He answered curtly. "Report?"

He listened as someone spoke. The lines between his eyes deepened. My stomach sank. I had a bad feeling about this one. Ash's contributions to the conversation were succinct and sporadic.

"Where?" he asked. "How?" He listened some more.

I cocked my eyebrows and mouthed, "What's happening?"

He raised a hand and motioned for patience, even though I had none of that to spare. Then he proceeded to test me further by listening for several long minutes.

"Affirmative," he said after a while. "Negative, not yet."

By the time he ended the one-sided conversation, he'd been on the phone for a good twenty minutes and we'd arrived at the cottage. There were three vehicles lined on my driveway, including a state-of-the-art RV that I recognized on the spot.

"What's the deal?" I said tentatively.

Ash parked the truck, engaged the break and looked at me for a second too long. "Don't be mad at me and try to roll with the punches."

Something huge was coming down the pipeline. "Uh-oh."

He bracketed my face with his hands. "Whatever happens, remember this."

He kissed me, and I don't mean a peck in the lips. He kissed me in a way that said hello and goodbye, good morning, good afternoon and good-night, please understand, I'm sorry and yeah, another big fat do-try-to-roll-with-the-punches.

For a moment, my brain cut out. I was back at the hot springs and at the brink of bliss. All of that from a kiss? Then he stopped kissing me and I went into immediate withdrawal. Before I had time to react, he handed me his phone. A text message glowed on his screen. It could've been copied from a first-grade reader. My stomach plummeted as I read three simple words.

Rat in trap.

TWELVE

NEIL BARKED WHEN we entered the cottage. The small sitting room was crowded. My eyes traveled from one man to the next, trying to make sense of the scene. Manny Rivera sat in his high-tech wheelchair, working on some type of cleverly attached console. Wang Ho paced the foyer's small perimeter as if guarding the door to the cellar. Will Jackson lounged on my couch, squinting through his thick glasses and playing what looked like a high-tech video game on his laptop.

"'Good morning, Vietnam!'" Will shouted, startling everybody, including himself. "Well, hello, beautiful," he shrieked like a parrot.

Eyes bright with interest, the three men leveled their stares on me, a trained, systematic, professional assessment with traces of…what? Curiosity. Compassion? I cringed under their scrutiny. I'm sure I looked quite unhinged, standing at the threshold wearing only a giant flannel shirt and black tennis shoes.

Ash surveyed the room. "Three-sixty?"

"Perimeter secured." Manny's fingers punched the screen before him. "No hostile contact on the radar, no prospects for contact for twenty-nine—no—make that thirty clicks."

Ash turned to Will. "Status?"

"Unchanged," Will said in a perfectly normal voice. "Target is on the ground, full entourage accounted for, all devices within designated range, visual confirmed."

Time slowed down to a trickle as one by one, the re-
alizations hit me. All that brainpower in the room. They
hadn't come to Copperhill just to shovel ashes and clear
debris. They hadn't spent all of their time at the ranch
either. They'd scouted, secured and monitored the cottage and who knew what else.

"Showtime," Ash said to Wang. "Bring him up."

"Bring who up?" I said as Wang disappeared down
the stairs.

"Hang on." Ash leaned over Will's screen as both
men scrutinized the streaming data. "Keep an eye on
the monitoring device signal."

Monitoring device signal? "Could somebody please
explain what's going on?"

Ash gestured with his stubble-darkened chin toward
the foyer. Neil growled. Wang came back, leading a
man wearing a hood across the sitting room. I stared,
speechless. If the hood wasn't shocking enough, the
man's hands were fastened with zip cuffs.

Wang guided the man to sit on the chair by the fireplace. My knees were already soft as melted butter, but
when Wang removed the hood from the man's head my
heart screeched to a complete stop. I took several wobbly steps backward. I sucked in the air, but not a drop of
oxygen made it to my lungs. My back bumped against
Ash, who propped me up with a hand to the waist.

"Breathe." Ash squeezed my shoulder. "Come on,
take a breath."

It took all I had to draw in the air. I forced myself to
look, to make sure I was seeing right. The man before
me would have been invisible in a crowd. He wasn't
short, thin or ugly, but he wasn't tall, fat or handsome
either. His small eyes could have been brown, hazel
or olive, depending on the light. His most notable trait

was the way in which he wore his hair, short and spiked
to cover his thinning crown. He was average in every
way and yet I recognized him immediately: Agent Paul
Steiner from the United States Federal Witness Protection Program, a man whose word I'd trusted once, until
he failed me.

"We caught Spiky here snooping around," Manny
said. "The son of a bitch tripped the wire like a moth-
erfucking elephant. He pinged it so hard my ears are
still ringing. Says he's a Fed. He's got the badge and the
regulation gun, but he's missing the suit, not to mention the warrant."

Steiner assessed me with a cold glare. "Look who's
back on the map," he said flatly. "If it isn't Rose Rojas,
in the flesh."

Rose Rojas. The name hit me like a fist to the gut.
My knees buckled and I might have stumbled to the
floor if Ash hadn't been right there to brace me against
the blow.

"Easy," he said.

I pointed at Steiner with a shaky finger. "Don't call
me that," I muttered. "Don't you ever, ever call me by
that name!"

"After all this time, I'm overjoyed to see you again."
Steiner leered. "You've given me the runaround for so
long that I don't know if should welcome you back into
the fold or read you your Miranda rights. How about I
give you the choice right now? Tell these idiots who I
am. Tell them to release me immediately. Tell them the
truth, Rose, that you and I are old friends."

Friends? I had to will my mouth to close and my
brain to work. Whatever his definition of friendship
was, it wasn't mine.

"Make it right," Steiner said. "I don't know who these

thugs are, but it's to their advantage and yours if they stand down, right now."

I blocked out Steiner's presence in the room, grappling with the implications of everything I had just learned. Neil circled around me, interposing his body between me and the rest of the people in the room. My stomach burned with a surge of acid. The fragile panel that guarded my sanity cracked. The fury inside me flared. Oh, yes, no doubt about it, I was so upset, I couldn't think straight. Betrayal. Ash hadn't been straight with me. Devious, conniving, underhanded. Was he as treacherous as Red?

Ash tried to hold my hand. "Don't freak out on me."

I snatched my hand away from him. "Me? Freak out? Why?" I squeaked like an out-of-tune violin. "Because you went behind my back and treated me like an idiot? Because you ignored all of my warnings and got involved in something that doesn't concern you? Because you brought this incompetent liar into my cottage?" My stomach squeezed with another realization. "Was this the real reason for last night? You wanted to keep me out of the loop?"

"That's not true and you know it."

"You didn't have to stoop so low."

"Not another word." The look in his eyes steeled. "We'll talk about this later."

I more or less snarled, "You deceived me."

"You're being paranoid."

"Paranoid? Me?" My nails dug into my palms. "How could it be paranoia when you've been keeping secrets and he's suddenly here?"

I couldn't help the shudders racking my unsteady limbs. I hugged myself in an effort to stop the shakes. My eyes fell on Steiner again. He looked from Ash to me, watching us intently. If only I could vanish him with my glare.

"Oh, boy," Will said in Bugs Bunny's voice. "I think you're in deep doo-doo."

"Do me a favor, kid," Ash said. "Can you try to zip it?'"

"On it," Will said.

Ash cleared his throat. "I know this is a shock to you."

"A shock?" I scoffed bitterly. "No, I'm used to people lying to me all the time. Ask Agent Steiner here. You and he should get along fine, because you're both into lying and scheming."

Ash's nostrils flared. His lips set in a straight line as he beamed his sanctimonious "you should know better" glare at me. I didn't care. He'd lied to me. The look on Steiner's face did nothing to appease my fury.

"I never lied to you," Steiner said. "I was only doing my job."

"How—" My voice broke. I took a deep breath and tried again. "How did you find me?"

"It wasn't easy," Steiner said. "I've been looking for you since you escaped."

"Sure you have," I said. "So you can try to get me killed all over again. What gave me away? Was it the letter I sent you?"

"Letter?" Three deep, crooked lines etched his wide forehead. "What letter?"

"The letter I sent to your office," I said impatiently.

"It was an envelope containing a packet of something called Red Rush," Ash put in.

I stared at Ash in complete disbelief. He'd been watching me closely the entire time and he knew, he somehow knew that I'd mailed out that Red Rush packet.

"Red Rush?" Steiner said. "What the hell is that?"

"According to our analysis," Ash said, "Red Rush is composed of synthetic cathinones that mimic the primary psychoactive active ingredients of delta 9-tetra-hydrocannabinol, also known as THC."

"You mean like K2 or Spice?" Steiner said.

"Meaner, stronger," Ash said. "Red Rush appears to have magnified chemical capabilities that impact the brain along the line of LSD. It's ten times more powerful than previous synthetic drugs and as addictive as crack and heroin. The envelope was mailed to your office a few weeks ago."

I was about to freak out. Ash had been on to me the entire time. He had researched and analyzed Red Rush? And he hadn't mention any of that to me? I clenched my jaw and glared at him.

"Mayday, Mayday." Will imitated the sounds of machine gunfire and sputtering propellers. "We're going down."

"No letter, no Red Rush," Steiner said. "I didn't receive anything like it."

"Then how did you find me?" I said. "How did you figure out where I lived?"

"You forget I'm a Federal Marshal," he said. "I don't have to tell you shit."

Ash rumbled quietly. "The lady asked you a question. I suggest you answer it."

Steiner took measure of Ash before his stare settled back on me. "Have you forgotten who provided you with your documents? I'd flagged all your possible identities in multiple databases. A few days ago, we had a hit. The Veteran Administration Caregiver Support Program submitted a request for payment with your name on it. I traced it all the way here. That's how I found you."

Gunny had taken matters into her own hands. In doing so, she might as well have killed me. My jaw muscles ached.

Ash cursed under his breath. "Does anybody else know you're here?"

"I came out here on my own, following a hunch," Steiner said.

"Right," I said. "You probably left crumbs for Red all along the way."

Steiner's glare turned frigid. "You can't possibly hold me responsible for what happened. It wasn't my fault."

"Weren't you the one who approached me in the first place?" I said. "Weren't you the one who promised that Adam and I would be safe if we cooperated with your investigation?"

"Wait," Ash said. "Who the hell is Adam?"

"My, my." Steiner tsked. "So you don't know much after all."

Ash's demonic glower could have cremated Steiner on the spot.

"I don't know," Will sang. "I don't know where I'm gonna go when the volcano blows."

"Adam was my brother," I said, suppressing the pain that struck me when I said his name aloud. "Agent Steiner here said he'd be safe for good if I testified against Red. Only he didn't keep his end of the bargain."

"It was a secure safe house," Steiner said. "Nobody could've foreseen what happened. I lost agents and friends in that attack too."

"I was there," I snapped. "Remember?"

Steiner's throat worked up and down and, for an instant, I saw a glimmer in his eyes, a glimmer of...empathy? Then it was gone, replaced by his standard glare. "Whatever happened in the past is irrelevant."

"Irrelevant?" I said, incredulous.

"Irrelevant, yes. You made a deal with the Justice Department and you will deliver on that deal."

"The deal was off on the day that Adam died."

"Wrong," he said. "You're still alive. The agreement stands. You must do your part. We invested a lot of resources in securing you so that you could assist us in putting Red away. You're the only one who can provide testimony to convict him."

"Sure, let's get Lia killed too, why not?" I curled my lips in disgust. "You've been trying to get Red for years. You've devoted your entire career to that purpose and yet you haven't been able to take him down. How is it different this time around?"

"Red has beaten every other indictment we've thrown his way," Steiner said, "but since you testified before the grand jury the last time, we've got him on house arrest and monitored 24/7."

"Great, freaking fantastic," I said. "If you have Red, then do your job and throw the book at him, put him in jail and leave me out of it."

"We can't convict him without your testimony," Steiner said. "No one else will testify against Red. We've already failed to produce you as a witness in court several times in a row. The judge is losing patience and we're out of excuses. If you don't show up to testify in two weeks, the charges against Red will be dismissed. He'll go free. Do you understand what I'm saying?"

Yes. My soul turned to ice. I understood very well.

"You are the key," Steiner repeated. "This might very well be our last chance to put him away."

Two weeks. The dark hole inside me expanded. Why

now? Why couldn't they rely on someone else? Why did it have to be me?

"I told you everything I know."

"And now you have to tell it to the judge and the jury."

"Will Red…" How I hated to say his name aloud. Was I considering Steiner's idea? No way. It hadn't worked before. Why would it work now?

I steeled my voice and tried again. "If I were to do this—and that's a big 'if'—will Red be at the trial?"

Steiner nodded. "It's his right."

Face-to-face with Red? Was Steiner crazy? I'd never survive that, assuming that Red allowed me the unlikely opportunity to make it alive to the courthouse. My stomach squeezed. Surely my guts were being shredded. I leaned on the wall and bent over my belly.

Ash squeezed my shoulder. "Lia?"

"Don't touch me." I shook off his hold.

"A whole lot of good people have died trying to convict this son of a bitch, including your brother," Steiner said, as if he needed to remind me. "You owe it to him. You owe it to all of those who died."

I groaned.

"Shut the hell up," Ash spat. "She can't handle it right now."

The tears just sprang out of my eyes. The pain was too much to bear. The jackass really knew how to get to me. Guilt churned inside me along with the fear. I chewed on my lip until it hurt. It was really too much. I could never face Red and hope to live to tell the tale. He'd never allow it. Neil leaned against my legs and whimpered.

"Breathe," Ash said, rubbing my back. "You don't

have to do what he says. We'll take it one step at a time. You can make your own decisions."

I jerked away from his touch. "I don't want to hear it from you. As for you—" I turned to Steiner. "You're mad if you think I'll go back to relive my nightmares. You had your chance. You failed. Adam is dead. It doesn't matter to me anymore."

"But—"

"Get out." I backed out of the sitting room, unable to stand the pressure building in me any longer. "Go away. Get out of my house, all of you."

"Take cover," Will shouted in a Scottish accent. "She's gonna blow!"

I ran up the stairs and slammed the door to my room. I locked the door and wedged a chair under the knob. I sunk my face in my hands and sobbed. Neil whimpered, sniffed and scratched on the other side of the door. This had to stop. No more tears. I shed the flannel shirt and began to dress hastily, muttering to myself like a nutcase.

My hands trembled violently. The rest of my body shook too, as if I suffered from hypothermia. Yes, indeed, hypothermia of the soul. I wasn't just angry. I was furious. I was terrified too. Steiner had showed up. Here. To wreck my life. Gunny Watkins had betrayed me and she didn't even know it. No good deed went unpunished.

And Ash? I groaned. Ash had crashed into my life like a wrecking ball. Hired his friends. Staked out my hideout. Did he sleep with me to add to his subterfuge or had he really wanted me?

I chewed on my pinkie nail until my cuticle was raw. Maybe Ash was somehow Red's man. Maybe he'd been paid to get to me through my pants. Red was sly. Red was calculating, ruthless and cruel and his reach extended way beyond the obvious.

Oh, my God. Ash was right. Paranoia was taking over. It clawed at my brain and gnawed at my reason. *Get a hold of yourself.* I stopped nibbling on my nail and clasped my hands together. Breathe and cope, cope and breathe. Think, think, think.

Red would resort to the vilest methods to get to me, including torture and murder. The mere suspicion, let alone the knowledge, that someone else had used the body he claimed as his would drive him to raging insanity.

No, Red would never allow another man in my bed, not even one of his cronies, not even if it was to trap me.

And Ash? I had to trust my instincts about him. I had to trust reason. He would never be someone else's crony. It was against his nature, impossible. Logically, he had no motive to be in cahoots with Red. He didn't need money. He'd been in a hospital for the past few months and, before that, he'd been in Afghanistan. He hadn't come to Copperhill by chance. He was Wynona's grandson and he belonged here.

Why then had he gone to all this trouble?

Because he loved me, that's why. Even in my fragile state of mind, it was obvious. He loved me so much that he was willing to take on enormous risks and impossible odds to keep me alive. No one had ever loved me like that. I didn't know that courage like his existed. The emotions clobbered me all together, infuriation, joy, terror, elation and relief, lots of relief. I was thinking again and I could trust my heart.

True, Steiner might have caught me by surprise if it hadn't been for Ash's surveillance, but what really incensed me was that Ash had lied to me. Okay, maybe not lied outright, but he'd distracted me with his antics and broken trust by keeping things from me.

Or had he?

I remembered the conversation we'd had at the restaurant weeks ago, when I had accused him of snooping.

"I'm talking about minimizing risk factors and establishing factual operational parameters," he'd said. *"I can't ask questions and you won't tell me who you fear or why. What other option did you leave me?"*

What other option indeed?

The option to stay out of my life. How was that for a good, sound, safe, intelligent option? The courtesy of respecting my wishes and refraining from putting him and his friends in the middle of a deadly fray. The opportunity to stay alive.

But, no—oh, no—he was just too smart for his own good, too brash not to pick a fight with titanic bullies who'd crush him without a second thought. I shoved my legs into my blue jeans. Ash might have a death wish, but he was not going to fulfill it under my watch.

A soft knock came from the door.

"Lia," he murmured from the other side. "We have to talk."

"We have nothing to talk about," I said.

"Please open the door."

"Go away." I hurled my boot against the door.

The impact shook the wall, rattled the mirror and sent it crashing to the floor, a huge clatter that reverberated throughout the cottage.

I stared at the broken mirror on the floor. I wasn't a violent person. I wasn't usually enraged either. My life had always been on the line. It had always been expendable. I had been running for so long that today should've been business as usual.

But it wasn't.

Since coming to Copperhill, I'd experienced freedom, self-sufficiency and a good life. Then Ash had crash-landed in my life and everything had changed again. I had a lot more to lose now. I'd tasted the sweetness of companionship and friendship, the power of passion and affection. I'd tasted Ash.

I swallowed a sob. He was maddening, calculating, scheming, overprotective, stubborn, and maybe even controlling, but he was also good, wholesome, honorable, smart, steadfast... How was I supposed to give him up?

Ash's voice came again, even but strained. "Lia, baby, I know you're mad, but you've got to listen to me. You're not thinking clearly."

For once, I was thinking very clearly. He was not going to die because of me. This amazing, brave, extraordinary human being who'd become the exclusive focus of my affections would live a long, satisfying, joyful life, so help me God. And that's why I had to give him up. Because that was the only way he was going to live beyond me.

Out in the pasture, Ozzie began to bleat, and Izzy and Ivy soon joined the breakfast racket. I had all but forgotten about my crew. After today, I'd never see them again. I'd never see Neil either. Or Ash. I swallowed another sob.

"I'll take care of the animals," Ash said against the door. "Be back in five."

Five minutes. That might be all the time I had.

I laced my boots while considering my options. I had several escape routes prepared for this eventuality. I selected the one that offered the best chance for a clean escape.

I forced myself to move fast. I wiggled the boards blocking the old fireplace and retrieved the escape duffel I'd stowed there. I was relieved to find everything intact, despite Ash having been through it. I packed a few last minute things, then stuck my arm up the dark flue and pulled the rope ladder that I had concealed up the chimney. Good. He hadn't messed with that, either.

The rope ladder was old and tattered, but it worked. I'd bought it at a firehouse yard sale within days of moving into the cottage, in case I had to escape from the second-story windows. Clearly, it had been a good investment.

I hooked the ladder over the windowsill. I took a last look at my room, at the little cottage where I'd claimed my dreams. And then, despite the pain pummeling my chest, I wiped the tears from my face and climbed out the window.

THIRTEEN

I STOLE ALONG the ravine and followed the dry creek bed to get to the lake. I crept under the barbed wire fence to the property next door and walked for about another mile, where an old, abandoned shed crumbled at the edge of the beach. Along the way, I passed the dilapidated dock where Neil, Ash and I had taken so many happy lunches. Like the shattered mirror, my heart splintered into jagged shards.

The old door creaked when I cracked it open. The morning sun illuminated the bow of the weathered rowboat I'd hidden beneath some rubble and an old tarp. It was an ancient thing, missing the middle seat, probably dating to the 1920s, but I'd tested it several times and it would take me across the lake, from where I could walk to the nearest truck stop.

I pulled on the boat, but it didn't budge. I squinted into the darkness. I couldn't see a thing back there. I leaned my weight against the heavy door and, pushing with all my strength, widened the opening. A perfect rectangle of light advanced over the space, illuminating the entire shed.

I gasped.

Ash sat on the boat's back bench as quiet as the dead. Next to him, Neil wagged his tail and barked.

"Hush, boy." Ash petted the dog. "Lia here is executing a top secret escape. No point in ruining it just because you're happy to see her."

My bag fell out of my grip. "H-How did you know?" The air just rushed out of me. "Never mind." This was Ash I was talking about, the most thorough creature in the universe.

"As a contingency plan, a watercraft made total sense to me," Ash said. "I just had to figure out where you hid it."

I braced myself on the door. "Why did you follow me here?"

"I have questions," he said. "I need answers."

"Ash, I—"

"Why are you running?"

"Excuse me?"

"I asked you a simple question," he said. "Why are you running?"

"Because of Red," I said, "but you know that."

His eyes narrowed. "Are you sure?"

"Of course," I said. "Why else?"

"The way I see it," he said, "running is a habit of yours. It's the way that you deal with everything."

I straightened. "Are you calling me a coward?"

"Your words, not mine." He leveled his stare on me. "Sometimes, running is the right call. You could very well be running from Red, but knowing you, you could also be running away from...other things."

"Other things like what?"

"You could be running away from our future."

Our future? The mere idea set my heart aflutter. We had a future? Together?

"Running won't make you safe," Ash said. "Or happy."

"But it may keep me, and especially you, breathing for a few more days."

"Maybe," he admitted. "But don't you get tired of running?"

Yes, I did, but I didn't dare to dream about a life without running, because I knew, deep inside, that it wasn't possible.

"I have to say this to you, Lia." The lines between his eyes deepened. "I can't stand it when you get like this. It pisses me off. Period. I have a hard enough time with my temper. Today has been…challenging."

The strain etched on his face smacked my brain. I wavered. I hated the pain and frustration I'd added to his life.

"I also don't appreciate you patronizing me with your condescension—"

"I don't—"

"You do too," he said.

"When?"

"When you keep me out of the loop," he said. "When you take it upon yourself to make decisions for me."

I scoffed. "How do you think I felt when I saw your guys and Steiner in the cottage?"

"That's different."

I cocked my fist on my hip. "How?"

"I tried to work with you, but you wouldn't let me. You're so stubborn—"

"Stubborn? Really? This is Mount Everest talking."

"You've got major trust issues," he said. "I get that, fine. You're used to going at it alone. Okay. I can buy that too, if I have to. But maybe you also doubt me, because you don't know me so well, or because I'm on injured reserve."

I realized that I'd struck at the heart of his insecurities. At some level, he believed I was running away because I thought he was weak, incapable or disabled, or worse, because I didn't want to be with him. He feared I was running away from the very concept of us.

Was he right? Could I be that sick?

"I don't doubt your abilities," I said, "I know you've got skills."

"I set out to prove that you can trust me," he said. "And I did. Do you remember that guy that came to the bar that night, the one who I told you was my business partner?"

"Yes?"

"Together we own a global security consulting firm," he said. "Through it, I hired the guys, secured the cottage, set up surveillance and caught Steiner. Did I do wrong?"

I grappled with the enormity of his actions. Where could I begin to unravel the mess in my mind?

"I appreciate your good intentions," I said. "But you're squandering your money and you've got to believe me. You and the guys are in terrible danger."

"Each person made their own decision," he said. "Each person was chosen because they have the qualifications and expertise to do the job. As to my resources, they're mine to use as I see fit. What would you have done in my place?"

Most sane people would have walked away from trouble like mine. I myself favored running away as far and fast as possible. But Ash? He wasn't like the rest of us.

"I need to know, for good." His eyes fixed on my face. "Do you want to be with me? If you do, I'm willing to find a way to make it happen. But you've got to answer my question honestly. Are you running away from me?"

"No—yes—maybe—" I hesitated. "Maybe I'm—I

was—a little scared of us, of the way I feel about you. It's…overwhelming."

"Tell me something I don't know," he said.

"But now…" I swallowed a sob. "I can't stay."

"What if you could stay?"

"If I could stay?" I hugged myself. "I wouldn't leave you. Ever."

The smile on his face brought back the light into my world. He reached behind the craft and plopped down his fully loaded backpack in the boat. "Mind telling me where we're heading?"

I croaked. *"We?"*

"Yes, *we*," he said. "You wanna run? No problem. We run."

"We can't run," I said. "We'd be too easy to find."

"Because I have a cane and a dog?"

"Because you coming with me would defeat the purpose of me running in the first place."

"Which is, of course, to keep me out of this and safe," he said in a flat monotone.

"And the guys," I said, teetering at the edge of hysteria. "And Neil, don't forget Neil."

"I'm thinking Iceland." Ash clasped his hands and steepled his forefingers together. "Astonishing geography. Or Barbados, if you prefer a tropical climate. Oh, yeah, you'd look great in a bikini."

"Don't make this harder than it already is."

"I've got excellent contacts in Poland." He tapped his fingers against each other. "Top-notch special forces friends over there. Or we could go to Madagascar. We touched down there en route. It seemed like a fascinating place."

"We can't go anywhere," I said. *"I'm* the one who has to go."

"See, now, that's a problem." He straightened his fingers and cracked his knuckles. "Should you be tempted to go anywhere without me, you'll keep getting the same result: me, anticipating your every move."

"You can't—"

"Oh, yes, I can and I will," he said. "It'd be a monumental waste of time and energy if you ask me, a huge strategic mistake, not exactly where I'd choose to concentrate my resources right now. But Neil and I, we'll do it if you force us."

He was so damn stubborn, not to mention devious, bringing Neil into the picture like that. But I believed him. He wasn't one to make idle threats. He'd do exactly as he said and then he'd get killed. Neil tilted his head and whimpered, shifting his attention between Ash and me.

"Ash," I said. "I don't want to go, but I have to go. Surely, you understand."

"Yeah, sure, if we're running, we ought to get going." Ash checked his cell. "On the other hand, unless they hear from me, the guys will wait a minimum of twelve hours before releasing Steiner, and, as of three minutes ago, our target and his assets remain stationary."

I couldn't wrap my head around that one. "How could you possibly keep track of Red?"

"I told you," he said. "These guys are good and I'm using the resources of one of the most advanced global security firms in the world."

Of course it would be the most advanced global security firm in the world if Ash had anything to do with it. But the world didn't turn on an axis of kindness. Free lunches didn't exist. Even if Ash was a founding member, his partner would expect something from him in exchange for using the firm's resources.

"So what's the catch?" I asked. "What do you have to do for them?"

"I'm expected to become an active partner."

"But you love being a SEAL," I said. "You weren't sure about leaving the service."

"It's like you said, Lia, I'm leaving all of my options open. I agreed to become active in the firm, but I haven't given anybody any starting dates just yet."

He'd done all of this…for me?

"I can't let you or the guys get killed on my account," I said. "I just can't."

"I know you have trouble with this," Ash said, "but you need to understand. You're dealing with a high level of expertise. Will's skill set is exceptional. He's got tabs on Red. He's hacked into his devices. He's actually hooked into the signal from Red's ankle monitor. We've even got visual on his place. So…"

"So what?"

"So we have some time, not a lot, but a few hours to make good decisions." He offered me his hand. "Let's make them together."

Stepping into the landlocked boat was both victory and defeat. Kneeling before Ash was a reprieve from my heart's execution. I relished the way he took me into his arms and welcomed me against his body. I let out a long breath. Was this how a hermit crab felt when it found the perfect shell?

I leaned my head on his shoulder and found joy in his heart's steady song. Ash signaled and Neil abandoned ship. The dog bounced out of the boat, trotted out of the shed and plopped down outside to guard the building, obsidian fur gleaming under the sunlight.

I looked up at Ash and found him waiting. He kissed me. The contact squelched my worries, eased my anxieties and melted away the fear. In his arms, I could be brave. It was reckless, but how could anybody blame me for wanting this?

"If you die, I'll kill you," I mumbled against his lips.

He chuckled and kissed me again. "I've proven myself hard to kill before, but I'll be careful. I wouldn't want to be haunted for eternity by your merciless spirit."

"I'm not kidding, Ash. I've survived a lot of stuff, but I can't survive you dying on me."

"Funny how death doesn't bother me overly much," he said. "A life without you, now that's terrifying to me."

A moment ago, a life without Ash had been exactly my best prospect. Now I had to kiss him while holding back tears. I'd never loved anyone the way I loved Ash.

"No need to stress right now," he said, caressing my face. "It's going to be okay."

His mouth distracted me from his hand's doings. I didn't notice when my coat came off, or when he unzipped my jeans. By the time I did notice, he'd already unbuttoned my shirt and unhooked my bra.

"Um…this might not be the best moment for this kind of thing."

"I disagree." He kissed me some more.

"Here?" I looked around the dusty shed. "Now?"

"Here, now," he said. "Say yes, Lia. You need this. Christ help me, I need it too. If I don't have you right now, I might just pass out from lack of blood to the brain."

"Is that so?" I stroked the bulge between his legs. "I do believe I just found all your blood."

He grabbed my hand and pressed it against his groin. "Say yes, Lia, and hurry up, please?"

I cherished the look on his face, the excitement in

his eyes, the boyish grin that was not boyish at all, but
sexy as hell. I relished the way he looked up at me and
waited, the fact that he wanted me to need him as badly
as he needed me. I liked that he would back off on the
spot had I said no.

"Yes."

The look in his eyes obliterated any option that involved living my life without him. He unfastened the
sleeping pad from his backpack and unfurled it on the
bottom of the boat. It took him hardly any time to finish undressing me. He tugged off my boots, peeled off
my jeans and, after stripping my shirt, hurled it over-
board, along with my bra.

I blushed, looking down on my naked self.

"No worries." He stripped out of his own clothing.
"Now we're even."

Between kisses, he laid me down on the mat at the
bottom of the boat. He kissed my feet and, with care,
hung each one by the heel on the boat's back bench.
It was hard to lie still when I was so intimately exposed, and yet I wasn't afraid. The Mona Lisa smile
etched on his face praised, reassured and promised at
the same time.

He kissed my toes, shins, knees and thighs in a slow
progression, working his way up my body, delighting
me with his lips. My pulse quickened and my breaths
sharpened. He kissed my sex and then licked me as if
every fold in my body tasted like an exquisite delicacy
and my clit was a treat. Talk about bliss. I clenched the
gunwales and puffed through his tongue's caress, melting under his mouth's exquisite heat.

"Oh, God." I whimpered, delirious, entwining my
fingers through his hair and curling my hips against his
tongue. "I'm going to come."

"Not yet," he mumbled, pausing for a moment.

"But I can't wait."

"Believe me, the wait will be well worth it."

I moaned and I begged and still he held me in place as his tongue deepened its reach to taste the very heat he'd baked into me. His gaze probed mine, lustrous and engaged, assessing my reactions. Lips parted, I blew out little breaths. I had no choice but to keep my legs apart, arch my back and stand the tasting, flowing with all kinds of flavors delivered exclusively to his mouth.

When he'd had his fill and I was incapable of coherent thought, he stopped, leaving me perching precariously at the edge of a monumental orgasm.

"Don't stop."

He chuckled with a perverse lack of mercy. "I'm not done with you yet."

He kissed my belly button, my hands, nipples and cheeks. His erection trailed his kisses, brushing against my thighs and tripping against the crook of my legs, unleashing the shivers that pebbled my skin and sent severe pleasure advisories to every part of my body. By the time his lips hovered over my mouth, the tip of his cock pressed against me.

"Promise me," he whispered, "No more running from me, no reservations, no secrets."

"Ash, I—"

He growled. "Promise me."

"I do, I promise."

"I want in," he said. "We do this together."

I murmured against his mouth. "Together."

"I'm going to let you come," he said, "but I'm not letting you go. Do you understand?"

"I do," I said. "You're not letting me go."

He stared into my eyes. "Are we a done deal, then?"

"We're a done deal."

He glided in, searing my flesh with pleasure's fire. My body seized on him and wouldn't let go. His tongue and cock worked in tandem, probing my body at the same time, like twins meeting twins. He breached me slowly, thrilling my body with his exquisite progress. I learned what it was like to belong with someone and to own them in return.

"Christ, Lia, can I fuck you?" he rasped. "Can I fuck you right now?"

He didn't have to ask me. The question alone had me whimpering with lust. How could his touch bring so much joy to my body? I wrapped my legs around his waist and arched my hips, freeing him to his desires, freeing my body to his. He curled over me like a dolphin on a wave. I rippled, rolled and swelled beneath him.

The muscles of his powerful buttocks contracted beneath my hands. My fingers dug in his flesh, my teeth raked his skin and my tongue licked his body's exquisite salt. His fullness satisfied the void inside. His presence in my body ended all prospects of loneliness. In his arms, I was worth something. In my arms, he was everything that mattered and my body's elation matched my heart's euphoria. His cock pumped into me, an increasingly frantic drumming that reverberated throughout my body until I could no longer ride the crest of my own wave.

"Lia," he called out my name as he came.

"Yours," I whispered.

AFTERWARD, WE WALKED together to the dock, listening to the breeze whispering as it combed through the trees. The morning was crisp. The sky gleamed with the perfect blue. Neil found a stick and dropped it at our feet. Ash hurled it a good distance away and Neil took off after it. Ash sat on the dock and tapped the tattered boards between his legs. I settled with my back against his chest, rested my head on his shoulder and sighed like a satisfied kitten.

"It's time," he said quietly.

"Time?" I said.

"It's time for you to share with me everything you know. I wouldn't ask if it wasn't important. But information is key to good intelligence. Every detail is vital. I've managed to gather some valuable intel, but it's time for you to tell me the whole story."

My stomach lurched. "I… I don't know if I can do that."

"Sorry, baby. You've got to try. If Steiner found you, chances are Red can find you too."

I gulped. "I wouldn't even know where to begin."

"How about we start with the basics?" He wrapped his arms around me. "What's your real name?"

It was a simple question, one that I should have been able to answer easily. But it had been a long time since I'd heard my own name, and I'd spent many years painstakingly hiding my identity from everyone. A straw might have allowed more air to pass through my strangled throat. I struggled to speak, but my body refused to make the sounds.

Neil trotted back to the dock, dropped his stick and, stretching out next to me, rested his chin on my lap. I ran my fingers through his coat, smoothing out the wet spots and combing the sable bristle into a semblance of order.

"Lia?" Ash squeezed his arms around me. "You can trust me. You *need* to trust me."

I forced my breathing into a steady pattern, one

breath in, two out. The exercise helped even my pulse. Breathe and cope, or just cope, for God's sake. After several attempts, my voice finally trickled out, small, frail and reticent.

"I was named after my mother and grandmother," I said. "Two first names and two last names: Rose Amelia Faulker Ventura. Most people knew me as Rose, but my little brother called me Lia, short for Amelia, and my parents followed suit. I think you know me by my best name. Lia is what I like to be called."

"Nice to meet you, Rose Amelia Faulkner Ventura," Ash said. "I love Lia too." He paused. "Where were you born?"

"Tampa, Florida."

"How did you first meet Ruiz Ramon Rojas?"

I craned my neck to look at him. Of course Ash would know Red's real name by now, but he must have understood my need to know how he'd figured it out.

"We started with Red Rush," he explained. "In order to discover who was behind it, we followed an intricate maze of subsidiaries through several layers of corporate umbrellas that led to a number of empty shells operating offshore. It took a while, but we zeroed in on a holding company operating out of Panama. The principal of that company turned out a name: Ruiz Ramon Rojas."

"You guys are amazing." They really had to be extraordinarily skilled to be able to navigate Red's complex corporate maze. "Red usually covers his tracks really well."

"Believe me, his tracks were thoroughly covered," Ash said. "But we've got grit. Red Rush is only one of Red's many lines of business. The FBI, the ATF, the Justice Department and DEA all have investigations in progress. Even Homeland Security and the CIA had some interesting things to say about the son of a bitch. When did you first come in contact with him?"

"I met him in Colombia, but I don't know that I want to remember."

"Okay, then fill in this blank: how does a girl from Florida end up in Colombia?"

"Oh, that." I sighed. "My mom died when I was very young. After she died, my father was never the same. Trained as an agricultural scientist, he became very religious and believed he was meant to bring God to the poor inhabitants of the jungles of South America."

"Did he travel to Colombia?" Ash asked.

"He tried to get hired by several missions operating out of Colombia, but none of them ministered in the Amazon, where my father wanted to go." I stroked Neil's soft fur. "My father decided to go on his own, ignoring the warnings from the State Department and the Colombian government about the dangers from the drug trade and the guerrillas. When I was about twelve and Adam was ten, my dad gathered his savings, packed us up and off we went."

Ash's eyebrows clashed in the middle of his face. "And nobody objected to his taking two young children into such a remote and dangerous area?"

"There was no one to object," I said. "Both Mom and Dad came from only-child families. My grandparents were dead and we'd been homeschooled since we were little. I don't know that anybody noticed when we left."

"So your father believed in taking big risks?" Ash said.

"He saw himself as a man of faith," I said. "He believed that kindness was especially needed in areas of conflict. Drug traffickers and warlords needed God more than the rest of us. He thought they acted out violently out of necessity, because they grew up in poverty and didn't have access to education and organized religion."

Ash took that in, wearing the neutral expression he used to spare me from what I was sure wasn't a stellar opinion of my father's choices. "What happened when you got to Colombia?"

"We started with a one-room hut, a small garden and a field in a jungle clearing, where my father wanted to experiment with growing crops. My dad believed that people were inherently good and would welcome anybody working to bring prosperity to their communities. How wrong he was."

Ash squeezed my hand. "And Ruiz Ramon Rojas?"

"Him." My throat went suddenly dry. "He used to come around a lot."

"Can you tell me how you first met him?"

"I can try."

Neil lifted his head and whimpered.

"It's okay, boy," I said. "It'll be okay."

I raked my fingers through Neil's fine fur. I could do this. I had to do this. There was no way I could verbalize what I felt, but as I spoke, I gave Ash dates, names, places, the information he needed. I'd tried hard to forget the past, but now the memories crystallized in my mind like a movie in high definition. I was back in the jungle, remembering the first time I ever saw Red.

FOURTEEN

THE SWELTERING SUMMER evening challenged my lungs' attempts at processing the jungle's humid air. We'd been in Colombia for quite a few months, and finally, some families from the nearby village had come to visit. My brother, Adam, was playing with the kids. My father and I were cooking dinner over the open fire. Sweat moistened the back of my cotton shirt and the wisps of hair that escaped my ponytail. Sweat also coated my skin and pooled above my mouth in salty drops that flavored my lips.

I loved shaping the corn flour mix into small flat cakes and dropping them on the griddle. It was like a game to me. We'd just finished a lesson on ancient Egyptian history and I pretended I was a pharaoh. I stacked the ready arepas in little pyramids at the edge of the grill, my very own Valley of the Kings. I'd just flipped the last lot when I looked up. A group of armed men oozed like leeches out of the jungle.

They were a violent-looking bunch wielding guns, machetes and knives. Some wore regular clothes. Some wore military fatigues, like their leader, who slung his AK-47 over his shoulder and trampled over the vegetable garden, squashing ripe gourds beneath his boots as he strutted to our fire.

I stared at him openmouthed. Fear kept me frozen in place. Was he the jungle's dreaded *Muan*, the dark, twisted monster that, according to the locals, stole

women and took them to his lair at the bottom of the
Caquetá River? Tall, dark-haired and barrel-chested,
he seemed fierce and enormous to me, and yet, when
he moved, he reminded me of a jaguar—graceful, elegant and deadly.

The people from the village were no fools. *"El dia-
blo de Caquetá,"* they murmured among themselves as
they grabbed their children and scattered into the forest.

The Devil of Caquetá?

I could tell by my father's expression that he was
afraid too, but he pasted a smile on his face and rose to
greet the strangers.

"Bienvenidos," he said in his poor Spanish. "You're
welcome here. In the name of God, please, join us."

The devil's black eyes took in my father's slight build
and dismissed him instantly. His stare moved on, skim-
ming the house and the cooking fire, before tripping
over me. The darkness I spotted there shocked me. It
was like staring into a black hole. His mouth twisted
in a knowing smirk.

The men made themselves at home, helping themselves to the garden, digging with the point of their
machetes into the fish we had on the grill and stealing
the arepas from my pyramids. A one-eyed brute with
yellow teeth grabbed my arm and tried to drag me into
the jungle. I wrestled from his grasp and screamed.
My father attempted to get to me, but the knife that
flew through the air got to the one-eyed man first. He
dropped to the floor. His blood soaked the ground.

Only the buzz of the mosquitoes interrupted the
clearing's silence. My sweat turned cold and my skin
pebbled with the shivers racking my body. I'd never
seen a dead person before. I'd never seen that much
blood either. My fingers sank into the dirt, rooting me

to the spot. I wanted to run, or at least crawl away from
the rivulets of blood trickling my way. I couldn't.

Everyone's eyes were on the leader, who sauntered
over with a smirk on his face to inspect his handiwork.
He stood over the dead man, poked him with the tip of
his boot and shook his head.

"Looking without my permission cost him an eye,"
he said in a deep, silky, Spanish baritone. "Touching
cost him his life." He winked at me then turned to face
his men. "The gringos stay. Nobody touches them."

The men cheered and went back to eating and drinking. My father slumped with a look of relief. Other men
might have interpreted the situation differently, but my
father decided it was a breakthrough. These were the
godless creatures he'd come to help. And now, they'd
accepted us into their ranks.

"Hola, gringuita." The leader helped me to my feet.
"Como te llamas? Name?"

"R-rose?" I managed to say, shaking the dirt off my
skirt.

"Rosa." He tapped my nose playfully. *"Rosita. Mi
Rosita Americana.* You scared?"

"No," I lied.

He laughed, a set of distinctive cackles that sounded
like caws.

"Me, Red," he said in halting English. "How old
you?"

"Almost thirteen."

"Wow." He nodded approvingly. "Almost woman.
You make good arepas?"

"I make very good arepas," I said. "Ask my dad."

My father nodded eagerly.

"Que bonita." Red's smile beamed instant warmth.

"You get Red a good arepa. Yes? Red give you—how do you say—prize?"

"A prize?" I smiled. "Cool!"

I rushed to fetch Red some arepas. When I returned with the food, I tugged on Red's sleeve and thrust the plate before him. He grabbed an arepa and, black eyes on me, mauled a huge chunk out of it.

"My prize?" I asked.

"Prize, yes." He leaned over my shoulder and lowered his voice. "You get to live."

This time, the smile on his face chilled my heart.

FOR THE NEXT two years, Red visited with us almost every week. I told Dad that Red's visits were a bad idea. He disagreed. He believed that Red needed a good role model and a mentor, and that having him around made us safer. In Dad's mind, Red's protection was key for our success.

Red spoke some English, but he wanted to speak like a native. My dad threw himself into the teaching effort with enthusiasm, procuring English books, encouraging Adam and me to talk and read to Red, so he could practice. Reading for Red was unnerving. He stared at me with those black eyes as if consuming my words.

Sometimes Red came with his men. Sometimes, he came alone. Sometimes he liked to surprise me when I was about, springing out of the jungle when I least expected, with a heart-stopping *boo*!

"Mi Rosita," he would say. "You look so pretty when you're scared."

He became a regular around our fire, talking to my dad, asking lots of questions, about God, life in America, politics and growing up gringo. He was smart and curious. My father thought he was a fantastic student.

Sometimes Red brought me and my brother presents, pretty shells from the coast, sweets from the city and fruits he probably stole from the poor farmers at the market. One time he brought me a titi monkey, a stunning red-furred creature with enormous crystalline eyes. It had a broken leg and I did my best to heal it, but the poor little monkey was too hurt. It just slumped in its cage, refusing to eat. It died shortly after.

I felt uneasy around Red, but I took my cues from my father and acted politely. He always looked at me thoroughly, as if he wanted to know what I wore beneath my clothes. One day, I caught him going through the laundry lines in the yard. He stuffed a pair of my panties in his pocket. From then on, I thought he was officially creepy.

NOTHING WAS DIFFERENT on the night that changed my life forever. Red came, he drank my father's Diet Coke reserves and talked until it got late and Dad sent us to bed. Adam and I climbed under the nets and lay sweating in our narrow cots, listening to the buzz of the mosquitoes and the murmurs of the conversation outside. The last thing I remembered before I fell asleep was the huge black moth perched on the beam above my bed.

I woke up to sounds of a grown man whimpering. It was my father, and he was strapped to a chair.

I knuckled my eyes. "Daddy?"

"Mi Rosita," Red's voice whispered, too close to my ear. "You've been a bud ripening on the vine, but now you're a grown woman. The time has come for you to bloom."

He raped me in my own bed, in front of my father and brother.

"You gringos think the world is such a wonderful

place." He taunted my father while he assaulted me. "In God you trust? Now you know better."

The pain was excruciating, but I didn't cry. I didn't want to upset Adam and my dad, who sobbed despite the gag. I closed my eyes and tried to imagine that I was caught in a nightmare and about to wake. But when I opened my eyes again, the ugly moth was still perched above me and so was Red.

"Now, children," he said, when he was done with me. "If you ever try to escape, if one of you ever refuses to do what I say, this is what will happen."

He ran the edge of his massive blade against my father's throat. Adam buried his face in my shoulder and cried. I must have gone into shock. All that blood. I looked away, but Red clutched my chin painfully and forced me to watch in horror as my father died a slow, ugly death. God never came to his assistance. I'd turned fifteen years old the day before.

I SAT ON my bloodstained bed, chewing on my pinkie nail, barely dressed in my torn jammies, hugging Adam, watching Red. He went through our little house systematically, collecting all of my father's papers, documents and books. I couldn't figure out what he was doing or why, but then again, my mind was out of commission.

After a while, Red commanded us outside, where his men waited. With a flick of his lighter, he set fire to the thatch roof. His men did the same to the garden and the field. By the time Adam and I stumbled into the jungle, everything burned like hell and our Colombian existence had been wiped off the face of the earth.

At the other end of our grueling trek through the dark and bug-infested jungle was a dirt road and a fleet of Range Rovers. Despite my efforts to cling to Adam, my brother and I were separated and put into different cars. I rode with Red, who blasted the radio. He beeped the horn as he flew down the dirt road, scattering donkeys and poor peasants who jumped out of the way in fear for their lives.

Somewhere around midmorning, we arrived at a sprawling compound surrounded by tall walls and armed guards. Hacienda Dorada, a sign above the gate said. As the gates opened, I spotted numerous buildings in the compound, many houses with nice cars and children playing in the yards. After living in the jungle's squalor for two years and surviving the night's horrors, the place seemed surreal.

Red drove to the top of the hill, where a modern house built with straight lines and lots of glass overlooked the sprawling compound and the jungle. He wasn't a poor peasant, like my father had believed. He wasn't an uneducated, neglected child who'd grown up without love and affection either. On the contrary, he'd come from money, lots of it. He'd had a proper education. He went to church on Sundays. He had lots of people who worked for him, servants, relatives and business associates who circulated the halls of the expansive house on the hill.

I was locked in a room on the third floor, which was separated from the rest of the house by a private staircase and a massive set of alarmed, bulletproof, steel doors. It also contained Red's private study and expansive suite. My room was nicely furnished, but I sat in a corner on the cold tile floor and shivered until the evening, when a couple of stone-faced maids arrived. They bathed me, combed my hair and dressed me in a festive sundress that contrasted with the gloom in my heart.

Dinner took place at a long table on the terrace with

Red, his parents, brothers and sisters, their families, his wife—yes, wife—and even some of his children. Servants dressed in starched white uniforms carried silver trays piled with food to the table. Nobody but Red acknowledged my presence, nobody wondered who I was or how I'd come to be there, nobody asked any questions. They ate, drank and laughed. My take? They all suffered from communal insanity.

I struggled to comprehend this unreal reality. Had the man sitting next to me at the head of the table really killed my father? Was the linen-clad don presiding over this family meal the same brute who'd raped me the night before?

After dinner, he took me to his room.

"Mi Rosita." He caressed my face and smiled. "You're very dear to me, very dear indeed. You're a rare species, one that needs to be cultivated, trimmed and pruned. I'm going to take good care of you. That stupid gringo kept you in the stinking jungle. But I'm no savage. I was patient. I waited until you grew up. Yes? Now I'll give you everything. See? Nice house, nice dress, nice everything. If you do what I say, you'll be a very happy woman. Understand?"

I nodded.

"Take off your dress, quickly now, do as I say."

I just couldn't.

"Be reasonable," he said. "Do you want to see your brother again?"

Thus began a war of wills. He always won, of course, whereas I always lost. It was a struggle he relished, an endless negotiation that traded his pleasure for my pain, his gratification for my degradation.

My brother proved to be all the leverage Red needed to force me to cater to his needs, even if it took several levels of convincing. On the punishment side, there was the belt, which he enjoyed using liberally. For greater offenses, or just because he was in a foul mood, there were also restraints and beatings, some severe, resulting in serious injuries and broken bones. My face was out-of-bounds, because Red prized appearances above all else, and my appearance in particular. Extended stays locked in the cellar's dark bunker were particularly terrifying. That's when the madness came. God knew, I feared going mad every day I lived with Red.

On the reward side, there were assurances that terrible things wouldn't happen to my brother if I complied, letters and visits, and even gifts for him if I excelled at pleasing Red. I was also allowed to read books, watch television and exercise daily, all of which I did voraciously. These activities became my lifeline and my only connection to the world outside. They kept me sane when nothing around me made sense.

Confined to my room except for when Red called on me, I lived alone even if I dwelled among lots of people. From the high windows, I watched other kids play in the yard. Sometimes, I even caught sight of my brother, playing with them. But I wasn't allowed out. It was a measure of Red's obsession that I was isolated and cut off, reserved for his exclusive use.

A maid who tried to help me escape was found drowned in the pool. A gardener who once offered me a rose in the garden was hung from the gates. One time, when I managed to find Adam and we escaped from the compound, a peasant gave us a ride to town. When Red's caravan of Range Rovers caught up with us, Red hacked the kind man to pieces with a machete.

The doctor who tended to my injuries on a regular basis never asked me what happened or why I kept getting hurt. The private tutor who schooled me every day taught me the history of Martin Luther King Jr. but never discussed the terms of my slavery. I was the compound's most visible invisible woman.

I learned a lot about Red in the early years, mostly by watching, listening and paying attention. The Devil of Caquetá was the most powerful drug lord in Southwest Colombia. He controlled not only the region's cocaine production, but also the distribution routes to North America.

He worked in tandem with the guerrillas and had an extensive network of politicians, attorneys and associates on his payroll. He used my father's passport when he traveled abroad, something he began to do with more frequency. By now, his English was not only perfect, it was eloquent. All those nights listening to my father's stories had served his purpose. He'd stolen my father's identity to set up his next gig.

But I only began to comprehend the range of Red's extraordinary ambitions on the day that the judge showed up at the house, the day after my eighteenth birthday. The maid insisted I wear a new dress, white lace trimmed with red roses. I disliked it instantly. The shouts of Red's wife reached my room. After a while, the screams ended and I never saw her again.

The maid nudged me downstairs. Red waited at the bottom of the marble staircase, holding a small bouquet—roses, of course. He led me into the salon, where the judge handed me a pen and pointed to the blank line at the bottom of the document on the desk.

I looked to Red.

"Sign and your brother will get a new dirt bike," he said.

I penned my signature and traded my life and whatever little remained of my dignity for a dirt bike.

"Today you become a Rojas and I become an American." Red put his hand around my waist and posed for the photographer who appeared out of nowhere. "Smile for the consulate, *querida*. America, here we come."

FIFTEEN

ASH'S HOLD DIDN'T waver as I told my story. He listened to every word I said, processing and absorbing the information with his usual intensity. It helped that I didn't have to look at his face. Instead, despite the pain shredding my insides, I spoke factually, keeping my eyes focused on the lake and the black-capped chickadee hanging upside down from a nearby branch. Upside down with evil at the horizon. That's what my world had been like. All that grief wanted to drown me.

"Christ, Lia," Ash said. "You never cease to amaze me. You're a formidable contender."

"Me?" He wouldn't think so if only he realized how many times I'd failed at running away from Red, how many mistakes I'd made and how often I'd had to please Red, despite myself. "I don't feel very formidable."

"But you are." He kissed the top of my head. "Now bear with me. What happened once Red came to the United States?"

"Miami, New York, Chicago, LA." I remembered going to all those places as if sleepwalking. "He worked the country like a global CEO. The Rojas Cartel flourished in the United States. Marijuana, cocaine and heroin were Red's 'core' products, as he liked to call them."

"I found many state and federal investigations on both Red and the Rojas Cartel," Ash said. "Why didn't those investigations lead to indictments?"

"He was always ahead of the game." I combed my

fingers through Neil's coat, leaving tracks on his fur along his spine. "Red schemed and bribed everyone in his path. If a case was about to go in front of a judge, he'd find out the judge's weaknesses, document them on camera or telephone recordings and use the information to blackmail the judge into dismissing the case. He did the same thing with police commissioners, prosecutors and legislators. He used to have an ultrasecret safe at his Miami house where he kept a single, encoded thumb drive that contained those files."

"Interesting." Ash paused, thinking over the information. "Why shift if things were going so well?"

"Things got tougher in Colombia." If only I could forget that time of my life. "A new administration cracked down on the illegal drug trade and the guerrillas, hurting Red in the pocket. The DEA and the FBI teamed up with the Colombian government against the drug traffickers. It's not like he stopped trafficking drugs, but in order to expand, he needed to diversify."

"So he went into synthetic drugs," Ash said. "Like Red Rush. I bet you he saw a huge opportunity. Synthetic drugs are both legal and popular, despite the fact that they kill people every day."

Ash's understanding of Red's newest venture impressed me, especially considering that he'd undertaken his entire investigation based on a hunch and a single packet of incense. I glanced up at him. The lines radiating at the corner of eyes intensified his face's expression. His eyes narrowed on the horizon, but his mind wasn't taking in the landscape. I could almost hear his brain whirring in his skull, processing and converting the information, but into what, I wasn't sure.

"So let me see if I get this," he said, blue eyes beaming with intensity. "He had the contacts, the distribution channels and the money to fund the expansion. Most important, synthetic drugs were flowing into the United States legally, mostly from Asia. But that was a problem. At any time, his merchandise could be intercepted and regulated by customs officials or border patrol. So he asked himself: What if they could be produced locally?"

"He was just beginning to think distribution when I escaped."

I fought the memories streaming in my mind. I'd paid for Red's frustrations on the flesh. The war on drugs had translated into a war on me. Who knew that global conflicts could inflict localized bodily damage?

"You okay?" Ash said, massaging my stone-stiff shoulders.

"Hanging in there."

"We're making lots of progress here."

If we were making so much progress, then why was I having so much difficulty drawing air into my lungs and keeping the ghastly memories from crushing me?

"So," Ash said. "The reason why the Justice Department is so interested in Red is because his 'products' are killing more people than all of the other mixes put together, but the authorities can't stop it from getting into the country because he's mixing it locally."

"Exactly."

"And that's also why Justice is so interested in you," Ash said. "It's why Steiner offered you witness protection. The cartel has closed ranks on cocaine and heroin distribution and they can't put Red away for selling bath salts, incense and potpourri. However, they could put him away for good, if they could prove that he's manufacturing synthetic drugs right here in the good old U.S. of A."

"That's the whole story in a nutshell."

"That's part of the story for sure," Ash said, toying with my hair. "But perhaps it's not the whole story."

I forced myself to focus. Ash needed the information. It was important.

"When did Agent Steiner first contact you?" he asked.

"About five years ago," I said.

"And how did he manage to break through Red's surveillance?"

"He was very clever about it," I said. "When I turned twenty-one, I begged Red to allow me to go to college. It took me months to convince him." I shuddered when I remembered the kind of things I had to do in order to persuade him. "Eventually, he let me enroll in an online program, even though he policed everything I did and restricted my internet access. I'm not sure how Steiner found out about it, but he contacted me online posing as a teacher's assistant and provided me with an encryption that allowed me to fool Red's watchdogs."

"Your tax dollars at work," Ash said. "How did Steiner manage to nab you?"

"It wasn't easy, that's for sure," I said. "And it took a long time. Even before I agreed to cooperate with his investigation, I told him I had three conditions."

His eyebrows came up. "You negotiated with the Justice Department?"

"First, I told them they had to reunite me with my brother," I said. "Second, they had to provide us with multiple sets of identity documents."

"So that's how you got the stash I found in your go bag." Ash nodded. "What was your third condition?"

"I told Steiner that I wanted my marriage to Red

invalidated, annulled, ended. He thought I was being finicky. I thought I was being principled."

"Principled gets my vote." Ash planted a kiss on my temple. "Was Steiner able to find Adam?"

"It took months, but eventually, I got a clip from Adam, via Steiner. He'd been sneaked out of the compound in Colombia and brought safely to the United States."

I'd been elated with the news. I'd gone about with a smile on my face for three days straight, even after Red beat me raw for what he called an "attitude leer." I kept smiling inside despite the fact that I couldn't walk for a while.

"I wonder how Steiner managed that rescue." Ash frowned. "It's shit-hot stuff. Special ops had to be involved. I'll have to put my ear to the wind. What happened next?"

"It took another few months to plan my escape," I said. "Meanwhile, they wanted stuff."

"What kind of stuff?"

"Information about what Red was doing and where, bank accounts, passwords, names of associates, things of that nature. They were building their case. I became adept at getting what they wanted. Red's devices were well protected from hackers and digital spies, but, given the right circumstances, they weren't always protected from me."

Ash's eyebrows rose on his forehead. "You got all of that for them?"

"I did." I'd also gained a lot of confidence, not to mention some very useful skills.

Ash whistled. "Not too shabby. When did you finally get away?"

"About four years ago."

"How?"

"There was a headliner boxing match at the Tropicana in Las Vegas," I said, remembering those last fateful days. "I knew Red would force me to go with him, because he liked to show me off to his buddies and he knew how much I hated watching grown men pound each other to oblivion. I passed on the information to Steiner. He neutralized my bodyguards and spirited me away from the women's lounge. And so, on a hot summer night, I walked out of Red's life for good, ten years, four months and seventeen days after the night he killed my father."

"Jesus, Lia." Ash shook his head. "You're made of steel. If I were wearing a hat, I'd take it off."

Relief flooded through me. Someone believed me— Ash believed me—and telling the story gave me a new sense of freedom. Out on the lake, a pair of otters played in the water, chattering, fishing and splashing as if they had no cares in the world. Neil yawned and pressed his head against my hand, encouraging me to keep petting him. Animals were such creatures of the present.

"Let me guess what happened next," Ash said. "Lots of hurry up and wait, holdups and bureaucratic shit clogging the pipeline."

"Sounds like you know the Witness Protection Program."

"I've worked for the government long enough," Ash said. "I know how the shit goes down. Or not."

"Adam and I were reunited." I smiled thinking about the few wonderful months we'd spent together. "He was fine. He hadn't suffered Red's wrath like I had. They moved us a lot. We did secret depositions, met with lawyers and agents, moved some more. Twice, we had

to go before a judge and one time I went before a grand
jury. Right after that, that's when it happened."

"What happened?"

"Red found us." My chest ached. "And he killed
Adam."

"Jesus." Ash wrapped his arms around me like a
shield.

"We were playing cards in the kitchen of our safe
house." My voice came out as a forced squeak. "We
were in a suburban neighborhood in Dayton, Ohio.
Adam and I were paired up against two of the agents
assigned to us. Other agents were on duty at the house.
Word was the indictment against Red was about to come
down and security was tight."

I paused. My mouth was woolly. My eyes stung with
tears. Neil lifted his head from my lap and licked my
hand. *Steady. Breathe. Press on.*

"I looked up from my game," I said. "Adam—God,
Ash, he'd been such a beautiful child. He'd grown up
to be a strapping young man, so full of life, a sunny
soul for sure."

Ash held me close. "I bet you he was a lot like you."

"No, not like me." I blinked away the tears. "Not broken or bitter or neurotic, but optimistic, hopeful, a good
person, so much better than I could ever be."

How could he be gone? Why him? Why was I alive
when he was dead?

"You can cry if you need to, baby," Ash said.

I shook my head. *Keep it together. Tell the story. Get
it done.* I took a deep breath.

"That day," I said, despite the pain squeezing my
heart, "Adam had just picked a card from the pile when
I noticed something small and green flickering on the
side of his head. I thought it was a bug or something.

I leaned across the table to wipe it off, but the window burst. Adam's face froze right before his head exploded."

I closed my eyes. My throat burned with the sting of tears flowing down my face. Hadn't I cried enough? My mind was stuck on that awful day. My own screams echoed in my ears. Bullets plinked. Glass clinked. The air in the room had grown too warm, tainted with the sweet-and-sour scent of the blood that splattered the walls and drenched the carpets.

Ash shook me softly. "Lia?"

"Adam was gone," I said flatly. "The agents were gone. I called for help but nobody came. Everyone in the house was dead. Everyone but me."

"Snipers?" Ash said.

I nodded.

"Ah."

He now understood why I'd thought he was a hired sniper that day when he shot to scare away the mountain lion.

"I moved fast," I said, blood pounding in my ears with the same sense of urgency that had seized me back then. "Once I realized everyone around me was dead, I knew that all of my efforts had been for nothing. I'd gotten to know those agents. They were nice people. They had families. And Adam…" I fought the tears. "He was gone for good."

Ash squeezed my hand.

"I don't know exactly how I got out," I said. "A survival switch flipped somewhere inside of me. I remember grabbing the go bag I'd packed with the documents and darting out of the back door. I remember thinking I had seconds to live. I hid in someone's garage for a few days. Red and Steiner were both looking for me."

"What did you do next?"

"I didn't sleep or eat for those first few days." My belly churned with the memory. "There was a car in the garage, and a man who left in the morning and came back every night. He had no clue I was there. One morning I stole into his backseat and rode along when he went to work. I sneaked out of the parking garage and made my way out of the city. After that, I wandered the country for a few months."

"Where did you go?"

"Most of the time, I lived on the streets. On good days, I stayed at homeless shelters."

"That must have been really tough for you," Ash said.

I shrugged. "It was better than being with Red."

"Is that where you found out about the Underground Railroad?" Ash asked.

I opened my mouth and closed it several times before I was able to speak. "How on earth could you know about that?"

"I talked to Reverend Martin," Ash said. "He never admitted that you came to Copperhill via the Underground, but he did admit to being part of a network of people who strive to provide safe passage to victims on the run."

"Let's clear up something." I steeled my voice. "I'm not a victim anymore."

Ash's eyes met mine. "Got it."

"A counselor at a homeless shelter in Chicago hooked me up with the Underground," I said. "For a year, I traveled from one safe haven to another, never staying more than a few days at a time. Copperhill was supposed to be another stop along the way. The reverend placed me with Wynona. She suggested I should stay. She didn't know my story, and I told her I couldn't stay with her because I didn't want to put her in harm's way. But you know your grandma. She was as stubborn as you are."

"Oh yeah." He smiled wistfully. "Nona was a force of nature."

"She found me the job and the cottage and insisted I stay, at least for a while. She was so good to me. She gave me the strength I needed when I was tired and discouraged, and very close to giving up. I was so lucky to meet her. Without her, I wouldn't be around anymore."

"I'm glad you got to meet her." Ash kissed my shoulder. "I'm glad you stuck around too."

I let out a long breath. "Now you know everything. Are we done?"

"Almost, but not quite." Ash hesitated then pulled out his cell from his pocket and put it in my hands. "Lia, we need confirmation. Is this Red?"

I looked at the grainy picture on the screen. It probably came from a security camera somewhere. Red was obsessive about not having his picture taken. This one dated from a few years back. *Steady. Breathe.*

The man in the picture was indeed Red, dressed in a smart blazer, blue jeans and the shiny, long-tipped Italian loafers he preferred. He stood next to his yellow Maserati. An unruly lock of hair fell over his forehead, while the rest of his mane curled about his face, giving him the playboy halo effect that made him so attractive to the opposite sex. His full lips stretched in an indolent smile and his heavy-lidded eyes smiled at someone beyond the picture. His hand clawed around a woman's elbow.

I stared at the woman in the picture. She was but a slip of a person, a walking skeleton really, exactly the superthin type that the ultrarich coveted. Her platinum blond hair was styled short and straight in a pixie cut that had been all the rage. She wore a red minidress that matched her lipstick and showcased her long legs, cut low to display sharp clavicles and the rise of puny breasts deflated by emaciation.

I had no sympathy for that woman. "She looks like a whore."

"She's never been that," Ash said hoarsely, "or anything remotely like it."

Neil whimpered and put his paw on my leg.

"She hated that dress." A heavy weight settled on my chest. "But he liked to dress her like that. And he had her hair dyed in that ultrablonde tone. Real American girls were blonde, he liked to say."

A memory flashed in my mind, a terrible snippet of the woman, slashing at her long bleached hair with a disposable razor and Red, going nuclear and taking his revenge. After she came out of the hospital, Red hired a stylist to fix the mess.

Neil got up and rearranged himself on my lap, settling most of his weight on my legs, thrusting his big head into my hands, rubbing himself against my fingers.

"Lia?" Ash's arms tightened about me.

"Please don't touch me." I shuddered. "Not right now."

"It's okay." He loosened his hold but didn't let go. "You can give me the cell now."

My fingers tightened around the phone and my eyes returned to the woman on the screen. Dark smudges underscored her eyes and makeup failed to hide her sickly pallor. My heart hammered my ribs. *Cope, cope, cope.*

"She wasn't well," I mumbled.

"You can see that in the picture," Ash said.

"She was mourning," I said. "Red had just killed her baby."

Ash's body stiffened against my back. "Her baby?"

"Red was pleased at first when he learned she was pregnant," I said. "Then he got jealous."

"Jealous of his own child?"

"He beat her until the baby died inside of her," I said as if reading from a grocery list. "She almost died. The doctors said the damage was extensive. It was unlikely she could get pregnant again. She wanted to die."

Neil's moan sounded like a wail. His caramel eyes were fastened on my face. He pressed his head against my hands and nuzzled my neck. I had a memory of the woman's attempts at starving herself. Her heart was broken. She didn't want to eat anymore, kind of like the titi monkey. From then on, she struggled with a severe eating disorder. I remembered Red, yelling at the doctor, and the doctor forcing the feeding tube down the woman's nose.

"I'm so sorry," Ash murmured in a strangled voice.

"He marked her." I fingered the thickened patch at the back of my neck where Red's brand had once been inked. "He branded her as if she was common cattle."

Ash massaged the spot that still burned sometimes. "But she freed herself."

"It was the first thing she did when she went on the lam," I said. "She worked as a day laborer picking strawberries to make the money to pay for the tattoo's removal."

"She's very brave."

"She's not so brave." I held on to the dog and gnawed on my lips. "Sometimes, that woman in the picture? She dreams of a sleep without nightmares, of a life with no memories. Father. Brother. Baby. How does she go on when everybody's gone? Sometimes, when she remembers who she was, she doesn't want to go on anymore."

"She's still alive." Ash hugged me against his chest. "She's still in the fight."

"Then why does she feel so worthless?"

He let out a long breath. "It takes work to heal." The pain of his private struggles permeated his words. "War drains the life out of the soul."

"She didn't go to war like you did."

"She did." He retrieved the cell from my hand. "She just doesn't realize it, yet."

My stare fastened on the horizon. It divided the sky from the lake as surely as the wall I'd constructed to separate my new life from that wretched woman's life. She seemed to have existed eons ago in another universe. I sank into the gloom, drowning in a pool of misery, until Neil *woofed*, three resonant barks that slung me out of the darkness. I remembered Agent Steiner, sitting in the cottage. The past had caught up with me and I couldn't avoid it forever.

Ash spoke quietly. "Do you want to testify against Red?"

"I don't want to," I said. "But I need to do it. Steiner is right. The only way I can be free of Red is if he's behind bars."

"Is that what you think?"

"Over the years, I witnessed Red committing several murders with my own two eyes, including my father's. It's all here." I tapped on my temple. "I've witnessed torture, money laundering schemes and drug smuggling operations. My testimony is the only way to stop him from killing more innocent people."

"If that's what you want to do, that's what we'll do." Ash entwined his fingers between mine. "But you have to promise me: you will not run away from me. You will trust me and, no matter what happens, you will fight to stay alive."

I looked up at him. The plea in his gaze brought more tears to my eyes. I swallowed the sob choking my throat. It was so unreal to be here, having this conversation with someone who cared, someone who was willing to put his life at risk to help me. It was humbling, but inspiring. It was uplifting, but also terrifying.

"I can try," I said, "but Ash, you have to trust me. This is my fight. You can't shut me out or go behind my back. I have skills too. I haven't survived this long for nothing."

"As long as we're dealing with Red, we have to be fluid and smart," Ash said. "We've got to be clever. We have to compartmentalize the information, especially when Steiner is around."

My eyes widened. "Do you think he's on Red's payroll?"

"It's a possibility we have to consider," Ash said. "We have to commit to doing whatever is necessary to achieve our objectives. Do you understand?"

"I'm *not* letting you die," I said. "I'm *not* letting any of the guys get hurt on my account."

"None of us signed up to die," he said. "But you've got to be a team player and you've got to follow directions, even if they don't make sense to you."

"He always wins, Ash. He always gets his way."

"Not this time." He scooted me around until I faced him. "This is very important, Lia. What do you have that Ruiz Ramon Rojas wants?"

I almost choked. "Excuse me?"

"You heard me." His glacial blue eyes burned through me. "At the safe house. He had all those agents killed. He killed your brother. He didn't have you killed. Why?"

I hesitated. "Ash, I—"

"The truth," he said. "That's our deal."

I stared at the lakeshore, at the mountains rising above it, at the spectacular scenery they offered together. Neil nuzzled the crook of my arm. I'd buried my secrets so deep, I had trouble admitting to anything. But one look at Ash told me he wouldn't accept anything but the truth.

"The thumb drive," I said. "The one Red kept in the secret safe with all the information on his bribes? I stole that from him before we left for Las Vegas. He'll want it back before he kills me."

SIXTEEN

Ash and I fleshed out the beginnings of a risky strategy. I didn't like parts of his plan but I agreed to most of it because he was adamant and, other than running, I didn't have any better ideas.

When we got back to the cottage, Ash huddled with the guys for a while. I went upstairs for a much-needed shower. Neil hesitated at the landing but came up with me at Ash's signal. That's how I ended up with a Peeping Tom sticking his big black nose and furry face in my shower. When I was done, lunch waited on the kitchen table, where Manny and Ash munched on sandwiches, gathered around Will and his laptop.

Without taking his eyes from the screen, Ash pulled out a chair and parked a loaded plate in front of me. I didn't think I was hungry until I bit into my sandwich. Once I got a taste of the crunchy vegetables, shaved mortadella and fresh mozzarella, I discovered I was famished. To think I had once refused to eat. Even my palate was evolving.

"Are you ready for this next part?" Ash said, seeing that I'd finished with my meal.

"As ready as I can be."

"Tell Wang we're ready for Steiner," Ash said.

"Sure." Will left the kitchen, followed by Manny.

"I want you to have this." Ash pressed a firearm into my hand.

I stared at the small automatic pistol in my palm. "What do you have against my shotgun?"

"This will give you better protection," he said. "It's a Beretta Nano, light and easy to shoot. It belonged to my grandmother. She would've wanted you to have it."

"Oh." Wynona was gone, and yet she still watched over me.

"I'll teach you everything you need to know about it. Once you've learned how to shoot it safely, I want you to have it with you at all times. Promise?"

My stomach went cold. "Do you think Red will attack us here?"

"It's a possibility," he said. "But we have an advantage. We'll know if he's coming. We're prepared for all contingencies."

I wanted to believe Ash, but he didn't know Red like I did. Red was beyond smart, beyond vicious. His billions bought him top-notch resources, and that included people. His lack of scruples was what made him so dangerous and powerful. He had brutality on his side and he never hesitated to use it.

The door to the cellar banged open. I jumped three feet high.

"Easy," Ash said.

Wang escorted Steiner into the kitchen. Ears perked and tail up, Neil barked then tried to sniff the man.

"Down, boy," Ash said and the dog lay at his feet obediently.

"You won't get away with this," Steiner said, eyes burning with indignation. "You can't imprison a federal agent."

"Sit down," Ash said.

"You can't order me around—"

"Sit. Down."

Ash's glare, combined with a rumble from Neil, persuaded Steiner to comply. He plopped down on a kitchen chair, grumbling like a cranky toddler. His eyes gleamed with surprise when Wang released his hands from the zip ties, stole a sandwich from the tray and slipped out the back door.

Ash took a chair opposite Steiner and gestured to the food. "Help yourself."

Steiner looked to me.

"They're really good," I said.

He selected a sandwich, bit into it and gulped loudly. "Kidnapping is a federal offense."

"Who the hell kidnapped you?" Ash poured a glass of water and parked it in front of Steiner. "You were trespassing on private property. People don't take well to trespassing around these parts. So stop whining and listen. The lady here has some things to say to you."

"Look, Rose—"

"She wants to be called Lia," Ash put in.

"Fine, Lia, you've got to listen to me," Steiner said around a mouthful. "This is our last opportunity to put Red away—"

"I'm going to testify."

Steiner's mouth hung open, not a pretty picture with all that food in transit. "You are?"

"I intend to be in that courtroom in two weeks."

"You will?" He stared at me for a few more seconds, before he resumed his chewing. "Good, very good. You've made the right decision. You won't regret it."

I wasn't so sure about that.

Steiner's eyes blazed with excitement. "I'll get you into a safe house with a full protective detail by to-night."

"I'm staying put."

Steiner frowned. "You need to be in a safe house."

"You may recall that the safe house didn't work out very well for me the last time," I said with as much backbone as I could muster. "It worked even worse for Adam and the other agents."

"Fuck." Steiner chucked the last of his sandwich on the platter and glared at me, lips twisted with frustration. He took a deep breath before he could speak again. "I swear, I'll make this place more secure than Fort Knox."

"This place is fine as it is." I startled him yet again. "This time around, I have some other ideas."

"Have you forgotten who we're dealing with?" Steiner's cheeks flushed a deep shade of pink. "You need a protective detail, double—no—triple the size of the one assigned to you before."

"I don't want a protective detail," I said. "It'll only add to the body count if Red finds us."

Steiner stared at me as if I'd gone off the deep end, which—part of me admitted—was a strong possibility.

"Wait," he suddenly said. "You're not deluded into thinking that these cowboys stand a chance against Red, are you?"

I stared at him wordlessly.

Steiner squeezed the bridge of his nose. "Please tell me you don't believe in fairy tales?"

I said nothing.

He cursed under his breath. "It won't work. Who the hell are they anyway?"

"Ash is my boyfriend." I cringed inside, knowing I was exposing Ash to immense danger, but he'd been firm on this point. My stomach roiled with a surge of acid reflux that burned all the way up my throat, but I stuck to the gamble. "The other guys are his friends."

"Your boyfriend?" Steiner snickered. "Here's news: banging you doesn't qualify him as a protective detail."

"Watch your mouth," Ash muttered, "that is, if you want to keep your teeth."

Steiner threw his hands in the air. "This is ludicrous."

"They have some training," I offered cautiously.

"Is that supposed to impress me?" He groped for the pack of cigarettes in his pocket.

"No smoking, please."

He ignored me and put a cigarette in his mouth anyway. "Don't tell me that you think this collection of broken toy soldiers can protect you better than the Witness Protection Program?"

I straightened my back and stuck out my chin. "I won't testify in court unless you agree to my terms."

"I won't agree to madness." He pulled out a lighter.

Ash reached over, snatched the lighter from Steiner's hands and dropped it in his pocket. "The lady said no smoking. She meant it."

Steiner's tone sent shivers down my spine. "Are you two out of your minds?"

"A protective detail here will only alert whoever might be looking that you've found me."

Steiner's forehead furrowed. "What are you trying to say?"

Ash's stare shifted from Steiner to me, a silent request to go along, before his attention returned to the agent. "There's a high degree of probability that there's a mole in your office."

Ash hadn't mentioned his hunch to me before, but he'd asked me to be flexible, so I let this one play out. The cigarette stuck to Steiner's slack slips.

"A mole?" he croaked. "You think there's a spy in

my office? You think Red has a source at the Justice Department?"

"I'm sure of it."

The cigarette fell out of Steiner mouth and bounced on the table. His expression shifted from shock to indignation. "What kind of cockamamy operation do you think we're running at WPP? We're fireproof. My staff is solid."

"Then how can you explain what happened in Ohio?" Ash said. "How do you suppose Rojas found the safe house and had Adam and your agents killed?"

"Rojas has vast resources at his disposal," Steiner said. "His outfit is the largest and most influential drug cartel currently operating in the United States. His empire is valued in billions. He can afford the best hired guns on the black market. I can assure you, Rojas didn't get his information from inside Justice."

"I suppose there's a small probability that your theory is correct," Ash said. "But consider this: Lia sent you a warning, an envelope with a packet of Red Rush, remember? Where is it?"

"It can't be," he mumbled. "Is it possible? Do you think someone intercepted my mail?"

"Are you willing to stake your only witness's life on it, knowing there's a chance that someone in your office betrayed you?"

The agent met Ash's stare but didn't answer.

"I didn't think so either," Ash said.

Steiner slapped the table. "Now you have me doubting my own people. For the sake of this discussion, let's assume for a moment that there could be a mole in my office. Why are you talking to me?"

"Because we'd like for you to stay," I said.

"Stay?" His eyebrows met over his sharp nose. "You lost me. You want me to stay here?"

"Yes," I said.

"You mean you want me to go rogue?"

"Rogue? No," Ash said. "We want you to do your goddamn job."

"Let me get this straight," Steiner said. "You don't want a protective detail, but you want me, a highly trained federal marshal to organize a bunch of fools to protect my only witness in the most important federal trial of my career against one of the most vicious drug lords in the United States. Am I in the ballpark?"

"No," Ash said. "We don't need you to protect Lia."

"Sure." Steiner jeered. "'Cause you think you can protect her better than I can."

"Yes," Ash said with mind-boggling confidence.

"Then why the hell do you want me to stay?" Steiner said.

"Lia needs a bridge into that Brooklyn courtroom," Ash said. "That's where you come in. I'm willing to allow you to stick around, provided that you can follow *my* rules."

"*Your* rules?" Steiner's thin lips quivered with indignation. "This is preposterous."

"Take it or leave it."

"But I have to coordinate with my office."

"I'll only testify under the condition that you keep my location secret." The safety of Ash and his friends depended on that simple proposition. "And I mean completely secret."

"What about my boss?" Steiner said. "He needs to know that you'll be at the trial. He'll need to notify the U.S. Attorney's Office. I'll also need to coordinate with the task force, FBI, DEA, ATF, Homeland Security—"

"Too many people," Ash said. "Too many chances for leaks."

"Red has deep pockets and a huge reach," I said. "If you decide to partner with us, you can talk to your boss. He can make the necessary arrangements, but he doesn't need to know our location. In fact, if he really trusts you, he'll probably agree that it's better to do this our way."

"This is not how we operate," Steiner said.

"I think your boss can be persuaded," I said. "He needs me to testify. He knows what happened in Ohio. He realizes the dangers and risks associated with someone revealing our location. You'll also make it very clear to him that I'll only testify under *my* terms."

"And if he doesn't agree?"

"Then I'm gone," I said. "You know how well I can disappear."

Steiner plucked the cigarette from the table and, rolling it between his fingers, seemed to think about everything I'd said.

"There's something else," Ash said. "Something vital to the success of our plan."

"And that is?"

"We want you to deploy a decoy," Ash said.

"A decoy?"

"We want you to set up a safe house and a protective detail elsewhere," I said. "It has to be an authentic setup."

"To confuse Red." Steiner understood. "To direct his attention away from here."

"The decoy also provides you with the opportunity to flush out the mole in your office," Ash explained. "Whoever is passing on information will surely be on

the lookout for something like that. He or she will tell
Red. At that point, Red will face some choices."

"What kind of choices?" Steiner asked.

"He could bite on the lure," Ash said. "If he goes
after the decoy, if he sends his underlings, then you'll be
in the perfect position to catch him as he strikes and to
prove he has broken his bail terms. You can throw him
in jail where he belongs even before the trial begins."

"A decoy and a trap." Steiner tucked the cigarette
back in the box then slid the box in his front pocket. "It
could work. What if there's no mole? Or what if Red
decides not to go after the decoy?"

"Then we know his plan of attack for sure," Ash said.

Steiner's smirk sobered. "The courthouse."

Ash nodded. My stomach roiled some more. The
thought of facing Red made me want to vomit on the
spot. The thought of Red harming Ash and the guys
brought me to the verge of hyperventilating.

"You're good." Ash rubbed my back in little circles.
"No need to get stressed yet."

"I'm good," I repeated like a freaking robot. "I'm
good."

"The courthouse will be a complex target to defend,"
Steiner said.

"But you'd have enormous resources to deploy," Ash
pointed out.

"We could set up the perfect trap," Steiner said.

"We could," Ash said. "But you have to be prepared
to get Lia in and out safely."

"We can do that."

Right. More promises from Steiner. As if I could
believe him.

"Your preparations should include me as well," Ash
said. "I'm coming with Lia."

"No way." I fisted my hands on my lap. "Absolutely not. That's not part of the deal."

Ash looked to Steiner. "It's either both of us or none of us."

"Ash Hunter," I said, digging my nails into my palms. "You're *not* coming to the courthouse, so help me God."

"Us," Everest repeated, intractable. "Steiner, are you game?"

"Do I really have a choice?" Steiner said.

Ash handed him a prepaid phone. Steiner dialed a number and talked to his boss. He was factual and to the point and he didn't let any of the details regarding my location slip out. There was some heated back and forth, but when he hung up after a long conversation, his boss had agreed to our plan.

A silent countdown began in my mind. I was resigned to this plan, but I was also terrified, because failure would be catastrophic, not only for me, but for Ash and his friends. I worried that despite Ash's best precautions, he was still underestimating Red's capabilities. But this was also my only chance to defeat Red and make sure Dad, Adam and my baby hadn't died for nothing. If the worst happened, I was going to go down fighting to the end.

"The decoy will be set up and running by tonight," Steiner reported. "My boss will be monitoring the staff, looking for leaks. The legal team has been advised that the witness will be present."

Ash called in the rest of the guys. "He's in," he said.

Manny put a radio on the table along with a headset.

Steiner admired the headset. "Good stuff. Expensive too. How the hell did you get your hands on these?"

"None of your business," Manny said.

Steiner cocked an eyebrow. "Is that how it's going to be?"

"That's exactly how it's gonna be," Manny said.

Wang handed Steiner's gun over to Ash.

Ash slid it across the table. "Do you remember how to use this?"

Steiner caught it. "I've used it before, a time or two."

"Those situations are the only reason you have your gun back."

"Wait." Steiner glared. "How did you get into my personnel files?"

The guys' faces were as blank as a beige wall.

"I see." Steiner smirked. "Top-of-the-line equipment, professional-grade weapons and the attitude to match. You were all Special ops, weren't you?"

Nobody spoke.

"Don't get overly confident," Steiner said. "You people better be on alert. You better listen to me."

"I'm a good listener," Ash said. "I hope you are too. *My* watch. *My* rules. If you break my rules, Lia's gone. Clear?"

"Crystal." Steiner holstered his gun. "At least you trust me with this."

"Don't be so sure," Ash said. "Trust is something you earn around here. Or…"

"Or what?" Steiner said.

"Or perhaps this cowboy is convinced that he can draw faster than you."

THE SLEET SLAPPED a steady beat on the barn's roof. The atmosphere of the gray, soggy day exuded ozone and the scents of wet loam and pine forest. The aspens had long lost their leaves and the weather was squarely in winter's quarter. I raked some fresh straw into Ike's stall. The work helped me cope with the anxiety and so did the guys.

Ash's friends were a good bunch. The men of Manny's family had served in the Navy for six generations. Manny hated that the streak had come to an end with him in a wheelchair. Wang was the youngest of seven brothers. He'd enlisted at seventeen and served five back-to-back tours in Afghanistan. Will had a toddler son he adored, but his girlfriend had asked him to leave because the child got scared every time his father had an outburst.

They made for a very efficient unit. They took turns monitoring the equipment, patrolling the property and keeping eyes on me. Most of the time, Ash stuck with me, but today he and Wang had gone to check a malfunctioning camera on the property's east boundary while Manny monitored the computers. Will, who shared my fascination for animals, stood in the next stall, brushing Ivy's coat into a high polish. I flashed him a quick smile.

"Eh—sexy lady!" He broke out into "Gangnam Style." He pressed his hand against his mouth and looked startled, but he continued to sing at the top of his lungs, driven by his odd compulsion. "Eh—sexy lady, oh oh oh oh."

He was embarrassed, but I wasn't going to allow this sweet and gentle genius to be humiliated by his condition.

"Man, you're good." I danced to his song. "Keep going. I like the way you sing."

His horrified expression transformed into a cautious grin. He let it all out, dancing with me, adding some pretty cool sound effects. I swung my hips as together we tried to remember the steps. We were having a grand old time, when Steiner barged in.

"What the hell are you two doing?" He stood by the barn doors, glaring, the kind of look that took the fun out of the moment, embarrassed Will to no end and wilted my dancing into a self-conscious shuffle.

"We were just dancing," I said. "It's not a crime, you know."

"Right." Steiner drew on the cigarette in his hand, expelling a toxic cloud of smoke.

"It's better than sharing your cancer with the world." I shot him a reproving look. "No cigarettes in the barn. Fire hazard. And don't even think about leaving the butts lying around. Nicotine filters can kill animals if ingested."

He was about to make what I was sure would be a snide remark, when the radio came online.

"Base here," Manny announced over the radio. "Contact approaching. Over."

"Base this is Zulu," Ash's voice crackled over the radio. "ID? Over."

"Stand by," Manny said.

Will grabbed his tablet and pulled up the camera angles, imitating the sounds of a submarine pinging under the sea. Steiner put out his cigarette and joined us. I looked at the screen, laughed and, taking the radio from Will, clicked it on.

"Finally," I said. "If it isn't the elusive Fish and Wildlife. See the markings on the truck? I must have called them—oh, I don't know—fifty times?"

"Sexy lady?" Will retrieved the radio from me. "That's, like, very bad radio form."

"Oh." I leaned over the radio and pressed on Will's thumb. "Sorry."

"Base, this is Zulu," Ash's voice came again. "Requesting confirmation. Come in, base."

"Base here," Manny replied. "That's affirmative. Plates check, ID verified, over."

Steiner's eyebrows rose in a question. "Fish and Wildlife?"

"We had a mountain lion prowling around a while back," I explained.

"Simba." Will pulled up some pictures of the animal on the screen, most of them grainy and green since they were taken through the cameras' night vision lenses. *"Hakuna matata."*

Steiner groaned. "Settle down, will you?"

"Lay off him," I said. "He can't help it." I turned to Will. "You guys didn't tell me the mountain lion was back."

"Ash's rules of engagement," Will said. "If it wasn't bothering you or your animals, we were not to interfere."

"Right." I looked at the live feed of the Fish and Wildlife truck. "Well, here come the experts."

"Base, we're headed to intercept," Ash's voice announced.

"Roger that," Manny said.

Steiner took the radio from Will. "Zulu, this is Romeo, over."

"Come in, Romeo."

"Recommend alternative course of action," he said. "We don't want to stir the hive."

Steiner was right. We didn't want to attract attention or compromise our cover when we only had a few more days to go before scrambling for the courthouse.

"Stand by." I could almost hear Ash calculating the

probabilities and weighing the options. "Base, can you verify additional contacts, over?"

Manny took a moment to reply, probably to check all his monitors. "No additional contacts to report, over."

"ETA?"

"Fifteen minutes."

"Roger that," Ash said. "Heading for the crib. Out."

"Let's see." Steiner glanced at his watch. "Ash and Wang are about two miles out. Bets anyone? How fast can the cripple run?"

Will snapped and began to sing "Let It Go" at the top of his lungs.

"See what you did?" I glared. "Were you raised by gorillas?"

"You liked me fine when I first approached you as a teacher's assistant," Steiner said. "And after that, when I was your only real friend."

"You were my lifeline for a while," I said over Will's racket. "That's true."

"Are you ever going to forgive me for what happened to Adam?"

I looked him straight in the eye. "Probably not."

Will's song suddenly cut out. I turned around. My heart stopped. His face froze into a rigid mask, his eyes rolled to the back of his head and his body shuddered like a man possessed as he crashed on the ground. I ran over to him.

Steiner's gun was out and he was casing the barn, the doors, the windows, looking for an assailant. "Stay down."

Terror jabbed at me from all directions. Steiner's aim swung toward me. I shrank back, grappling for my little Beretta. For a full four seconds I knew that Steiner was in Red's pocket. Hands shaking, I struggled to click off the gun's safety.

He lunged for the radio. "This is Romeo, we've got a man down, I repeat, man down." He took a knee by the barn doors and scanned the pasture. "Is the kid hurt?" he said. "Is he bleeding?"

I set my Beretta aside and checked on Will. His body rattled as if he was being electrocuted, but I couldn't see any signs of wounds or bleeding.

"I don't think he's been shot," I said, trying to hold him still. "Will? Are you okay?"

Across the pasture, the back door of the cottage flung open. I spotted Manny rolling his wheelchair through the kitchen door with an automatic rifle on his lap. But as soon as he made it over the pavement, the chair got stuck in the mud.

"What a clusterfuck." Steiner stole across the barn. "Are you sure he's not hit?"

"I think he's having a seizure."

Steiner examined Will. "You're right." He turned Will on his side. "Come on, kid. You're going to be okay."

"Shouldn't we put something between his teeth or something?"

"That's an old myth." Steiner cradled Will's head, holding him in place while stroking his back. "Work through it, Will. You can do it."

I gawked at this new Steiner I hadn't met before. The tremors racking Will were subsiding. His arms twitched, his eyes closed, his body relaxed.

"My little brother had seizures." Steiner folded his coat and tucked it beneath Will's head. "He died when he was twelve."

"I'm sorry," I said.

"Nothing to do about it," Steiner said. "Some of us were born to suffer. There now. It's done."

"Is he going to be all right?" I asked.

"In a few hours," Steiner said, "after he sleeps it off."

He raised his gun again as Wang sneaked in through the back window and Ash stole quietly through the front doors.

"Stand down." Steiner lifted his hands in the air. "False alarm."

Gripping both his cane and his weapon, Ash leaned against the barn door and took his weight off his bad foot. "Wang, go help Manny." He caught his breath and whistled.

Only then did Neil enter the barn, greeting us excitedly, bouncing, barking and panting with his long tongue hanging out of his mouth.

"What the hell happened?" Ash said.

"Will had a seizure." I said, trying to keep Neil from licking and sniffing Will on the ground. "How's your foot?"

"Fine," he rasped, but I could tell he was in pain.

Steiner made a show of looking at his watch. "Two miles in eight minutes and forty-two seconds. Not too shabby. You're still holding yourself to SEAL standards. Honestly? I didn't think you had it in you, cowboy."

"Next time," Ash said, "I'll call in the false alarm and you run."

THE FISH AND WILDLIFE officers were courteous, efficient and knowledgeable. They took our statements, walked the property and asked lots of questions. Ash gave them a detailed description of the mountain lion, down to the distinctive white butterfly markings on its chin.

"That's the one," the officer said. "A rancher reported

that it's been feeding on his sheep. We think it's best to relocate it. We'd like to set up a trap on your property, if you don't mind."

Ash agreed to the officer's request and so did I. I wanted my animals safe and the lion relocated. It would be helpful all around...*if* I survived my visit to the courthouse. Promising to return soon to set up the trap, the officers left. Based on their workload and on how long it had taken to get them out here, I didn't expect them to come back until next summer.

As soon as the truck drove away, I spotted Steiner and Wang carrying Will to the RV.

"Steiner says he's going to be fine," I said. "Should we take him to the hospital?"

"He doesn't want to be in the hospital," Ash said.

I glanced at him. "He reminds me of someone I met once."

The grim lines on Ash's face deepened. "There's nothing they can do for him anyway."

"The seizures can't be controlled?"

"Will's best hope is that, in time, his brain will stabilize and the seizures will decrease in frequency."

It really sucked that there was nothing we could do to help him. I ached for Will.

"Come on." I hooked Ash's arm around my shoulders and made for the kitchen. "Let's take care of you."

"I'm fine," he said, but he allowed a portion of his weight to lean on me and signaled for Neil to follow.

"Well, I'm not fine." I kneaded my chest. "My heart just about gave out. That didn't go according to plan."

"When the shit hits the fan, it never goes according to plan." He kissed the top of my head. "Remember that, Lia. That's why we have to be fluid."

"Fluid, sure." I opened the kitchen door. "I about peed in my pants."

He had the gall to laugh.

"Sit and take off your boot," I said. "I'll be right back."

I dumped all the ice trays I kept in the freezer in a bucket, added water and dragged it over to the kitchen table. Neil immediately stuck his muzzle in and tried to drink the water.

I nudged the dog aside. "I'll get to you in a sec." I pointed at Ash. "You, in goes the foot."

Ash grimaced when he tested the water. "Brrr." He shivered, but he shoved his foot in the ice bucket anyway.

"Ashton Hunter, I swear, if you fractured, fissured or otherwise hurt even the smallest bone in your pinkie toe, I'm going to be one pissed-off broad." I knelt next to him, dipped my hands into the freezing water and gently rubbed his foot.

He flashed me one of his fake-innocence looks. "Why so set on terrorizing me?"

"I don't want you to undo your healing," I said. "You didn't have to run so hard and fast."

"I tightened the brace," he said, as if that should make a huge difference. "It was good training. We faced several contingencies at the same time and we had to hustle."

He'd tightened the brace. Right. As if that was going to keep him from hurting. For a bright guy, sometimes, he had no sense at all.

My fingers tripped on a couple of stitches that hadn't been there before. "What's this?"

"Oh, it's nothing." Ash waved dismissively. "I cut my foot the other day when we were working at the ranch, but don't worry, Jordan was there. He disinfected the cut and stitched it up for me."

"Why didn't you tell me?"

"I didn't want you fussing all over me."

"Hmm." I inspected his foot, looking for signs of infection. "Looks clean, but I'm sure it bothered you when you ran today."

"Some," he admitted. "I may have been able to run faster without the cut or the cane."

"I think you ran fast enough."

"I've been thinking," he said. "Maybe the doctor is right."

I looked up at him. "About what?"

"Not having to live with the pain."

My belly contracted into a knot. He was talking about amputation. "You don't have to decide right now."

"That's true," he said, "but today made me think that, with all the biotechnological advances out there, I could do better."

Yep. That was Ash for you. He wasn't so much thinking about escaping the pain as he was thinking he could run faster with the right prosthesis.

"Perhaps you ought to do some research about that," I suggested.

"I have," he said, surprising the heck out of me. "There's some kick-ass technology that could maybe help. By the way, Steiner did well."

"Maybe that means that he's not a plant and you can relax around him?"

"Relax?" He shook his head. "Hardly. We're a man down and Red's sitting tight on a courthouse hit. We'll be moving out soon. Red hasn't taken the decoy's bait, but that could also mean that he knows it's a trap. No, I don't think this is the right time to relax."

"Maybe there isn't an informant in Steiner's office after all," I said. "Maybe you were wrong about the mole and Red has no way of knowing our location."

"Maybe." Ash sounded skeptical.

The front door of the cottage opened. Manny came through in his motorized wheelchair with Wang and Steiner in tow. By the tone of their voices, they were having an argument.

"It's fixed," Manny announced, joining us at the kitchen table.

"What's fixed?" I asked.

"I've changed the Rover's tires to account for sleet, snow and mud," Manny said. "I won't get stuck again."

"Awesome," Steiner muttered. "Next time, we won't have to call Triple A."

"It's the cold weather." Wang pried off his prosthetic arm, laid it on the table and, after pulling out a tiny screwdriver from his keychain, unscrewed the component's compartment. "It's fucking us up."

Steiner perched an unlit cigarette between his lips. "What's wrong with your arm?"

"My thumb." Wang twisted the tiny screwdriver in his hand. "The fucker's jamming."

"Must be hard," Steiner said. "Without opposable thumbs, entire species drop down a notch on the evolutionary ladder."

Every pair of eyes around the table homed in on Steiner, including mine.

"Please ignore the jerk sitting next to me." I said. "He was dropped on his head as a baby."

"Can I just beat the crap out of him now?" Wang said.

"Patience, dude," Manny said. "Get in line."

"I for one won't be waiting for the cavalry the next

time we get into a bind," Steiner said. "Not when it's Scarecrow, Tin Man and the Cowardly Lion riding to the rescue."

"Agent Steiner!"

Wang slammed the screwdriver on the table. "Who the hell are you calling a coward?"

"Steady as she goes," Ash said. "He just wants to mess with your cool."

Steiner sneered. "Listen to the Wizard of Oz, munchkin."

"What the hell is wrong with you?" I said.

"What's wrong with me?" Steiner glared. "I think you ought to be asking what's wrong with you. You've got to listen to me."

I lifted my chin in the air. "And what is it that you have to say?"

"Haven't you learned anything from what happened today?" he said. "You need a protective detail."

"I have one."

"You call these clowns a protective detail?" Steiner's chair screeched against the floor as he shoved it away from the table. "You need to wake up, or you're going to get knocked off the game, 'cause—guess what, Dorothy?—you're not in Kansas anymore."

He stalked to the door and wrenched it open, allowing a burst of cold to chill my little kitchen. He slammed the door on his way out, leaving the guys around the table in utter silence and my stomach churning with an impending sense of doom.

SEVENTEEN

I CHECKED ON Will before I went to bed. He slept comfortably in the RV and Manny swore he'd woken up and eaten a full meal earlier. He seemed to be recovering well. Wang was on watch duty, monitoring the surveillance equipment. Steiner snored on the couch. When I finally made it upstairs, Neil was fast asleep on his cushion and Ash was working on his laptop. He lay on the bed where I'd left him, wearing only his T-shirt and underwear, with his foot wrapped and propped up on a pillow.

"What are you working on?" I asked while I wiggled out of my blue jeans.

"Oh, nothing." He set aside his laptop on the night table and watched me undress.

"Hey," I said. "This is not a peep show, you know."

He smirked. "If you're taking your clothes off, it's *my* show for sure."

I was very self-conscious about my body, but I was getting used to Ash's attention. His interest gave me a confidence boost. The glee in his stare had me giggling inside. Astonishing. How could a lopsided smirk make me feel so giddy?

"Tempers around here are running high," I said, while I slipped on my pajama pants. "Steiner put up quite the tantrum."

"Can't say as I blame him," Ash said. "I wouldn't

have liked it either if my team had fallen apart so easily."

The way he said it. The irreverence in his voice. The way his blue eyes sparkled with mischief set off my alarms.

"Ash?" I narrowed my eyes on him. "Did you guys set up Steiner to test him?"

His shoulder rose up and down. "I didn't say that."

I cocked my fists on my hips. "Ashton Hunter, you better tell me the truth right now. Did Will fake his seizure?"

"Unfortunately, no," Ash said, his mirth gone. "Will's seizure was for real and so was the untimely arrival of Fish and Wildlife. But the circumstances did precipitate the opportunity to test Steiner's reliability."

"So you left Steiner alone with me to test his loyalties?"

"How little you know me." Ash's gaze sparkled with a trace of irritation. "You were never alone with him. The whole time you were at the barn, Wang was stationed nearby, with his rifle trained on Steiner."

I gaped. "Wang wasn't with you?"

"He was where he was supposed to be, with you," Ash said. "He was concealed from everybody. Don't forget, he's a trained sniper. He loves that shit. He reported Will's seizure on an alternative com channel. Manny's rover didn't get stuck in the mud. He held back on purpose, to see what Steiner would do if he thought he was alone with you."

"What about you?" I said. "Did you fake that run? No way. I know you were hurting when you got back."

"Neil and I were checking on that faulty camera," he admitted. "We did run all the way back."

Holy Mother. "Why didn't you tell me any of this?"

"I've been telling you all along," he said. "We have to be fluid. You're a bad liar and a terrible actress. Steiner would've known if you didn't believe the situation was real."

Maybe he had a point, but I wasn't a happy camper.

"Don't be mad at me." He put out his hand. "Come over here. Please?"

The kindness in his eyes. The fact that I was sure he'd acted for my benefit. The electrical buzz disrupting my brain waves... I groaned, but I took his hand anyway and ended up wrapped in his arms and happier for it.

"I don't like it," I mumbled against his lips.

"I know." He kissed me some more.

I tore my lips from his mouth. "I want to be on the private channel too."

"Okay." He kissed me again.

"Okay?" I mumbled between kisses. "You promise?"

"Promise." He tucked a lock of hair behind my ear. "Now, Lia, please, I've gone too long without you. I find that particularly trying. Can we do something about that?"

The delicious shiver was back with a vengeance. "We can't," I said. "This creaky old house is full of grown men who will know very well what's happening in this room at the first sound."

"They think it's happening right now."

"Really?" I said. "Why would they think such a thing?"

"Because we're together and alone and sex is what happens when people like you and me are together and alone." He kissed me again. "Because they know I want you every time I see you and that I'm having a hell of a hard time keeping my hands off you."

The space between my legs flooded like a creek after monsoon rains.

"Oh, well," I mumbled between kisses. "In that case, maybe we can be really quiet?"

"Let's play, Lia," he said. "We need some R & R. Are you up for a little game?"

I cocked an eyebrow. "What kind of a game?"

"A game where I call the moves and you make them."

I eyed him skeptically. "Sounds like a one-sided kind of game."

He grinned and wiggled his eyebrows. "What if I promise I'll make it worth your while?"

"Do we have to play that one?" Uneasiness crawled up my spine. "I mean, can we play some other game?"

"Of course," he said. "You name the game and I'm there. I just thought we could combine a good time with a bit of therapy."

"Therapy?"

"Trust therapy, to be specific," he said. "The kind of therapy that helps *you* trust *me*."

The intensity in his eyes. Yes, this was somehow important to him. I should at least try it. Still, I wavered. Making love with Ash was always a thrilling experience, but I wasn't sure how I'd react to commands, even if I knew they were pretend commands. The nature of his request brought up treacherous memories of pain, degradation and grief, recollections of fear that tensed my muscles, tightened my shoulders and gave me a bad case of cold feet.

Ash read my reaction. "Forget I said anything." He hugged me against his chest and kissed the top of my head. "My bad. How about we watch a movie instead?"

I looked up at him. The concern that deepened the lines on his face filtered through my fears and soothed the old grief that pained me. This was Ash. I could trust him. I did trust him. And he was right. I so wanted to be free of the fear. I wanted to reclaim my emotions, heal myself and learn to enjoy different kinds of sex like a healthy adult. I wanted to please Ash too. Was it wrong? I didn't think so. For once, I wanted to be normal, carefree and maybe even daring in the bedroom. Could I start to work on all of that today?

"Um…" I chewed on my lip. "Maybe we could try this game of yours and see what happens?"

"We don't have to," he said. "Best course of action is to wait until you're totally comfortable with me."

"I do feel comfortable," I said, "with you, I mean. It's me I doubt sometimes, but you could be right. A little trust therapy could help."

He studied my face. "I don't want to rush you."

"No, really, I want to try this game of yours." I squeezed his hand. "We can't operate out of fear, right? That's what you said. We have to operate out of our strengths. I'm willing to give it a try. Are you?"

He sighed. "I'll only try it if you promise me that the moment you feel iffy, you'll let me know. You can say no to anything and quit at any time. Those are my conditions and they're nonnegotiable. Are we clear?"

"Okay." His condition made me feel safe about trying out something new. It helped that my body craved Ash so much that I was ready for him now.

"All right then." He planted a kiss on my lips. "Let's play."

I shivered inside. "What should I do first?"

"Stand up. Good." The intensity in his eyes ramped up. The planes of his face set into stern lines. His voice turned suddenly exacting. "Take off your top," he said. "I want to see you naked."

His bluntness startled me. A bubble of fear surged up my throat. All those years of snarled commands slammed me hard. *Steady.* This wasn't that. *Breathe.* I stole a look at Ash. He winked at me. A rush of affection lent me the strength to step up to this brand-new plate. *Cope.* The raw sexuality exuding from him was irresistible. Goose bumps prickled my skin in a race that convened at the sensitive nexus between my legs. A game, that's all it was, a game he wanted to play. Surely I could play it too?

I drew in a deep breath and took off my top slowly, revealing my tummy first, then my midriff, before I pulled the shirt over my arms. A sudden bout of shyness flushed my cheeks. I'd been naked with Ash many times before, but this was different. I was having problems with the idea of blatantly exhibiting my scarred body. *Therapy.* The first thing I had to do was get comfortable in my own skin. My body was fine as it was. My body was mine. I chose who I wanted to share it with. Ash was the one.

He reached up and, lowering my face to his, kissed me, infusing me with wallops of unmistakable affection. My heart swelled. My pussy began to melt on the spot. Ash grinned. We hadn't even started and he was already cheating.

"How are we doing?" he asked.

"Good." I let out a nervous giggle. "What next?"

"Go on," he said, back to the firm tone. "You know what I want to see."

I reached back and unhooked my bra. I held the bra in place as I slipped one arm out from the strap, then the other. The affection in his eyes reassured me. The authority in his voice lent me the confidence to set the bra aside. His gaze caressed my breasts like a brush of fine silk. My nipples perked under his scrutiny.

"Lovely." He built me up with his praise. "Very fine indeed." He paused and spoke more forcefully. "Now, take off your bottom. Come on, get to it."

Feeling more confident by the moment, I turned around, slid the flannel sweats down my legs and dropped them to the floor. I peeked over my shoulder, watching him watching me. I liked the intensity I spotted in his eyes. His stare consumed every movement I made, wasting nothing, appreciating everything. If he wanted to see me undress, then undress I would.

His boxers tented over his generous erection. I could almost feel his gaze trailing my body's curves like hands, tapering into my waist, widening around my hips and gathering beneath the halves of my ass. Excitement moistened my panties and pulsed in my sex.

"Turn around," he said gruffly.

I straightened my spine and squared my shoulders before I turned to face him. The passion I spotted in his eyes made me feel beautiful, wanted and admired. I drew taller.

He swung his legs over the edge of the bed and pointed at a spot before him. "Over here."

I walked to the space between his knees. He rolled my panties down my legs as if unwrapping a candy bar. He kissed my belly button. Every cell in my body buzzed with the contact. His lips followed a crooked trail to my pubis, where his mouth brushed over my bristle before his tongue tasted the length of my sex and his lips pursed on my clit. My knees buckled.

This game of his was delicious. Therapy was a lot more pleasant than I had anticipated. I didn't care if our game leaned toward crass or vulgar. I didn't want to think about whether it was right or wrong. I stood on the tips of my toes and offered more of me. I relished the chance to please him. Whatever he wanted, I needed to give. Whatever he craved, I wanted to satisfy.

I swayed on my feet, dangerously close to collapsing.

"Careful now." He helped me to the floor. "On your knees."

I dropped to the braided carpet with a sense of relief. I didn't think I could stand on my own any longer. I landed between his legs, gasping for breath in the shelter between his knees. My arms entwined about his good leg. I kissed his calf, the inside of his thighs. I rose on my knees and kissed the erection testing the fabric of his shorts.

I nuzzled his underwear, burrowing my face in his groin. I rubbed my head against his bulk and breathed in his arousal's enthralling scent. I delved into his boxers' slit and pressed my mouth to his cock, sliding my lips over his erection's solid heat. I'd never had him in my mouth before. My mouth watered in anticipation.

He let out a strained breath. "Are you sure?"

"Totally sure." I tugged playfully on his boxers' elastic band.

"Christ, Lia, you're killing me over here." He took in a deep breath and steeled his voice. "You want it?" He pulled his cock out of his boxers and offered it to me. "You can have it."

My lips parted to take him in. They slid down his shaft in a long journey that filled all the space in my mouth and dead-ended at the back of my throat. His entire body replied to my tongue. He groaned in a way that had me trembling too. I loved the feel of him in my mouth. I twirled my tongue around his girth, enfolding him against my palate.

He sat at the edge of the bed watching me. Beneath partly drawn lids, his eyes sparkled with blue fire. Occasionally, a gasp or a hiss would escape him, but most of the time, his lips were white and pressed tight together, as if his body had resolved to trap both sounds and seed.

As I worked my mouth over his cock, he entwined his fingers in my hair. He grew so excited I had difficulty swallowing the whole of him. I discovered that I could drive him to madness with my mouth. Naked, on my knees, with his cock jamming in and out of my lips, I'd become the world's most powerful woman.

"Man, you give good head," he rasped. "You suck like an angel."

I shifted his cock from my mouth to my hand and stroked him in my fists. "Do you want to come?"

"Oh, yeah." His face scrunched up as if in pain and his body balked with the strain of holding back.

"Come then."

I returned him to my mouth and took full charge of his pleasure. I gulped him down to the root, retreated and plunged again, wearing down his restraint with each swallow. His fingers dug into my scalp. His breathing stopped. Then he groaned and his body folded over me in the throes of a powerful orgasm that rattled his body and delivered his load deep in my throat. He tensed and released several times in my mouth. He poured into me for a long time. I watched him take his pleasure in my body and rejoiced at the sight. Perhaps I was good at this game after all.

When he was done, I licked him clean and smiled. The look he gave me was full of praise and lust. He caressed my face, thumb lingering over my lower lip. Then he kissed me and I melted like butter on the grill.

"That felt...phenomenal." He hugged me between his legs.

If he felt phenomenal, then I felt phenomenal too. It struck me then that his therapy was working for me, because I hadn't once felt fear or regret and I'd been so focused on pleasing him that the memories had stayed away. I felt light, as if the past couldn't touch me. I felt renewed.

"More?" he said.

"More," I agreed.

He lifted me up and settled me on my hands and knees on the mattress. He knelt just behind me. His weight bent the mattress and the old frame protested with a chorus of squeaks. He reached over my back, casing my body with his as he grabbed my hands and wrapped my fingers around the bronze spindles. Then he lifted off me and caressed my pussy, which flowed for him like an open spigot.

"Christ, Lia, you're so wet," he murmured. "You've made me so hard all over again. I want to take you like this."

I moaned when his fingers breached me, my body tensing with pleasure. "I want to feel you inside of me."

"In that case..."

He glided into me slowly. Then he stopped to give my body time to accommodate to his bulk, a throbbing, delicious presence that filled me up completely and had me shivering with pleasure.

"I'm going to move now." He journeyed through me in slow, exquisite strokes that had me whimpering with need and my hips angling for more. "Jesus, you feel so good."

The only sound I could muster was a groan of delight.

He steadily increased his pace, deepening and strengthening his strokes in a way that thrilled my body. He drove me to the edge and then…stopped.

"Ash?" I protested.

He leaned over me, pushed my hair out of the way and nipped at my earlobe. "Remember our game?"

"I do," I rasped, caught in a surge of lust.

"So now I want to love you really hard."

I swallowed a dry gulp and braced on the mattress. "How hard?"

"As hard as you'd like." His breath was warm on my ear. "As hard as you'd let me love you."

"Okay." My body trembled with anticipation.

"Hang on," he said.

I tightened my hold on the rails and groaned when he started again, stern, demanding, delicious strokes that traveled through me and sent pangs of bliss to every corner of my body. I balanced precariously on my knees, absorbing his strokes and yelping softly, trying not to scream out loud from the pleasure.

He was ferocious at this game; he played to win. His strokes grew into a rhythmic pounding. My flesh shook with his passion. My body smarted with pleasure. But I was determined to play well too. I loved this kind of therapy. My hands tightened around the bars with each stroke and yet I didn't let go. I answered his strokes with the swirl of my hips.

"Christ, I love the way you feel."

He brought his hand around to stroke my clit. I buckled but he held me in place and made me endure his excruciating touch. He was strong, stern and forceful and I liked that he wasn't holding back. He wasn't making love to me as if I was frail, damaged or delicate. He didn't tiptoe around his wants or hold back on account of my history or my fears.

On the contrary, he defied and defeated all of that with his passion. He restored and rebuilt me with his confidence in my body. He loved me hard, as if I was indeed a good fuck, and that made me exactly so. In his hands, my body was hale, whole and sturdy, a tool for his pleasure, which might have been unfair, except for the fact that his pleasure also meant mine.

"You're mine," he said. "Say it. Who do you belong to?"

"You," I rasped. "You."

"This is mine," he said, caressing my ass. "These are mine." He squeezed my breasts in his hands. "And this little jewel is mine too," he added cupping my pussy in between delicious thrusts.

"Yes," I whimpered. "It's all yours."

I groaned, flowed and reared beneath him, about to go off.

"Not yet," he said. "You have to ask me."

"Oh." This game was harder than I thought. "Can I?"

"No."

I protested, begged and even tried to coax him by rocking and twisting my hips like a belly dancer, but although he urged me on and matched my moves with a charge of his own, he wouldn't budge. He pushed me into that mindless state where pleasure ruled. I dangled over the precipice by his will's capricious rope.

I tried to explain that I had to come, that I couldn't bear it any longer, that if I didn't come I might die on the spot, but he just laughed it off and kept up those divine strokes while I panted the short little breaths that kept me in the game, but not by much.

"Christ, you're a joy." He kissed my back and shifted his weight. "Hold on real tight."

I clung to the bed as hard as I clung to my sanity. *Pant, pant, pant.* It was all I could do as he packed me to the rim with pleasure's explosive charge.

He tilted my head, grabbed my chin and claimed the space between my parted lips. His tongue dipped into my mouth with the same ferocious rhythm as his cock. He deepened his kiss then raked my lower lip with his teeth as he bore down on me.

The room quaked around me. My body absorbed his delicious pummeling. His cock ground ever deeper into me. I gritted my teeth, braced my knees wide on the mattress and arched my back to meet his strokes straight-on.

"That's my brave girl," he rasped. "Hell, yes, you're a sex goddess. You hear me? The universe's best fucking ride."

The universe's best fucking ride was ready to go supernova. "Please?"

He kissed my ear, flattened a hand on my back and, pressing down, pumped into me with renewed zeal. "You may come. Now."

I let go like a BASE jumper leaping from great heights. The long, protracted orgasm kidnapped my body and overthrew my brain. I plummeted out of control. My body rattled as a tremendous force tore me apart, obliterating reason, memory and thought, enveloping me in brilliant flashes of blinding pleasure. This type of therapy? I could handle it every day. I pressed my cheek against the pillows, bit down on the sheets and roared until I ran out of voice and air.

I didn't remember a lot after that. At some point Ash must have pried my fingers from the headboard. If it wasn't a dream, I think he made love to me again later on, this time slow and tenderly, with due consideration to the better-used parts of me. I woke up, late in the night, snuggled in his arms, utterly satisfied with the new additions to my growing collection of earth-rattling orgasms, and brimming with his seed as he'd promised.

He was awake. He kissed me as soon as my eyes fluttered open.

"I had to love you like that," he whispered in my ear.

"I know," I said. "Who won?"

"Won?" he said.

"Who won the game?"

He chuckled. "You looked like you did well for yourself," he said. "As for me, you won't hear any complaints. Hell, all my prizes were extraordinary."

I fell asleep smiling.

EIGHTEEN

THE NEXT THREE days stretched like the dark molasses syrup Wang thickened in a pan for his pancakes every morning. The nights, on the other hand, passed rather quickly. Maybe it was because Ash and I kept busy in bed, starved for each other. Maybe sex was my new way of coping with stress. Perhaps we were having trouble regulating the attraction between us. Whatever it was, I was glad for it. It kept me from lying awake all night, worrying about the guys, the courthouse and Red.

But as the date for the trial loomed closer and Steiner finalized the arrangements for my transfer to New York, sleep evaded me altogether. I fought with Ash, who in his Everest state insisted he was coming to the courthouse. He was by far the most stubborn person I've ever met.

With only two days to go before our departure date, I was groggy when I came downstairs. A chorus of grunts answered my halfhearted morning greeting in complete contrast to Neil's happy *woof*.

"Good morning, handsome." I scratched Neil behind the ears. "You too," I said kissing Ash on the cheek in passing.

I grabbed the largest coffee mug I could find and filled it to the rim. The guys didn't look much better than I did. Dark stubble and bleary eyes prevailed around the kitchen table. The unlit cigarette hung from Steiner's lip. Wang's prosthetic arm lay on the table as he fiddled with the electronic components. Manny and Ash gathered around Will's laptop.

"It's like 3.3 milliseconds," Will was saying. "You can't possibly get an electronic monitor off in milliseconds."

"If you can detonate a charge in 3.3 milliseconds," Ash said. "Isn't it at least theoretically possible that the lapse indicates a disruption pattern?"

"It happened once, yesterday, so it's not a pattern," Will said. "It looks more like a minor signal fluctuation."

I looked at Manny. "What are they talking about?"

"Will found a slight anomaly in the data of Rojas's electronic monitoring device," Manny explained. "Heads up, guys. ETA three minutes."

"ETA?" I said. "Who's coming?"

"Fish and Wildlife is on the way," Manny said. "That mountain lion must really be eating lots of sheep, 'cause they're back, and they're bringing the trap they talked about."

The live shot on Manny's laptop showed the truck approaching on the road, the same one from a few days ago, this time towing a trailer with the trap strapped beneath a tarp.

"I'll take Fish and Wildlife." Ash checked his Sig Sauer's magazine before clicking it back in place and shrugging on his vest. "Manny, you're on coms. Will, cover me."

Everyone around the table inserted their earpieces and clicked on their coms, even Steiner. Belatedly, I did the same. Outside, Izzy and Ozzie began the breakfast racket. I put on my boots and grabbed my gloves and jacket.

Ash gave me a look. "Aren't you forgetting something?"

"Ah, yes, I need my keys to unlock the shed." I grabbed them from the peg and dropped them into my pocket.

"No, not the keys," Ash said.

"Oh." I fetched my gun from the coat rack, checked the clip—to show Ash I'd learned something—and tucked it in the back of my pants. I headed for the back door, where the bleating and the braying had achieved epic proportions. "Those rascals can con anyone into believing they haven't been fed in years."

"Wait up." Wang grabbed his rifle and, fitting his prosthesis on the go, opened the door ahead of me and scoured the yard beyond the animals gathered by the door. "I go first, remember? You'd think by now, I'd have you better trained."

"Me, trained?" I laughed. "Never."

Steiner rolled his eyes and pushed off from the table. "I'm coming too."

The air chilled my nostrils and stung my lungs. My breath came in visible bursts. A leaden cover of clouds hung low in the sky, roiling over the mountains and trailing dark skirts of precipitation in the distance. Followed by my animals, I went to the trough first. A layer of ice had formed over the water.

"Hey," I yelled over to Steiner. "Can you grab the shovel by the kitchen door?"

Steiner, who'd just lit a cigarette, cursed under his breath and went to get the shovel. I was chiseling at the ice with a small trowel when I heard Ash's voice over the com, terse and controlled.

"Athena," he said. "I repeat. Athena. Athena. Athena."

The com in my ear went silent seconds before a windowpane exploded. White plumes burst out of the cottage's windows. Shouts echoed all around me, together with the unmistakable plink of gunfire. Several canisters landed in the yard, streaming tendrils of smoke that streaked my view.

My heart shot up my throat. I didn't have to be Special ops to understand what was happening. I couldn't see Ash anymore. I got a whiff of spice in the air. My lungs buckled and my eyes stung. Smoke bombs? Worse, some sort of toxic gas?

Another canister landed nearby. Thick dark clouds drifted in my direction and choked the breath out of me. I pressed my hand over my mouth and, crouching low, moved toward the barn. The shots were louder now. An engine throttled somewhere to my right. Time screeched to a halt as I squinted through the smoke.

With a bang and a whoosh, the red flash of flames ignited. It came from somewhere on the other side of the cottage and it must have hit something, the RV maybe. A wave of heat reached all the way across the pasture. A goat bleated pitifully.

Ike trotted across the lawn and disappeared beyond the broken fence. A burst of wind sent the plume of smoke directly at me. It stung my nostrils, scalded my lungs and brought tears to my eyes. My home, my animals, my friends. Ash, where on earth was he? I tripped, fell and, croaking on all fours, dry heaved.

Steiner staggered out of the smoke halfway between the house and the barn. His eyes were red and swollen and his clothing was ripped and stained, but he clutched the cigarette in his mouth, the shovel in one hand and his gun in the other.

I grappled with my gun. I aimed it at the smoke, at

the noises beyond the smoke, at Steiner, who stumbled wide-eyed toward me.

"Really?" he said. "Are you aiming at *me*?"

Wang skid-landed by my side, bracing his assault rifle against his shoulder, which was also aimed at Steiner. "Keep your head down and move toward the tree line," he barked. "Now!"

I staggered to my feet just as the Fish and Wildlife truck barreled through the smoke. It roared across the field, spraying the pasture and the cottage with automatic gunfire. Steiner turned, aimed and shot. The truck never slowed down. It ran over Steiner as if he was but a pothole on the ground. Then it turned toward us, front grill soaked with blood.

Wang and I ran, weaving toward the shed where the trucks were parked. I glanced behind me. Three men rode on the trailer hooked to the truck. They'd been concealed beneath the tarp. Two of them were armed with heavy machine guns. The third man held an RPG launcher on his shoulder. It was aimed in our direction.

A projectile sped by and slammed against the shed ahead of us. It exploded, cutting off our escape route. Jagged fragments came at us like blades slicing the air. Wang tackled me from behind. We hit the ground hard. The blow knocked the air out of my lungs.

Beyond the smoke, the battle continued. Shots sputtered from every which way. I slithered out from beneath Wang. A nasty gash bled on his temple. I groped his torso, looking for injuries. His vest looked normal, but it felt compact and hard to my fingers. Had he been wearing a bulletproof vest all this time? More gunshots. I had to hurry. I checked his pulse. He was alive but unconscious. I knew exactly what would happen if our attackers found him.

I took advantage of the black smoke streaming from the burning shed and dragged Wang behind the pile of rusting oil drums piled up at the back of the property. I tipped one of the steel drums and, after stuffing Wang in it, rolled it behind some of the other drums.

The survivor's switch in me flipped. My personal contingency plan kicked in. Nobody else was going to die instead of me. Red wanted me alive for the moment. Right? So all I had to do was lead the killers away from Wang, Ash and the rest, so they could make their escape.

"Over here!" I waved and ran up the hill.

Shouts chased after me. I sprinted toward the forest, leading the men away from the cottage. I heard the truck's engine accelerate, but when I looked back, the wheels sank in the muck, spinning without traction. I raced up the slope and dove into the tree line.

I had no air left in my lungs. My legs shook with the effort, but I ran some more, even though I kept tripping. I wasn't sure where I was heading. Away. To the woods. To give the others a chance.

I'd been such a freaking fool. How could I have believed that anybody could stand between Red and what he wanted? Running was my life's only fate. Running was all I could do. So I ran, for the guys, for Ash, for me.

I heard the men before I saw them. A new group trampled through the trees, cutting off my escape. Shouts echoed in the forest along with heavy footsteps and the crackle of radio communications. A helicopter buzzed the top of the woods. Some of the men lingered along the trail, doing what, I couldn't tell. One of them spotted me and called out the alarm. I took off in a different direction, but they were closing in on me like the rope of a tightening noose.

I stepped quietly over a creek. My feet crunched on a thin layer of mud. *Snap.* The sound hit me an instant before the pain. The steel jaws of a trap closed about my leg, cut through my boots and bit into my ankle.

I suppressed a scream. The pain. It was unbearable. Bastards. Planting leg traps. That's what those men pretending to be Fish and Wildlife officers had been doing in the bushes, seeding the forest with the cruel snares. They didn't give a hoot about the innocents who'd get snared. I clenched my gun and, cursing under my breath, tried to shake off the trap.

The steel teeth sank deeper, scraping against my shin. The men converged around me. I aimed my gun from one man to the other, but none came closer. They seemed to be waiting, for what, I couldn't tell. The roar of the helicopter shook the earth. After a few moments, another man showed up at the clearing, this one surrounded by a group of bodyguards. He stepped forward and took off his cap, freeing the hair that framed his face with a halo of curls. My breath caught in my throat.

At long last, the Devil of Caquetá had caught up with me.

"Rose," he said in his velvety bass. *"Mi Rosita Americana."*

Red's grin chilled me down to the marrow. Lord help me. Red was here. Frantically, I considered my choices. Surely by now, Ash and the others had made their escape. I prayed that was so. Only one option left. I pressed the Beretta's muzzle to my temple.

"Now, now," Red said, palms in the air. "You really don't want to do that. You might be in a bit of a pickle, but surely an out can be properly negotiated."

I remembered that I had promised Ash I'd fight to stay alive. I also remembered the type of negotiations Red favored. Any settlement with Red would translate into unspeakable horror for me. My courage shattered like an egg hitting the floor. *Sorry, Ash.* I broke a promise and put my finger on the trigger. I wasn't going back to Red.

NINETEEN

THE SOUND REACHED me first, moans, groans and whimpers disrupting my mind's darkness. I blinked. My lids rustled like sand over my eyes. The lights in the room were dimmed and for a moment, I couldn't make out anything around me. My arms couldn't move. My hands were fastened securely behind my back. My cheek peeled off a warm surface when I lifted my head.

I swung my legs around and managed to sit up groggily. My head throbbed with a dull ache, coupled by a sharp pain when I planted my foot on the plush carpeting. Then, the memories began to pour in. I recalled the attack, the escape, the trap snaring my ankle, those men catching up with me. I remembered my finger curling on the trigger and then…nothing.

My pulse drummed in my ears. I forced my eyes to work. I sat on a semicircular leather couch among a bed of embroidered pillows. Behind me, several similarly shaped sofas rose in four tiered levels. The ceiling arched into a softly illuminated cupola, decorated with frescoes copied from Michelangelo's Sistine Chapel.

Flanked by elegant curtains, an enormous television screen dazzled my eyes. The screen was dark, showing only the pause button. Before I could make sense of where I was, I heard the sound of a throat clearing next to me. I turned around and died inside.

"Don't look so surprised."

Red shared the couch with me. For a moment I contemplated the idea that we had both died and this meeting was taking place in hell. But then he cupped the back of my head and forced his lips on my mouth.

Terror rattled me to the core. Was this a nightmare? A flashback? A hallucination? I struggled in his arms, testing the duct tape binding my hands. It didn't budge. I tried to shake off Red's hold, but the harder I fought the harder he clutched me. His fingers dug into my scalp. His mouth became more aggressive.

I gagged when he forced my jaw opened and pushed his tongue into my mouth. I tried to hold back, but I couldn't. I croaked. I gagged. Then I threw up all over him.

He slapped me so hard that I flew off the couch and landed against the wall. The room flickered before my eyes. A trickle of warmth dripped from my nose. Blood. It was true. The monster that inhabited my nightmares had returned.

"See what you made me do?" He dropped the remote on the couch and, wrinkling his nose, wiped the vomit from his shirt. "Here I was, enjoying our sweet reunion and off you go, acting up like a shithead. You deserved that, wouldn't you agree?"

Nobody deserved to be beaten, enslaved and abused. Nobody. But saying so would only provoke Red into more violence. I was trapped and bound and I didn't expect to live very long. I huddled against the wall and I swallowed my rebuke.

Red called out. Someone scurried into the theater room and cleaned up the mess. My field of view narrowed on Red's sleek loafers as he came to stand next to me. I expected his foot to crash against my face anytime now. Instead, he drew a monogrammed handkerchief from his pocket, knelt beside me and, tilting my head back, pressed it against my nose.

"Querida..." He blotted the blood from my nostrils. "You're such a reckless bitch. You beg for violence. All those years trying to tame you seem like such a waste. I rescued you from the jungle. Remember? I protected you. I gave you the best of everything. Tell me, Rose, why did you betray me? Why did you run?"

Red's skewed version of my story stung. I stared at him, unable to connect with his faulty reasoning. Was I stuck in *The Twilight Zone*? Did he really believe all of those lies?

He picked me up from the ground and settled me on the sofa. I hated the way he arranged me on the cushions, as if I was his rag doll and he could pose me in any way he wished. He took off his dirty shirt and loomed above me, the large, imposing, barrel-chested bear of a man I remembered. He scratched his belly, ruffling the dark line of hair dipping into his pants, inspecting me with his black eyes.

"You look good," he said. "You must be eating at least occasionally these days."

On second thought, since I'd last seen him in Las Vegas, his belly had expanded and so had his waist. A few platinum strands streaked his black hair and mixed with his chest's dark, coarse curls. The years had deepened the lines on his face. He looked older.

"You've got a glow about you." His nostrils quivered like a predator sniffing for game. "I'm going to enjoy getting reacquainted with this version of you."

The chills that rattled my body shattered my composure. I pulled on the duct tape binding my hands in outright desperation. I truly wanted to die.

An attendant came into the room and offered him a

clean shirt. He put his arms into the sleeves and pulled it over his shoulders.

"Don't worry." He reached out and caressed my face. "I'll give you what you want, very soon, *querida*. You won't have to wait long." He buttoned his shirt. "But before we get to that, we've got a few things to talk about."

Talk about?

"Just kill me." I lost it. "Just be done with it and kill me."

His elegant eyebrows rose in surprise then curved in mock resignation. "My poor Rose." He ran his knuckles over my cheek. "So soft you are, so pretty and delicate, inside and out. How could you possibly think that I'd want to kill you? I assure you, I want to work on our relationship. The judge will understand."

"No judge in the world would ever believe anything you said," I spat out in defiance.

"You're mistaken, *querida*." He flashed his bone-chilling smirk. "The federal judge who is expecting your testimony has been presented with extensive documentation detailing your lifelong mental health issues. Several experts will testify that you suffer from depression, paranoia and acute anxiety disorder. They'll detail the severity of your eating disorder over the years, your propensity to hurt yourself and your suicidal behavior."

I could barely get the words through my throat. "Suicidal behavior?"

"Just a little while ago one of my men had to sneak behind you and knock you unconscious to prevent you from shooting yourself," he said. "What do you think the judge will say when all of that evidence is presented in court?"

Ice crusted over my spine. He was messing with my history and my mind. Red planned on taking me to that Brooklyn courthouse himself. He also planned to invalidate my testimony with a fabricated interpretation of the behaviors that his abuse had triggered in me. My story was so foul, so cruel, violent and vicious, that most people would find it hard to believe.

It was a brilliant strategy on his part, one I'd failed to anticipate, though it was exactly the kind of twisted scheme he favored. Worse, it could very well succeed. He'd use the force of his personality to charm both judge and jury. He'd conceal his vile nature behind his good looks and put on a show. He'd have tons of paid witnesses, whereas I'd have no one to corroborate my story. He'd expose all of my weaknesses while I'd have no way to show any of my strengths.

"I can't wait," he said. "The judge will dismiss the charges against me. I'll be a free man. After that, we'll pop over to family court, where my attorneys have already initiated the legal proceedings. Soon, you'll be declared mentally impaired and legally incompetent. You'll become my ward."

Oh, my God. Was it possible? Was I still married to Red?

"So you see, *querida*," he added, flashing his self-satisfying smirk. "I plan on taking care of you for the rest of your life."

He meant it. He wasn't going to kill me. He planned on keeping me for his use for as long as I lived. Steiner hadn't delivered on his promise to annul the marriage and Red would be my caretaker for the rest of my life.

I started to hyperventilate. I couldn't find my breath. *Steady. Cope. Breathe. Okay, forget the rest, just breathe. Breathe.*

I forced myself to wade through the panic. *You're still alive.* Ash's words echoed in my mind. *You're still in the fight.* Focus. I had to get out of this place. But how could I escape Red in my present circumstances?

I recalled everything I knew about Red. He was smart, ruthless and violent, but he also loved the sound of his voice and enjoyed boasting and singing his own praises. After murder, gloating was his favorite hobby. He was a narcissist and stroking his ego always worked. He'd always craved my submission.

Did he still want it?

The attendant cleaning up opened the door as he left. I caught a glimpse of the balcony beyond the doors of the state-of-the-art theater room. I spotted mountains, a golf course and ski runs before the doors closed. I recognized those mountains. We were somewhere in the ski resort, not far from town, in one of the multimillion dollar homes that overlooked the resort's best views. If I could manage to find my way out of the house, I might be able to run.

"Are you following what I'm saying?" Red plopped down next to me and perched his arm over my shoulder. "Do you understand how things will work from now on?"

I swallowed my pride and nodded.

"Good." He drew me to him. "When this is done, we'll have a second honeymoon at Hacienda Dorada. We haven't been there in a long while. It'll be good to rekindle our memories. You'd like that, wouldn't you?"

I forced the word through my lips. "Yes."

Red prodded me with a look. "*Sí,* what?"

"Sí, mi amor."

"Better." He patted my head as if I was a child or a dog. "You'll be back to normal in no time. But before we go on, there's the small matter of the flash drive you stole from the Miami house." His stare and his voice hardened. "Where is it?"

"I… I don't have it."

"Now, Rose." His fingers toyed with my neck's fragile vertebrae. "Be reasonable. Don't make me hurt you. Where is it?"

"I mean it," I said. "I don't have it."

"It's not at the cottage," Red said. "The only reason why we didn't destroy it outright was because we didn't want to risk damaging the flash drive. But we tore the place apart. We looked, dear. We didn't find it."

His fingers tightened around my neck. My throat buckled beneath his grip. Dark spots flickered before my eyes. I couldn't breathe.

"I need the flash drive back," Red said. "You'll give it to me or else—"

A buzzing interrupted his threats. In his pocket, his cell vibrated like an angry cricket. Red tore his glare away from my face. He looked at the number and took the call.

"Go ahead."

I fixed my gaze to the floor, but I listened to the conversation while wrestling with the duct tape binding my hands.

"What do you mean, you haven't found any stragglers?" Red barked into the cell. "Those sons of bitches scattered like frightened chickens. They have to be around. Bodies. You owe me some additional bodies. Are you sure you have control of the scene?"

Scattered? Thank God. If the guys had scattered, then they'd survived. I prayed hard that all of them had escaped. Ash had to be alive. He was skillful. He was resourceful. I clung to that hope, because if he was dead, then my life had no meaning whatsoever.

"Correct," Red said on the phone. "No, I don't want police sniffing around. If they come by, tell them you're Feds. You've got those IDs I paid good money for. And keep looking for the thumb drive."

So I hadn't been out for that long. Red's men were still at the cottage.

"I want to get out of this fucking place too," Red spat into the line. "Notify the pilot. We're New York-bound as soon as we're done. Yes, I know you advised against coming here, but I don't give a fuck. We can't leave without the thumb drive." His eyes fell on me. "We'll find it. I guarantee it. No matter who has to bleed."

God help me. I was short on time and long on terror. I worked on the bindings.

"I'll deal with it personally," Red said testily. "I don't care about your risk management assessment." He paused to listen. "I told you, I have to do it myself and yes, you moron, it means we do it here." He paused again. "No, I won't wait. You've got twenty minutes to get back here." He hung up and let out a weary breath. "Risk assessment is such a cliché."

I forced the word out of my throat. "H-how?"

"You want to know how I found you?" His lips turned up in a smirk. "How about a kiss, a real kiss from my obliging wife, in exchange for the juicy details?"

He was eager to negotiate with me again. I didn't want to fall into the old pattern, but I saw no way around it. I leaned over, closed my eyes and, holding my breath, pressed my lips to his. He mauled me in return, scratching my skin with his beard's coarse stubble.

The scent of him invaded my lungs, sweet cologne and spicy breath mints. My body cringed. My muscles bunched up. My lips smarted, but with that kiss, I made an important discovery: he still wanted me. It was sickening, but at least I had something to bargain with.

"What is it about you?" He dipped his nose in the crook of my neck and inhaled deeply. "Is it the way you smell? Is it the way you look at me with those huge Bambi eyes, as if daring me? Is it the way you move, like a thoroughbred filly, always in heat, craving the bit and the rider?"

He pushed my jacket over my shoulders and wrenched my shirt apart. *Pop, pop, pop*, the pearly snaps gave way one after the other. He perused me brazenly.

"What's this?" He examined the obsidian charm at my throat. "Did I give you this?"

I gulped dryly. "No?"

With a brutal tug, he wrenched the pendant from my neck and threw it across the room, leaving me smarting with a bloody scrape on the side of my neck and a sense of total loss. I'd worn Wynona's necklace for almost two years. It had always meant courage and freedom to me, but it had also come to mean love. It was Ash's stone.

Red entwined his fingers into my hair and pulled my head back, until my neck was completely exposed. I flinched when his mouth landed on my body. His lips and tongue left a wet trail over my strained neck. His teeth nipped on my skin as he settled on a spot and suckled until it hurt.

I bit down on my lips. For all I knew, he could have been a vampire feeding on my terror. Horror quickened my breaths and left me panting at his mercy.

"I do like it when you do that," he murmured hoarsely. "I like the way your chest heaves and your breasts strain against the cups of your bra." His knuckles brushed against my rising and sinking breasts. "You look so tempting, *querida*. So seductive when you're scared."

His cold hand crawled beneath my bra and settled over my breast. His fingers cradled my flesh, toyed with my nipple and squeezed until it hurt. I straddled the edge of sanity, but I refused to scream or cry. That's what he wanted. Instead, I fixed my eyes on the fresco on the cupola and tried to regulate my breathing. *Cope and keep at it*. The duct tape wasn't yielding and I needed more information if I was going to escape.

When I spoke, my voice sounded even and flat, as if his touch had no impact on me whatsoever. "How did you dupe the monitoring device?"

"I'm still wearing it." He stretched out his leg and, letting go of me, pulled up his fine trousers to show me.

It was such a relief to have his hands off my body. I slumped on the couch, covering myself as well as I could, glad that I'd managed to steer his attention away from me.

"Your friends forgot I've got access to resources they can only dream about," he said. "The world's foremost technology experts like their money and I pay top dollar. As far as the Feds are concerned, I'm still caged in my New York apartment. It was simply a matter of transferring the electronic signature from one device to another and presto, here I am."

The signature transfer was probably the slight fluctuation that Will had detected, the one he and Ash had discussed. Ash had been right to be suspicious of the anomaly.

I probed deeper. "Did Steiner give me away?"

"I lost count of how many years Steiner spent trying to nail me," Red said. "What a pathetic little man. He had no weakness, but he had no joys either, and noth-

ing I could use to control him. Why would anyone want
to live like that?" He shook his head. "I'll admit he had
some competencies. He did manage to get Adam out
of Hacienda Dorada. But people on my payroll regu-
larly sorted through his mail. That's how I came to be
in possession of this."

He pulled a packet of Red Rush from his pocket.
It had my handwriting on it. My will to live wavered.

"You didn't like my new line of business?" he asked,
tapping the fragrant packet against my nose. "Weren't
you impressed by my new venture? Why did you try to
warn Steiner? What's in it for you?"

"I'd explain it to you," I said. "But you wouldn't understand."

"Watch your mouth." He slapped me so hard that
my cheek burned and my neck hurt from the whiplash.
"See? You made me lose my temper again."

I ground my teeth. If only my hands were free.

"You think I'm a bad man," he said. "You think the
world is black-and-white, that good and evil have clear
distinctions. But the world is not simple, *querida*. In
Colombia, I'm a national hero. I build schools, fund
churches, feed thousands of poor families and sponsor
great works of art. How's that evil? Explain it to me.
Come on, speak up. How can I be evil when I do so
much good with my money?"

"You get people hooked on drugs," I spat between
clenched teeth. "Kids who can't think of anything but
their next fix. Men and women who get sick, overdose
and die when they buy what you sell. You kill people
for a living. You force others into lives of violence, de-
pendence and misery. How's that good?"

"Free will." He pocketed the incense packet. "Supply and demand. It's their choice to buy what I sell. I simply provide the product they want."

"An illegal poison that destroys a person's capacity to think."

He scoffed. "Drugs have been used since the dawn of mankind. This moment in time is no different from, let's say, Prohibition."

"It's not the same."

"But it is," he said. "Listen and learn, *querida*. When you met me, I was but a local warlord who couldn't even speak good English. Look at me now. The world is changing again. Yesterday's vice is today's virtue. The unacceptable has become commonplace and complete acceptance is the only standard of morality."

"Murder is murder."

"I'm a businessman," he said. "There are plenty of opportunities for legal business ahead. Uncle Sam likes his share and as long as he gets it, he'll square off with us. People today prefer settlement to war. The drug lords of yesterday are today's entrepreneurs and tomorrow's senators and presidents. The voters are generous. I'm the tax base of the new economy."

I shook my head, rejecting a world ruled by drug lords, murderers, sex traffickers, kidnappers and psychopaths whose crimes were ignored for the sake of the almighty dollar.

"I know what you're going to say," he said in his silken voice. "You had to warn Steiner in order to keep the Feds happy. But don't worry." He twirled a strand of my hair in his finger. "I have some ideas on how you're going to redeem yourself. As to Steiner, he was incorruptible and he had good habits. He never gave us anything much."

"Then how did you find us in Ohio, when you had Adam killed?"

"Ah, that." He smiled, happy to torture me by showing off his competences. "Steiner's assistant was very helpful with that. She also helped with his mail. Poor lady, she had a disabled son who needed pricey special care. I was the answer to her prayers. But she had to be careful. Steiner kept a tight watch on his staff."

I remembered the truck running over Steiner. Tears came to my eyes. He'd been a difficult person, bitter, unfriendly and cold, but he'd died for me. I said a silent prayer for his soul. We'd never trusted him and yet he hadn't betrayed us.

"No way you traced that package of Red Rush to the cottage," I said.

My defiance stung him into the type of reply I needed. "You forget who you're dealing with," he said. "The postmark on the packet narrowed my geographical search and then, about three days ago, my technology associates discovered someone trying to hack into my devices."

Three days ago? The timing seemed wrong. Will had hacked into Red's devices weeks ago.

"My technology experts were able to track the hacker all the way back to his computer." Red gloated. "He was quite good, but no match for my experts. They hacked the hacker and were able to deliver his files to me."

They had gotten into Will's computer?

"There were some interesting files in the hacker's computer," Red said. "I found out, for example, that the Feds had set up a decoy safe house to try to nab me. So I stayed away from the trap. The info also told me this guy was for real. He knew stuff no one else knew."

I tried to wrap my mind around that one. Nothing

made sense. Why would Will have such sensitive information available in his computer?

"But it was one particular file that convinced me to expedite my plans," Red said. "I can be patient. I was prepared to meet you at the courthouse. I can put up with a lot and, in your case, I have. But there are certain things that a man of principle can't tolerate."

A man of principle? Is that how Red saw himself?

"Watch." Red grabbed the television's remote and clicked on the screen.

The dark screen gave way to movement. The paused movie resumed. The theater room's superb acoustic design enhanced the sounds, lusty groans, intimate moans and lots of whimpering. The clip was a grainy, single-angled compilation. It started with a man sitting on a bed. I couldn't see his face, but he was commanding someone to get naked. A few moments later, a woman stepped into the screen, wearing nothing but a pair of panties. I didn't recognize her until the man stripped her panties off, pulled her down on her knees and put his penis in her mouth.

My face ignited. I tried to look away, but Red clutched my chin and forced me to watch.

"You liked it, didn't you?" Darkness ruled Red's eyes. "You weren't so eager when you were with me. You balked as if I put out rancid milk. But you sure seemed to like his come."

Part of me was angry, mortified and humiliated. The smarter part of me was baffled. Think. My mind traveled back to that night. I recalled how Ash had set the laptop aside on the night table. The lid had been opened. The camera had been pointing in the direction of the bed. A game, that's all it had been, therapy. Had Ash recorded our lovemaking on purpose? Why?

It struck me then. Red's experts hadn't hacked into Will's computer. They'd hacked into Ash's laptop instead.

I knew precisely what would come next on the TV screen: me, on all fours on the bed, while Ash took me from behind. My mouth open with soundless pleas, my body rattled with the pounding, my breasts flailed with the force of Ash's strokes.

"You cried when your lawfully wedded husband did that to you," Red said. "What was it he gave you that I couldn't?"

Love, friendship, trust, encouragement, empowerment, confidence, pleasure...the gifts were too many to list. But these notions didn't fit in with Red. He favored pain and anguish.

To be fair, the clip on the screen showed no evidence of the tenderness and affection that had defined my game with Ash. It featured none of the kinder words he'd had for me, or his therapeutic approach, or the earnest ways in which he'd pleasured me.

The clip had been edited to show only selected parts and to eliminate any semblance of tenderness between us. The man on the screen was forceful and commanding. The woman was lewd and obscene. And yet there was something fascinating about the way he claimed possession of her body and the way in which she granted him tenure.

"You're mine," Ash said. "Say it. Who do you belong to?"

"You," I rasped. "You!"

I squirmed. I'd pay for this. It was very possible that, despite Red's intentions to deliver me to that courthouse, the end of the clip would coincide with the end of my life.

Red's stare was glued to the screen. White droplets of saliva pooled at the corners of his mouth. He was furious, I could tell, but his crotch bulged with the shape of his erection and his body was abuzz with arousal.

I scrambled to make sense of my situation. A crazy idea began to coalesce in the back of my mind, too reckless to be rational, too calculated not to be logical.

"The most effective defense is an intelligent attack," Ash's voice echoed in my mind. *"Most fights are better fought sooner, rather than later. If all the intelligence suggests that an attack is coming, then it's coming. I'd rather fight on my own terms and turf, than when it suits the other guy best."*

Had Ash baited Red's technology experts by making them think that he—not Will—was trying to hack into Red's computer? Had he lured them into his files only to give them access to the clip he knew would provoke Red into action?

It was inconceivable, dangerous, daring. It was the kind of complex, intricate strategy that only a highly confident, top-notch professional with extensive combat and intelligence experience would consider, someone trained in the harshest and most hostile environments in the world, someone exactly like… Ash.

But if Ash had gone to all the trouble to bait Red—in the only possible way that Red could be baited—why then had Red's attack on the cottage succeeded? Ash was skilled, careful and calculating. He understood Red's capabilities. Where had he gone wrong?

The clip ended. The screen went suddenly dark. I could smell the fetid rage puffing from Red's pores. He turned to me. I braced for a hit. Instead, he put his hands on my shoulders and planted a chaste kiss my forehead.

"See what happens when you go out into the world

without me?" He drew my stiff body into his embrace.
"You're weak, Rose. I've always known that, since the
first time I saw you across the fire, trembling in fear.
You're fragile. You need me. You must be supervised,
trained and disciplined in order to achieve your po-
tential."

Was that really how he saw me? No, this was the
rationale he used to justify his dark cravings. I wasn't
nearly as weak as he thought I was.

"This really upsets me." He shook the remote in the
direction of the screen. "I feel as if I've shirked my
responsibilities, as if I failed you and let your father
down."

I swallowed a full-blown sob. "You killed my father."

"One thing doesn't belay the other," he said as if
his twisted logic made perfect sense. "I should've kept
better track of you. I should've been tougher on you,
stricter. I should've found you earlier, before you tres-
passed on our vows."

"I never swore you anything."

"But you signed the papers, remember?"

"You made me."

"Rosa, Rosita." He caressed my hair. "I know what's
best for you. I also know you missed me a lot. This
video? It's not your fault. That jackass took advantage
of my absence and your weakness. He wanted to take
my place. He thought he could own you like I do. That's
not something I can tolerate."

I stared at Red, horrified by the depths of his delusions.

"What he did to you?" Red ran a finger down the
center of my body, along the line of my undone but-
tons. "That's what I'm going to do to you. Only better.
Oh, yeah, so much better—"

A knock on the door interrupted his lust fest. I let out the breath I'd been holding.

Red adjusted my shirt and buttoned up a couple of snaps before he yelled. "Come in."

The door opened and a group of four men came in, carrying a bundle between them. Red got up from the couch and watched as the men placed their load on the ground and left without making eye contact.

Another man came into the room, a tall, droopy-eyed fellow with a luxurious head of blond hair, dressed casually in a leather jacket, but with a weapon clearly bulging from his holster. I recognized him right away. His name was Samuel, and he'd been third in command when I escaped Red. I guessed he'd moved up in the ranks since.

"Boss," Samuel said tentatively. "This might not be the best time for this sort of thing. We need to get back to New York before the Feds notice."

In a blink, Red had Samuel by the throat and against the wall. "Don't ever presume to tell me what to do. You work for me. My buck pays for that spurt of piss that just wet your pants. Understand?"

"Sure, boss," Samuel croaked.

Red released his grip and gestured with his chin to the bundle on the floor. "Get to it."

Samuel straightened his collar, cleared his throat and pulled out a knife. He cut off the ropes and rolled out the tarp. A beaten-up body tumbled out, covered in blood and torn clothing. Samuel prodded him with the tip of his boot. After a harsh poke the man gulped in air and broke into a coughing fit.

I tried to make out the face beneath the crust of blood. His eyelids fluttered, and all of a sudden, the blue eyes that had pierced through my life's darkness fastened on Red like a pair of laser range finders.

No, no, no, a voice keened hysterically in my mind. My heart dropped into a bottomless canyon. The broken man sprawled at Red's feet was Ash.

TWENTY

ASH SHOWED NO hint of fear or alarm. That is, until he saw me. For an instant, I caught a flicker of surprise in the slight, almost imperceptible widening of his eyes. Then his stare was back on Red and his expression turned blank.

I fought back tears. Ash's hands were cuffed behind his back. His feet were shackled with chains. His T-shirt was torn and his pants ripped at the knees. He wore no coat. The puffy eye, the swollen lip, the bruises on his arms. He'd been beaten. It was exactly what I'd tried so hard to avoid. I swallowed a moan of despair and cursed a world where the good suffered and the wicked thrived.

Red clasped his hands behind his back and paced around Ash.

"You could've lived," he said. "You could've had a long, productive life, but on the day you touched her, you died. You just didn't realize it."

"We all have to die sometime." Ash pushed himself up on his elbows and leaned against the wall. "Some of us just go sooner than others."

"A philosopher?" Red chuckled. "The Navy Cross. The Purple Heart. I can see that you've had occasion to consider death closely."

Ash tilted his head. "You read my file?"

"Getting your military file was a piece of cake for my guys," Red said. "I like to have the advantage of knowing my enemy before I destroy him."

I shivered with gut-chilling fear.

"It must rankle you a bit," Red said. "Despite all your precautions, I found her because of you."

"There's a lot about you that rankles me," Ash said, perfectly calm. "That you found me is a minor irritation in the big scheme of things."

"A minor irritation?" Red let out one of his awful caws and pulled out a knife. "We'll see what you think when I'm done with you. I hope you're a fan of blades?"

"I respect blades," Ash said. "I like them even better when my hands are free."

"What are the chances of that?" Red said.

"I'd thought I'd give it a try." Ash flashed a furious smirk. "On the off chance you craved a fair fight."

"A fair fight?" Red laughed. "A uniquely American concept. Allow me to clue you in. If you take the fair out of the fight, you win. And just in case you haven't figured it out, I always win." Red motioned to Samuel. "We'll start with his toes."

Samuel crouched next to Ash and fiddled with his boots.

"Wait." I leaped to my feet. "What are you doing?"

"My dear Rose." Red tsked, keeping his eyes on Ash. "She's so damn sensitive, always has been, since she was a little girl. I try to save her the grief, but she has this annoying habit: she's curious. It's like she welcomes the suffering that comes with the knowledge."

He smiled and turned to me.

"Allow me to enlighten you, *querida*," he said. "First, I'm going to cut off your friend's toes, one by one. Then I'm going to geld this stallion. That should make him less mouthy and better behaved. When I'm done, I'm going to rip out his eyeballs and make him eat them, to make sure he'll never dare to look at something of mine again."

My stomach turned in horror.

"When he's gelded and blinded," Red said, "I'm going to very carefully carve out his heart and lay it on his chest while it's still pumping, so we can all witness it quaking during the grand finale as I cut off the filthy cock he used to trespass on *my* property. At that point, I'm going to slice his heart like a ripe tomato and watch the motherfucker die."

I stared at Red, terrified. My stomach ached. His sick mind was capable of all of that and more.

"Red, please," I said. "You can't—"

"What?" Red said. "You didn't think I was going to let this son of bitch get away with fucking you, did you? And just to add to this teachable moment, you'll watch the whole thing, right here, with me."

I felt the blood drain from my face. The room spun around me. My stomach had turned into a heavy chunk of concrete. I tugged on the duct tape, praying for superhuman strength. The tape held up.

Samuel took off Ash's boot and ripped the brace from his foot but, before he could peel off his sock, Ash's body snapped like a rubber band. His knees crashed against Samuel's head. The man careened backward and crumpled against the wall. Red whipped out his gun and centered it on Ash.

"No!" I cried out.

"Shut up." Red kept his gun on Ash. "What the fuck was that about?"

Ash smirked. "I don't like strangers messing with my stuff."

Samuel stumbled from the floor, holding his gun in one hand and his forehead with the other. He groaned when he spotted the blood on his fingers. "Mother-fucker." He grabbed his gun by the muzzle and was about to bring it down on Ash's head when I stopped him.

"Don't hurt him," I said. "He's not part of this. I'm the one you want."

"Hey, lady." Ash squinted through his swollen eye. "Stay out of this one. Will you? Let me take care of these clowns."

"Who the fuck are you calling a clown?" Samuel looked to Red.

"If you walk like a clown and act like a clown, then you're a clown," Red said. "Do you think you can manage to do your job without fucking it up? I told you he was a marine."

And a SEAL, but Red didn't say that and neither did I.

"Red, please," I said, when Samuel approached Ash again, this time with a lot more caution. "I swear, if you let him go, I'll give you the flash drive."

"Oh?" Red said. "What do we have here? She suddenly remembers she does have it after all."

Ash sneered. "She doesn't have shit."

"I do too." I had to convince Red that I had the drive for sure. "Without it, I was of little value to the Feds. It was the only way I could ensure that they would offer me witness protection and deal with me fairly. And if you hurt that man, you'll never get it back."

Red's voice oozed with glee. "Is that so?"

The blow caught me between the ribs and slammed me against the couch with the force of a Mack Truck. All the breath swooshed out of me. Thirty seconds was a century when one couldn't breathe, when every nerve in my body screamed and every cell begged for oxygen.

"Have you forgotten, *querida*?" Red said pleasantly, grabbing a fistful of my hair. "I can be very persuasive in person."

My scalp burned under Red's grip. His fist got me again, this time across the face. My brain rattled in my skull. My mind struggled to grapple with the misplaced sound filling the room. It was getting louder.

Red's fist froze in midair. A few drops of sweat glimmered on his flushed face. His head swiveled as his black eyes shifted from me and fixed on Ash.

Ash's face split into an unrecognizable grimace. Was he…laughing?

"What the fuck is wrong with you?" Red said.

Ash laughed louder.

"Didn't you hear me?" He stomped across the room, dragging me along by the scruff of the neck. "Shut up." He landed a foot between Ash's ribs.

Ash made a strangled sound and curled around his knees, convulsing on the floor with more laughter.

"Why won't he stop?" Red said. "Stop laughing." He hurled me at Ash. "Make him stop."

For a moment, I just lay there, catching my breath. My scalp smarted and my face throbbed, but Ash's body heat warmed my cheek and the scent of him appeased my lungs. His heart drummed hard against my ear. I lifted my face until we were eye to eye.

"Ash?" I said. "Pay attention. Stop laughing. You're making Red mad."

"I'm trying." He slid out from under me and sat up between chuckles. "I'm really trying. It's just that…" He laughed some more and this time, when he shifted his body, I ended up behind him. "It's so funny."

"What is it you find so funny?" Red demanded.

"You," Ash said. "You pathetic, wretched bully. You

think you're shit-hot and instead you're hot-shit. You make a living off preying on the weak and the helpless and beating on women. What you saw in that clip? It was a woman enjoying herself, a reaction you'll never get."

He was provoking Red, funneling his attention away from me. But Red wasn't used to anybody challenging his authority. His lips trembled with rage that usually led to murder. I gritted my teeth and begged God with all I had to spare Ash's life.

I suppressed a gasp when Red grabbed a fistful of Ash's hair, switched opened his blade and pressed it against Ash's exposed neck, right above the spot where his pulse beat steadily.

"Please, *mi amor*." I knelt on the floor and kissed Red's feet. "I beg you. I'll get you the flash drive. Right now. You were right. It's in the cottage. But nobody will ever be able to find it except me. It won't take but a moment. *Por favor*. Let me get it for you."

Red's kick sent me reeling backward. "This motherfucker's not going to survive me."

I bounced off the wall, shook off the impact and crawled back to Red on my knees.

"I can get you the drive," I said. "And the day after tomorrow? I'll tell the judge whatever you want me to say. I'll tell him that you're right and I'm crazy. I swear, I'll never try to run away again, but please, don't kill him."

I kissed his calves, his thighs and pressed my face against his groin, giving up the little that I had left, my pride, self-respect and dignity, willing to turn into the lowliest creeper in the universe if it meant Ash's life. Ash's eyes were beaming with defiance, but I kept groveling. I had a mission too. He was *not* going to die today.

"I'll do whatever you want," I said. "I mean it, Red. Whatever. Tie me, cut me, bleed me, beat me; I swear, I'll beg for more if it pleases you. But if you want the drive, if you want me, you must let this man go."

I managed to shock Red into a stunned silence. In all my years of captivity, I'd made a lot of concessions and I'd done a lot of things I loathed to do, but I'd always fought him. Never before had I offered him what he wanted most: complete and total submission.

The offer must have enticed him, because his eyes fell on me and his groin visibly hardened. I knew he needed that thumb drive. He couldn't return to business as usual without it. He didn't let go of Ash, but the cold tip of his blade slid down my cheek and crept across my chin.

"Remember your oath, Rose." The blade tickled my trembling lips. "I'm going to enjoy everything you promised me." He sheathed his knife and released Ash, flinging him against the wall.

Ash slumped in the corner. Our eyes met. A warning gleamed in his stare. He and I both understood that I'd only bought him a little time. Deep in my heart I knew that Red would keep him alive, but only until he had the drive. After that, Ash was a dead man.

"To the cottage," Red barked.

Samuel hesitated. "I'm waiting for the all clear."

Red snarled. "We're leaving right now."

"But—"

"Now!"

That sound. Ash was at it again. This time, his chuckles were full of scorn. "You're upset, Red, I get that," he said. "I'd be upset too, if I were you."

"Shut up."

"You wonder how she performed so well for me,"

Ash said, "especially when you can barely get her to react to you. You wonder why she liked it so much with me, while she hated it so much with you."

"You have a death wish." Red glowered. "You like to run your mouth. Your gloating is premature. I'm not done with you yet."

"Nor I with you," Ash said. "You and I? We have unresolved issues."

"And you need to learn some respect." Red moved quickly. He leaped in the air, only to tramp down on Ash's injured foot with his body's full heft.

The crunch of bones breaking resonated beneath the acoustic cupola. Ash's foot crumpled beneath Red's brutal stomp. With a groan, he rolled onto his side, curled into a shuddering ball and went still.

I opened my mouth to scream but wailed instead. I crawled on my knees over toward Ash, but a pair of sturdy legs blocked my way.

Red spat on the unconscious man. "Speaking of unresolved issues…"

He lifted me up and forced me to stand on shaky legs. My entire body shivered in shock. My knees refused to hold me and my swollen ankle throbbed with jolts of pain. And yet my pain was nothing compared to Ash's agony. He'd tried so hard to heal his foot.

"I'm tired of this bullshit," Red said. "We're going. Bring him."

Samuel balked. "But, boss—"

Red barked. "I said bring him!"

Red dragged me out of the room and through an expansive living room. He surprised the armed men lounging about, who rushed to pick up their weapons and follow their boss across the house to the back door. My eyes struggled to adapt to the brilliant sunlight streaming through the windows. I blinked to clear my sight. Ahead of me, I spotted a guard flanking the inside of the glass-paneled door and beyond it, a trio of Suburbans parked on the driveway.

"Grab the keys," Samuel commanded and the guard rushed to follow his orders.

I craned my neck. Samuel and another man carried Ash between them. Pain distorted his face, but his eyes were open. Thank God. At least he was conscious. My eyes welled with tears. His foot dangled listlessly from his leg.

"Hold on, boss," Samuel said. "We need a security sweep."

"No more delays," Red said. "We're going now."

Red threw the door open and stopped in his tracks. Standing right before us, dressed in a white coat embroidered with the High Mountain Veterinary Clinic logo was Jordan Meddler. Our eyes met briefly before his expression changed.

"Hello." He smiled brightly, taking us in as if the sight of a half dozen armed men surrounding two tattered prisoners was commonplace in this neck of the woods. "Sorry to startle you. I'm looking for one of my patients, a scrawny Maltese with a shabby coat, a sour disposition and an injured paw." He put his hand in his pocket. "Let me show you a picture."

The clicks of a dozen safeties echoed in the room.

"Easy, boys," Samuel muttered behind me.

Jordan seemed blessedly oblivious to the danger. "Ah, here it is." He whipped out his cell and, after scrolling through the screen, held up a picture of a mutt. "Have any of you seen it?"

Red tightened his hold on me. "Out of my way."

"That's not a Maltese," Samuel pointed out.

Several of the other men grunted in agreement.

"It's not?" Jordan stared at the picture and frowned. "You're right. I think I have a flyer with a picture of the lost Maltese somewhere," he added, holding his cell with one hand and grappling with his pocket.

A canister flew out of his jacket and clattered on the floor, trailing a hissing plume of smoke that blurred my view of Jordan as he lunged toward me. Red jerked hard to the left and, dragging me along, dove for the stairs. We tumbled down the steps into the basement and crashed against a rack of skis.

The rack fell on us. Something hit my head hard. I lay there, stunned, but Red dug himself out from under the pile of skis and pulled out his gun. He dove to the side of the stairs and exchanged fire with someone shooting from the top floor. More gunfire echoed from above. Glass shattered, men shouted, steps thundered upstairs where an all-out battle took place.

I took cover in the corner and yanked on my bonds, but still, the duct tape wouldn't give. I looked down on the skis piling around me. I had an idea. I knelt on the ground and straddling the ski, secured it between my knees. I leaned back and bore down, jerking my hands back and forth, rubbing the tape against the edge.

Perhaps my earlier efforts had succeeded in weakening the duct tape. Maybe I had to thank the speed demon who kept his skis in top shape even in the preseason, or the diamond stone that had sharpened the edges of his skis to perfection. For once, hard work and luck favored me. The duct tape ripped and my hands went free.

I bolted toward the stairs. I glimpsed a few staggered faces behind the weapons at the top of the steps, Jordan, the sheriff and a couple of his deputies. Red caught up with me on the third step. He tackled me like an offensive lineman and wrestled me off the stairs while shooting at the men above.

"I'll kill her if you come down," he yelled.

"No more bloodshed," the sheriff yelled back. "Let her go."

"Don't get your hopes up," Red said to me, spraying the top of the stairs with more bullets.

I lunged in the opposite direction. If I could just lure him away from Ash and the others. But Red caught my leg and slammed me against the floor. I reeled. I might have gone out for a few minutes. When I came to, I had to fight to stay conscious. Red's gun barrel was pressed on my forehead. He talked on his cell.

"Get the bird in the air," he said. "Do it now."

"They're not going to let you go," I said. "You need to surrender."

"Shut up and stay still." The gun's hot barrel burned against my skull. "They're not going to kill me, not while I have you."

"Wherever you go, the Feds will follow."

"Our trip to Hacienda Dorada just got expedited." Red flattened against the wall and sneaked a look out the window. "We'll fly out to Colombia today. Nobody can touch me there. You're coming with me."

I knew he had every intention of following up on his newest plan. I'd lived with the man for over ten years. He'd defeated every challenge to his rule, every enemy he'd ever faced. He'd kill to escape. He'd also kill to take me with him.

Red's cell chimed with a newly arrived text. The roar of a nearing helicopter told me what the message was about.

"Get up." Red lifted me up from the ground. He used his strength to manhandle me, wrapping his elbow around my neck. I perched my hands on his forearm and pulled down, trying to breathe, but his hold was solid and my world wobbled as unsteady as my knees.

"Now, pay attention," he said. "And do exactly as I say."

He kicked open the basement door and burst through the threshold, using me as a shield. The sun dazzled my eyes, but I blinked several times and took in the sights around me. We stepped into a sloping yard wedged between luxury homes. It opened up onto the backyard and the resort's golf course, which followed the gentler contours of a green ski run.

"Out of my way." Red pressed the gun to my temple and shouted, "Unless you allow that helicopter to land right now, she dies."

Radios crackled. Several armed deputies backed out of the side yard. The helicopter's engines roared as it buzzed the house. The flag that identified the seventh hole bent and snapped violently as the helicopter landed on the green. A pair of patrol cars screeched into position around the helicopter, but nobody interfered with the landing.

It wasn't just the local sheriff surrounding the house. The FBI was there as well, wearing their distinctive jackets and protective vests, taking cover behind cars, structures and bushes. I also spotted men on the roof of the neighboring houses. Red saw them too.

An unnatural calm took hold of me. Those snipers were my companions on a one-way journey, gauging their shots as we advanced, calculating their trajectories, making the choices they'd have to live with for the rest of their lives.

In a moment of complete clarity, I realized everything. *"The most effective defense is an intelligent attack and the most effective attack is the one that disables your opponent fast and for good."* Ash had made the hard choices from the outset. He'd studied the situation, evaluated the options and weighed the strategies. He'd known that Red wouldn't be easy to defeat in court. He'd anticipated that Red would use his money, power and influence to prevail. At that point, Ash had decided that the only viable way of freeing me was to confront Red on Ash's terms, turf and time, and for good.

Along the way, he'd also made decisions about who to trust with what. Not only had he taken advantage of his firm's intelligence capabilities, but locally, Ash had relied on the sheriff and Jordan to back up his plan. He must have also used his personal contacts to identify someone trustworthy in the FBI, because they were here, now.

Part of me was mad that Ash hadn't shared the full plan with me. The other part understood that in more than one way, he had. We had to be fluid. We had to be smart. He'd told me the truth from the beginning. He'd compartmentalized the information to orchestrate a complex plan because it was the only way to beat Red's extensive surveillance. And it had worked. Almost.

His complex strategy also explained why he'd made that sex clip, managed to get it to Red without raising suspicion and lured him to the cottage. The clip was possibly the only object in the world capable of provoking Red's fury beyond caution, the only way of getting Red to show up when and where Ash wanted him.

As I stood there, surrounded by all those armed men, watching the helicopter's rotor blades spinning as it waited on the green, the explanations crystallized in my mind. The defeat at the cottage had also been part of Ash's plan. So had been Ash's capture. That's why the guys had been wearing bulletproof vests. That's also why they'd scattered during the attack. The only reason why the cottage had fallen to Red in the first place was because Ash had wanted it so. Yes, I was sure: Ash had plotted to get himself caught in order to ensure Red's capture.

"Easy now." Red's gun knocked against my jaw. "One step at a time. Walk toward the helicopter."

I put one foot in front of the other, moving slowly, limping on my swollen ankle. It was hard to breathe with Red's arm so tight around my neck. I was thinking furiously. Once caught, how had Ash managed to lead the others to Red's location?

Of course. Jordan's presence at the back door hadn't been coincidental. He'd known about the plan. A memory of the day that I discovered the stitches on Ash's foot flashed in my mind. Ash had said that Jordan had taken care of the tiny cut. Jordan—who had plenty of experience embedding pet microchips—had implanted a microchip locator in Ash's foot.

It explained not only the cut and the stitches, but also Ash's behavior in the theater room. He'd tried to distract Red as he waited for the others to get a lock on the microchip and get into position for the takedown.

Complex as it was, his plan had worked nearly perfectly. Except for one glitch: me.

Ash had never intended for me to get caught. I was sure about that. *Athena* had to be the name of the contingency plan that the guys had put in place to lead me away from the fray. Ash expected that I'd escaped with Wang, whose primary mission had been to protect me in case of trouble and to facilitate my escape. My capture had thrown Ash's plan into disarray. And now these men would allow Red to escape, because he had me.

"Scram," Red shouted to the FBI agents nestled behind the terrace. "Do it now or I'll shoot her."

The men scampered out of sight. The helicopter got closer with every step, and so did a life of servitude in Hacienda Dorada.

Time slowed down to a crawl. My mind opened up to a world vibrant with detail. I could see the spectrum in the sunlight. I could hear the subtle swoosh of the clouds rushing by. I could taste the salt of the mountains' minerals on my lips and whiff the scent of three seasons dying beneath a layer of frost.

I closed my eyes and breathed in the mountain's cool air, the fragrance of peace, beauty and freedom. I gave thanks for a life that had tossed me a huge bonus of happiness right there at the end. Ash was out there, far or near, it didn't matter. He was alive and his rifle's range would close any distance with deadly accuracy. He was a man who owned his hard choices, lived with them and suffered them in his nightmares, even when he understood his choices to be right.

I spotted him then, kneeling next to Wang behind a patrol car casing the seventh hole. My pulse raced. Ash braced his rifle over the hood and squinted through his scope. The telescopic sight would show him the details on my face and my expression all the way to the white of my eyes.

"It's whether you want to make your own decisions or whether you want to play someone else's game; whether they're gonna kill your guys or you're going to kill the ones who want to kill your guys before they kill you."

Time to make my own decisions. Time to fulfill my

personal resolutions. No prison would ever prevent Red from selling drugs and destroying the lives of innocent people. No protective detail could ever keep him away from me. As long as we both lived, I was his to keep.

But I had a chance to end it now, even if Red's death meant mine too. It seemed like a fair trade to rid the world of evil, protect the ones I loved and free myself for good. I was the only one who could do all of that.

Ash might have recognized the resolve on my face. His head popped up from behind his scope. His eyes went wide. His lips pursed. "No, no, no."

I mouthed the words. "You go out fighting."

I'd practiced the motion with Ash a thousand times before. It took but a second. I braced myself for the pain, then planted my front leg, claiming my real estate. I bent my knees and wrapped my hands around Red's elbow while pulling down with all my body weight. At the same time, I wrapped my right leg behind his and threw my body toward his shoulder.

The dog came out of nowhere, a sable blur that rocketed out of my peripheral vision and collided into Red like a high-speed projectile.

Neil?

The thoughts raced through my mind. How could it be? He'd been taught to stay away from fighting. Ash took every precaution never to allow the dog near danger. We were a good twenty miles from the cottage.

But it was him, and he sank his teeth into Red's forearm, just an inch or two above the hand holding the gun, growling like a wild beast. The three of us went down together. Fur flashed before my eyes. Fangs pierced flesh and ripped tendons. Shots rang out, so loud that they hurt my ears. There was howling, snarling, screaming and blood, and yet the fierce three-way struggle continued.

The wolf bred into Neil took over. His attack became primal. Red punched Neil on the face and kicked the dog to the side while I struggled to free myself from his clutch. For an instant, he let go of me, grabbing the dog by the collar and angling his arm to aim his gun at the beast leaping for this throat.

I tackled Red with all my strength. Additional shots rang out from his gun, loud and yet somehow muffled to my bewildered brain. I lunged for Neil, enfolding him in my embrace as we tumbled together away from Red. More shots rang in the air, sharp and clear. Red's body jerked with the impact of the snipers' bullets. *Thump, thump, thump.* People shouted. The helicopter tried to gain altitude, spun out of control and crashed against the mountain. Fire, smoke and debris raged in the wind of the explosion, breaking windows and setting a patrol car on fire. People dove every which way to take cover.

I huddled with Neil against the wall, hugging the dog to my chest. For a moment, the world went mute. Then Neil whimpered and nuzzled me with his big head, caramel eyes fastened on my face. A loud *swoosh* filled my ears. His breath came in short, sharp pants. So did mine.

"My dear friend." I petted the lovely, courageous boy. "I would've never allowed him in my house if it hadn't been for you. You were the best caretaker ever."

I stared at the blood dripping from my hand. So much blood. It smeared Neil's fur, coated my arms and soaked my shirt. I fumbled through my coat and found the little flashlight attached to the keychain and unscrewed the top of the battery compartment. It was hard. My hands didn't want to work. But it seemed important that someone should have the thumb drive that slid out and onto my hand. So many people had died because of the information it contained.

The sights before me blurred. The pain burning inside me eased. I let out a long rattling breath. Relief. Red was gone, unable to kill anymore. The rest of my friends were safe. Ash was alive. I'd defied the course of my life, challenged the expected outcome and gained my best years in the bargain. No more running. No more hiding. No more fear.

It was done.

TWENTY-ONE

DYING WAS A hell of a lot easier than healing. In that, we all agreed. The guys gathered around my bed had a lot of experience in the subject. They swore I was the worst patient in the history of medicine.

"You went at the ventilator like a banshee," Manny said.

"I couldn't talk with that tube down my throat," I said, still hoarse from the experience.

"And then she tried to rip off the IV," Wang said gravely, his forehead still scarred from the blow he'd taken to the head.

"I wasn't really awake yet."

Some of the doctors and nurses at the hospital may have agreed with the guys, but Ash just smiled. Sitting next to me in my hospital bed, he kissed my hand. "The way I see it, you took two bullets to the lung and came out of an induced coma. You give them hell if you need to, baby."

"The problem with Lia is that she refuses to follow directions," Wang said, refilling my cup. "She's never met an instruction she liked."

"I'm right here," I said, "No need to discuss me in the third person."

"The real problem with Lia is that she hates rules." Manny sneaked a chocolate bar out of his pocket and, snapping off a square, offered it to me. "Hospitals have a lot of rules and she refuses to comply."

"Now see?" I seized the tiny piece. "You really know how to ease a girl's sour moods."

"*She* refuses to comply?" Jordan plucked the chocolate out of my hand. "You guys are a bunch of desperadoes and a terrible influence on my patient. Lia, I'm not letting them keep you here a day more than is absolutely necessary just because your blood sugar tests are all over the map." He dropped the chocolate into his mouth and swallowed.

"Dude," Manny said. "You're gonna hog the diabetes all by your lone self?"

"Drink this instead." Wang delivered the cup of apple juice to my hands. "I got you a different kind today. See if you like it."

The guys' kindnesses brought tears to my eyes.

"Oh, no." Will burst out into a song. "Don't cry for me Argentina…"

"Goddamn it, stop it, Will." Manny eyed the door. "We're going to get kicked out of here again. Hurry up, somebody go find the mean nurse. You can cuss at her, if you like, but please, Lia, whatever you do, don't cry."

"Stand down, everybody." I wiped the pesky tears from my eyes. "I'm fine. I explained this to you yesterday. These are the good kind of tears."

"Tears freak me out," Wang said. "I might need a drink after this."

I laughed and winced at the same time.

"Doing okay?" Ash said.

"Fine."

"You look tired," he said. "Visiting hours are done for today, guys. Our gal needs to rest."

The guys said goodbye and marched out in single file, with Manny leading the parade in his rover and Jordan lingering behind.

"Don't worry about your animals," he said. "They miss you, but they're all doing great. I'll come back to pick up the Maltese in a few hours."

Ash threw an empty cup at Jordan, but he ducked it and slipped out the door, laughing.

"Of all the fine breeds out there," Ash grumbled, "the asshole had to pick a Maltese?"

"Don't you dare make me laugh," I said but I was already laughing.

"Okay, then." He reached over and grabbed his tablet. "Some serious stuff instead. How about we take a look at the plans?"

"What plans?"

"The plans for the house we're going to build."

What on earth? "A house?"

"Our new house at the ranch," Ash said. "The one where we're going to live. What? Do I hear an objection?"

"No, no objections," I said. "I'm just a little surprised, that's all."

"Why?"

"Well, to begin with, I didn't know you'd come to a decision regarding the ranch."

"I did," he said, turning on the tablet. "I re-signed the lease with Woods the day before yesterday. The new contract is plenty profitable and offers robust growth rates for the trust."

"I bet you Wynona is doing a happy dance in heaven."

"No doubt about it." Ash grinned. "She's a happy angel. Now take a look at this." He brought up the floor plan on his screen. "What do you think?"

"Wow." The elegant facade of a sprawling stone, glass and log home was featured on the screen, complete with an extensive floor plan and a site plan that included a redwood barn and fenced-in fields for my animals. He'd thought of everything.

"It's great, Ash, and it looks really nice. When did you have these plans drawn up?"

"I did it while you were under," he said, "I couldn't sit still. Or sleep. Or eat. I had to do something. So this was the next best thing."

I caressed his face, tracing the stubble along his jaw. It was just like him to focus on hope amid the grief.

"Ash, I—"

"Don't you dare say anything nice to me," he said. "I may yet break and you'll have to pick up the pieces and do something with the mess."

"You're fine," I said. "You're more than fine, you're holding your own. Think about it. You've gotten through the last couple of weeks without Neil by your side."

"I won't lie," Ash said. "I miss that insubordinate son of a bitch. I can't wait for him to come home. Jordan says he's recovering well, but I swear, between you and him, I've got no more terror left in me."

"But he's going to be fine, right?"

"Neil's a trouper and a pro and tough as they come. He followed our scent for twenty miles. He must have galloped all the way. I think Neil would've died for sure if Jordan hadn't been right there on the scene when he got shot."

"Lucky dog," I said.

"That I am." His eyes lingered on me. "Lia, I... If you hadn't made it..."

"I made it," I said, bracketing his face between my hands. "Are you sure you're okay?"

"I'm good," he said. "That's what's strange. I haven't needed Neil to deal with stuff. I haven't had problems coming and going to the hospital, or into town, or wherever the hell I've had to go."

"That's good progress."

"It is," he said. "I've also been talking to the shrink on the phone. That helps. But enough about my crap. Now it's all about you. By the way, Gunny Watkins came to visit while you were out." He gestured toward the flowers on the table. "She's responsible for that horrendous cactus over there."

"A cactus, eh?" I cracked a smile. "Perfect...coming from her."

"She said they're a reliable plant. Resilient too. She said they're her favorite."

"I hear they're hard to kill."

"In that case," he said, "I find them sexy as hell."

I laughed and planted a kiss on his lips. "What did the doctor say about your foot?"

"We all know it's got to go." Ash looked out the window, before returning his stare back to me. "I'm just biding my time until you come home."

I caught a glimpse of the pain the decision caused him, but also of the determination that made him such a remarkable fighter. "Are you okay with that?"

"You know I hate goddamn hospitals," he said. "Healing is serious business. I see tough times ahead. But after what we've been through, I think we've got it down."

I had to agree. "We're learning for sure."

"So here's my plan," he said, taking my hand.

"I should've known." I smiled. "You always have a plan."

"Your hospital, Neil's hospital, my hospital." He lifted my fingers one by one. "Then healing and then on to that stuff you promised me."

"Oh?"

"That nonsense about the best is yet to come and all that."

I frowned. "I have no idea of what you're talking about, but I'm not encouraged if you think it's nonsense."

"Hey, you promised me and you better deliver."

"Deliver what?"

"Lia!" He reared up. "Have you forgotten so easily? You promised me an alternative future."

"An alternative future?"

"Yes, don't you remember?" he said. "That day, after pizza, at the supermarket parking lot? You said the future could hold as much adventure, challenge and satisfaction as the past. You said that the future could be even better than the past."

"Ah, yes, I remember now. That future."

"Well, I'm here to claim your version of the future," he said. "In fact, I demand it."

"Lucky for you," I said. "Futures are always up for grabs."

"So tell me again," he said, with a crooked smile. "I need to hear it."

"Ashton Hunter, we're a done deal," I said. "And so that you know, I'm looking forward to discovering the future with you."

"In that case." He dug in his pocket and held out his hand. The obsidian pendant rested on his palm, sporting the stylized outline of the frog skeleton. "May I?"

I nodded, because words couldn't convey the joy in my heart. His hands were strong and steady as he fastened the pendant around my neck. He couldn't speak either. The smile in his eyes dazzled me with a glimpse of the future he demanded. He kissed me and every part of me rejoiced, not because the future lacked in challenges—no way—but rather because we were both free of the past and ready to tackle a new adventure together, *our* alternative future.

* * * * *

*To purchase and read more books by
Anna del Mar, please visit Anna's website
at www.annadelmar.com*

Summer Silva never imagined that the search for her missing sister would leave her abandoned on a wintry back road, barely escaping with her life from a cold-blooded killer for hire...

Read on for an excerpt from THE STRANGER, book two in the WOUNDED WARRIOR series by Anna del Mar

TROUBLE WELCOMED ME to Alaska. It ambushed me in the guise of an invisible patch of black ice that launched my car spinning into a triple Lutz. I pumped my brakes. Nothing. My rental careened over the ditch and bounced down the steep ravine. The rocks pummeling the undercarriage rattled my brain. I was distantly aware that the shriek piercing my eardrums came from my throat. My headlights illuminated the spruce that materialized before me, down to the huge, corrugated trunk that collided with the hood, bringing my involuntary detour to a jarring stop.

Silence. Only the sound of my ragged breath and my pulse, pounding in my temples, interrupted the atmospheric quiet. I pried my fingers from the wheel and stared at my shaking hands. They flickered in and out of focus until I managed to even out my breaths.

The good news? I was alive and, although the wreck had probably relocated some of my internal organs, nothing seemed broken. The bad news? The air bag hadn't gone off and pain throbbed in my thigh and somewhere behind my ear. Crap. I'd come to Alaska to find my wayward sister, but my search had hit a major snag. Time to figure out how bad of a snag it was.

My hand was still quaking as I reached into my purse and found my cell. Zero bars. I groaned. What was the point of technology if it never worked when you needed it most? I snatched my purse and pulled on the door handle. The door refused to open. I scooted across to the other seat and opened the passenger side door, grateful to crawl out in one piece.

The cold hit me like a slap to the face. My nostrils flared and my lungs ached with the arctic wallop. To a tropical gal like me, the air smelled as though someone had stuffed a live Christmas tree in the freezer. Delicate snowflakes floated in the air like tiny speckles of silver. This was the first time I'd seen snow in real life. It was pretty, kind of magical really, but the cold crawled under my skin, stiffened my muscles and clung to my bones. I pulled my hood over my head. Had it been this cold when my plane landed in Anchorage?

My wrecked rental was wedged between the slope and the spruce like a deflated accordion. I had no prayer of backing it up the hill. I tackled the ravine, scrambling on all fours, and followed the wheel ruts up the slippery incline. It wasn't easy. I wore a narrow pencil skirt under my Burberry trench coat, and a pair of four-inch heels I now wished I'd never bought.

It served me right for allowing my stepmother to choose my outfit for the Darius project presentation. Louise was a sucker for shoes—the taller, the better. Note to self: never again relinquish your feet to someone else's sense of fashion when it's you—and you alone—who has to suffer the resulting torture.

I'm not sure how long it took me to climb back to the road, but by the time I reached the top, my toes had gone numb, my hands ached and my fingertips had turned white. The road I'd been driving on looked totally benign, not like the camouflaged skating rink that had hurled my vehicle into the ravine.

I clapped my hands together to warm them up. The sound echoed for miles around me. Stuck in the Alaskan wilderness. Unreal. It was an unlikely predicament for a gal who'd much rather be at the beach. Shark attack? Sure, it wouldn't surprise me if that ended up being part of my obituary. But frozen alive? Only if it involved a freak accident in Publix's frozen food section.

"Summer Silva, get your act together," I said out loud to break the eerie silence. My father hadn't clung to a capsized raft for three days in the Florida Straits in order for me to die on my first day in Alaska.

I straightened my coat, shoved my hands into my pockets, and began to walk. A layer of slush-covered ice crackled beneath my heels. Crap. My feet slid every which way and my legs wobbled. *Steady, Silva.* I could handle the unwieldy shoes…on firm, unfrozen ground. The only ice I'd ever dealt with came out in little cubes from the automated dispenser in the freezer door.

Five minutes later, the cold skewered me and not a single car had made an appearance. I leaned into the bitter wind. I wasn't made of sugar and spice. I was tough, and I meant to get out of this one, but I was majorly pissed. I was so going to give Tammy a piece of my mind when I found her.

I envisioned my sister lying on a white pelt in front of a roaring fireplace. I mouthed off into the deepening darkness. I was the levelheaded one. I was the one who always followed the rules, cleaned up the messes, did the responsible thing. And yet, right now, I was the one freezing my ass off on a desolate Alaskan road.

The headlights caught me by surprise. They sprang out from behind the curve and pierced the dusk. I waved my hands to flag down the speeding vehicle. As it got closer, I made out a Ford F-450 Super Duty, black as night, the type that would've made my truck-obsessed sister drool with envy. The truck drove right by me before the taillights lit up and it skidded to a stop, then accelerated in reverse.

The window whirred down to reveal the warmth and comfort of the softly illuminated cab. The leather-scented, heated air wafted from the window and teased my frozen senses. A man sat at the wheel, enveloped in a black thermal jacket that I would've gladly traded a thousand bucks for, on the spot. His face might have been handsome, if it hadn't been distorted by the scowl that wilted my poor attempt at a smile.

He more or less growled. "Who the hell put you up to this?"

"Excuse me?" I clutched my hood against a sudden burst of wind.

"You better come clean right now," he bit out in a tone that matched the frosty temperature. "A name. I want to know who the hell hired you and what you were expected to do."

"Hired me?"

"Don't play dumb with me." He eyed me like a wolf eyed a meal. "Who was it? Was it someone related to me? I swear, if you don't tell me this goddamn minute, you're going to be sorry."

I stared at the man in the cab, unable to comprehend his rage. What on earth was he talking about? The fury blazing in his striking amber eyes frightened me. As it was, I was so cold I couldn't think, let alone make sense of what he was saying. I rubbed the sore spot behind my ear. Maybe I'd hit my head harder than I thought. Maybe this was a dream or a nightmare. Oh, God. My stomach clenched. I really hoped I was awake. I shoved my hand up my sleeve and pinched my arm. It hurt. In fact, a lot of me was either throbbing or aching. A good sign, yes?

"Well?" he said. "Are you going to speak up or are you dumb, deaf, and mute?"

"Um, no." I rubbed my arms. "I usually have a lot to say. It's just that…well… I'm cold and you—I'm really sorry to have to tell you—but you sound like a crazy person."

He launched another blistering glower in my direction. "For the last time," he said, his tone intractable, "who the hell put you up to this?"

"Nobody," I said. "I don't know what you're talking about. My car skidded off the road and I've got no cell reception."

"Your car?" He looked up and down the road. "I don't see a car. Where is it?"

"Back there somewhere."

I'm not sure whether my treacherous heels slid on the ice or if fatigue did me in, but my feet went out from under me and, though I clung to the window, I landed on my knees.

"Ow," I might have said aloud.

"What the hell?"

I let go of the window and my dignity at the same time. I surrendered to the elements and settled precariously on the frosty ground. The cold iced my shins, traveled up to my core, and chilled my spine. I was about to pass out from exhaustion. I'd been up for over seventy-two hours. On top of that, I was suffering from a bad case of jet lag. If all of that wasn't enough, the wreck had jarred my senses. I wasn't in good shape and I knew it.

But I couldn't allow myself to go unconscious. No, sir, no way in hell. I knew the risks of passing out in front of a stranger too well. I just needed a moment to gather my strength, defrost myself and get my act together. I leaned my forehead on the door and, basking in the warmth radiating from the undercarriage, forced myself to stay alert. Surely, I could get some help, the crazy man would go on his merry way, and I could move on to finish what I'd come to do.

The engine quit. The truck quaked with the slam of a door. Angry steps crunched on the road. A pair of hiking boots parked by my side. I looked up and cringed. The man's scowl pummeled me. From my perspective on the ground, he soared above me, tall and imposing, a giant really. His knees cracked when he crouched next to me.

"Did Alex hire you?" he said. "Alex Erickson?"

"Who?"

"Are you telling me you don't know who Alex Erickson is?"

"I don't."

His breath came out in angry puffs that condensed in the air. "Do you know who I am?"

"No clue," I said. "Am I supposed to know?"

"You tell me." He looked like he was about to spit fire. "If no one put you up to this, then what the hell are you doing out here in the middle of nowhere?"

"Not taking a walk in the park, that's for sure."

My throat made this weird noise, a cross between a sob and a giggle, a sound that combined confusion with hilarity, fear with absurdity. But I wasn't going to cry. No freaking way. I wasn't going to panic either. The part of me that felt utterly ridiculous kneeling on the frozen pavement in the middle of nowhere won out. I pressed my hand over my mouth, but the quiet giggles leaked out anyway.

The man rubbed the back of his neck and frowned, a dip of full eyebrows that screamed vexation. "Do you think this is funny?"

"Funny?" I couldn't stop giggling. "No, not funny, more like hilarious."

"Jesus Christ." He raked his fingers through his long-ish hair, leaving a bunch of straight, flaxen strands in disarray. He didn't know what to make of me, but he sure knew how to scowl.

The shivering, combined with his radioactive glower, stifled my giggle attack. I forced myself to pay attention. Determination whetted the man's features and set the line of his jaw into a straight angle. A shade of stubble covered the lower half of his face, imbuing him with a golden glow that echoed the gleam in his eye, but there was nothing soft in his stare, not a hint of humor or friendliness.

At least he looked clean and groomed, unlike the rugged, hygiene-challenged bunch I'd met in the back-to-back episodes of *Alaska's Bush Men* I'd binge-watched on the plane. Alaska had never been on my long list of places I wanted to visit, and after watching the show, I'd questioned my sister's sanity along with that of people who lived away from even the most basic human comforts. Now I wondered about this surly stranger too, the first off-the-grid Alaskan I'd met.

"Is your cell working?" I said. "Could you please call the police?"

"There's no reception on this stretch of road." The copper-hued eyes probed my face. "If you really need help, I'm all you've got."

Great. Just great. The world whirled around me. I steadied myself against the truck. Three days ago, I'd been in the middle of the most important presentation of my professional life when Louise had called to tell me about my stepsister, Tammy. I'd already been short of sleep and high on stress, but since then, I'd been on the go, trying to get to Alaska.

The earth beneath my knees shifted again. I tightened my grip on the truck and took a deep breath. I wasn't one to fall apart so easily. *To bad weather, a brave face,* my father used to say, quoting an old Spanish proverb. I might be out of my comfort zone, but I hadn't given up on my pride just yet. I straightened my coat and, balancing carefully on one knee, planted one foot first, then the other. I rose slowly from the iffy crouch.

"Oops!" My heels skidded in opposite directions. I fell, bounced on my butt, and ended up sprawled on the ground all over again, rear smarting from the impact. I cursed under my breath.

"Dammit." The man hooked his hands under my arms, lifted me up, and set me upright. "There. Do you think you can stand on your own?"

"Maybe," I mumbled, rubbing my ass. My legs buckled, but I steadied myself on the truck and willed my feet to stick to the ground.

"You're shivering." He opened the car door. "Get in."

"No, thank you." Even if I was freezing, there were rules about cars and strangers. "Can you please call for Roadside Assistance?"

The man actually scoffed. "No reception, remember?" He eyed me impatiently. "Lady, you do know that there's a storm barreling down on south central Alaska, right?"

"The clerk at the airport did mention that."

"But did he mention that anytime now, a Bering Sea superstorm is expected to bring blizzard conditions with winds in excess of sixty miles an hour?"

"Yeah, no." I swallowed a dry gulp. "He didn't put it quite as bad as that."

"It's going to get a hell of a lot colder," the man said. "Emergency services went on lockdown about fifteen minutes ago."

Fabulous, just fabulous.

"What I'm trying to tell you," he explained in a strained tone obviously intended for the dimwits among us, "is that—assuming you're not a trap—I'm your only option at the moment. So get in the damn truck, before you freeze your ass off."

Dressed in his black jacket and blue jeans, glinting with all that gold in his eyes and hair, he looked perfectly normal. Minus the scowl, he might have even been good looking. But his bad temper and my flash-frozen brain made for a bad combination. Plus, there was a good chance he was more than paranoid and grouchy. Maybe he was off the grid in more ways than one.

"Look," he said. "I've had a long day and I'm in a shitty mood."

I rolled my eyes. "No kidding."

"I wasn't expecting this. You. Whatever."

I perched my fist on my hip. "Do you think I was expecting you?"

"Just get in, okay?" He gestured to the cab. "I want to get indoors before the storm hits."

"Oh, I don't know." I considered both, the brawny guy and his burly truck. "Where I come from, hitch-hiking is dangerous."

"Too bad," he said. "In Alaska hitchhiking is a common form of transportation."

"As far as I know, you could be a serial killer."

"So could you." He held the door open for me. "And my risk is higher than yours since, according to the Discovery Channel, female serial killers have been proven to be more dangerous than male serial killers."

I'd either met my match or found the only other person in the world who watched as much Discovery Channel as I did.

"Get the hell in," he said impatiently. "We're running out of time."

The weather was getting colder. The wind had picked up and the snow fell in bigger, wetter chunks. I was shivering violently, but still, I hesitated.

"Can you please take me to the nearest gas station or hotel?" I said, trying to keep my voice from quavering.

"The nearest gas station is sixty-five miles that way." He stuck out his thumb and pointed behind him. "The nearest motel is seventy-eight miles in the opposite direction. There's no time to get there. My cabin is close by and I have the full intention of being there by the time the storm hits in…" he paused to look at his watch, "…anytime now."

The mention of the word "cabin" did nothing to appease my fears. I'd seen plenty of "cabins" in my reality show marathon. I didn't want to spend a moment—let alone hours—chewing on squirrel parts in a rustic shelter without heat, electricity, or plumbing, especially in the company of a pissed-off guy whose actions so far put the *strange* in stranger.

"What is it going to be?" he said. "I'm willing to play the female killer odds if you decide you don't want to turn into an icicle. It's your choice, but I'm hauling ass right now."

What's the use of choices when one has none?

I said a little prayer, shuffled on the ice and, balancing carefully on my unwieldy heels, climbed into the front seat. He helped me up, shut the door, and walked around the truck. My head began to hurt, pangs of pain stabbing behind my eyes. Not good.

The man climbed in next to me in the cab. "Strap in."

He switched on the ignition, pressed on the pedal and accelerated down the icy track as if truck skating was an X Games signature event and he was going for the gold. My knuckles tightened around the door handle. I bit down on my lips, but the backseat driver in me was out of control. Whether he was a serial killer or not was irrelevant. We were both going to die today.

He glanced in my direction. "You got a name?"

"Yes." I pressed my frozen fingertips against the heating vent, reveling in the blessed heat.

"Well?" he said in that demanding tone of his.

I stared at him, mystified by his persistent state of grouchiness. "Well what?"

"Are you going to tell me what your name is or what?"

"Oh." I was close to frozen stupid. "My name is Summer, Summer Silva."

"Summer in Alaska?" He stared at me for an instant, then burst out into quiet laughter. "You're a little late. Summer arrived in Alaska just in time to meet winter."

Maybe it had something to do with the fact that I hadn't slept in a while, but yeah, no. He wasn't going to laugh at my expense. I narrowed my eyes on him.

"That's quite the glare." He suppressed another round of laughter. "I didn't mean to be rude."

"Well, you are rude, a lot rude in fact, accusing me of God knows what and acting like a total jerk."

"Sorry," he said. "It's just that… Summer in Alaska." His lips twitched. "You've got to admit. It's pretty damn good."

"Are you drunk?" I said. "Because if you are, maybe *I* should be doing the driving. I imagine they've got laws in Alaska, including some about drinking and driving?"

"You're turning out to be a piece of work," he said,

smirking. "Bossy too, for someone riding in my god-damn truck. Here I am, doing you a favor, not letting you freeze off your pretty little stuck-up ass and yet you're being a smartass and giving me attitude."

"Are you for real?" He had a lot of nerve calling me a smartass. "You're not exactly attitude free yourself."

"And yes," he added, ignoring my comment, "we do have some laws here in Alaska, although not nearly as many as they've got in the lower forty-eight. As to your question, nope, I'm not drunk, haven't had a drop all day. Should've, but didn't."

"What's that supposed to mean?"

"I mean that if there was ever a good day for drinking, today was it." He stomped on the clutch and shifted gears. "But no, unfortunately, I'm not drunk. That and the shitty day probably explain why you're getting a double dose of sarcasm."

"Sorry about your shitty day," I said. "But you need to mellow out. Do you always go around trying to bully people into doing whatever you want?"

"Pretty much." He flashed what could've been a semi-contrite glance in my direction. "Look, I apologize for my lack of manners." He offered his hand. "My name is Seth, Seth Erickson."

I shook his hand, mostly because, sarcasm aside, he was making an effort to be civil. Plus, he was a fellow Discovery Channel watcher. His hold was firm, hot, and supremely comforting to my fingers. My entire body wanted to shrink into his grip if only to bask in his radiant heat. My fingertips tripped against the unusual texture at the bottom of his hand. I spotted a patch of mangled skin scarring his palm, crawling up his wrist and disappearing into his sleeve. He caught me looking and covered most of the scar with a self-conscious tug of his sleeve.

"You've got some icy fingers there." He tapped on the console's screen and punched up the temperature of my heated seat. "Tuck them under your thigh. Trust me. It's the quickest way to warm up those puppies."

He was right. Trapped between the heat of my body and the seat, my fingers began to thaw.

"Where the hell are you from?" he asked.

"Miami."

"Ah." He smirked. "That explains it."

"Explains what?"

"Your inability to cope with ice. And the outfit."

I looked down at myself. "What's wrong with my outfit?"

"No gloves, hat, boots, or a proper coat," he said. "When I first saw you I thought you were either crazy or—well—you know."

"No, I don't know."

"I thought maybe you were a plant, someone looking for attention, or more specifically, *my* attention."

I stared at him for a full thirty seconds, unable to figure out what he meant. "What are you talking about?"

"Nobody in their right mind out here wears skirts and high heels on the roads, except the occasional call girl, playing a pre-ordered role or meeting a very specific customer…"

"Oh no you didn't." What was wrong with this man? "You thought I was a whore?"

"I couldn't see beneath the coat…"

"Are you like…freaking insane?"

He cleared his throat. "It was probably the heels that gave me the wrong impression…"

"You're out of your mind, you know that?" I snapped.

"First you think your family is out to get you. Then you think I'm…what? A prostitute? Which implies that you think someone in your family was going to set you up with a… Jesus!" I rubbed my temples, wishing that I'd never come to Alaska and also that I'd ditched those damn shoes. "I really want to go home."

"Don't get upset." His eyes betrayed a hint of concern. "I would've bought the look if I'd seen you down in, say, Ketchikan getting down from one of them fancy cruises. For future reference, Alaska 101: dress warm, keep dry, stay warm. That coat might look fine for a fall afternoon on Fifth Avenue, but in Alaska? It'll kill you faster than a dip in the Bering Sea."

Great. Advice from Mr. Sunshine himself. His condescending tone annoyed the hell out of me. "Okay, fine, maybe I'm not properly dressed for the weather, but that's only because I had no time to plan for this trip. I'm not as stupid as you're making me out to be."

"No offense," he said, "but all the tourists are gone. What the hell is someone like you doing all the way out here at the end of September?"

"It's kind of a long story."

"I don't know why," he muttered, "but I'm itching to hear it."

"If you must know," I said, "my sister ran away with a guy she met on the internet. He's from Alaska and I came to find her."

He flashed me a skeptical look. "Is your sister stupid?"

"No," I said, but at times like these, I wondered. "Tammy is just…impulsive."

"Has she done stuff like this before?"

"Well, yeah, but it's not really her fault."

"What do you mean it's not her fault?"

"She struggles with bipolar disorder."

"Hey, lady, Summer—right?" he said. "There's no excuse for stupidity. I've met people with all kinds of injuries and disorders who know better than to run away with a stranger they met on the internet."

"I know, but Tammy is…"

My cell rang to the tune of chirping birds. Reception. I had reception! I groped through my purse until I found the phone.

"You might get a minute or two if you're lucky," Seth cautioned. "After that, nothing for a while."

My tepid fingers fumbled over the keypad, accidentally hitting the speaker in the process. "Hello?"

"Did you find Tammy?" Louise's voice blared in her best Brooklyn accent, shrill, loud, and capable of busting an eardrum or two. "Where is she? Is she okay?"

"Calm down." I tried to turn off the speaker but my stiff fingers succeeded only at increasing the volume. "I'm on my way to find her now. There might be an itsy-bitsy delay. The weather is not cooperating, but don't worry, I'll find her."

"Are you locked in a fancy hotel room?" Louise demanded. "You won't find Tammy from behind a bolted door."

"Of course not." Louise could be such a witch when she was anxious. "I promised you I'd find Tammy and I will."

"I sure hope you're not enjoying room service while your sister is gone and I'm here, suffering, imagining all the terrible things she could be going through…"

"Please, don't be a drama queen," I said. "We don't have any evidence to suggest that Tammy is in immediate danger."

"Find your sister!" Louise's voice flickered in and

out of range. "Find her! I don't care what you have to do, just do it…"

The phone lost all its bars again and the call dropped. The narrow reception zone had ended. Part of me was grateful for the reprieve. The other part knew I was cut off again. The headache throbbing behind my eye intensified. The sights blurred before me.

"Hey," Seth said. "You okay?"

"Fine." I dropped my cell in my purse and straightened my back, fighting the exhaustion.

"Who was that very loud woman?"

"My stepmother."

"Is she right in the head?"

"She's just worried about Tammy."

"Something's not adding up here." He rubbed his wide back against the seat like a great big bison scratching against a tree. "Your sister's an idiot. Your stepmother demands that you drop everything and go chase her. Your family? Sounds like a major clusterfuck."

"Look who's talking." I sniffed. "My family may be a little different, but we love each other. We don't hire people to try to set each other up. Sure, we can be loud and a tad dramatic on occasion, but honestly? Your family sounds a million times more screwed up than mine."

His mouth twisted into the sarcastic smirk he favored. "You might have a point there."

"Yeah, you bet I do." I leaned back on the headrest. After a two-day journey, a three-hour drive, and a car wreck, I felt as if someone had taken a bat to me.

"You're looking very sleepy there," he said. "Talk to me. Are you all right?"

"I'll live," I mumbled, rubbing the knot behind my ear.

"Are you hurt?" He turned on the cabin lights and leaned over to inspect my head as he continued to drive.

"Is that a bruise behind your ear? Hell, I didn't notice before." The truck swerved in the road. "Did you hit your head when your car went off the road? Are you sure you're all right?"

"Just concentrate on driving straight, please." I inched away from his touch and switched the cabin lights off. "I'm a little tired, that's all. I haven't slept for a few days."

"A few days? That's not good." He groped behind the seat, opened the top of a small cooler and, after grabbing a bottle, handed it over to me. "Here you go."

"No, thanks." I wasn't about add alcohol to my troubles.

"It's not for drinking." He pressed the cold bottle to the side of my head. "It's to keep the swelling down."

"Oh." I took the bottle from him and held it against the lump.

"Hang on tight," he said. "That's a real nice hand-crafted lager. I wouldn't want it to go to waste."

"Got it," I said. "Hanging on to the brew over here."

He smiled, a genuine, eye-lightening grin that eased the angles on his face and radiated charm and warmth. Could a guy who smiled like that really be a jerk or a serial killer?

The world around us turned into a white maelstrom. The wind wrestled with the truck. The road became invisible under a new layer of snow. Seth geared down and kept his eyes on the road as we negotiated some hairy turns and the road's deteriorating conditions. In all my twenty-nine years of life, I'd never seen weather like this.

"We're not beating the storm, are we?"

"This is just the beginning." He tilted his head and surveyed the sky. "It's going to get bad soon, thirteen hours of very nasty wind, snow, and ice."

My timing sucked. "And I thought this was bad."

"This is nothing." He slowed down to maneuver over a bridge. "I don't suppose you get blizzards in Miami. But don't worry, we're almost there."

"Goody," I mumbled.

I knew my chances of getting to a hotel tonight were nil, but I needed to keep it together, at least until we got to the cabin. With a little luck, it might be a two-room cabin, with a door and a lock between me and the rest of the place. A door chain would be nice, but I could always improvise.

I eyed the man riding next to me. Maybe under all that hubris, he'd turn out to be a decent human being. After all, he had stopped to help me. I toyed with the idea of giving him a quick rundown of my condition, but my hackles went up. No way. He was a stranger and a guy and maybe even a little off, with all that paranoia. I knew from experience what would happen if I warned him. No need to add premeditation to humiliation.

All of a sudden, my vision narrowed. My thoughts slowed down to a crawl. My body slacked and my eyelids slammed over my eyes like hurricane shutters. I ran out of time and energy at the same moment. Oh, crap. I knew exactly what was happening to me.

"Hey, Summer." Seth's voice came from far away. "We're almost there." He shook me softly. "Wake up. Stick with me, girl."

I had no time to explain.

"Make sure you lock the door," I mumbled, before I conked out.

Don't miss THE STRANGER by Anna del Mar,
Available wherever Carina Press ebooks are sold.
www.CarinaPress.com

ABOUT THE AUTHOR

ANNA DEL MAR WRITES HOT, smart romances that soothe the soul, challenge the mind, and satisfy the heart. Her stories focus on strong heroines struggling to find their place in the world and the brave, sexy, kickass, military heroes who defy the limits of their broken bodies to protect the women they love. A Georgetown University graduate, Anna enjoys traveling, hiking, skiing, and the sea. Writing is her addiction, her drug of choice, and what she wants to do all the time. The extraordinary men and women she met during her years as a Navy wife inspire the fabulous heroes and heroines at the center of her stories. When she stays put—which doesn't happen very often—she lives in Florida with her indulgent husband and two very opinionated cats.

Anna loves to hear from her readers and can be contacted at:

Website: http://www.annadelmar.com

Email: Anna@annadelmar.com

Facebook: https://www.facebook.com/
AuthorAnnadelMar/?ref=hl

Twitter: https://twitter.com/anna_del_mar

ACKNOWLEDGMENTS

FROM BEGINNING TO end publishing a novel is a team sport and I've got some of the best players ever in my corner. I'm greatly indebted to my personal editor, the amazing Nancy Cassidy, who read through the first drafts of this novel and led me with great wisdom and incredible generosity all the way to Carina's doors.

At Carina Press, I had the enormous good fortune of landing on the desk of Kerri Buckley, editor extraordinaire, multi-tasking queen of the writing universe, and precision surgeon of the story. Without Kerri, I'd be going in circles. Thanks Kerri!

I'm also thankful to Stephanie Doig, Heather Goldberg, and all the folks at Carina whose names I haven't come across but whose talents and contributions I sincerely appreciate. Angela James, Kerri Buckley and the team at Carina Press represent everything that's right, fun and inspiring about writing and the publishing industry. I can't thank them enough for their hard work and enthusiasm.

I'd be remiss not to gush about the usual suspects, my parents, who gifted me with the joy of reading, my sisters who bring laughter to my life, my children who are the inspiration for everything I do, and my husband, who is always willing to grab the helm and steer the ship to port when I go MIA. I'm blessed with their love.

Finally, I'd like to thank you, the reader, for giving my novels a chance. I know that there are a lot of great authors writing some awesome romances out there. Thank you for choosing to read one of mine.

REQUEST YOUR FREE BOOKS!

2 FREE NOVELS
FROM THE ROMANCE COLLECTION,
PLUS 2 FREE GIFTS!

YES! Please send me 2 FREE novels from the Romance Collection and my 2 FREE gifts (gifts are worth about $10). After receiving them, if I don't wish to receive any more books, I can return the shipping statement marked "cancel." If I don't cancel, I will receive 4 brand-new novels every month and be billed just $6.49 per book in the U.S. or $6.99 per book in Canada. That's a savings of at least 18% off the cover price. It's quite a bargain! Shipping and handling is just 50¢ per book in the U.S. and 75¢ per book in Canada.* I understand that accepting the 2 free books and gifts places me under no obligation to buy anything. I can always return a shipment and cancel at any time. Even if I never buy another book, the two free books and gifts are mine to keep forever.

194/394 MDN GH4D

Name	(PLEASE PRINT)	

Address		Apt. #

City	State/Prov.	Zip/Postal Code

Signature (if under 18, a parent or guardian must sign)

Mail to the **Reader Service:**
IN U.S.A.: P.O. Box 1867, Buffalo, NY 14240-1867
IN CANADA: P.O. Box 609, Fort Erie, Ontario L2A 5X3

Want to try 2 free books from another line?
Call 1-800-873-8635 or visit www.ReaderService.com.

*Terms and prices subject to change without notice. Prices do not include applicable taxes. Sales tax applicable in N.Y. Canadian residents will be charged applicable taxes. Offer not valid in Quebec. This offer is limited to one order per household. Not valid for current subscribers to the Romance Collection or the Romance/Suspense Collection. All orders subject to credit approval. Credit or debit balances in a customer's account(s) may be offset by any other outstanding balance owed by or to the customer. Please allow 4 to 6 weeks for delivery. Offer available while quantities last.

Your Privacy—The Reader Service is committed to protecting your privacy. Our Privacy Policy is available online at www.ReaderService.com or upon request from the Reader Service.

We make a portion of our mailing list available to reputable third parties that offer products we believe may interest you. If you prefer that we not exchange your name with third parties, or if you wish to clarify or modify your communication preferences, please visit us at www.ReaderService.com/consumerchoice or write to us at Reader Service Preference Service, P.O. Box 9062, Buffalo, NY 14240-9062. Include your complete name and address.

ROM15R

REQUEST YOUR FREE BOOKS!

2 FREE NOVELS PLUS 2 FREE GIFTS!

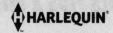

ROMANTIC suspense

Sparked by danger, fueled by passion

YES! Please send me 2 FREE Harlequin® Romantic Suspense novels and my 2 FREE gifts (gifts are worth about $10). After receiving them, if I don't wish to receive any more books, I can return the shipping statement marked "cancel." If I don't cancel, I will receive 4 brand-new novels every month and be billed just $4.74 per book in the U.S. or $5.49 per book in Canada. That's a savings of at least 12% off the cover price! It's quite a bargain! Shipping and handling is just 50¢ per book in the U.S. and 75¢ per book in Canada.* I understand that accepting the 2 free books and gifts places me under no obligation to buy anything. I can always return a shipment and cancel at any time. Even if I never buy another book, the two free books and gifts are mine to keep forever.

240/340 HDN GH3P

Name	(PLEASE PRINT)
Address	Apt. #
City	State/Prov. Zip/Postal Code

Signature (if under 18, a parent or guardian must sign)

Mail to the **Reader Service:**
IN U.S.A.: P.O. Box 1867, Buffalo, NY 14240-1867
IN CANADA: P.O. Box 609, Fort Erie, Ontario L2A 5X3

Want to try two free books from another line?
Call 1-800-873-8635 or visit www.ReaderService.com.

* Terms and prices subject to change without notice. Prices do not include applicable taxes. Sales tax applicable in N.Y. Canadian residents will be charged applicable taxes. Offer not valid in Quebec. This offer is limited to one order per household. Not valid for current subscribers to Harlequin Romantic Suspense books. All orders subject to credit approval. Credit or debit balances in a customer's account(s) may be offset by any other outstanding balance owed by or to the customer. Please allow 4 to 6 weeks for delivery. Offer available while quantities last.

Your Privacy—The Reader Service is committed to protecting your privacy. Our Privacy Policy is available online at www.ReaderService.com or upon request from the Reader Service.

We make a portion of our mailing list available to reputable third parties that offer products we believe may interest you. If you prefer that we not exchange your name with third parties, or if you wish to clarify or modify your communication preferences, please visit us at www.ReaderService.com/consumerchoice or write to us at Reader Service Preference Service, P.O. Box 9062, Buffalo, NY 14240-9062. Include your complete name and address.

HRS15